THE WEST IN HER EYES

Janet Hancock
July 2024

JANET HANCOCK

Published by Resolute Books in the United Kingdom 2024

ISBN 978-1-915981-67-7

Copyright © Janet Hancock 2024

The right of Janet Hancock to be identified as the author of this work has been asserted by her in accordance with the Copyright, Design and Patents Act 1988.

All rights reserved. No part of this publication may be reproduced or transmitted in any form or by any means, electronic or mechanical, including photocopy, recording, or any information storage and retrieval system, without permission in writing from the publisher.

Typeset by Charlotte Mouncey – www.bookstyle.co.uk – in Adobe Gramond Pro 11.8pt on 14.95pt

Printed and bound in Great Britain by Clays Ltd, Elcograf S.p.A.

www.resolutebooks.co.uk

We were young, we were merry, we were very, very wise,
And the door stood open at our feast;
When there passed us a woman with the West in her eyes,
And a man with his back to the East.

    Mary Coleridge – *Unwelcome*

Thank you, Richard and Val, rigorous readers.

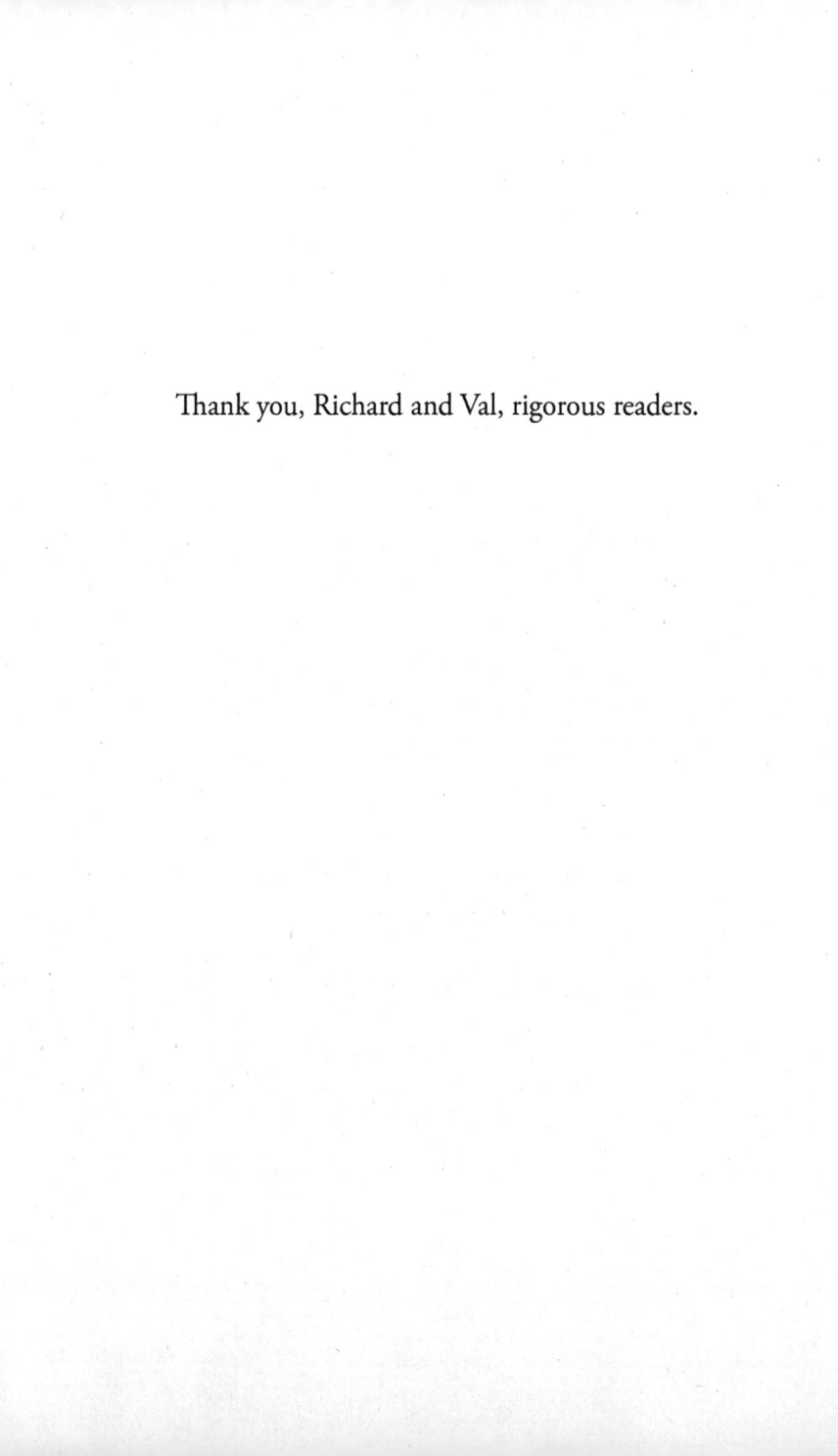

A note on Russian names

Russians have three names: a given name; a patronymic – the father's given name with the ending –ovich (male) or –ov(n)a (female); a family name, which in some cases can have a masculine or feminine ending.

In the early 20th century, when *The West in Her Eyes* is set, the standard form of address was the given name and patronymic. Only among family and close friends would the given name alone be used.

Most Russians have a diminutive of the given name: Sasha (Alexander), Masha (Maria), Kolya (Nikolai), Borya (Boris), Fedya (Fyodor). In chapter 3 of *The West in Her Eyes*, Esther recalls copying her mother, cuddling her twin-brother Lev when they were small, calling him Lyova, Lyovka, Lyovushka. The possibilities appear to be endless, depending on the level of affection.

Vocabulary

Some Russian, Persian, Turkish and French words have become part of English usage, e.g. soviet, harem, concierge; others can be understood from context. Words not found in an English dictionary, or with a different meaning in English – such as divan, impasse – are italicised in the text. There is a small glossary at the end of the book.

Nomenclature

Place names are those in use at the time of the book. Some are different from today. In Russia: Tsaritsyn (Volgograd), Tiflis (Tbilisi, Georgia), Ekaterinoslav (Dnipro, Ukraine),

Kiev (Kyiv, Ukraine). In Persia (Iran): Enzeli (Bandar Anzali), Teheran (Tehran). In Anatolia (Turkey): Trebizond (Trabzon), Angora (Ankara), Smyrna (Izmir), Brusa (Bursa), Constantinople (Istanbul).

At its most powerful, the Ottoman Empire included many races: Arabs, Kurds, Greeks, Albanians, Armenians. By the beginning of the 20th century, the declining empire was often referred to as Turkey and its people as Turks, regardless of their ethnicity. Modern Turkey comprises the Ottoman provinces of Anatolia and eastern Thrace, recognised by the Treaty of Lausanne in 1923 after the war of independence.

PART ONE

In exile, one lives by genius alone.
    Vladimir Vladimirovich Nabokov

ONE

Paris, 1998

This morning I took a taxi across to Père Lachaise and put tulips on my mother's grave. Yellow ones, always her favourite; many of the home-made clothes I wore as a little boy in the twenties were that colour, or just a pocket stitched onto a patterned shirt.

I asked the driver to leave me in the dappled rue des Rondeaux. It was early, a May day when chestnuts are in bud and winter rains seem banished forever. Inside the cemetery, my shoes crunched the gravel along shady avenues lined with aristocrats' and artists' tombs. A residue of overnight showers glistened on the grass, but the breeze was warm, the air alive with birdsong. An occasional cat peered at me from behind an urn or stone angel. The only human company was a man wrapped in a blanket, sleeping the length of a mausoleum.

On a few graves were fresh flowers. From time to time, I have found some by Mama's name and wondered who put them there: somebody who remembered her when she had been someone, or perhaps a former pupil. Today, however, I wanted to be the first, for it is her centenary. I was not disappointed. I laid the bouquet on the black marble and paused over the gold lettering: her name and my father's, and their years of birth and death.

He had died first. She delayed having the engraving done. She had already turned eighty and possibly knew it would not be long before she joined him. It was to be twelve months.

During that time, we discussed the wording: nothing fancy, dear, she would insist, as if purchase of the plot in Paris's most prestigious burial-ground forbade further extravagance. No cherubs or eulogies, she emphasised.

She never really lost her accent. She would smile and wrinkle her elegant nose, close her eyes, open them, the iris so dark a brown as to be black.

Those were the occasions I wanted to say: tell me, Mama, what you remember of the old days.

But I never could. What arrogance would it have been on my part to force to the surface and prise from her things hidden for fifty or sixty years? And to what end? To satisfy a curiosity I had never been able to shake off.

Opposite the grave is a seat, near the monument to Armenians who died fighting for France in both world wars. I am alone – my wife is dead and my children grown-up – so this morning I sat and looked out across the acres, the cobblestones and green expanses around obelisks and shrines, a walled-in, miniature Paris ensconced within the live one. I mused at secrets embedded in this seemingly boundless garden.

When I was a child, my father used to sing to me and recount tales of the mountains. Yet, there were times when his brow furrowed, harshness settled in coal-coloured eyes, and he retreated to his study for hours.

'Papa's sad,' I would say to Mama.

'He's busy, darling.'

Yes, but downcast. He might emerge in the early evening and take me on his knee; moments I loved most, in his circle of protecting arms. I would touch his thick hair – steel-grey, cut every four weeks, and parted on the left – and discover all sternness gone from his expression. I would twirl the thin gold ring he wore on the third finger of his left hand; my mother's was identical. We listened to her together, and he appeared to be staring at some horizon only he could see.

I had no brothers or sisters; when I was old enough to think about such matters, I could never understand why I was the sole offspring of such a loving marriage. It meant I was often with adults. Otherwise, books were my companions; imagination made fertile ground of ignorance. I raced through Perrault's *Stories of Olden Times*, fairies and giants and wishes come true. I was first among my school-friends to have Hergé's *Adventures of Tintin*. I flung myself into Dumas' *Three Musketeers*. I devoured sagas such as *Ermak*, of Cossack guards in flowing robes of barbaric splendour, Tartars galloping upside down on long-tailed ponies; sledges and droskys speeding over the steppes, Circassian slaves pursued by wolves.

I never asked my father about the past for fear of provoking melancholia. I did sometimes try to prompt my mother. A glimmer of a smile would move her lips as she looked at a point beyond me. I felt there were things best left, that the memory has many rooms and windows, a few open to the world, others locked. She might reply: it's years ago.

I was probably ten when I went to stay with her family in the south during the summer. She put me on the train, and one of my uncles met me in Nice. He was considerably younger than her and busy each day with his own concerns which, much later, I realised involved taxi-ing middle-aged Americans around the town and its hinterland, in return for favours and exorbitant gratuities.

I was rather in awe of him: he spoke with the long vowels of the Midi, strange to my Parisian ears. I wanted to find out if he'd ever seen a wolf; such a casual enquiry might lead to a story. But at mealtimes, or if I saw him in the yard – when the standard greeting was to ruffle my hair and exclaim: *ça va, jeune homme?* – my courage failed me.

My grandparents gave an impression of age. I did not know them well enough or feel sufficiently at ease to beset them with questions. My grandmother talked to her plants and chickens as if they were children.

One morning, however, when I was gathering eggs, my uncle came in. I blurted out, 'Do you remember the old days with Mama?'

He smiled and narrowed eyes that were the same black as hers. He chucked me under the chin, put his face close to mine, and said, 'Did you know some camels have two humps?'

When I returned to Paris, they were added to my gallery of exotica. That autumn and winter, I cut pictures of them from the newspaper or *Je Sais Tout*, and made a scrapbook. My mother happened upon me one wet afternoon engrossed in copying out a paragraph about the double-humped Bactrian ... *in central Asia, especially eastern Persia ... can carry loads of up to 300 kilos* ... I finished writing the sentence, turned to show her, but she had gone.

I looked the places up in the atlas. They swirled around my

mind with sheikhs like the evil Bab El Ehr in *Land of the Black Gold*. I decided my parents were special, unlike those of my school-friends whose mothers had never had a job and fathers had always worked in a bank, owned a shop, or been a schoolteacher. Mine must have done something unusual, brave, even dangerous. I became proud of them.

By the time my father died, Mama was taking fewer pupils. Arthritis was encroaching on her fingers, but she did love to have people to tea. At four o'clock, anybody who knew her was sure of a welcome, lapsang souchong in Limoges cups, and madeleines and millefeuilles. When frost covered chestnut-branches in the Luxembourg Gardens, and you could see your breath, glasses of fragrant, colourless liqueurs – fiery mirabelle or *framboise* – would be served from cut-glass carafes. She relished conversation. Any young people she encouraged in pursuit of their dreams, while they revered her expertise, judgement, and generosity.

On one of the tables in the salon always stood a framed photograph of my parents and myself, taken at the end of the year I started school. It was my favourite. It was also the earliest. Even after my mother's death, when I had to go through her papers, I never found pictures of her and my father on their wedding day or myself as a baby. Neither were there any letters.

Something I did come across, wrapped in tissue paper, was a piece of silk, the size of a tray, embroidered with vine-leaves and yellow tulips. Nestling inside was a girl's slipper, pink, the end where the toes would have fitted scorched open.

I still have them in my bedside drawer.

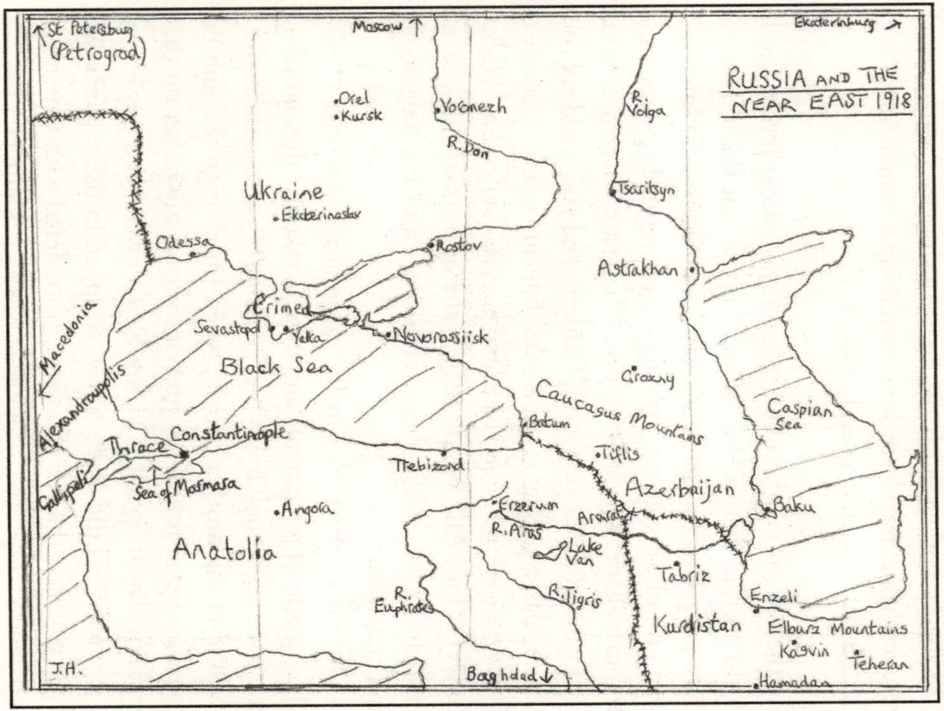
RUSSIA AND THE NEAR EAST 1918
St Petersburg (Petrograd)
Moscow
Ekaterinburg
Orel
Kursk
Voronezh
R. Don
R. Volga
Tsaritsyn
Ukraine
Ekaterinaslav
Odessa
Rostov
Astrakhan
Crimea
Sevastopol
Yalta
Novorossiisk
Macedonia
Alexandroupolis
Black Sea
Grozny
Caucasus Mountains
Caspian Sea
Batum
Tiflis
Constantinople
Thrace
Trebizond
Gallipoli
Sea of Marmara
Angora
Azerbaijan
Erzerum
Ararat
Baku
R. Aras
Lake Van
Anatolia
Tabriz
R. Tigris
R. Euphrates
Kurdistan
Enzeli
Elburz Mountains
Kasvin
Teheran
Baghdad
Hamadan
J.H.

TWO

Baku, Russia, July 1918

In the days before war and revolution, when fuel was plentiful and the tsar's edict covered land from the sea of Murmansk in the north to the Caspian in the south, steamers plied their course each day from Baku down the coast to Persia. They might arrive back as much as forty-eight hours later if the water was a writhing white plume which tossed ships of all sizes.

Stepping onto Russian soil and into this city of more than a quarter of a million souls, could be Jews, Persians, Armenians. Along the puddled dock, broadly built sailors, stripped to the waist, unloaded cotton, watermelons, and red, purple, yellow shiny fruit; silk, wine, rice, to be transported by train throughout the empire. Beyond them, trawlermen swung their knives, roach- and salmon-scales glinted, fluids splattered bloodied wooden boards, buckets filled with guts and slime. Moslem Tartars and Christian Armenians worked side by side most of the time, for the tsar's rule imposed peace on Azerbaijan and other fringes of his realm.

Revolution, the liberation of the masses, has made people afraid. At nine o'clock on a moonless Friday evening, nobody is outside without reason. Even cats have found hiding-places.

A dog is busy with his bone, indulging fortune, oblivious to the night. The sweetness of crude oil, pumped from sandy, outlying wastes, lingers in the air. A shout rises and dies in the distance. Although the curfew, imposed by the Bolsheviks when they seized power three and a half months ago, does not begin until ten, the Marine Boulevard – once lit by electric light, the place to see and be seen – is in darkness.

If you are one of the plucky ones, lurking between sail lofts, hoping to pick up some bruised fruit or a discarded sturgeon-head, you will notice five people making their way across the cobbles to the landing-stage, where a man in a khaki greatcoat stands by a boat, holding at shoulder-level a hurricane-lamp. You may think of running over to help in exchange for a few kopeks, for here are quality: a *baryn*, hunched inside a similar coat; two young *barynii*, shawled and with wide-brimmed straw hats; a couple of lads in sailor suits. They each carry a bundle.

But you'll need to be quick. The men shake hands. The one who has been waiting bows to the ladies, bends to speak to the boys. The boatman offers assistance as the man with the lamp guides the women onto a wooden ladder. The *baryn* passes the children to them. The men climb aboard. The boatman pulls up the steps, starts the engine. The vessel edges round, chugs away south, pushes a swathe through lively, lead-coloured water; foam sprays, pearl, iridescent for a few seconds, before dropping back to the sea.

Soon, everybody is a blur, and it is impossible to tell if they are looking at the port or facing the way they are going.

Against wet timbers, Esther wraps herself into a sheepskin from the boatman. It smells of tar, fish, unwashed people. She wonders how many shoulders it has covered. No matter. Often during the last months, things that were unthinkable have become normal. What is important is survival; people make whatever plans they can. Some cross the mountains to the Black Sea, hope to board a ship to the Mediterranean; friends who used to visit for five-course meals.

She is sitting at the side of the boat. The tower of Nargin island still sheds light enough onto the mainland, sketches ghostly outlines of florid buildings accomplished from oil-wealth, and the cathedral dome surmounted by golden balls; a horse-shoe-shaped city: land to the north and west soars from the bay of the peninsula like an amphitheatre, retreats into the night.

Seawater splashes her face; the Caspian, silhouette of a sea-horse, whose fruits she has eaten all her twenty years, whose smells, squalls, and caprices are under her skin. She passes her tongue over her lips. They taste of salt. She wipes them, and her cheeks, with the back of a hand as she might tears even though there are none. Three years ago, she cried all there were in her when Papa forbade her to go to the conservatoire in Petersburg. He had, he was certain, lost his eldest son, her twin, and was not going to let his daughter travel in troop-trains two thousand miles across Russia during wartime. In any case, he tried to reason with her, the school was unlikely to be open.

She uses the old name, Petersburg, rather than Petrograd, to remind herself of visiting the capital with Papa the spring before the war started; hours of auditions, interviews, written tests, before being awarded her place for the following year when she would be seventeen.

After his decision, she wept to Livvy, her brothers' English nanny, 'My heart is breaking. I can't live. Like a plant must have water, sunlight, I need that opportunity.'

Livvy replied, 'You can help me with the boys. And I should think they'll be glad of you at the Red Cross, packing parcels and rolling bandages for your soldiers at the Turkish Front.'

Her face forgot how to smile even though the war could have ended at any moment and Doctor Bagratuni continued to come to the house for her forty-five-minute piano lesson. The fighting dragged on, however. Her teacher became frail, his visits fortnightly, monthly.

Last November, the *bolsheviki* in Baku – flushed with their comrades' success in Petersburg – requisitioned Papa's Rolls-Royce. He arrived home on foot. The family should not draw attention to themselves, she decided; it wouldn't do for Beethoven and Chopin to be heard resounding from the first floor so she sat at her Steinway and skimmed her fingers over the keys. The final time was this afternoon; she smoothed shut the polished rosewood lid and whispered: I shall be back.

She places her fingertips on the damp wood of the boat's side. She stretches both hands to their fullest extent, agitates them in a Chopin étude, the one called 'revolutionary'; hears the magic in her head.

The oil derricks of Bibi-Eibat line the water's edge like prison guards. Grandfather, *dedushka*, was one of the pioneers nearly half a century ago. He had set out from Rostov-on-Don, within the Jewish Pale, in his only suit, made by his father; hundreds migrated to Baku from throughout the empire, hoping for riches. There, it turned out safer to be a Jew than in other areas. All that people were interested in was the black gold.

His beard and moustache used to prickle her face when, as a little girl, she was lifted up for a kiss. After he was murdered in 1901, by a Tartar workman taking literally subversives' call for a show of force against employers, she moved with her brother, and Mama and Papa, from their apartment to *dedushka*'s three-storey house; he had had it built from sandstone in the European style with large balconies. She would scamper along the landings, simply because they were there and she could. One day, Papa shushed her; Mama was resting. Mama always seemed to be lying down and never played with her and her brother. The following year, Mama's chaise-longue was empty; Papa said she had died and gone to a better place. She cried and wondered why somewhere without her should be an improvement. Papa scooped her into his arms, her head against his shoulder. She never ran again.

In the study is *dedushka*'s strongbox, containing the deed to oil-bearing land leased to him by Tsar Alexander the Second in 1872. *Dedushka* had no sons; Mama was his eldest daughter, Papa his senior engineer.

In the space of seventy-two hours in March, smoke spiralled from the Tartar Quarter of the city as Armenians massacred three thousand before rampaging through the outlying districts. The *bolsheviki* seized control, declared themselves the only people able to restore order, and outlawed Tartar and Armenian units; they went out to the oilfield to inform Papa – trapped but safe – and helped him bury the dead. But they have nationalised the oil industry, stolen Papa's refinery and holdings, and given them to the Council of People's Economy.

She shifts position, away from Baku. This is not farewell.

The boatman is Azeri or Persian, or from one of many tribes that have always inhabited the Caspian coast; born with the sea in his veins. He's talking to Papa and Mr MacDonell, Baku's British vice-consul until the revolution, rough speech she can't follow.

Whatever he has said, Papa and Mr MacDonell agree. Over his red, yellow, and blue kaftan, the man pulls a matted sheepskin with sleeves. She wonders why he is stopping the engine. The boat bobs as if it were flotsam on water which has the appearance of glass. He hoists a black sail, turns his broad, beardless face towards the stars. The bottom of the kaftan flutters. Above them, like a bird's wings, the sail spreads, catches the wind, and the vessel glides.

Her canvas sandals are spattered; Livvy bought them in the bazaar months ago. She wriggles her fingers into the left one. The letter is protected by muslin and sewn in.

Her hand brushes the hem of her navy linen skirt. That's moist, too. Inside, Nadia stitched paper money: real roubles from before the revolution – although they'll only buy a fraction of what they used to – and those issued by Kerensky last year.

Papa looks at her.

'They'll soon dry,' she says to him. In Baku, Mr MacDonell had access to supplies and gave Papa a greatcoat. It isn't new – dark patches suggest epaulettes have been removed – and makes Papa look more ordinary than the oil baron Yefim Solomonovich Markovitch.

He nods. 'The boatman's cut the engine to save fuel.'

'It'll take longer to reach Enzeli.' Persia, a hundred miles south and neutral in the war, is to be their sanctuary.

He shrugs, as if time no longer matters and what are another twenty-four, forty-eight hours? He glances beyond her to the boys, curled asleep against their mother under a sheepskin. 'Nadia must be exhausted,' he says. 'So much sorting and sewing.'

There is fondness in his voice; into calico lengths, Nadia packed them all a change of clothes and a blanket for Papa. She helped Nadia conceal valuables in pockets inside skirt linings.

She leaves the boat's side to sit alongside Papa; jewelled flowers and animals cut by Fabergé in turquoises, cats'-eyes, aquamarines, weight her. She takes Papa's hand. 'We shall go back.'

Sunken eyes meet hers. She sees sadness, an absence of hope, and creases that recent months have etched onto his face. Papa's hair, once black and parted on the right, is sparse and white.

His mouth shows the semblance of a smile. 'I wonder.'

'Yes,' she insists. 'You must believe, Papa. Life as it was before the war.'

'Even the house is no longer ours.'

That much is true. Home is now to be shared by decree or abandoned at any moment. Last week, officials from the housing commissariat allocated Papa five refugee families, one in each spare room, thirteen people, including two babies who cried most of the night. Filthy, starving, garments clinging to them like scraps of material to a wooden post, they were Russian Armenians who had been on the road for six days, fleeing the Turkish Army.

In the marble hall, dust settled in corners and along edges. Smells of washing and humanity pervaded the air, rather than polish and spices. Eating all together in the navy and gold dining-room, with silver cutlery, from the Limoges dinner service – every piece decorated with Nadia's initials, Papa's gift to her on their wedding day in Paris – seemed the old order's final unravelling. Meals, however, didn't take long: pancakes from minced vegetable peelings fried without fat, preceded by soup that was no more than flavoured water.

'Serge, Sonia, and Elena should have come with us,' Papa says. 'They would have been safe in Persia. If the Turks capture Baku, what chance will there be for Armenians, not to mention vengeance for the March Days?'

The enemy and their booming guns are only a few miles from the city. Her throat catches at the mention of servants she has known all her life; in Baku, they had sought sanctuary from persecution before she was born. *God go with you, baryshnya*, Sonia said this evening in her guttural accent; *pray your return will not be delayed; we will look after everything*. Sonia held out one hand, and the second, and their arms were round each other; also Elena the cook, eyes like black cherries above the folds of her cheeks. Serge, Sonia's husband, bowed.

Sonia always smelt of lemon and used to cuddle her after Mama died and would talk to her about Mama: *she never recovered from your grandfather's murder*, Sonia admitted, folding sheets, matching corners where Mama had embroidered entwined M and W; *it was fruit killed her, though, too much, and overripe; her delicate digestion couldn't take it; he adored her, your papa, gave her whatever she craved*.

With hands that are thin, veins distended under wrinkled skin, Papa draws out of his pocket a leather pouch twisted closed with a string of the same fabric. He undoes the fastening. 'I've never shown you this, Esther. *Dedushka* gave it to me the morning I married your mother, promising it would all be mine one day. Dip your fingers in.'

She does as Papa asks, to humour him. 'Sand?'

'From the oilfield. He told me he dug it out as soon as his claim had been granted. It has allowed us our good life in Baku.'

'The Turks, the *bolsheviki*, everybody who wants our oil will be defeated.'

Papa secures the bag, puts it away. 'The Ottomans, maybe. They are the invader. But the upstarts ... that is another matter. Will the genie regain the bottle, once it is released? You know I always looked forward to change,' Papa clenches his fist in the palm of the other hand, 'to the time when reasoning men would advise the tsar. But this has been an ambush. And now we have Russians fighting each other, like a gangrene spreading through the body.'

She wiggles her toes, feels the letter. 'I know everything's going to be all right.'

Papa touches the side of her cheek, unaccustomed tenderness that thuds her heart. 'Dear girl,' he says. 'You're so like your mother. She was innocent, idealistic, and only a little older than you are when she died. You're all I have left.'

No, she wants to say, we must not give up faith that Lev is alive; if he's in Russia, he will have joined those against the *bolsheviki*. But Papa stands, and she watches him pick his way across wet planks, avoiding several barrels, to Nadia and their sons.

Nadia once said the births of Papa's children always yielded a bonus. His four offspring are two sets of twins.

Next morning, fog surrounds them. The boatman offers her water in a tin mug. A dried sprat passes from his fingers to hers. She forces her lips, teeth, tongue, onto its saltiness. When the air clears, the sun is climbing. For hours the boat drifts, sea a gleaming metal sheet waiting for a breeze; she remembers times when oil might be set ablaze on its surface to flare skyward red, pink, orange, as though forewarning a day of judgement.

The second dawn, a yellow strip, like a cloud, marks the horizon. It broadens as they progress; she can make out buildings squatting along the shore, the Elburz mountains behind. She sits with her brothers and Nadia; eyes clay huts, searches for something with which to identify, investing this land with hope, the breath of Persia on her face.

The boatman has started the engine and steers the boat, hooting its mournful arrival, through a channel to the landing-stage. Beyond, is a lagoon. Except for a few dunes, everywhere is flat.

Anton hangs onto his mother's skirt as he has for most of his six years. Jacob, identical only in appearance, points and says to Mr MacDonell, 'High up is white.' His English is fluent; he and Anton adored Livvy.

'That's snow,' Mr MacDonell tells him. 'You haven't seen it before, have you?'

Jacob's eyes widen with excitement. 'Can we go there?'

'I shouldn't think so,' she finds herself saying. 'We shan't be here long.' Papa and Nadia are looking at her. Embarrassment burns her cheeks. She is not required to venture an opinion when Mr MacDonell is with them; their departure with him was arranged by Livvy's new husband, a British engineer of Papa's. Mr MacDonell is going to Teheran to lie low after an accusation of anti-bolshevik conspiracy in Baku, even though the tribunal let him off. She wonders what he was involved in and whether he knows about the messengers' network.

The splintered pier seems as if a rope-pull might bring it crashing into the water, but it holds. Papa and Mr MacDonell clamber onto steps wet and slippery from the splash as the boat came alongside. Papa leans down to help everybody. She lifts her skirt above her ankles and trusts the letter isn't sodden. She grips Papa's hand.

A man waits to greet them. He wears a morning coat and high, brimless sheepskin hat, on the front of which is a badge embossed with a silver lion holding two swords in its mouth, the sun rising behind its back. He regards his visitors with big, round eyes as he speaks.

Mr MacDonell replies and gives him the family's passport.

Two barefoot men, clad in what she thinks could have been uniforms, talk to the boatman.

The official leads the passengers along the dusty quayside, past single-storey clay structures, doors wedged open by briars and sand, and from which any paint peeled away years ago. Damp heat hangs in stale-smelling air. She yearns for the syrupiness of Baku's crude oil; the wind's scream; yelp of a cat or dog tussling over scraps, territory. Here, there is just the ebb and flow of men's voices.

They stop at a building which bears a faded Cyrillic notice across the top: *Lianozov Brothers: production of caviar and salted fish*. The port was constructed by Russians.

'I have to ask you to wait here for the moment,' Mr MacDonell says, 'while I see about transport and accommodation, and news from the hinterland.'

The only furniture is two wooden benches. Nadia and the boys sit on one. Papa stands by them. She remains in the doorway, breathes in dankness and putrefaction, evening's decline; watches Mr MacDonell and the Persian walk along the track.

She has to find General Dunsterville and give him the letter.

Pretend you're a secretary, Maria told her the other day; your English is surely up to it, having Livvy with you all this time.

Of course it is; Livvy joined the household as her summer companion a month before the war started, and stayed on to look after Jacob and Anton.

Maria is the daughter of Doctor Bagratuni, an old Armenian family in Baku; she went to school, with ambitions to work in an office, but the first winter of the war trained as a nurse, cut off her hair, packed a few belongings in a carpetbag, and joined a Red Cross unit. Only after three years, when it was disbanded, did she return to Baku, and was accepted as a typist at the bolshevik Council of People's Commissars.

'They have committees for everything, Esther,' Maria said at the end of her first week, the two of them strolling along the Marine Boulevard at six o'clock.

Maria had tied a scarf round her head and frowned at her friend's parasol. 'Let's hope we don't see any Red Guard; they'll have that off you.'

'Habit,' she defended herself. 'There's no shade.'

They rounded the curve of the bay, the ornamented yet austere seven-hundred-year-old wall of the Tartar Quarter on their right. 'Everybody who's never been anybody is now somebody, member of this or that,' Maria explained; she always gesticulated when she chattered; the skin on her hands looked red and scaly – no doubt from skivvying in the war – and nails bitten. 'They're glad to employ anyone who doesn't ask questions or make a fuss. My typing's improving, but I keep my eyes and ears open. When Shaumian, chairman of the soviet and director of the military revolutionary committee, strides in, we all have to take notice.'

She wanted to spit. 'That rogue used to be a foreman at Papa's oilfield until he was exiled to Siberia for making trouble; he came back after Kerensky's amnesty last year. Papa's desk is covered with papers from the soviet: rules for hiring and sacking workers, pay, number of hours they can work, not more than eight out of twenty-four.' She snorted. 'I suppose it's to show that one of them can write. Three thousand oil workers have formed a union. They send deputations to Papa to what they call negotiate, to avoid another strike.'

'He's up to capacity after the March Days?'

'From the villages, the cousins and younger brothers of those who were killed.'

'By making sure opponents of the *bolsheviki* have what they need – supplies and information – ordinary people like us can help defeat this rabble,' Maria impressed on her.

'How? I feel so helpless. It's breaking Papa. He even walks differently, shoulders stooped, owning nothing and knowing his every move is being observed. Shaumian told him starvation would continue in the city until the likes of our family were eating grass. The effrontery! He's offered Papa a salary. We can take three hundred roubles a month from the bank.'

'Which doesn't go far,' Maria sympathised. 'Come and visit Papa. He never goes out. There's just me and two ageing servants. He'd be delighted to see you.'

She went the following evening to the stone house in the Armenian Quarter. Doctor Bagratuni, white-haired, sat with a shawl over his knees. 'Ah, Esther,' he welcomed her but did not get up. 'Which piece have you chosen?'

She settled into a Chopin nocturne she had learnt with him when she was nine or ten. A few minutes later, he was nodding in his chair, but she played a couple more, eking out this first time at the piano since her decision last year not to draw attention to herself and her family; she used to practise for hours. Those days will come again, she repeated to herself, when the beasts have been defeated and I can go to the conservatoire.

'Which is your way home?' Maria wanted to know.

'The Mikhailovskaya.'

'Try the Olginskaya,' Maria said, arm through hers, ushering her into the hall, 'and off to the left, the Lalayevski, number one.' Maria showed her an envelope. 'Knock on the door. When somebody opens it, say that Maria is indisposed but did not want to forget the birthday. The reply will be: she always remembers. Give him this.' Maria slipped it into her pocket.

Nerves tickled her stomach, different from the usual hunger pangs. 'But you're all right.'

'Course I am, silly.' Maria picked up a faded, frayed scarf near the door. 'Put this round your head and shoulders. Push your hat inside your front. That's better: more down at heel.'

Three, four times a week, she would go the Bagratunis, when Livvy was walking out with her fiancé. 'Maria again?' was all Papa queried.

'Her father likes me to play for him.' A nudge in the pit of herself brought a flush to her cheeks. It wasn't that she'd told Papa an untruth, just kept something back.

'Maria's a sensible young woman and has served her country well,' Nadia observed.

Papa sighed agreement. The fight had gone from him. He no longer insisted his daughter be accompanied. His skin, taut over high cheekbones, had lost its olive colour and acquired the appearance of candle wax. His moustache, however, remained trimmed above thin lips.

The *bolsheviki* are certain to be watching me, Esther, Maria told her; I would be trailed if I went out alone at this hour.

But not her. She often carried messages in her sandal. Sometimes, she went to kitchen doors as if begging, and thought of people who rummaged through rubbish in her own yard and really did implore Elena for refuse; who tore up roots from waste ground around the oilfields.

She passed Red Guard who sauntered in uniforms they had worn in the tsar's army, top button undone in defiance. Scum! she breathed, eyes averted. Once, they were packed into a dusty car, a couple more on either step, two lying along mudguards, red cockades in their caps, flags flying from bayonets fixed to rifles. A Maxim machinegun poked through the rear window frame. She realised with a plunge of horror in her belly that it was Papa's Rolls-Royce.

When she told Maria she and the family were going to Enzeli, the final missive was not simply placed inside her sandal but stitched in. The general must stay there, Esther, Maria emphasised, biting off the thread, and be ready to come to Baku; it's imperative he doesn't lose heart and move south or into the mountains.

They stand in the doorway looking at the water – dark now the sun has set – and at the boat which brought them. There is no sign of anyone. Airless heat clings to her like tentacles. She unfastens the top of her white linen blouse under her chin; puckers her nose at her smell, wonders how long it will be before she can wash. She longs to unpin her hair from beneath the straw hat and soak it in water.

Papa has removed his greatcoat but still perspires in his suit, one of several he had made by Knabe in Petersburg in 1914.

She notices a speck, the only flaw in Nadia's complexion. Nadia has all buttons done up, hat at an angle on hair that has not lost its lustre. With his breast-pocket handkerchief, Papa dabs at Nadia's left cheek as if she were a piece of porcelain. Papa and Nadia's love is a living entity encircling them both. She sees it all the time in glances, the touch of a hand, a glow in their eyes, as though whenever Papa looks at Nadia he is struck afresh by her beauty. She can't imagine feeling that way about anybody. In any case, war has claimed all the young men.

Jacob kicks at the dust, covering his boot with sand. She holds both boys' hands, follows Papa and Nadia past the landing-stage and along the track. It widens into a road, off which opens a park. There are several tents and a few men in khaki uniform. The British? Is General Dunsterville here?

A rickety car noses its way towards them. It halts a dozen paces ahead. Mr MacDonell climbs out and indicates the driver. 'He doesn't dare stop the engine. It took him half an hour to start it.'

She glances at patched tyres. Papa helps Nadia and the boys into the back. The conveyance gasps asthmatically, trembles with the extra weight. She is squeezed against Jacob. The driver wears a kaftan the colour of the road, material the same shade wound round his head. Mr MacDonell gets in next to him. A rumble of protest and the vehicle judders forward.

Mr MacDonell turns towards his passengers. 'Some of our troops are still here, in pretty poor shape with fever. Gales long ago silted up the Caspian with mud and sand. Pestiferous, unhealthy climate, below sea level. Europeans can't take it. If the chaps pull through, they'll join General Dunsterville in the mountains.'

'So he isn't here?' she exclaims.

Nadia's expression wants to know why his absence should concern her.

'Can't blame him,' says Mr MacDonell. 'He'd been dug in since the end of June, waiting for the Bolshies in Baku to ask for British help against the Turks. Couldn't go without being invited. That would amount to invasion. Very tricky in these sensitive times, diplomatically speaking. But the Bolshies'll never request aid from a British imperialist. Too proud. The general couldn't justify keeping platoons hanging around in this bug-ridden swamp so he decamped. Much healthier summer quarters.'

'The sick need quinine,' Nadia comments. 'If only I'd brought a few grains. Could they do with an extra pair of hands?'

'We're short of everything,' Mr MacDonell admits. 'No railway in Persia. Communication-lines hundreds of miles long.'

How am I to meet the general? she agonises. If the British don't lead us in driving out the *bolsheviki*, who will?

THREE

Enzeli, Persia, July 1918

She has unstitched the roubles and valuables, and hidden them in the bundles. She has never washed clothes, but it is something to do and justifies her not accompanying Nadia to the British camp. When the car arrived for Mr MacDonell this morning, Nadia went with him. You ought to come, too, Esther, Nadia said; you'd understand them better than me. She couldn't. She's always hated blood or anything messy. In Baku, as Livvy had suggested, she did help Nadia at the Red Cross, packing parcels for Russian troops at the Turkish Front; each contained home-knitted socks, soap, and square packets of cheap *makhorka* tobacco. *For glory and honour*, she wrote inside, unmindful that many men wouldn't be able to read. She also rolled bandages but refused to tend sores and blisters of Armenian refugees.

She carries salt- and sweat-encrusted garments, and Papa's blanket, through an archway and down stone steps to the courtyard; thinks how different Baku must have been for Nadia, newly married to Papa: the heat, dust, wind, smell of oil. And water delivered each day.

Nadia had completed four terms at medical school in Paris when she married Papa there; Nadia's family, the Ginzbergs, had fled pogroms in Ukraine, chants of: lynch the Jews, save Russia. Nadia used to hug her and Lev, call them little squirrels, get onto hands and knees to play with them. Their Mama Nadia, who would check homework and sometimes make them begin again. Once the Ginzbergs had returned to Ukraine, part of each summer would be spent there.

Nadia suffered miscarriages before Jacob and Anton. After the births, her stepmother – the word Mama dropped by tacit agreement – would consult her about new curtains, and what they might eat when they entertained people to dinner. There were always pictures of Mama and *dedushka* in the salon, but Nadia was Papa's, Jacob's and Anton's.

She will never give up the piano as Nadia did Paris and medical school.

She and Lev were eight when Papa took them to the French capital in springtime. They stayed on the boulevard Malesherbes with Papa's uncle, *dyadia* Pavel, who wore a monocle.

Their first morning, rain streamed down lace-curtained windows. In the salon was a piano. She had never seen one before. She lifted the lid, touched a white note with her index finger. The sound was like a voice. She pressed another ... higher; to the left ... lower. She tried the black ones, sat on the stool in front of the piano, used her right thumb and all four fingers to play until she reached the wooden block at the end. She placed both hands over the keys. They were waiting to talk to her, but she must start the conversation. How? *Dyadia* Pavel came into the room. She turned to him, said: I want to do it properly. Two days later, Madame Giraud gave her the first of weekly lessons which taught her to release music from the black and white ivory, back straight, seat at exactly the correct height.

After a month or so, at nine o'clock each weekday, another lady arrived, whom she was told to call Mamzel; reading, writing, and history and geography were learnt in French; a man was in another room with Lev. What had begun as a few weeks' holiday was to be extended, but schooling not neglected: Papa had met Nadia, invited to dinner one evening with her parents, friends of *dyadia* Pavel.

As soon as Mamzel had gone, or after walks in the Bois de Boulogne with Papa and Nadia, and Nadia's mother, she would rush to the piano to continue a dialogue she never wanted to stop.

Following the wedding in late December, the journey to Baku was the main topic of conversation. 'Can't I stay here and play music?' she sobbed to Papa.

He put his arms round her, and she breathed in the liquorice-scented tobacco smell of his coat. Him. 'You'll be able to in our salon,' he promised her. 'I've ordered a Steinway for you.'

A few minutes from the sea, the house Mr MacDonell brought them to last evening is built of sun-baked bricks around the courtyard, facing inwards, shut away from the road. Pigeons coo on the roof, interrupted by the cry of a passing pedlar. This morning she woke to the scent of newly baked bread and woodsmoke and, outside the room she shares with the boys, water in a flower-shaped ewer with a ladle; everywhere basked in a soft, hot brilliance.

In one corner of the courtyard is a peach-tree, on the opposite side acacia, and clumps of grey sage and jasmine by a fountain. In the shade, she shakes open Papa's blanket to air; in Baku, Sonia always did this with bedding. Something falls to the ground. She picks it up, unwraps muslin to find a piece of parchment, the Romanov double-headed eagle seal broken. The document grants Aaron Davidovich Weinstein, *dedushka*, fifteen hectares north-east of Baku for oil exploitation. Underneath is Tsar Alexander's signature, followed by an amendment dated 1901when the lease was transferred to Yefim Solomonovich Markovitch, signed by Tsar Nicholas. Papa's identity, allowing the possibility of a return to Baku and his need to re-establish right to the land. Yes, Papa. She rewraps it.

Rose-scented water in a bowl has been left for her. She kneels and immerses the clothes two or three at a time. A baby toddles past. Jacob and Anton flop beside her. 'The skin on your fingers has gone crinkly, Esther,' Jacob comments.

She looks, hopes they dry smooth.

Children peep through several archways.

'*Dobrayeootra*,' Jacob hails them and asks their names. 'Let's begin a game. You don't have to be shy.'

The youngsters scuttle out of sight.

'Not very friendly, are they?' says Jacob.

Women in blue robes flecked with stars stand at the top of the steps; hold their veils in place, titter, whisper, until an unseen voice causes them, too, to go inside.

Anton peers at the water. 'The white things have changed colour.'

'That's from the skirt,' she tells him. 'It won't stop us wearing them.'

A large brown dog appears, settles, and tolerates Jacob stroking it while it sleeps.

'*One two, buckle my shoe,*' Jacob recites.

'*Three four, knock at the door,*' Anton joins in.

'*Five six, gather sticks.*'

Under the peach-tree, they practise their numbers and sing more English songs Livvy taught them.

'Miss Livvy used to take us along the Marine Boulevard in the mornings,' Jacob remembers. 'She said the exercise was good for us.'

'I used to walk there with her at six o'clock.' Those summer weeks before war, she and Livvy would breathe in the sweetness of acacias that lined the streets, as they made their way down steep cobbles to the Boulevard; wind whipped up dust. In the opposite direction might be donkeys laden with panniers of cargo from the port.

'Why did you?' Jacob wants to know.

'It was what people did.'

He frowns at her in disbelief.

Her arm through Livvy's beneath their parasols, she would acknowledge the salutations of other young women and their companions.

'Tell us about when you and Papa went to Petersburg and met Miss Livvy,' Jacob prompts.

She describes the city: hooves pounded wooden pavements, tugboats wailed on the Neva, which rippled in sunlight; constant traffic of yachts and barges. 'The tsar's palace is the colour of wine, and fronts the river as long as our road in Baku. He will go home when the *bolsheviki* are overthrown, and we shall, too.'

'They are bad men,' Jacob says. 'Is Lev defeating them?'

'I'm sure he is.'

Moy Lyova, Mama used to call him, so she did as well. Lyovka, she would pet him, Lyovushka, while he sat like a doll, not moving, until a smile transformed his face, he reached out to her, and they rolled on the carpet together. Her first friend and playmate. She has brought, removed from its frame, the photograph of him she kept in her room; Papa commissioned it when they were two years old. Lev stands on a chair in white suede boots and a dress the same colour, sultry, appraising eyes and broad forehead surrounded by dark curls touching his shoulders. On their fourth birthday, Papa announced Lev's hair should be cut; she cried because they were no longer alike.

They grew up separately. Lev became a studious boy, wore spectacles, always had his head in schoolbooks. At the age of eleven, he won a place at the *gimnaziya* in Baku when the Jewish quota was raised to ten percent. Her education was more fragmentary, and depended on the nationality and interests of governesses. She lived for the piano.

When she and Papa returned from Petersburg with Livvy, they found a different Lev: he'd been to the oilfield and joined men marching to the city; the legacy was a wound the length of the left side of his face which Nadia had stitched, and cleaned and dressed every morning and evening.

Lev argued with Papa in support of the men. There was another row, about a book Nadia had come across on Lev's desk and shown to Papa; something the boys at school must have been passing round, written by a revolutionary. Papa ripped it up.

The war began a few weeks later. Lev had a further twelve months' studying. He was expected to be top of his year, win the gold medal, go to university. Instead, he was expelled for clashing with the director; this, Papa discovered from a secretary after telephoning the *gimnaziya*, for Lev had disappeared. Before the end of August, there were three lines he'd scribbled on a torn-off piece of paper to say he was in the Army. Jacob cried himself to sleep. She consoled herself with the realisation that Lev's decision to fight for his country, under-age, meant he'd cast aside his summer behaviour.

Snatches of conversation from unknown rooms; soundless, slippered feet whose owners leave for their unbidden guests trays of food: chicken cooked in pomegranates, golden rice, curdled cream, jam in a green glass jar, and brown bread the texture of biscuit.

In the evening, she climbs steps to the roof, sits with Nadia and the boys on intricately woven rugs and emerald velvet cushions. She gazes at the mountains to the strain of chords struck on some stringed instrument, and chanting, timeless, exquisite, soothing.

In the courtyard, Papa and Mr MacDonell talk; they are joined by the owner of the house, a tall, dignified, black-bearded man who, Papa says, has a tobacconist shop in the bazaar and does business with the British. The three men drink tea. Their host inserts an amber mouthpiece into one of the tubes of a narghile, inhales, drawing smoke through bubbling water. Papa and Mr MacDonell prefer cigarettes. These, and charcoal from the hookah, glint like fireflies beneath stars and a high, dazzling moon.

'I wonder what they're saying,' she whispers, not to disturb her slumbering brothers. Perhaps there will be news of General Dunsterville.

'What do men always discuss? Business, war.' Nadia adds, 'A British lad died this morning. Jack. He seemed so young. Little more than a boy. Mam, was the last thing he said. They all spoke about their mothers.' Nadia's voice falters, eyes solemn. 'It made me think of Lev and whether he uttered our names before his final breath.'

'He may not be dead.'

'But ... never to hear from him.'

'Letters surely didn't always get through. Everything in Russia broke down.' Which could, of course, mean that notification of Lev's death was sent, but the family never received it. She would rather hope he is somewhere.

Only she and Jacob talk as if he is alive. The servants used to glorify his sacrifice on the European Front in defence of Mother Russia.

The second day, Mr MacDonell escorts Nadia from the British camp and departs straightaway in the car.

Nadia comes in and unpins her hat. 'He wants to start at first light tomorrow. To Kasvin. He says he has things to prepare.'

She and Nadia wash clothes again as they don't know when they will next have the chance. Nadia's hands are reddened from scrubbing and carbolic, and the job is done in less than half the time. They sew roubles and valuables into their skirts once more.

Later, she sees Mr MacDonell in the courtyard, stacking bedding in canvas bags alongside a sheepskin blanket. Children watch from an archway until a voice calls them.

She goes out to him. 'Mr MacDonell.'

He is stowing water bottles into a green bucket. He looks

at her and smiles. 'Esther Yefimovna,' he greets her in that English way which combines equal measures of courtesy and friendliness. His neck has a scar level with his collar. According to Nadia, he refers to it as Baghdad Boil, result of a sandfly bite.

'How long will it take us to reach Kasvin?'

'I anticipate one overnight stop. The road winds through mountains. We should arrive by the end of the morning.' He pauses, as if he expects her to explain why she asked; she feels herself blushing. 'We shall have a mounted escort. There was a bit of bother from the tribe that lives on the wooded slopes. All resolved now. No danger.'

He is her idea of very British: capable and sensible, like Livvy; dependable, never likely to panic. General Dunsterville – if she ever finds him – will be the same, she decides: a Mr MacDonell in army uniform.

When weariness weighs on her eyelids, she flexes her fingers to play the opening chords of the Chopin 'revolutionary' étude. She stretches on a mattress laid over rugs but wakes several times, frets about the letter.

Eight children stand in line and wave them goodbye. Mr MacDonell drives, Papa next to him. The guard consists of four khaki-clad Persian troops in peaked caps, riding two on either side and armed with rifles.

She settles Jacob on her lap. 'Are we important?' he murmurs.

'Yes.' Nerves flutter her stomach.

The car goes round the lagoon – which is enclosed by two sand-spits and suggest the jaws of a monster's pincer – before following a dried-up river-bed. Boulders: fat-bellied giants, sleepy and sated, or crouching beasts, uncertain, disquieting, throw shadows on the sand. The desert's breath burns her face in spite of the hat brim.

She retches, turns away from a horse's glazed eyes fixed on her in Kasvin, the ancient Persian capital.

'Don't make that noise, Esther,' Jacob objects.

She cradles his head against her shoulder. Anton, snuggled into Nadia, hasn't moved.

Dogs tear at the pelt, fight over entrails in the broad street. In Baku at the end of last year, people gouged flesh from horses that had fallen dead.

Vultures hover. Nearby, lie two human bodies. She clamps her hand over her nose and mouth, but the stench has insinuated itself onto her tongue.

The car edges past mud walls and the occasional wooden door. Shops have nothing for sale in dusty windows. Two men sit at the roadside in rags, palms held out in supplication. A third has curled into a heap.

'Local dealers hoarded grain and kept it off the market to sell at high prices when famine bit.' There is apology in Mr MacDonell's voice. 'We've requisitioned the stores, but it's too late for some people.'

We. The British, who go to other countries and take charge, as they must in Baku.

Soldiers, legs encased in khaki cloth, dismantle wrecked vehicles. 'Left by your troops when they retreated last year,' says Mr MacDonell. 'Parts have already been put to good use by our chaps. Constructed what appeared to be an armoured vehicle except it wasn't, just paint and planks, and a couple of machineguns aloft.'

She regards him. He talks as if it's a game.

'We're going to HQ,' he explains. 'Was a hotel. I'm sure they can rustle up some tea, and the ladies could relax. I shall report to General Dunsterville.'

Her heart clamours. So he isn't in the mountains!

Mr MacDonell adds, 'I would prefer to reach Teheran by dusk, but it won't be practical. We'll set off again in the early evening and travel through the night.'

Teheran? She and her family don't need to go there. They can stay here and return to Baku with the general.

'What are you doing, Esther?' Nadia wants to know as she washes the boys' hands and faces. As well as water, a tin basin was brought, and a clean towel. The room has two chairs and a table.

She is snipping Maria's stitching. 'I think these must have shrunk on the boat. I'm just loosening the soles.'

'Cheap things.' Nadia doesn't look up from drying Jacob's face. 'They'll have to last you a while longer.'

She separates the letter from its muslin, pushes it inside her blouse, refastens the buttons. She puts the sandal back on her foot. 'I'll only be a minute.'

A sandy-haired soldier is in the corridor. 'Yes, miss?'

'Where is Mr MacDonell?' she demands with more hauteur than she feels. 'He said he would be speaking to the general.'

Maria used to refer to British troops as tommies. This one is probably no more than her age, spotty on cheeks and chin red and leathery from the sun, khaki sleeves rolled to above the elbow. A shadow of sweat is spreading under each arm. 'Mr MacDonell,' he repeats.

She has no time for conversation so walks away through a fug of tobacco and unwashed clothes. A typewriter clacks, carriage clanging like the trams in Petersburg. She wonders what is being written and who will read it. Can she try every room until she sees the general? How will she know it's him? Or should she go into the street: glare, heat, corpses? Panic claws at her. Her heart is banging.

A door opens. Mr MacDonell emerges. 'Esther Yefimovna?'

I am proud of you and so is Russia, Maria said. 'Mr MacDonell, I have something for General Dunsterville.' The words tumble out.

'For the general?'

'From Baku.'

Help me, she wants to beg. But she looks at him to show she is serious, not nervous, and will be treated as such.

'This way,' he indicates.

Further on, he stops. 'Please wait here.' He knocks and goes in.

With shaking, clammy fingers, she removes the letter.

After a few minutes, Mr MacDonell comes out, unsmiling, preoccupied. He turns to whoever is in the room and says, 'Miss Markovitch, sir.'

She finds herself alone with a tall, imposing man in khaki who stands behind a desk. On one corner rests a topee hat.

'General Dunsterville?'

'That is correct. And you are?'

'Esther Yefimovna Markovitch, sir.' Her tongue feels too big for her mouth. She swallows, offers the envelope. 'This is for you, from loyal Russians in Baku.'

It's done.

He takes the message. 'Thank you,' he replies in Russian. His eyes remain on her face. 'You've brought this all the way to Kasvin, for me?'

His manner of talking – and in her own language – of concentrating on her, convince her that nothing is more important to him than what she has given him. Here is the man to send the *bolsheviki* packing. She recounts to him how she and her family left. 'Papa stares at the mountains for hours. Those of us who love our country, the *real* Russia,' she puts her hand over her chest, 'need you to drive out these enemies, these … riff-raff! There are thousands waiting for you.'

'I salute your bravery and patriotism, Esther Yefimovna. We shall be in Baku soon. A detachment is preparing to sail from Enzeli, and I shall follow shortly. Apparently, the bolshevik leader in Baku, the so-called Lenin of the Caucasus, has resigned rather than surrender to the Turks or ask for our help in overcoming them. The new committee has invited us.'

Her heart is pumping gasps. 'I must tell Papa. It will make him happy.'

The general smiles.

'So we can go home,' she enthuses.

The humour fades. 'I wouldn't advise it. The Turks are infiltrating the oilfields. Our job is to stop them. The *bolsheviki* will seek control again. Baku is not a place for civilians. But, perhaps, one day.' The general puts the envelope on the desk. 'Thank you for this.' He walks towards the door. She notices his trousers are tucked into boots that come up to his knees, and marvels that he doesn't seem hot. 'I admire your dedication. Your country endures.' He looks as if he might say something else but decides not to. He holds out his hand. 'Goodbye, Esther Yefimovna. And good luck.'

Back to the others, and she shouts Shaumian's resignation before even closing the door. 'It's going to get better!' She halts. Mr MacDonell is there. Everybody's eyes are on her. Nadia's are red and swollen; she is seated, the boys beside her like sentries.

'Maybe I should leave you,' Mr MacDonell addresses Papa.

'No. Esther has to be told. Please stay.' Papa indicates the second chair. She sits, trembling. Has Mr MacDonell revealed what she has done?

'Esther,' Papa begins, 'Mr MacDonell has grave and terrible news.' He pauses. Dear Papa, face more haggard than ever. 'The *bolsheviki* have slaughtered the tsar, the tsarina, and their children.'

'No,' she whispers.

Mr MacDonell enlarges, 'The intelligence officer attached to our forces in Meshed has received dispatches. However, no bodies have been found. The imperial family had been – have been – held under house arrest since April in Ekaterinburg, Siberia.'

The enormity of his words seeps through her consciousness. Hot bile rises into her mouth. Murder. It isn't possible. Nobody would dare. Not even the *bolsheviki*. The tsar *is* Russia. How can anybody as much as touch him? Without him … the abyss. And General Dunsterville said nothing.

'I am very sorry.' Mr MacDonell speaks as if referring to a relative's death. 'Obviously, I wouldn't recommend a return to Baku. These are ruthless people. Your own lives could be in danger. Although the Bolsheviks have relinquished power, the oilfields are too valuable a prize to let slip through their fingers. They will attempt another coup when the Turks are put to flight.'

'The greater our duty to be there,' she contends.

'Esther,' Papa reprimands her.

Instead of acquiescing to his rebuke, as she should, she regards him. 'Papa, there are countless faithful Russians wanting to rout the *bolsheviki*.'

'Esther,' Papa raises his voice.

Mr MacDonell interrupts, 'In Baku, the only job for you, Esther Yefimovna, will be at the hospital. Have you seen shrapnel wounds? Would you know how or be prepared to clean and dress them?'

She studies her precious hands in her lap.

'If you will excuse me,' Mr MacDonell finishes, 'there are matters to attend to. We depart for Teheran in a couple of hours.'

When Mr MacDonell has gone, Papa says, 'Esther.' Her eyes meet his. 'Even though I have lost everything, I am still head of the family.'

'We would be safe with the British,' she persists.

'No! I will not tolerate my daughter talking about accompanying soldiers. We have Mr MacDonell's guarantee, which he is giving us out of generosity and some expense, and we will continue to Teheran. You were brought up, Esther, for family, country, tsar. From now on, you will stay with Nadia and your brothers. There is nothing more to add.'

'There is, Papa: your parents, grandparents I never knew, Moscow moneylenders, and your younger siblings, all expelled from the city and herded south when you were a student in

Paris. Did you ever try to find out what had happened to them? No. There were more important concerns: your new life in Baku and marrying Mama.'

Nadia has drawn in her breath in shock. 'Esther!'

'These are not normal times, Nadia. The *bolsheviki* are all over Russia. Papa has told us so himself. A gangrene, he called it. You of all people should know what that means.' Her voice cracks, scrapes her throat. 'Papa, the *bolsheviki* will never be overpowered by people running away –'

'Esther, enough!' Papa's anger smothers her. 'That is my final word.'

She looks at Nadia, beseeching; Nadia, who admired initiative in girls like Maria.

Nadia's eyes are downcast; she gathers her sons to her as if they are cold.

FOUR

Grozny, Russia, July 1918

They're a scruffy, unkempt lot, some little more than boys, legs and feet bound in reddish-brown rags, coats like as not stripped from corpses. They arrived this morning with a curious assortment of weapons, including a revolver and a German cutlass, battered, greasy caps perched on the backs of lice-ridden heads, hair stuck to foreheads and unbuttoned collars, until the razor was brought out. Red Guard, they call themselves, with their ideals – which amount to: we can do what we like, we're the masters now – slouching along, cigarette between lips milky from endless chewing of sunflower seeds.

He watches this latest dozen sit in sullen silence on baked ground. Pigsty-smells they brought with them infuse his nostrils and mingle with those of grease and earth, as they clean the three rifles they will have to share. He's been here since the spring of last year, forming units to defend the revolution. Now, all men aged eighteen to forty are being conscripted.

'Every bullet you shoot must hit a fat, bourgeois belly,' he warns. 'Protect your cartridges more than your eyes: you can still see with one. You can't survive without ammunition.'

Some look up with scowls as though he cannot be serious. On one face is something more hostile, a who-do-you-think-you-are, Jew, telling us what to do? The wretch wears a lady's hat, no doubt looted with the pair of rusty-looking hunting-rifles.

'Having a peek at the scar down my cheek, are you?' he challenges. The lad blinks, glances away; at least there's no cigarette sticking from his mouth. 'My first badge of rank; sixteen, I was. How old are you?'

'Eighteen.'

'Are you sure? And your name?'

'Fyodor Petrovich.'

'Fancy yourself, do you, in that get-up?'

Nobody laughs, but tired shoulders relax, and grins stretch across grimy faces that have little to smile about. Fyodor Petrovich pulls the hat off.

'I marched with workers wanting better pay and housing,' he tells the rascal. 'And eight hours' labour a day instead of eleven. Have you seen a Cossack's whip, heard wounded men scream?'

Fyodor Petrovich looks round at the others as if to garner support, but they are all concentrating on the rifles or fiddling with their feet. His 'No' sounds as though it has been dragged from him.

'Long leather strips with metal at the ends. As the horse reared up, the Cossack lashed at me and spat: filthy Yid.'

'Did we elect you?' the lad asks.

'No and I didn't choose you.'

'I thought that's what they did,' volunteers a boy with a hardly broken voice, 'voted in their officers.'

'For a while, yes, when we'd got rid of Nicholas Romanov's.' He recalls those heady days after receiving order number one from the Petrograd Soviet of Soldiers' and Workers' Deputies. No more morale-sapping rumours about trouble in Russia and on the European Front. Order number one. The sound of it! With the implication there would be more. All decisions were arrived at through discussion. 'Not now, though,' he tells the group. 'You're in the Red Army. You will spread the revolution by force throughout Russia and beyond.'

Someone nods towards Fyodor Petrovich. 'He was supposed to be getting married.'

'She'll wait for you and take pride in you. Russia will be proud of you. But you'd best stop thinking about who you left behind. Private thoughts are as bad as your own money: likely to cause reaction and dissent. Every worker is your family, and that's who you're fighting for.'

'We haven't got enough weapons,' Fyodor Petrovich points out.

'We shall have. And uniforms.' He indicates the rifle-barrel Fyodor Petrovich is peering down. 'Give it another poke all the way to the bottom. You should be able to feel the indentation along the inside.'

Fyodor Petrovich rams a stick into it. 'Was it the whipping made you join? I'm sure you were clever. You could've been a student.'

'The whip, and a book: *Speeches of a Rebel*, by Prince Peter Kropotkin. Yes, a prince! Escaped from prison to England. Night after night, I devoured what he'd written. My stepmother found it in my room, showed it to my father. He tore it to pieces in front of me. I didn't tell him it had come from one of his employees.' This he never tires of recounting. These are not private thoughts.

Fyodor Petrovich is looking at him, interest sparking. 'I can't read.'

'*The conflict between new ideas and old traditions flames up in every class of society*,' he quotes. 'I'll give you more when you've finished this job.' It's like talking to his young brothers.

No private thoughts.

'And there was the school director,' he continues, 'who said Jews were afraid to fight for Russia. I wasn't having that so I stood up, banged my desk, told him with the whole class listening how Jews were stopped from becoming army officers, lawyers,' he counts off his fingers, 'civil servants, teachers, and revolution was the only thing open to them. He kicked me out. I never went home. Lied about my age and joined the Army.'

Fyodor Petrovich passes the rifle to his neighbour. 'All my brothers did. The priest blessed them, every young man in the village, and the banners. Said it was for Russia's glory. Nobody came back. My mother hardly stopped crying.'

No private thoughts. The mind, and therefore the memory, is now public property, to be managed and directed. His family probably think he's perished, these four years. He has, the quiet, studious boy they knew; the son his father wanted to mould and send away to university. They are all dead to him, too.

FIVE

Teheran, Persia, July 1918

'Haven't you brought the post?'

In the marble hall of the Russian Legation, a woman perhaps Papa's age, in a white lace dress with a fichu collar, stands as if to bar further entry unless they produce some letters. Has this person any idea how things are in Russia? she wonders.

Mr MacDonell inclines his head, almost a bow. 'Madam, there hasn't been any in Baku for months. Russia has lurched into civil war.'

'Baku, you say? So far south? The heat must be intolerable. We never go beyond the Crimea. We have a summer residence near Livadia. Our children used to play with the tsarevich and his sisters. I suppose you find all sorts in Baku, wanting the oil.'

She thinks of *dedushka*, grateful for the gruff old man she little remembers. 'We holidayed near Yalta,' she replies, but the woman claps her hands until almond-eyed, barefoot servants run into the hall.

Mr MacDonell leaves, responsibility over. She and her brothers follow Papa and Nadia up staircases. Hot water and towels arrive, and tablets of *Violette de Parme* soap. Two cots are pushed into the room the boys are to share with her.

She lays out her second skirt, black linen, and a pale-grey silk blouse to wear for dinner; turns back the red damask bedcover, caresses monogrammed, lace-edged lawn sheets. A whiff of violets lingers on her fingers, reminder of days peaceful and unchanging.

'The tsar and his family killed?' someone repeats at the table. 'Malicious rumours.'

'You haven't seen the *bolsheviki*,' she retorts, 'and people dancing, singing in the streets, and the imperial eagles torn down from Baku's city hall, thrown into the gutter.'

Papa and Nadia look at her. She has not apologised for her outburst in Kasvin. She holds their scrutiny, the daughter who has shown a steelier side than expected.

'The sooner these troublemakers are lined up and shot, the better,' somebody else comments.

She wonders where the residents are and what they are doing. She's not used to being alone, a glimpse of freedom. Nadia and Papa have gone to the American mission hospital to see if there is work. Jacob and Anton have joined other children in the legation for a couple of hours' lessons.

On the landings, she studies portraits of three centuries of Romanov tsars, gilt frames tarnished. Tsar Nicholas is attempting a smile; the tsarina is staring, no emotion visible. The two pictures are the same as those hanging in Papa's study at home. A longing for Baku and its smells overwhelms her, for life as it was, the imperial family in Petersburg. They cannot be dead.

Through a half-open door, she spots a dark grand piano. She steps into the room. Sun presses against shutters, shafts escaping in. Sofas and upright chairs are covered in crimson damask, or chintz, popular with the tsarina, people say, after her English mother.

She sits at the piano. Mahogany. A film of dust lies along the lid, which she lifts, heart racing. Scales. Doctor Bagratuni always made her begin with them, and arpeggios. One must never come to a performance cold, or as a horse at a gate, she can hear him declaring. She starts with middle C, left hand an octave below, and plays to the end of the keyboard, grimaces at the sadness, sourness, of an untuned instrument. She tries a Chopin mazurka, a traditional Polish dance, Doctor Bagratuni's favourite, but stands up as if she would banish the previous few minutes.

The woman who greeted them yesterday is watching from the doorway.

She tells her hostess about her place at the conservatoire.

Arched eyebrows, a startled expression and she's gone.

Am I not believable? Because I'm a Jewess? Yet Jews, even their Christian wives, have never been presented at the tsar's court. She goes back to the painting on the landing, the Little Father of all Russians, and asks him: would it have mattered very much if you'd met us? We're not orthodox, she feels she ought to have explained just now; we celebrate Passover, and Papa gives money to the synagogue. But why should she excuse herself to these aristocrats, innocents who are here because nobody has directed them anywhere else?

'They treat us like outsiders!' she fumes after dinner, perched on her bed next to Nadia, the boys on the floor round their feet.

'To them we are nouveaux riches,' Papa says.

'We must find lodgings,' Nadia suggests; she has been given work at the hospital; Papa, too, as a porter; his knowledge of English is appreciated. Payment is uncertain; nobody knows when money will arrive. Papa fetching and carrying! He was never employed by anybody after *dedushka* and refused European companies' proposals to buy his land and property.

'I'll enquire tomorrow,' he promises.

Someone recommends a widow who lives in the myriad of streets between the main thoroughfares of Teheran's European Quarter.

Madame Lavirotte pads through a curtain of coloured wooden beads to offer two rooms plus meals, '… although there is nothing, madame,' she assures Nadia in quaint French. 'People are forsaking the city.' Of olive complexion, raven hair, and clad in a shapeless mourning-dress, stockings and slippers, Madame Lavirotte claims to be French yet is reputed to speak Russian and Persian, even a smattering of English and Arabic.

'We've been making do for a year or more,' she answers in Russian ahead of Nadia, hardly able to decipher Madame Lavirotte's mangled vowels.

Madame Lavirotte shows no indication of having understood, and pats Jacob and Anton on the head. 'Poor little ones.'

Half an hour later, the landlady appears at the doorway of the larger room with a wooden box; her eyes sparkle like jet. 'For the children.'

She takes the gift. 'Thank you, madame.' Inside are at least a dozen tin soldiers, chipped red and blue. 'Look, boys! What do you say?'

Jacob and Anton chorus their thanks, and get down on hands and knees. 'These are yours,' Jacob tells his brother, 'and the rest are mine.'

They are invited to continue lessons at the legation. An ikon in the corner, they receive the education of those far from home, that their culture and heritage should be kept alive. Rather than reading Madame Ségur's *Un Bon Petit Diable*, as she did at their age, they are put to Pushkin, Nikolai Gogol's epic *Taras Bulba*, Chekhov's short stories, and a few sentences to learn by heart each evening.

Whenever she escorts or fetches them, she is alert for Mr MacDonell; scans faces of officials such as the one who met them off the boat, and men in white or dark-blue turbans, on foot or bicycle.

Papa brings wood from the hospital and helps the boys build a fort. Another lunch-time, he has paper; her brothers draw soldiers and battles.

It's Papa who comes across Mr MacDonell; he lets the Englishman have the roubles he's been carrying in his pocket. 'He's certain he'll be able to use them in Baku,' Papa reports. 'We have these in exchange, Persian tomans.' Papa lays heavy silver coins on the table.

'Baku?' she repeats. 'When?'

Papa shrugs. 'I didn't ask.' A pause. 'He was wearing native clothing.'

'Time to sell things,' Nadia decides. 'Whatever you do, Esther, don't give the impression of being desperate, or accept the first price.'

A couple of items twice a week: miniature eggs in lapis lazuli; ornaments decorated with diamonds, emeralds, pearls; a ruby necklace, and mother-of-pearl box in which Mama kept hairpins; pink tourmaline earrings, a present one name-day; a silver cigarette container, the Petropavlovsk fortress in Petersburg engraved on the lid; a sapphire parure – necklace, earrings, brooch, bracelet – from Papa to Nadia at their betrothal in Paris. She feels the old life disappearing, birthdays, celebrations, never to be retrieved.

'There's still this,' Nadia says another morning; she produces a leather belt studded with diamonds. 'I've been wearing it under my clothes. Your father gave it to me when we left Paris for Baku.'

Nadia relinquishes it, and their hands touch. Nadia's are roughened; the skin below her eyes has darkened, as if they have retreated; there are lines at the sides of her mouth.

'How can you part with it?'

'No choice. I still have my wedding and betrothal rings.' Nadia has secured them on a string round her neck, beneath her blouse. 'We're together, safe. We have our health, a roof over us.'

'But you want to be in Baku, surely?'

'Only what's best for your father, and all of us. Think how much worse it could be. They talk at the hospital as if the tsar really is dead and turn away in embarrassment in case I've understood, and change the subject.'

She grabs her hat. The boys are waiting by the door. 'I can't imagine anything more dreadful than the tsar gone forever.' She knows this isn't what Nadia means but isn't able to believe the rumour; as if everything about Russia and their existence now is unreal, a disconnected dream; one day, it will come right.

In an open courtyard, shaded by large trees, belongings are laid in little chessboard squares on the ground, speaking of recent impoverishment and current despair, yet of a life once lived in gaiety: forlorn bits of ribbons, lace, silk waistcoats; a broken watch, kettles, gramophone, high-button boots with skates screwed on, remnants of sacrifice, price of a meal or room. She cannot see the valuables she has already brought here, and wonders who has bought them and for whom.

Nadia's belt will go elsewhere. Clutter and chaos eddy and absorb her: donkeys, only legs visible under their loads; dogs, bone-shapes showing through matted fur; scraggy brown and black sheep, ropes of camels, a youth carrying a chicken, a child driving a goose; someone wrapped in rags lying by a door; veiled women gossiping, a car or two. A man on a mule shouts a warning, and she presses her back against a warm mud wall.

She glances at strange, harsh faces of men in flowing garments; dark, intent, hooded eyes, no-one resembling Mr MacDonell.

She finds a recess, no bigger than a cupboard, in the leatherworkers' street, quiet and industrious. Smells of their craft mingle with those of perfumes and drains. The shopkeeper, beard henna-dyed beneath a green turban, squats beside his wares. Long fingers, nails stained orange, brush across brass weights and scales. She holds out her offering.

From between sleepy lids, lacklustre eyes light with interest. He takes and caresses it, smoothes the diamonds. She imagines Papa giving it to Nadia: I'll always love you; is that what he promised? The Persian is saying something, and she reins in her thoughts, concentrates. She has memorised the words for twenty, thirty, forty. The first will not be enough. The next will do. The last, she will consider she has done well. She looks at the man, does not understand, turns to walk away. He is still talking.

She returns to him. 'Forty,' she embarks.

His monologue persists.

She repeats her price.

He mutters. She nods. He counts out twenty silver coins and some two-toman notes. Thirty-six tomans. Sufficient to stay at Madame Lavirotte's for another ten days, by which time they might be able to go home.

She has an hour before she must collect Jacob and Anton. The Magasin Hollandais, the Comptoir Français, and other shops in the European Quarter have little for sale, so she makes for the bazaars as she has before. Not once did she patronise the ones in Baku: they were the province of Tartars and Armenians, ordinary people, trade; Livvy used to end up there a lot, a habit when not in your own country.

Here, they are covered by a domed roof, suggesting a clay umbrella, and meander without end, break now and then into open lanes and narrow alleys, creep like labyrinths beneath vaulted tunnels. Odours of grain and cardamom compete with those of dung and sweat. Shafts of sunlight burst through apertures. Lamps burn in dingy corners. Through a low door, she distinguishes men smoking and conversing. Two crouch at a table. One extracts coins from a pocket and gives them to the other. The second scrutinises and bites them, weighs his gain, deposits it in a bag, with sedate, dignified movements.

Merchants show no anxiety to sell, but observe as if more

concerned that nothing be stolen. She can turn over bundled silks, ancient filigree necklaces and bracelets, unbothered who might see her, people of whom she knows nothing, or they of her, passing around her, going about their business.

She strokes a Kirman rug, its arabesques and gardens woven in ivory velvety wool similar to one in the drawing-room at home; she thinks of the parquet floor, rosewood furniture, a French ormolu clock. Somebody is peddling rosewater. She used to wear it in Baku, eking out the last drops.

Because she entered the bazaars from the leatherworkers' street, she has no idea how to reach the legation. Panic beats at her chest. She must ask. 'Excuse me,' she launches in Russian to a woman. For a few seconds, kohled eyes regard her above the veil. The person moves away.

She tries French. *'Pardon, madame ...'* This one is enveloped in a mantle of indigo, face concealed by a white cloth; she pauses before sucking in breath – of shock? fear? – and scuttling on.

If they are too shy or scared to speak to an unveiled stranger, she must approach a man. Here is someone with a fur fez such as those worn by Tartars in Baku, and a long, dusty-coloured, loose-fitting robe. She addresses him in Russian.

Hostility glares from him; he sneers as he replies, and slides past her. Frustration, anger, burn her cheeks. What's the matter with everybody?

Ahead is a gate in the grey clay, and she is in a lane wide enough for two carts on sun-baked mud. She stops. In the distance, somebody is playing the piano. She walks on, slows, the music nearer, in a house behind a windowless, discouraging wall. Outside a wooden door, she recognises a Chopin nocturne she learnt with Doctor Bagratuni.

She lifts an iron handle shaped like a roaring lion. It creaks as if unused to such tentative treatment. Through the doorway is a courtyard, in the centre a bush, taller than a person, smothered in wide, single yellow roses that settle more like a butterfly than a flower. In one corner, an oleander wilts in August heat. Grapes cluster a vine's length on rough supports. She goes over to a rectangular cistern on her right. Water reflects the sky, and goldfish dart about. Unseen pigeons coo, and a bee blunders from a flower, across time hanging suspended. Stone steps lead to arches.

She listens to the final bars. Silence, until the sound of sobbing, and she feels embarrassed to be eavesdropping on grief. A rose breaks, and petals flutter. She hears a voice, gentle, consoling, and the weeping ceases.

Someone strikes chords on a stringed instrument, and she remembers she is in Teheran, lost, and should be at the legation. She begins to climb the steps to ask the way, but the ease with which she gained admission discomforts her. She cannot intrude further, especially as there is sorrow in the house. She returns to the door and the parched, dusty street.

She walks beside the wall and onto a thoroughfare furrowed by tramlines, the snow-capped Elburz mountains rising behind. The legation is on the only tramway.

'On Petersburg, the darkened city,
    November, chill and without petty –'
'Pity, not petty, Jacob. Try once more.' Who was it, she wonders, playing a Chopin nocturne and crying?
    'On Petersburg, the darkened city,
    November, chill and without pity,

blasted; against its noble bank –'
'Brink, not bank.' What tragedy has afflicted the household?
'*... against its noble brink
Neva was splashing noisy billows –*' recites Anton.
'It's not your go,' Jacob snaps at him. 'Tell us again, Esther, when you saw the Neva and Petersburg with Papa and met Miss Livvy.'
'After you've said it all correctly.' Has a baby died, a child, a loved one?

The next day, she keeps to the tramway beneath flat roofs, and blue and gold cupolas, stark against an azure sky. She looks for the lane where she heard the piano. Yes! The same music. She quickens her pace. When she arrives at the door, she twists the handle with more determination than before.

An old man is sweeping the courtyard with a broom of twigs. He wears a pale-blue kaftan and a yellow cummerbund. He glances up, stops what he is doing. His hands are scrawny; face thin, wrinkled, and topped by a skullcap.

'Good morning,' he addresses her in Persian. This she has learnt from Madame Lavirotte and how to reply. He smiles, revealing more gaps than teeth, and speaks some more. His voice is high, a woman's.

She shakes her head, points towards the direction of the Chopin. She spreads her fingers, wiggles them in imitation of playing the piano.

'Zeinab,' he tells her.

She repeats the name.

Pleasure disappears from his expression. He is not going to invite her in, and conversation is impossible.

'Please excuse me,' she says in French.

Zeinab. His wife? Sister? Daughter? Now with a name, the pianist and her suffering become an obsession. Maybe Zeinab is ill, or grieving; is she beautiful or aged?

She goes back the following morning to find the courtyard empty, rose petals on the ground.

'Zeinab,' she whispers. Twice.

She stares, as if at a vision. The young woman who has come through an archway to stand at the top of the steps is arrayed in buttercup trousers and shirt, the latter worked in silver and finishing at the elbows to reveal dainty arms the colour of amber. On top is a violet silk tunic embroidered with golden roses. On her feet are slippers in a darker yellow. A topaz necklace circles her throat. Black hair is arranged in several thick plaits, gold-braided and tied at the end with primrose ribbons.

A cloud of curls clusters around Zeinab's pale, oval face; small, upturned lips are parted in surprise.

In her skirt, blouse and hat, and canvas sandals, she can only feel plain opposite this bird of paradise. She has been holding her breath. She breathes out. 'Zeinab?'

Zeinab says nothing.

She puts her hand on her chest and introduces herself.

Zeinab's mouth moves in the start of a smile. 'Russian?' Zeinab responds in a language she, Esther, recognises. The Armenian servants used to speak it among themselves on the ground floor of the house.

'Anahid,' Zeinab pronounces. 'Anahid.'

A greeting? A plea?

Perhaps Zeinab understands French. *'Je m'appele Esther.'*

Zeinab comes down the steps, and attar of roses fills the air. 'You know French? My name is Anahid, not Zeinab.' Each word is placed with care, perhaps through lack of use. 'Anahid,' she emphasises, as if luxuriating in its sound, its feel on her tongue. 'Zeinab is what they call me here. I am Armenian. And you are Russian? Esther?'

'We had Armenian servants at home, the same ones since before I was born. And during the war, refugees in Baku, from Lake Van. The Turks had been hounding them.'

'That is my mother's area. I look like her; the blue eyes of Van.'

She explains why she and her family left Russia. *Bolsheviki* prompts no reaction from Anahid.

Maybe she's gabbling. With more thought, she describes to Anahid how she heard the piano and discovered the courtyard the day before yesterday.

Anahid puts fingers to her mouth; they are long, languid, a pianist's. Amusement flickers across her face. 'I will not tell him you said he was old.'

'His appearance was.'

'He is a eunuch.'

'A what?'

Anahid regards her for a moment. 'He is different from other men. He has no desires, cannot be bribed, and so can be trusted.'

And is therefore an ally, she thinks. 'It was you weeping?'

The street door opens, and the same man comes in, carrying a dead chicken by the claws. He stops, looks at Anahid. 'Zeinab.'

Anahid inclines her head in acknowledgement. 'Seyed Ali.' Anahid says more in Persian.

Seyed Ali turns to her. She feels his appraisal from under cowled lids. He nods.

'I have to go, Esther.'

'And I, too. Perhaps I shall see you again.'

'Maybe,' Anahid replies, without encouragement or emotion.

Before she steps into the lane, she glances back. Anahid and Seyed Ali are watching her.

Baba *always said the Russians were our friends, the bear across the mountains. Christian like us rather than the Turk. Call the bear your uncle until you have traversed the bridge, Achmet Bey used to caution* Baba. *Not all Turks are bad, for Achmet Bey was* Baba's *pal, but their ways don't resemble ours. Russian and Turk could never be comrades,* Baba *used to say; the tsar had designs on Constantinople, the Ottoman imperial city. I am Anahid. My name is Anahid Touryan, daughter of Stepan – my* Baba, *schoolmaster in Erzerum in the province of Anatolia – and his wife Vergeen. I must never forget I am Anahid.*

A Russian girl talks of the piano in a rich, velvety voice, rolling the 'r', and does not know what a eunuch is. She has an oval-shaped face the same as me, thick eyebrows, and long lashes over eyes so dark a brown as to be black. Her lips are thin, and skin firm over high cheekbones. Is she an angel, an answer to a prayer? But here is Seyed Ali and he has the Koran: I must listen and read with him and concentrate. I am Anahid.

Vitaly Ivanovich, a translator at the legation, teaches the children. 'Jacob Yefimovich is not attentive, Esther Yefimovna. He does not learn his passage.' Vitaly Ivanovich's pale, northern gaze rests on Anton. 'His brother, now. That is another matter.

We have a scholar in the making.'

'But I hear Jacob say it every evening,' she protests.

Vitaly Ivanovich spreads hands that have tapering fingers. 'So he has very poor retention.'

Walking to their lodgings, she impresses on Jacob, 'You must try harder.'

'It's not interesting,' Jacob complains. 'I want to be a soldier.'

'You're only six!' That he might be excluded from the class alarms her: she will be responsible for him and unable to visit Anahid.

As soon as Papa and Nadia return, they all sit at the table and she removes the wire mesh from the dish Madame Lavirotte has brought upstairs; jubilant at having found two eggs, the landlady has prepared an omelette and kept a portion for herself.

It is not quite set in the middle. On her tongue, she keeps every piece intact until it dissolves and she has to swallow it. She licks round her mouth for traces of yolk, wipes her plate with yesterday's bread, sucks any stickiness that clings to it.

She tells the family about Anahid.

'What's she doing in Teheran?' Nadia asks.

'I don't know. There's a sadness in her.'

With a spoon, Nadia catches a drop of yolk on Jacob's chin. 'Poor girl.'

After taking the utensils to Madame Lavirotte, she lets down reed blinds and undresses as far as her chemise. The boys have already gone to sleep. She unrolls her pallet, stretches out.

Anahid.

She closes her eyes.

'Are you dreaming of the piano, Esther?' Jacob is peering at her.

A breeze has risen, sighs between the screens. Nadia comes in and pulls them up. 'Still resting, Esther?'

She pushes Jacob away, stands, ruffles his hair. 'Homework.'

She goes to the window. Shadows lengthen, the intense light of sunset extends over the city, creeps like a tide up foothills. Snow-covered ridges glow for a few minutes, the sun a pink ball in darkening sky. An owl hoots. Night falls, stars emerge from their hiding-places, and the mountains revert to their changelessness and secrecy, as in days when no traveller passed here except a nomad driving flocks to pasture.

Papa has trimmed the oil lamp. While writing Cyrillic letters as though each one is important, Anton recites, '*He had, ten miles from the posting station, a fine property of two hundred souls.*' He checks the sentence, places his pen on the table, smiles at her. At *posting*, Jacob makes a blot.

Anahid.

SIX

Teheran, Persia, August 1918

'I've tried the door each day, Anahid. I wondered if Seyed Ali wanted to stop me.' They stand in the courtyard.

'It's possible. Sometimes he locks it. Or he forgets. He is not a bad person.'

'What did you mean when you said he was different?'

'He was castrated. That's why he sounds like a woman.'

When she was in Petersburg with Papa, they heard a man sing with a female voice. He was described as a castrato; she assumed it was how he'd been born. On her cheeks, she feels a flush of embarrassment, ignorance.

'It is the way of things here,' Anahid says. 'He runs the household well. He can read and write, and use numbers, so keeps the money, oversees the expenses. He controls the servants, looks after the wives.'

Where does Anahid fit into this ménage? Surely not as a maid, in such clothes; her tunic today is emerald green, embroidered with gold thread humming-birds. 'I came to ensure you were all right.'

'I am as you see me. If I cannot meet you, I will leave a note,' Anahid moves over to the vine, 'here.' She touches where roots push through and coil round.

'Why might you not be able to?'

'If Mirza Khan ...' Anahid shrugs. 'I may get up late.'

'Who is he?'

'My husband.' There is a fraction of a pause between the two words but Anahid continues, 'He has two more. They are older and have babies. I am his plaything.'

'Do you go out?'

'The three of us, occasionally, and Seyed Ali, to visit. When it's hot, so we don't have to veil and cover, we cross the rooftops.' Anahid smiles as if at some excitement. 'But we don't cultivate European women. Our lives are not the same.'

'What do you do all day?'

'Ready ourselves for Mirza Khan and talk about it afterwards.'

She is blushing again. What could there be for the women to recount?

'And we discuss the best type of henna: we favour red for the neck and palms, blue for the eyes.' Anahid takes her arm. 'Now go, Esther. There will be another time, and you can play the piano.'

They walk to the door; Anahid waits. She wonders if the Armenian girl has ever opened it.

Anahid embraces her, rests fingers on her face. 'You must protect your skin from the sun. In the kitchen, they produce a paste from avocado flesh.'

As she joins the street, Anahid's perfume lingers around her, makes her feel exotic and aware of possibilities she can't name because she knows nothing ... ways between men and women. Plaything?

How many years is it since I spoke French? How long have I been here? We used to study the language of Voltaire at school. Baba *knew some and would recite Lamartine, who had stayed in Constantinople and written a history of Turkey, which* Baba *had in the salon. He quoted Lamartine to Achmet Bey, who called on us because he loved Mama's rosewater* lokum *and swore that no other Armenian woman could flavour it so well.* Baba *and Achmet Bey sat in the salon, and I served them tea and* lokum *on a brass tray, and they smoked from a narghile – Achmet Bey had an ivory mouthpiece – and drank raki. In between* Baba's *declaiming, they sighed over taxation; Achmet Bey was a tailor, and my brother Edouard his apprentice. Achmet Bey said the governor would tax everybody out of business.*

This evening I have to go to Mirza Khan. His lips are soft and wet, and he murmurs against my hair that I will thank him for my fortunate escape. I never ask him what he means. He will keep me with him until we hear watermen cleaning the street, and the trot of the pony who brings water to the house just before dawn. I will sleep and when I wake, Seyed Ali will have prepared for me a bath of rosewater warm from the sun, and a dish of yogurt for breakfast. I am Anahid.

She finds a piece of paper in the base of the vine. *Mirza Khan is sick. He has a cold. I mix him tea from jasmine flowers, or mint-leaves for his digestion. I have to sit with him. I play the* oud *and sing to him.* She remembers the stringed instrument she heard. *I cannot read Persian so I amuse him by telling him stories I learnt as a child, and he falls asleep.*

... I have to sit with him ... a duty? Does Anahid love her husband? What does that mean? She has nobody but Papa and Nadia as an example. The summer the war began, she used to drag Livvy to films starring Moszhuhin. There was always lots of swooning and kissing. Moszhuhin, with painted eyes and mouth, looked so romantic. At sixteen, she imagined herself enamoured of him. Yet, it is a serious matter. Russians do not sprinkle the word in the English manner: I love to do so and so, or I'd love to see you.

She has only known Sasha. His father, too, was an oilman; he and Papa, and Baku's businessmen, made up fours for bridge. Their families entertained each other to meals, not two fingers'-width of lace tablecloth visible beneath plates, bottles, glasses. Sasha and his parents were among dozens of guests invited on her and Lev's fifteenth birthday. She and her brother stood in the reception line with Papa and Nadia. She wore a dress of heavy peach silk and long white gloves. Later in the evening, there was charades.

Sasha was at the *gimnaziya*, a year above Lev, and came to the house to see him. She would be practising the piano. There was an occasion when Lev was out. She finished a piece and turned to find Sasha leaning against the jamb of the open door, watching her. Blond curls reached his shoulders. 'It sounds awfully good, Esther.'

'I'm going to be a concert pianist.'

Sasha failed his finals at the *gimnaziya* and was sent away to a military school in Tiflis, capital of the Caucasus. One morning in her room, she recognised his voice in the hall. She crossed the landing to the top of the first staircase. 'Lev Yefimovich is not at home, Alexander Nikolaevich,' Serge explained to Sasha.

Sasha saw her and said, 'Oh, I'll talk to Esther.'

She went downstairs; she had on an ivory voile dress bought in Petersburg. He was in uniform, navy blue, a single row of gold buttons between the belt and high collar, cap under his arm. His hair was very short. He was holding a small package.

'Hello, Esther. How is the piano?'

'I have a place at the conservatoire in Petersburg next year.'

'That's splendid. I'm back for a week. I brought you these.'

They stayed there for a few minutes, Serge loitering as if unsure what he should do, smells of garlic and coriander percolating from the kitchen. After Sasha had gone, she unwrapped the parcel. It was a box of marrons glacés, and coloured marzipan in the shape of animals and fruit. A picture of children playing with lambs in a flowered meadow covered the lid.

He called once more before he returned to Tiflis. 'Can I write to you, Esther?'

'Yes.' She wondered how she would reply.

He wrote three letters to her one; described drill, parades, and polishing boots with petroleum jelly. *It is a wonderful thing*, she read after the war began, *to experience the glory of fighting for Russia.* They had advanced miles into East Prussia, he reported.

But news arrived in Baku of the First and Second Armies' destruction at Tannenburg. General Samsonov had shot himself having lost two hundred thousand men in ten days, many of them killed.

Including Sasha. Papa told her Sasha's parents had received notification of their son's death.

Where's the glory? she wept to Livvy; he was just nineteen.

'Lev must have perished in the battle, too,' Papa said, a propos of nothing months later, as if continuing a conversation that had already started. 'He and Sasha were probably in the same unit, both from Baku.'

She wondered if, for Papa and Nadia, deciding that Lev had died for his country nullified his rebellion those weeks before hostilities broke out.

Sasha's letters are still in her desk at home.

Leaves on Teheran's plane trees have a yellowish tinge. She helps Nadia sew bed-linen sides to middle for Madame Lavirotte.

Jacob raps Anton over the head. 'Food train late again! What have you been doing, you stupid body? And hair has to be cut! Every Saturday! This is not good enough, Corporal. Commander Lev Yefimovich will be here any moment to inspect the troops.' He cuffs his brother.

Anton puts his hand against his face. 'Don't do that.'

'Soldiers have to be tough,' Jacob insists: '"Yes, Captain," you say. "It won't happen any more, Captain."' He rearranges Anton's tin soldiers into rows of four. 'Stand straight!' he yells at them.

Nadia is snipping cotton. 'Play nicely, boys.' She adds, 'We saw Mr MacDonell this morning. He'll be in Enzeli soon.'

She bunches a sheet in her lap. 'We could go with him!'

'A lot of British troops are in Baku. There's a confrontation with the Turks. A siege, he said.'

General Dunsterville will win. 'We can set off as soon as it's all over.'

'And how do you suggest we do that?' Nadia wants to know, scorn in her voice.

'Ask. There must be someone who'll take us.'

'Esther, the *bolsheviki* will not rest until they have the oil,'

Papa reminds her. 'They call themselves the Red Army now. Nobody's going back.'

'Corporal, get this bread unloaded and the men fed,' Jacob instructs. 'We have the Red Army to defeat.'

Anahid embraces her on both cheeks. 'You're here.'

'Do you mind?' A week has passed.

'No. It is nice to talk to somebody ... different.'

'How is your husband?'

'He is better.' Anahid's voice shows no expression.

'Do you play the piano to him?'

'No. He bought it for me.'

'I haven't heard it since I met you.'

'It results in sadness, memories. Anyway, come and see.'

She follows Anahid up the steps. She hears tinkling; Anahid wears anklets of coloured discs.

'We have been dancing,' Anahid tells her, 'the other wives and I.'

Anahid leads her through an archway and across a tiled floor. Perfume pervades the air: vanilla, musk, ambergris. Carpets and tapestries hang from some walls. Recessed niches contain engraved copper and silver plates, and ceramic urns.

Anahid lifts the latch on a door. 'We are going into the women's quarters.'

The scent of dried roses wafts among swathes of red drapes; latticed windows, unseen female voices, a baby crying. Perspiration tickles her armpits and shoulders. Her stomach is a knot of nerves.

'Does your husband come in here?'

Anahid's eyebrows rise in surprise. 'Of course. Sometimes. It is his house.'

They arrive in a white room. She breathes in attar of roses and coffee. The ceiling is painted peacock-blue. A pink embroidered *divan,* scattered with satin bolsters and silk cushions, lines the perimeter. There are a few low, carved stools and small tables. In one corner, a tawny bird chirps and hops in a cage, causing it to shake.

In the centre stands an upright piano of walnut inlaid with satinwood. On the top is a vase of brilliant, single amber roses. Alongside the flowers is a dish, which Anahid picks up. 'Some *mastika?*'

'Afterwards,' she says, unsure what it is.

Abandoned on the *divan* lies a silk cloth stitched with vine-leaves and yellow tulips. Further along languishes a pear-shaped, stringed instrument, Anahid's *oud.*

Anahid reclines next to it, piles cushions, tucks her legs underneath her. 'Play for as long as you wish, Esther.'

She wipes damp hands down her skirt, steadies her breathing. She sits on the stool, wishes it were higher, flexes and wiggles her fingers. She starts with a few scales and arpeggios. The piano is tuned. She wonders where Mirza Khan purchased it.

She closes her eyes to distance her surroundings, goes into a polka, a jolly thing to make Anahid happy. And another.

She forgets Anahid. Just herself and this piano as one. She launches into the Chopin étude called 'revolutionary', his anguished response to the Russian capture of his dear Warsaw, nearly ninety years ago. The chords crash, tumble, climb once more and, not quite grasping what they are searching for, retreat as if pursued by a demon. Her wrists ache; the last time she performed this was for Doctor Bagratuni in July. The notes chase each other, one slip, but she recovers and completes the sequence. She pushes herself through the final bars, hands aloft in the triumph of completion.

Her heart is slamming. She stays seated, looks down until ready to rejoin the room.

Anahid sits cross-legged, arms clasped around knees, staring at her.

A dusky-skinned woman in a white shift, dark curls cropped close, stands in the archway, holding a baby; behind her crowd several girls, who flee at a snapped remark from her.

The bird is still, head on one side. 'You have soothed Kiki, Esther,' Anahid smiles. 'You have a great gift.'

The woman says something. Anahid's reply is met with a short laugh and wave of farewell.

'That was Lallah, Mirza Khan's second wife. She comments she's never heard this from me.'

'You play well. I have to perpetuate music inspired when Russia was powerful. As a boy of fifteen, years before he wrote this, Chopin performed for the tsar.'

'I imagined myself in a concert hall.'

'It is my greatest wish.' She tells Anahid about the conservatoire.

Anahid comes over to the piano. 'The war changed your life, and mine too. I wouldn't be here, otherwise.' The word how stays unspoken as Anahid adds, 'I will explain another time. You will be late for your brothers.' Anahid offers the dish again. 'Have some *mastika* now. It will relax you.'

She picks golden crystals and bites into them. They dissolve into a sweet, aromatic gum.

Anahid gives her a jar from a tray. Inside is a pale, yellowish-green cream. 'For your skin,' she reminds her.

The first we knew of the fighting was when the town crier passed the house. It will not last, Baba *maintained. Achmet Bey visited as if nothing had happened, but he and* Baba *sat with worry beads, faces solemn.*

Mama had been buried a few months. Achmet Bey went to her funeral. He stood at the back of the church, arms folded, out of respect for his friend Stepan Touryan, my Baba. I pickled eggplants, cooked pilav *and* köftes, *and looked after Baba and my two brothers, and rubbed my hands with half a lemon to keep them nice. I'm sure I didn't make* lokum *as well as Mama, but Achmet Bey was too kind to say. He was like that, Achmet Bey.*

In the spring – I remember that's when it was because apple- and cherry-blossom were on the trees, and the air was fresh – Baba and my elder brother, Edouard, Achmet Bey's apprentice, were taken. To fight in the Army, they were told, but the gendarmes tied their wrists with ropes and rough speech. Achmet Bey and his wife, Bedia Hanum, *cared for me and my young brother, Gaspar, in their home. They are rounding up Armenians of military age, Achmet Bey said; it is not good to be Armenian, but you will be safe here. I had to wear a black headkerchief, the* çarsaf, *to make me into a Turkish girl, one of Achmet Bey's daughters. I met my friends in secret by the river.*

Bedia Hanum *was affectionate, but Achmet Bey was concerned: the sultan's army was split between two Fronts – the Russians in the mountains to the east, and the British in the Dardanelles. Soon, he and his son would be conscripted. There would be nobody to protect me and Gaspar. It would be better for us in Persia, away from trouble. He gave us into the charge of merchants who sold him cloth, travelling through Erzerum to Tabriz on the old Silk Road. He intended it for the best because we were Armenian.*

Esther's eyelids, normally translucent, darken with emotion. The muscles in her face and neck are never still when she plays the piano. Her limbs loosen. She is oblivious to everything. She winces at a wrong note, shoulders tight, as though somebody has hurt her hands. She is a breath of outside, unveiled in the sunshine, and her European clothes.

I feel miserable recalling the old days. Seyed Ali is on his way. He will not want to see me unhappy. He will suggest a salve.

'Your expression is sorrowful, Zeinab. Your head is aching?'

'No. I was thinking –'

'It is not good. The Russian woman has upset you with her fiery music?'

'No. I could watch and listen to her for hours.'

'I will concoct a preparation for your eyes, and you must rest or Mirza Khan will not be pleased later.'

I was with him yesterday, too. I am Anahid.

'How did you end up in Teheran?' She and Anahid are sitting on the *divan*.

'The traders treated us well. Achmet Bey would have paid them. I lost count of the days. One night, there was shouting and screaming. I was rolled in a blanket, carried off, and after that it was a black space. Whenever I woke, I was bumping along in a cart, just room for me. When we stopped, I was given a drink and returned to sleep. I asked about Gaspar, but they shrugged as if they didn't know what I meant.'

'Who?'

'Persian camel-drivers. Smelly people. Eventually, I opened my eyes to find myself here. Seyed Ali was sponging me with rosewater and stroking my hair. I was terrified and wouldn't eat. I cried, kept repeating my brother's name. Seyed Ali was very patient; I found out, when I understood more, that he had told me I was safe in Persia. He sang to me when I was tormented by dreams.'

'How old was Gaspar?'

'Fourteen. Three years younger than me.'

'You and I are the same age.' She tells Anahid about Lev.

'There can be no-one closer than a twin, Esther. You were in your mother's womb together.'

Her cheeks are burning.

'Seyed Ali brought all kinds of dishes to tempt my appetite. He taught me a few Persian words, and introduced me to the other wives and their children.'

'Don't you get jealous? I can't imagine Nadia accepting anybody with Papa.'

'Lallah was. It's been better since she had the baby. Seyed Ali started calling me Zeinab and instructing me in Islam. But I never want to forget that I am Christian. I have no idea what happened to *Baba*, Edouard, Gaspar. Were *Baba* and Edouard forced to fight? Armenians have no quarrel with Russians. I need to remember the church we all used to go to; frescoes and ikons blackened by a thousand years of candlelight; chanting, incense, and the red carpet; that I am Anahid.'

I kiss his hand. He has long fingers and hennaed nails. I wait for him to speak. He is calm, with an ebony beard which never changes. He has an oval face, and strong brows which meet at the forehead. Dark lashes curl over brown eyes. He wears a silk robe on which are embroidered gazelles. He has come to the harem.

'Are you happy, Zeinab?'

'I wish only for your happiness, my husband.' Seyed Ali has told me to say this. My job is to please. Mirza Khan is not interested in my opinion, does not require me to think at all but just to be beautiful and feminine.

He rests a finger under my chin, and smiles. Walks on. He is going to Lallah and their daughter. Good. She will be sweet for the rest of the day.

I had been here weeks when I was taken to him. Lallah and the first wife had spent hours with me, washing my hair with an infusion of camomile flowers to make it glossy, and braiding it – Lallah tugged more than was necessary – rubbing my teeth with a green pecan-shell to whiten them, smearing melted sugar under my arms, and between and down my legs, stripping it off, trimming my fingernails and toenails before dying them red. They cracked an egg into each of three basins of steaming henna so it was golden, spread it on me, glazed me with jasmine-oil, kneaded me with olive-oil and ground almonds, told me about their introduction to Mirza Khan and how to satisfy him. Seyed Ali hovered at the edge of the room, wrung his hands, sighed, wrinkles re-arranging themselves when he caught my eye and winked encouragement. The massage and the feculence of henna lulled me into a stupor.

The first wife, who has four children and a tooth missing, and is rather plump, greased me between my legs. I tensed and tried to move away, but she tapped me on the hand and insisted I would find it easier, so I let her. She nodded in approval, said I really was a virgin and she wouldn't have to use chicken's blood, that my abductors must have kept me untouched to get a better price and Mirza Khan would be delighted because he had paid a lot of money for me. Of course I was intact. A good Armenian girl. Perhaps, if there had not been the war, I would have married an Armenian boy, one of the cousins from Lake Van or the son of Baba's sister in Kars; they were all at Mama's funeral, but I have no recollection of them. I would have embroidered a bridal sheet with Mama's patterns. Baba and the parents would have agreed concerning money and possessions, but I wouldn't have needed to be aware of those details.

Finally, I was dressed in a white robe, and Seyed Ali led me to Mirza Khan. It hurt a bit, and I cried. Seyed Ali told me afterwards that Mirza Khan was enchanted with me, resulting in all the clothes and jewellery, and the piano. He should give equal attention to his wives, but I have extra, his favourite. The first one doesn't mind. She is full of advice but says she is tired so I suppose he is too energetic for her.

I cannot speak of this to Esther. She has never been with a man so doesn't understand. She is embarrassed by any mention of the body and blushed when I said she and her brother had been in the womb together. Here, it is normal to talk about it. I am married, even though it was not in church. After the war, I may be able to leave and wed an Armenian although I won't be pure for him.

Poor Esther, to have lived through revolution. She is so brave. She calls here, hoping the door is unlocked. I will see her again soon. Maybe tomorrow.

SEVEN

Grozny, Russia, autumn 1918

Fifty men, the whole unit, stand in rows behind him alongside a slanting barn with woven brushwood walls. Ramrod-straight, hands at his side, he steps forward to within three paces of the commander, Dmitry Grigoryevich, and stares ahead as you had to in Nicholas Romanov's army. Another stride and he's an arm's reach from DG who – with sandy hair, freckled cheeks, and a mole at the end of his nose – is only a few years older than him. DG studied in Paris and Switzerland, and knows Lenin.

He focuses on the cart beyond DG, mouth closed, teeth clenched, so as not to betray the tingling in his chest that is spreading through his belly.

DG pins the five-pointed red star on his shirt; says, 'Leon Alexeevich Kovansky,' stretching out each name. 'You are the eyes and ears of the Party inside the Red Army. Look well, listen well. Russia is proud of you.'

It's done. He is a political commissar. Which means keeping you in line, too, DG, so watch it!

Never a great communicator, Dmitry Grigoryevich. Now if it were him attaching the badge, with a captive audience: ... *Russia is yours ... Mother Russia ... you will not put down your rifles until forces of opposition and reaction have been wiped out ... no foreigners in Russia, who have dominated our affairs for too long, involving the homeland in complications and battles always fought for the benefit of others ... after that, you will have your Mother Earth ... freedom to work your land and enjoy its benefits ... the oppressed will become the ruling class ...*

The words roll around his mind as the cart shed swims in his vision. Much of it comes from *Soldatskaya Pravda*, the newspaper which circulated among the troops eighteen months ago at the time of the revolution in Petrograd and Nicholas Romanov's abdication; now he's gone, German wife and useless children, too.

The thrill of the moment swells to pride, belief in the future. In his head, he repeats the three names he has taken. Stalin and Trotsky did it, as well as Lenin, as a sign of throwing off the old order, previous selves.

Leon he has chosen the same as Trotsky as they also share the given name from their original Jewish lives. Alexeevich, his new patronymic, is to remember Alexei, whom he will always think of as his revolutionary father; the textile-worker who lodged him in a cramped, second-floor flat after he left home at the beginning of Nicholas Romanov's war. Late into the night, door locked, last stub of candle sputtering on the table, they talked; or rather Alexei did, and he soaked it all up, sixteen-year-old heart opening like a flower in the sun. Working men of different countries should not be fighting each other, said Alexei, but joining forces, grasping hands across frontiers to confront the real enemy.

Alexei's name and street appeared on papers that were eventually produced for him so he could enlist. By that time, he knew how to play on men's dissatisfaction, for euphoria and patriotism in the early weeks gave way to inactivity and boredom as they waited to know where they would be sent. News came of millions of Russians shivering in icy mud up to their knees in ill-constructed trenches. Gloom deepened when they heard of the Russian army's collapse in central and southern Poland in the summer of '15. Fertile ground for what he had to do. The following year, he was posted to the Turkish Front.

Kovansky is because of a village on the Anatolian/Russian border. When he and his comrades learnt of the revolution in Petrograd, they began the trek back to Russia over the mountains. The first place where people understood Russian was Kovansk. Villagers shared what little food they had, and somebody tended the leg he'd twisted; another, in a heavy coat with no collar or buttons but tied with a sash, gave him boots, easier on stumps of frostbitten toes. In the corner sat a grandfather, legs folded under, cradling a baby, and he, Leon Alexeevich, for fleeting, unbidden seconds, recalled the father who had cuddled him when he was a small boy after his mother died.

They were escorted to the headman in a long, low building of piled stone; in a sheepskin cap, black cloak reaching his ankles, the man had only the previous day returned from Tiflis on horseback. 'They read out the declaration of revolution from Petrograd,' he said, voice shaking as if in unbelief. 'People were there from the entire Caucasus, even Baku oil-workers. They carried political prisoners shoulder-high through the square, twenty of them, who'd been in the dungeon for a dozen years.'

He wondered if Alexei had managed the journey to Tiflis. 'We shall all be comrades and free,' he told his host, 'and making peace with the Ottomans.'

He turns. Fyodor Petrovich slouches towards him, greasy cap perched on shaved head, same filthy rags binding legs and feet, and still smelling like a pigsty, but with determination blazing from his eyes. 'It's good,' Fyodor Petrovich says.

He clasps a proffered, calloused hand.

EIGHT

Teheran, Persia, late 1918

On days when lanes and thoroughfares are moon-white, grey sky heralds more snow, and a strange quiet and stillness haunts the streets. She grows used to the crunch of a fresh fall under feet shod in boots that lace past her ankles; Madame Lavirotte gave them to her, and a shawl. Another morning, sun shining and twinkling like fire along the summits of the Elburz mountains is just a whisper against her face; whiteness hurts her eyes. Air is thin, clear, a top note on a piano. Sometimes wind is icy. She dips the smallest fingertip into the avocado cream Anahid gave her and rubs it on her cheeks.

'Winter suits you, Esther,' comments Anahid. 'It brings a blush to you and liveliness to your expression.'

'I never expected to be here.'

The season does not diminish Anahid's appearance. Tunics have sleeves threaded with gold or silver, fastening at the wrists, and a succession of shawls, blue, emerald, scarlet, yellow.

Anahid cracks pistachios and melon seeds, and hands some

to her. 'Mirza Khan wants me to have his child. When I go to him, there are mandrakes in his room, big purple blooms. The heavy perfume is supposed to be good for barren wives.' Anahid tosses the shells onto hot coals encased in brass, sunk into a floor covered with a silky carpet of birds and flowers on an ivory background. 'He has only daughters. He longs for a son. If I conceive, I shan't ever leave, shall I? There are ways of stopping it. Lallah has told me. You mix herbs and make a drink. But if Mirza Khan finds out, he will be angry. And Seyed Ali.'

A flush of embarrassment warms her neck, moves upwards.

Anahid notices it; amusement hovers at the corners of her mouth. 'My monthly bleeding is very,' Anahid gestures for a word, 'irregular.'

'And mine.' How many times since leaving Baku? Once? Twice?

'If I'm not with child when the thaw starts, Mirza Khan promises to take me south to Hamadan. There is a giant statue of a lion, hewn from red stone. It is said to work miracles for women.'

A maid comes in, scatters twigs and garlic skins on the fire, which gives off a musky smell.

At the lodgings, the aromatic scent of olibanum and charcoal percolates from a copper brazier in the hall. They haven't had eggs again. Weeks pass with no meat, until a few scraps floating in watery soup.

News filtering through to the American mission is seized upon like food: the British withdrew from Baku in September, relinquished control to the Turks. 'They say the British general did this rather than his small force be wiped out,' Papa adds at lunch-time, 'as not one Baku unit supported him. Treachery is the poison of our times.' He shakes his head.

This hits her, a blow to the chest. She thinks of General Dunsterville's dignity months ago in Kasvin, his attention to her. How could he abandon her city? Couldn't the British have sent more soldiers? She aches at the idea of Turkish troops marching down the Olginskaya.

Papa's face is thinner; above the frayed collar, skin hangs loose. Some days, he doesn't shave, stubble grey. 'The British did evacuate their civilians to Enzeli,' he says, 'and any Armenians who wished to leave, for they could not expect quarter from the Turks.'

'It's to be hoped Serge saw sense and accepted the offer. Maria and Doctor Bagratuni, as well.'

Weeks later they learn that the Turks have signed an Armistice with the British on board H.M.S. *Agamemnon*. Ottoman forces have left Baku. The city is capital of the independent republic of Azerbaijan, under British protection.

'But for how long?' Papa muses. 'They have forsaken us once. They could do so again.'

'We must go back,' she tries. 'We're prisoners here.'

'You hear her, Yefim?' Nadia exclaims.

'Esther, you have freedom,' Papa points out. 'More than ever you had in Baku. You take yourself to the bazaars. You have made the acquaintance of a local girl and have carte-blanche to play her piano.'

'But don't you want to return, Papa? In the spring? I can never think of this as home. We're drifting on the surface, passing days, unable to dig and put down roots.'

Papa looks across at his sons. 'Now boys, where were we in the story?'

'Pyotr found the golden mare –' Jacob begins.

Anton continues, '– and became the tsar's best huntsman.'

Slushy brown puddles appear in the road. Snow shrinks up the mountains, lower slopes streaked with darker ground. Through one of the handsome tiled gates which open into the Meidan, a wide space north of the bazaars, she sees young green shoots on plane-trees.

In the courtyard of Mirza Khan's house, fat yellow buds, and already a few flowers, cover the rosebush. On the vine clusters unripe fruit, round, perfectly formed, waiting for sun and warmth.

'We depart soon,' Anahid tells her. 'Everybody. There are a lot of preparations. Seyed Ali is more agitated every day.' Anahid clings to her. 'I shall always remember you, my only friend. Will you be here when we come back?'

She hugs Anahid. 'I want to go home, but there is nobody to accompany us.'

Next morning, she hears female voices raised in excitement and alarm, followed by hands clapping, calling people to attention. A baby is crying. She returns to the street, closes the door on a household in tumult. Anahid's perfume lingers, in her hair, the collar of her blouse.

It fades, becomes a memory.

Three soldiers are on the corner of the road to the legation. She assumes they're British, in the same khaki as those in Enzeli and Kasvin last summer, shirt-sleeves rolled to above reddened elbows. They regard her as she approaches; tommies, solving problems, making you feel things are better. Except when they leave your country.

Their moustaches are neat, faces hardened and burnt by an alien sun, eyes pale and harsh, appraising her, an unveiled woman. She turns away, uncomfortable under their gaze.

Yet, discomfort dissolves, and she asks them, 'Have you been, or will you be going, to Baku?' The words sound strange. She has not spoken English since the journey with Mr MacDonell.

They glance at each other, at her. 'Baku, miss?' one of them repeats.

'You know it?'

'Heard of it. Hell-hole from what they say. Stink of oil. And a wicked wind.'

She stiffens, that her city should be so dismissed. 'The British are there, I understand.'

'For the time being.'

'It is my home.'

He looks sympathetic. 'You Russki, miss?'

Russki. A diminutive that trips off the tongue, describing millions of individuals whose lives have been changed. Have these men nothing more pressing than to loiter on a foreign street corner until ordered to do something else?

'Best out of it if you ask us,' another one comments. 'Bolshies are fighting anyone who gets in their way. Strikes me they'll want their oil back.'

'*Our* oil. Loyal Russians. Are you going to help us throw these ruffians out?'

They smile, shrug. 'We do what we're told, miss.'

A longing to see the sea and the house hurts her chest. She will not show weakness in front of these troops who are probably not much older than her and have no feeling for her country. Russki, indeed!

'Thank you,' she manages. 'Goodbye.'

They touch their caps. 'Goodbye, miss,' they chorus. 'Good luck.'

Shoulders straight, she walks to the pond in the middle of the Meidan. Plane-trees around it are in full leaf, young green not yet wilted in the heat. The square is surrounded by dozens of rusty cannons, muzzles turned outwards as if to meet an invisible enemy. She sits under one of them, sighs. What would she give for a plate of *pryaniki*, the little cakes Elena made with treacle or honey, or *krendielki*, strips of rich, sweet pastry twisted into different shapes. And the hors d'oeuvres: caviar, blini, pirozhki – small pastries filled with minced meat and vegetables, into which Elena sprinkled plenty of cayenne, ginger, garlic, coriander. Elena cooked dolma – lamb and rice wrapped in vine-leaves – and there would be sturgeon fresh from the Caspian. I hope you went to Enzeli, Elena, safe with Serge and Sonia. Are you in Baku now, waiting for us?

A man in uniform is coming towards her. His dark jacket is fastened to the neck with a single row of buttons in the same gold as the upright collar and epaulettes. On his head is a fez, the crown of which is gilded with braid. Her eye is drawn to his full moustache, turned up and waxed at the ends.

He slows as he approaches. She focuses on the ground. He passes by.

'Jacob, walk properly!' He tugs at her hand, jumps, skips, release of a morning's energy reined in at the legation. 'You're making me hot.'

'It is anyway.' He scuffs dust in the road.

'Look at your boots!'

'It's boring, Russian. I want to run about. We never play, Esther.'

A stone lands in front of them. Jacob pulls himself free. An urchin points in their direction, yells.

'Jacob, no! Stay here!' But he has picked up the missile, thrown it back, and a scoop of sand.

The lad bounds over to Jacob; the two grapple, kick, punch; Jacob spews Russian expletives. Where did he learn them? The other boy curses in who knows what language; he is Jacob's height and wears an ill-fitting, colourless garment tied at the waist. The top half has flopped open; she sees the shape of the child's ribs under stretched, swarthy skin. She tries to separate the boys, Anton clinging to her skirt, but they lash at her, and she steps away, shaken by such fury in children.

People shout, gather round. She hears horses' hooves, neighing, wheels. Through the mêlée, she makes out authority in a male voice. Hands heft the fighters, carry them to the side as a carriage rolls past. The aggressor thumps Jacob's shoulder, but the man pushes him on his way with a few curt words and a boot in the backside.

The uniform and waxed moustache: the person she saw in the square the other day? '*Merci*,' she thanks him in French, for he certainly isn't English or Russian.

He looks at her with eyes that are black, inscrutable, below thick brows which almost meet. He bows, mumbles, 'Madame', and walks in the direction from which she and her brothers came.

With nothing further to gaze at, onlookers drift away although some hurl comments as they go. She feels uneasy, not understanding yet sure she's being blamed for what happened. Anton is crying.

'Apologise,' she tells Jacob, 'and take my other hand. Heaven knows what we're going to say when we get home.' She bites her lip. It's the first time she has referred thus to their two rooms at Madame Lavirotte's.

Jacob grasps Anton's fingers. 'Don't snivel,' he says. To her he adds, 'There's no reason to be sorry. One of us has to be the soldier, and it's me.'

She buys a faded muslin parasol in the bazaars; while the boys are at the legation, she seeks shade under the plane-trees and wonders who it belonged to.

A shadow on the ground in front of her.

She regards the face of the man who rescued Jacob.

He inclines his head. 'Madame.'

She smiles. He hesitates. 'I have …' he tuts as if in frustration, '… little French, madame. I speak … German.' That word is pronounced with an air of accomplishment.

She struggles for language that has lain forgotten since Fräulein Lesser returned to Berlin in May 1914. 'So do I.'

'You seemed troubled just now. You were talking to yourself. Your children are not with you. Your son is well, I trust, after his …' he searches for a word, 'shall we say … adventure? … in the street last week.'

His speech in no way resembles Fräulein Lesser's. Memory, a fragment, flitters across her mind: early-evening walks with her governess, who always wore gloves made of dogskin, in the Mikhailovsky Gardens or along the Marine Boulevard. Amusement tickles her at the officer's assumptions, and a small laugh escapes her throat. He frowns, as though concerned he might have offended her.

She tells him who Jacob is. 'And yes, thank you, he is very well. Too full of energy.'

'Half a brother,' the officer muses. 'That is much to be regretted. He appeared so very complete.'

'We have different mothers.'

'Ah. We do not make such distinctions.'

Is he Persian, with lots of wives like Anahid's Mirza Khan? A shiver of alarm ripples through her, edged with fascination. An aura of tobacco hangs about him. She wonders where he lives, works, and how he spends his time.

'And so you have left your half-brother with his mother and come out to sit alone.'

She explains where the boys are, and Papa and Nadia. 'We should go back to Russia. Things are not good in Teheran.'

'Ah, Russia,' the officer says, sorrow in his voice. 'Persia is Russia's haven. Was not Dmitry Pavlovich, the tsar's cousin, despatched here for his part in Rasputin's murder?'

'You are informed.' Perhaps this man is a spy.

'You are not married?'

If he is Persian, he is accustomed to women veiled, never out of doors unaccompanied. Does he believe I'm not to be respected? Is he mocking me? Hasn't he spoken to a European woman before? He is looking at her. She averts her eyes. What is he thinking? Who is he?

'Your father is not worried about you?'

She regards him again. 'He trusts me.'

'Ah, trust.'

She is finding the conversation tedious, with its examination of her circumstances. She could, should, stand up, walk away. Instead, she hears herself asking, 'Who are you?'

'Captain Kemal Bey of the Ottoman Embassy.'

A Turk. The enemy until recently. Turkish boots on the cobbles of the Olginskaya ... along her own street ... inside her house? Now is the moment to go.

Bey. Anahid talked of Achmet Bey, who took her and Gaspar into his home. It must be a common name. Not all Turks are bad, Anahid said.

She introduces herself.

'Esther Yefimovna,' he repeats as if trying an unfamiliar sound, its feel as he speaks. 'Esther was a Jewish queen at the Persian court, was she not? and saved her people. More than two thousand years ago. And you, too, are a Jewess?'

'Yes, but it shouldn't matter. Where did you learn of her?'

'At school in Macedonia. During Alexander the Great's reign, after Queen Esther's time, all the Persian Empire was brought under Macedonian control.'

'How did you come to speak German?'

'In the war. I was injured, and recuperated in Austria. Have you been there?'

She tells him of Fräulein Lesser.

'So you dismissed her.'

'No. She went that spring to visit her sick father. Papa and I travelled with her as far as Petersburg. She would have rejoined us in Baku ...' She stands up. 'Captain Bey, I shall be late for my brothers.'

He smiles, as though she has said something humorous. 'Should I go ahead of you, Esther Yefimovna?'

'It's only a short distance. I'm quite safe. I'm sure you have work to do.'

'Work,' he echoes, with that habit he has of fastening

onto a word she says. 'Transferring papers from one desk or room to another in the belief we are furthering the ends of his imperial majesty.' He starts walking, keeps several paces in front of her. When he reaches the gate of the square, he turns to her. 'In truth, Esther Yefimovna, his imperial majesty has little knowledge of what is happening outside his own palace.'

She draws in her breath with shock that he should disparage his emperor.

'In fact, I am in disgrace, posted here out of harm's way.'

'How so?'

'After the Armistice with the European powers last October, I returned to the Military Academy in Constantinople as an instructor. I had poor regard for our commanders, like the peacock Enver Pasha who believed himself a great strategist and had a portrait of Napoleon on his desk; nor for the tottering regime he sought to shore up for his own advancement: a trail of muddled politics, scheming treachery, and greed, such as the occupation of Baku.' He nods as if acknowledging a wrong done to her personally. 'The war was the death-throes of old empires: German, Hapsburg, Russian, Ottoman, the clash of dynastic titans, dinosaurs in mortal combat.

'Our sultan, whose forbears once ruled half the world, still harbours grandiose dreams to unify all Moslems: Transcaucasia, Transcaspia,' Captain Kemal Bey counts on the fingers of his left hand, and she notices fine dark hairs below his knuckles, 'the north Caucasus and Volga basin, which would compensate loss of Arab territory. He is unaware or unwilling to accept that for a century the Ottoman Empire has been ridiculed as the sick man of Europe.'

He points to the rusty cannons. 'Persia is no better. Not a single fort does it possess, not one man-of-war, no soldiers except Russian Cossacks, a few British, and fat palace guards. Old men. The land is in tired, weak hands, which are stretched out like an aged beggar, when it should be the clenched fist of a young man.'

He sets off again, and she is obliged to follow, in the direction of the legation. He stops at the foot of the steps and faces her.

'This Armistice with Europe has forced the sultan to place his realm under British protection. The sick man rots, festers, decays in Constantinople. What honour is there in loyalty to such a regime? Your tsar, who dreamed of hanging the Romanov eagle on the gates of Constantinople, his new Byzantium, was murdered by those who seek reform; rough justice from an oppressed people. For our sultan,' Captain Kemal Bey shrugs, 'who knows his fate? Meanwhile, no doubt some ill-considered remark of mine at the academy was overheard and reported to my superiors. And so I am transferred to this backwater –'

'Enough! Please! You talk of pride. There are those who still have respect for their country. Our tsar was betrayed by bolshevik scum, comrades of those who took everything my father owned and have left him broken and old before his time. There are thousands of faithful Russians waiting to drive them from power and restore the imperial family.'

'And where are they, Esther Yefimovna?'

'Here.' She gestures towards the grey stone legation. 'Goodbye, Captain Bey.'

He bows from the shoulders, walks away.

Pulling Anton with him, Jacob runs down the steps. He looks along the road. 'An officer,' he says. 'Dressed the same as the one last week.'

She fusses over Anton, straightens his jacket, smoothes his hair, turns to Jacob. 'What are you doing, Esther?' Jacob demands.

'That's better.'

Captain Kemal Bey is out of sight.

She saw the Ottoman Embassy once at the end of one of the main streets in the European Quarter, not far from the entrance to the jumble of lanes which contains Madame Lavirotte's house. She will take a different route back, not across the square.

The vitriol in Captain Kemal Bey's voice is still with her next morning. If the tsar's death is a rumour, there is hope. But to hear it talked of in such a casual way – not, it is possible ... we believe that ... but, your tsar was murdered – is hateful.

Madame Lavirotte has told her that beyond the legation are some gardens, making her think of the Mikhailovsky in Baku: gas lamps, grass, paths, order. After she leaves the boys, she finds what the landlady must have been referring to. Mud walls are crumbling, gate jammed open by a tangle of briars with flame-coloured roses, red inside and gold outside. Plumes of acacia, and here and there a Judas-tree – a few magenta flowers remaining, the rest desiccated – trunk spindly like a donkey's legs, foliage staining white bodies of tall plane-trees. Birds call, 'Who? Who?' while lizards rustle through dead petals and undergrowth at her feet.

There are other blooms, pink, terracotta, sea-green, whose names she does not know, and peach-trees stripped of fruit. Water flows in runnels into a channel paved with blue tiles, which empties into a broken fountain between four cypresses.

She wonders if she is trespassing. Yet there is nothing to steal, damage already wrought by time and nature.

She walks to a pavilion, over the smashed façade which lies upon the terrace. She sits on a warm stone seat, stretches her fingers, plays scales and arpeggios. Future uncertainty weighs on her, unmoved even by the peace of these surroundings.

Someone has come into the garden and is approaching her. She stands up, recognises the uniform before the man's face. 'Captain Bey!' Disappointment that she cannot be alone is chased by anger and fear. This can be no chance encounter.

He stops a few paces from her. 'Esther Yefimovna. Good morning. Please do not be alarmed.'

'You've followed me. Why?' She steps back. Is even this refuge to be taken from her, tranquillity a threat? Perspiration prickles her. He can surely hear her heart clattering.

'I wanted to speak to you.'

'Don't imagine because I am not veiled and indoors, I am not correctly behaved.'

'I do not, Esther Yefimovna. You told me your father trusted you. I respect that.' He indicates the seat.

'What is it you have to say to me?' She sits at one end, he at the other, a distance of a couple of arms'-lengths.

'I felt after our conversation yesterday I must have sounded very bitter. I was impressed by your patriotism, your hope.' He puts a hand against his chest, and she notices black hair beyond his cuff. 'It can be a hurt, a physical pain, here, can it not, love for one's country and sorrow when there are those who seek to harm it? I, too, am a patriot, Esther Yefimovna, although I realise from the way I spoke you may think otherwise. Have you heard of Mustafa Kemal?'

He does not give her an opportunity to reply but continues, 'No, of course not. Yet, war always throws up its champions. He is a fellow-Macedonian, was hero of Gallipoli, saviour of Constantinople. Now he works in the Ministry of War. It isn't an empire we crave but a land for Turkish-speaking people, such as the first Turks, the Seljuks, who ruled until they were conquered by the Ottomans with their schemes of expansion.'

'Why are you telling me this? Empires are not a bad thing.'

He smiles. 'The original Turkish homeland, Anatolia, is what is important to me, without foreign interference, which is why the Armistice sticks in my throat: British and French in Constantinople, and a few months ago a French general riding through the city on a white horse, gift of local Greeks; British controlling all the Anatolian railway; French and Italians in the south and west. Not to mention Greek occupation of Smyrna. That is what wounds, Esther Yefimovna.'

'The British have been in Baku since the end of last year. We expect them to defeat the *bolsheviki* so we can return.'

'The British.' He speaks as if he would dismiss a whole nation. 'They are everywhere but cannot possibly *stay* there. Even they have to decide what is –' he hesitates, alights on a word, '– paramount. India, of course. Their jewel. They will use Persia if they can to protect their gem from the Bolsheviks. When Azerbaijan and her neighbours no longer serve a purpose, the British will let them go. If, when, the British leave Baku, who would you prefer to be in charge? Bolsheviks or Azeris?'

'Neither. The Russia of old. The tsar reinstated.'

'That is not progress, Esther Yefimovna.'

'The French had a revolution, did they not? And a new king? We ... Russia will survive, as did France.' She stands up. 'Captain Bey, I have to meet my brothers.'

He also is on his feet. 'Esther Yefimovna, Bey is not my name.'

'You told me yesterday it was. Captain Kemal Bey, you said.'

'Bey is a title, such as herr.'

Achmet Bey, friend of Anahid's father. 'But do you have no family name?'

He shrugs. 'It is not the custom. Perhaps this is something that will change.'

'So you are just Kemal?'

'Yes.'

'There must be a lot of them. The officer you mentioned, Musta –'

'Mustafa Kemal. In his case, Kemal was bestowed on him by a schoolmaster. It means perfection. I was known as Kemal, son of Irfan and Besmé of Dedeagach. And I was far from perfect. My teacher had a cane so long he could wallop us without rising from his seat.'

'And did he hit you?'

'Indeed.' The captain allows a smile, as if remembering some incident.

She notices his brows: coarse black hair becomes thinner, finer, the nearer it grows to the lid. The skin around his eyes and out to the temples looks soft compared with the rest of his face. The observation sends a tremor through her.

'I will stay ahead of you,' he says. She frowns, and he adds, 'This is the East, Esther Yefimovna. Men and women do not walk along the street together.'

'Why not? Is it shameful?'

'On the contrary. We respect our women, have care for their tender feelings, and therefore do not draw attention to them in front of others.' He inclines his head. 'Good day to you, Esther Yefimovna.'

What a strange man. She watches him stride towards the entrance to the garden. A man grieving for his country, or his ideal of it. A man whose ideas do not find favour in high places. She makes her way past the fountain.

A man with just one name. How silly!

A name that means perfection.

He's probably homesick; lonely, even.

NINE

South of Voronezh, central Russia, September 1919

A spring rout. The whole of the Red Army, one hundred and fifty thousand, driven from the Caucasus by Denikin's Whites. The humiliation still goads him, Leon Alexeevich.

Units scattered in all directions, with different strategies: north and east, to reach the bolshevik strongholds of Tsaritsyn and Astrakhan; what about the Don basin and Rostov? But the Whites advanced, pushed them to the black earth, the Russian heartland.

'We don't belong to any party,' he would hear from villagers with pudding-basin haircuts and straggly beards, high-necked shirts belted onto loose, threadbare trousers. 'Reds, Whites, they both take.'

'... we organise ourselves. If you strike anyone, he will retaliate ten times ...'

'... a broken bone, any injury, the one who did it loses his life ...'

'... also for stealing, arson ...'

'... we share out our land; don't trust the Whites because they'll pinch it back ...'

'... we have grain. But next year ...'

He looked at hope in eyes that had never been given any; determination on faces scarred and lined by subservience. 'The government of the soviets will guarantee your land, and freedom and peace to work it,' he said.

He has to have no doubt it will happen and to keep his men believing. When they were ejected from Grozny, the promised uniforms hadn't arrived. Each man wears a red band on his sleeve and under it, like a badge of rank marked with pride, a line for every wound incurred. He has six, starting with the lash to his cheek from that Cossack whip when he went to the oilfield demonstration the summer Nicholas Romanov's war began.

Dew lies on foliage, sparkling silver on cobwebs from grass to gatepost. Flat, fertile earth stretches as far as the horizon; the Russia they are fighting for. Flecked clouds hover in a pale-blue sky interrupted by the onion domes of a church.

He and his men, for they are his now – bound together by months of surviving, fifteen of them after a couple of desertions and two dead from fever – spent last night in yet another barn. At daybreak, a ragged boy – too young for the Army but strong enough to carry the iron pot – brought them kasha, buckwheat porridge that is the peasants' staple. They passed the bowl round, prised the scrapings with their fingers.

'... that'll pad your stomach ...'

'... almost as good as Mam made ...'

The youth lingered. 'They say it's city business this talk of revolution,' he ventured, voice squeaky.

'Don't you believe it, lad. How old are you?'

'Dunno.' He ran off.

In chill air, they leave behind them low hovels with dark, tumbledown roofs, slow stares of women and children driving a few bony cattle to pasture.

Apart from their feet on the rutted, sun-baked track, the only sound is larksong. They will continue the traipse north, hope for news or, even better, comrades.

He begins the refrain they always sing. It helps perk the men up.

'Lenin and Trotsky are our pair,
Just try them, just cover them!
Our pair can't be trumped!
What have you got, Denikin, that can match them?'

That'll be the moment, when they can sit down to a game of poker again.

The path narrows. On he leads the men, repeating the verse, hoarse bass baritones.

They come to a railway. The sun behind him, he sets off at the head of a single file. After about an hour, there is a bend. He stops, and the men group around him on the hard earth, chewing blades of grass.

'Anywhere near a river?' Fyodor Petrovich wonders.

If they are, the men can have a drink, unwind the filthy rags from their legs, or the strips of birch bark trussed to bits of old tyre, and soak their feet. He's as thirsty as the rest of them but concerned with a plan. Beyond the curve are trees, one with its trunk half-cutaway, branches almost touching the ground.

'We'll see.' He claps Fedya on the shoulder, sufficient pressure to show he's in charge, and yet encouragement when all Fedya wants is a drink, a pee, and a sleep.

With their knives, they hack at what's left and drag it across the rails. The thicket conceals them. They flop down, wipe rivulets of sweat with grubby sleeves.

'What if there's no train?' Fedya asks.

'Then we'll press on.' Twenty-four, forty-eight hours? How long? Are they in White or Red territory?

Another hour and he hears what he has been straining his ears for. Or is he imagining it? Two of the others glance up.

'Looks like we're in luck, Leon Alexeevich.'

The train's chugging increases until it slows because of the obstruction, screeches to a halt.

His men crouch, wait for his command. He has to see which side the occupants are on. Two people step from the train; boots glint in the sun. Whites. Must be, with that footwear.

'Yes!' he whoops.

Fedya and the others rush forward, knock out the Whites. More emerge from the train. 'Save your bullets!' Fedya yells. 'The knife's as good.' Minutes of shouting, grunting, screams. Silence.

A couple of Whites lie unconscious. He takes one, Fedya the second. A slash in the neck and, before blood can stain them, tear off the jackets: useful as they make their way north to the winter.

A dozen Whites are stripped, pockets emptied. His men put on the clothes. He lifts the covers on the first wagon. Boots, overcoats: new ones. He pulls a few down. Hidden inside the pile are rifles and ammunition. Excitement pulses through him; his breath catches. A haul to expunge the shame of Grozny.

'Climb aboard!' he urges. 'Two in front.'

The train starts, trundles.

'Vicious whirlwinds give us pause,' he begins.
'But all our warriors we will call,' the rest join in.
'The banner for the worker's cause
We'll raise both proud and tall …'

They'll keep going until they run out of fuel. Perhaps as far as Moscow.

TEN

Teheran, Persia, September 1919

Shadows in the square of cannons lengthen; leaves are dry, faded. She no longer requires her parasol but, carried closed, it lends a much-needed suggestion of elegance.

'Captain Kemal Bey!' Her heart kicks with surprise at seeing him after several months. Everything about him is unchanged: waxed moustache, immaculate uniform, short hair beneath the fez.

'Esther Yefimovna. How are you?'

She reaches for German unused since their last encounter, and has the feeling of stepping outside her present circumstances and into a new existence, circumscribed by the language she speaks to the captain. 'The same as before,' she says. 'And you?'

'I am very well.' He indicates the seat. 'May I?'

'Yes.'

'I have been in Anatolia.' There is pride in his voice.

'To your family?'

'Alas, no. They are in Constantinople. I came to look for you, Esther Yefimovna, as I have news of your city. I thought you would want to know as you spoke with such patriotism.'

'Of Baku?' she enthuses, blushing. The captain watches her, smiles.

His face becomes serious. 'British troops have evacuated the whole of Transcaucasia except for a garrison in Batum on the Black Sea coast. They are accused of bad faith, for the Caucasian republics expected their support against the Bolsheviks.'

'It is the second time they have abandoned us,' she observes. She drives from her mind the memory of General Dunsterville's imposing, reassuring presence. 'They are not to be trusted. You know someone who has been to Baku?'

A guarded expression clouds his eyes. 'No. But at the embassy ... diplomatic channels ...' His voice trails into silence, although he continues to look at her. 'Esther Yefimovna, you talk of returning. You have to ask yourself if the place it is now is somewhere you wish to be.'

'What do you mean? It is home.'

'Your brothers will have to be taught in Azeri at school. Teachers are also being recruited from Anatolia. Will your father be prepared to give authority to Azeris at his oilfield and refinery, and learn the language himself? It isn't the Baku you remember. It was clothed in the Russian mantle for a hundred years, but now that has been cast aside and the city reclaims its roots. It has more in common with Persia, by whom it was ruled for centuries, than it does with Russia. And there are the Bolsheviks.'

'In Baku?'

'Not openly. Yet no doubt waiting for their moment as they always have done. They want the oil. The Red Army, as they call themselves, was expelled from the north Caucasus by a White force less than a third of its strength.'

'That ragbag of boy soldiers? I'm hardly surprised. We'd see them loitering on street corners and along the Marine Boulevard, red bands on their arms, shirt collars unbuttoned, hair not combed or cut.'

'They are fighting on other Fronts. They will be back, push south to Baku and the Persian border.'

If not Baku, she muses, where in Russia will we go? To Nadia's parents in Ekaterinoslav, in the Ukraine? The summer the war started, she and Papa stayed there with Livvy during their journey from Petersburg, days of innocence and sunlight on golden corn. Nadia's father and brother are doctors. There has been no news for years. Perhaps they aren't there.

'I, too, have had to accept that my birthplace is part of another country,' the captain says. 'When I was born, Dedeagach was in western Thrace in the Ottoman province of Macedonia. Now it is in Greece and known as Alexandroupolis.' He pronounces the name as if unused to it.

'Turks have a heartland,' she points out. 'You speak of Anatolia. Russia has lost its heart. It fights against itself because the tsar is not there to unite and lead us. I have never lived anywhere but Baku. I do wonder what has happened to our house.' She explains to the captain about Serge, Sonia, and Elena.

He stands up. 'I will see you again if I have news of Baku.'

'Esther!'

She and Anahid run across the courtyard, hug each other. Attar of roses fills her nostrils. For days, she has tried the door, hoped to find it unlocked.

Anahid holds her at arm's length; she is dressed in bright pink and emerald green, braided hair threaded with gold, eyes blazing. 'I've missed you, Esther. You look sad. And you've lost weight. Have you been ill?'

Only a sickness of soul for home, life as it was. 'There's very little to eat,' she reminds Anahid, 'and nobody to escort us away from here.'

'Where to?' There is disbelief in Anahid's voice.

'Anywhere. But we can't do it once winter comes. Your return makes Teheran more bearable.' She glances at her friend's stomach: still flat; Anahid appears well and fuller in the face. 'How was the visit?'

'To Hamadan, awful. Mirza Khan bought amulets for my neck, wrists, ankles, and every day I had to go to this enormous statue of a lion and kiss his –'

'– Anahid! Stop!' Her cheeks are burning; embarrassment shakes her. 'I'm sure it shouldn't be spoken of.'

'I'm sorry, Esther. I forgot. You see, all the time among married women it is usual to gossip about these things. Anyway, it didn't work, and I am without child. After that, we went to stay at Mirza Khan's palace. Other people joined us. They hunted animals and birds.'

'It sounds like home, and the dining-room table groaning with food for guests. Oh, don't remind me.'

'You must have something to drink,' Anahid decides, 'tea, I think. And play the piano.'

She follows Anahid through the house to the harem; breathes vanilla, musk, secrecy. We respect our women, Captain Kemal Bey said. She wonders if oriental men are afraid of them, to keep them so secluded.

Anahid calls, claps her hands, speaks to the barefoot maid who arrives within seconds. When the girl has gone, Anahid says, 'I'm to have whatever I wish, which includes you here. I heard Mirza Khan snap at Seyed Ali; he is concerned maybe I've been homesick, not cared for, and that's why I haven't conceived. I'm worried, Esther: he says he'll take me to the best doctor in Europe. If I don't co-operate, he may change towards me, divorce me. I have to be compliant.'

Tea is dark, in porcelain cups, accompanied by a dish of cinnamon, and nuts and raisins on a copper platter embossed with almonds. Alongside is a silk napkin with birds embroidered in blue, red, yellow. The maid places the tray on a beaten brass table engraved with animals and Persian script, glances at her sitting straight-backed on the *divan*, and scuttles away. Kiki twitters in his cage, spills seed on the floor.

To loosen her fingers after several months, she practises scales, arpeggios, a short piece by Mozart she learnt as a child. Her mind is elsewhere. How can she broach the subject of Captain Kemal Bey to Anahid? ... an Ottoman officer saved Jacob from an accident in the street ... we have sat and talked a few times while my brothers are at their lessons ... he has given me news of my city. That is all her acquaintance with him amounts to, yet the words remain jumbled on her tongue and will not come out.

Perhaps it is because Anahid has a Persian veneer in spite of her upbringing: daughter of a schoolmaster who quoted Lamartine. Here, men are not people who bring you information; they are to be obeyed, pleased, allowed to treat you as a plaything. A gulf is opening between herself and Anahid.

When they return to the courtyard, Seyed Ali is tending the vine; it sags with fruit. He looks up at the sound of their

What can he tell her when he does not have her address?

They cross the street. He walks in front of her past a high, enclosing mud wall, the side of the shah's palace. At the entrance to the bazaars, she resigns herself to not visiting Anahid today and steps into the dark, vaulted labyrinth a few paces behind the captain. They stop to gaze at a tray of miniatures shaped like flowers of paradise, a king hunting, a lance, and a fleeing stag. The shopkeepers' hooded eyes follow them, alerted perhaps by a uniform and a lady in European dress, which could mean money. Nobody speaks to them, however, or presses them to buy.

'There is a Persian mission leaving for Baku,' the captain says. 'Azerbaijan is anxious to build relations with Moslem neighbours. Part of Azerbaijan is Persian territory.'

'And you are going, too?'

'No. My duties are elsewhere. But I have ... contacts. It occurs to me ... if you were to give me the address, I'm sure enquiries could be made. There is someone for whom I have rendered a service ...' The captain's speech becomes more halting as if he is not only searching for the best words but for what it is safe to reveal. 'I could ask him to find out, or even see for himself, on behalf of a refugee family who long for news of their home. No?'

'That's very kind. It's on the Birzhevaya, the street of the stock exchange. Number twelve.'

He pronounces the Russian name as if he must not lose any of it. 'And it's easy to locate?'

'Oh, yes. In the city centre.' She touches filigree necklaces and bracelets. 'I hate the thought of a second winter here.'

'Where would you go?'

'If not Baku? Perhaps to my stepmother's people in the Ukraine, or somewhere I can study the piano.' She tells him of her place at the Petersburg Conservatoire.

'Russians are fleeing the civil war, Esther Yefimovna. Several ships a week leave Odessa and other Black Sea ports. They discharge their passengers in Constantinople or the islands in the Marmara, sometimes the Gallipoli peninsula.'

They have wound their way to where they started, and continue along the side of the palace. Although the sky is heavy with cloud, she blinks in brightness after the bazaars' gloom.

Opposite the bank, the captain stops. 'I shall be returning to Anatolia soon,' he says. 'We have elections to parliament before the end of the year.'

'So your work here is finished?' Disappointment stabs at her chest. How will he give her news of the house if he has left Teheran?

'No. But my absence can be arranged. I shall be back.'

The city's soft whiteness imprisons them, plane-trees like ice-covered guards, a twig cracking in the silence.

She finds Madame Lavirotte tearing a book, feeding pages into the brazier. 'It was my husband's,' laments the landlady. 'We shall have to burn furniture next.'

At lunch-time, Nadia announces to the family, 'We can't stay here. They're saying at the hospital there's likely to be famine by spring. They may not be able to pay me or your father, Esther. Some mothers are using their milk for all their children. In the north west, near the border with Anatolia, there have been food riots, even a massacre.' With her spoon, Nadia indicates the soup. 'This is most likely horse. Goodness knows who had the meat.'

'That's what we ate our last year in Baku,' she reminds Nadia.

'Your father does not wish to live in a Baku that is capital of independent Azerbaijan,' Nadia's voice is like the icicles that hang from the roof, 'or for the boys to grow up there. We must go west for their future not east. But we have no money or transport. There are no trains in this … this – ' Nadia is on her feet, knocking her chair, rushing to her and Papa's room, slamming the door.

Papa follows her. Jacob and Anton look solemn. 'Mama is unhappy,' is all Jacob says after a while.

Papa and Nadia's conversation sounds low, quiet, until … is it a sob? Nadia never cries, always has a suggestion.

Papa returns to the table as if the weariness of a lifetime's labour pushes at him. 'The thought of not seeing the house, or what might have happened to it, is too much for her to bear.'

She stands up, goes to Nadia. The blind is down. Nadia is on the edge of the bed, weeping. She sits beside her stepmother.

'Do you think Mama and Papa have left, too?' Nadia whispers and leans towards her. 'Perhaps they've gone to Paris as they did before. We were all happy there. It was where your father and I met, you remember? Maybe you don't. You were only a little girl.'

'I do recall walks in the Bois de Boulogne, and the smell of roses and honeysuckle.'

Nadia's crying becomes more bitter, from deep within. 'Paris. We might as well talk of the moon.'

She puts both arms round Nadia. Strength she did not realise was inside her rises, flows from her.

There are dark rings under Anahid's eyes. 'My monthly bleeding again. Mirza Khan says he will take me to Europe as soon as the thaw begins. I don't want this, Esther, strange places and doctors examining me. And I will miss you.'

'We shall depart in the spring. You come, too.'

Anahid's mouth forms an O of apprehension. 'With you?'

'Why not? Do you wish to stay? Forever?'

'The longer I'm here, the more difficult it will be to leave. I never have to decide anything. Even my clothes, Seyed Ali will say wear this or that, and I expect it's because Mirza Khan has told him to.'

'So?'

'I'm safe here, cocooned.'

'But it could end, you've told me. If you're with us, you'll be all right. We'll face the future together.'

Her stomach flutters at the sight of trunks, valises, carpet bags in the hall of the legation.

Vitaly Ivanovich walks in. 'Good morning, Esther Yefimovna.'

She returns his greeting, indicates the luggage. 'You are going.'

'The minister has been withdrawn as he was the tsar's appointee.'

'The legation will close?'

'Probably another envoy will be sent. A representative of the regime.' Vitaly Ivanovich does not attempt to hide the distaste in his voice.

'The civil war has finished?'

'We hear there are still pockets of fighting. Denikin in the Crimea. But those who have seized power evidently feel secure enough to contact neighbouring countries.'

She keeps hold of Jacob's and Anton's hands, unwilling to release them until she has found out as much as she can. 'Where are you making for?'

'England. They have always been our friends.'

'Really? Twice in less than twelve months they abandoned Baku.'

Vitaly Ivanovich draws in his breath, raises his eyebrows. She doesn't want to antagonise him so asks, 'Which way will you travel?'

'Across north Persia and the mountains of Kurdistan to the River Tigris or even the Euphrates. Thence down to the port of Basra. It should not be difficult to get a ship to Egypt and from there another to England.'

Although unable to picture the route on a map, she memorises the names just as she did messages and addresses in Baku two years ago. 'It will take ages,' she ventures.

'We have time.' He turns to Jacob and Anton. 'And now, to our studies.'

She relinquishes her brothers. Vitaly Ivanovich could at least have shown some concern for her family and whether they might wish to join the group leaving the legation.

At lunch-time, she tells Papa and Nadia what he said. 'Do you want to go to England?'

'We know little about it,' Nadia replies.

'Just the people who used to work for me,' says Papa. 'Engineers. Accountants.'

'Mr MacDonell,' Nadia adds.

'And Livvy.'

'You speak English better than I do, Yefim. But are they sympathetic? Their king did not offer sanctuary to his cousins, the tsar and tsarina.'

'The dowager empress was evacuated there from Odessa last year, on an English battleship,' Papa points out.

'Is not her sister the king's mother? They do what suits them.'

She imagines Russians congregating in London, supporting the tsar, plotting return. England is a cold, foggy country, with chintz-covered furniture such as she saw inside the legation.

Later, she lies looking at vertical strips of moonlight which creep through gaps in the blind; listening to insects, the occasional cat. Of course, they could travel to Paris from England.

The next morning as she comes down the street from the legation, Captain Kemal Bey is standing on the corner outside the bank. Her heart skips. She greets him.

'Esther Yefimovna,' he says with a small bow. 'Without your parasol.' He smiles. 'Any day, we can expect the thaw.'

'There has been no fresh snow since last week.' She searches his face. 'You have news?'

'From Baku. Through diplomatic channels. It awaited my arrival from Anatolia.' She follows him across the road into the square of cannons.

'Should we sit for a few moments?' he suggests. 'There is no wind.'

She does as he asks, wonders what he has to say that she should hear seated. It must be bad. She pulls her shawls around her. 'Please tell me. Everything. It is best I know.'

'I'm afraid it is not good. My contact, in his message, wrote the number of the house on the Birzhevaya. Several in the street have been demolished, too damaged during rioting to repair. Yours was one of them.'

'Rioting?' she whispers. That would be when the Turks took control nearly eighteen months ago, thanks to General Dunsterville. The Tartars, fellow-Moslems, would have fought with them. What became of Serge, Sonia, Elena? Had Serge accepted evacuation to Enzeli with the British? What safe quarter could there be for Armenians in Baku if there was revenge for the March Days six months previously.

Dedushka's lovely house ... demolished? Marble hall and wide staircases ... velvet, damask ... and her Steinway. Hours of practice, weeks, months. Part of her. Gone forever with her home. She tries to picture the gaping space in the street.

What feels like a lump has lodged in her throat. She swallows, but still it is there.

'I'm sorry, Esther Yefimovna,' the captain says. 'Six thousand Armenians are estimated to have perished.'

Why hadn't they gone to Enzeli? She turns to him, compels words through her mouth. 'Your troops did this.'

'They did not prevent it,' he admits. 'It seems the forces of Nuri Pasha waited outside the city for two days allowing Tartar units to go in and ...'

'... settle scores,' she provides for him. 'You don't need to explain. There has always been trouble between Tartars and Armenians in Baku, but most of the time, under the tsar, different races co-existed peacefully. We were all Russian first, Tartar, Armenian, Jew, second. Even the *bolsheviki* at least kept order. While your army encouraged a massacre.'

Again, he apologises. 'I hold no respect for Nuri Pasha, who was as much a peacock as his brother Enver, full of grand schemes and his own advancement. The sultan is well rid of them ...'

His words disappear into the air for she has ceased to listen. If Serge, Sonia, and Elena had left Baku, the house might have been spared for nobody, as far as she knows, had scores to settle with Papa; he had been a good employer and built a pharmacy. Which means they stayed. They lived downstairs. When they had finished their work in the evenings, they would relax in the courtyard, laughter and guttural Armenian language rising into the warm air. Sonia would sew, Elena smoke a small pipe.

Serge had been *dedushka*'s coachman, witnessed the murder in 1901, knocked the knife from the Tartar's hand, wrestled him to the ground until help came ... Elena was Serge's brother's widow ... used to shoo Jacob out of the kitchen when he went in wheedling food from her ... attended the Armenian cathedral with Sonia and Serge every Saturday evening ... the old life, household members bound to each other and the comfort of routine.

The weight inside her throat shifts, forces tears to the surface. She is weeping, shaking. Elbows on her knees, fingers over her eyes, she sobs for the horror of it all, her own helplessness, and a world she does not understand.

'Esther Yefimovna —'

'Please leave me,' she manages to whisper. 'There is nothing more we can say.'

She is aware of him moving. He is gone.

Exhaustion is crushing her. She makes herself stand on feet the snow has numbed, and stamps them several times. She moves her legs, one in front of the other, out of the square, along to the legation. Is there any point in telling Nadia or Papa? To what end? And to have to admit how she learnt the news discomforts her: Papa will not take kindly to her having talked to an Ottoman officer, and unaccompanied. It must be a secret she will carry for the rest of her days.

Facing her, all of them, is a journey far longer than the one here from Baku. Her footsteps crunch, drag, on packed snow. She has barely energy to walk to the legation.

ELEVEN

Odessa, southern Russia, February 1920

This one's working hard, rides him on his greatcoat, thrusts with child-bearing hips; open blouse releases saggy breasts, brown nipples the size of grapes. The woman's face is in shadow, the only light a smoking candle-stump's glimmer on the floor by the bed. The room reeks of stale sesame-oil and garlic in a tenement that must once have been part of the rococo elegance of the Nikolaevsky Boulevard above the harbour. The parks are still there, but trees have been used for firewood; rows of bare trunks defy the darkness. Odessa, second capital of old Russia where, in a rehearsal for the real thing, the crew of *Potemkin* mutinied in 1905, and barricades sprang up on the streets, while the other side the Caucasus, Mademoiselle Dupont explained to a boy of seven the meaning of revolution.

He closes his eyes, draws on what's left of his cigarette. His coat came from the haul on the train; the Whites had probably got the supplies from the British. His unit joined comrades in Moscow. In the same rolling-stock, fitted with a Maxim machinegun, they fought their way south, taking towns; night air resounded with cries of: goodbye Nicholas – even though he had been dead over a year – and songs that became increasingly savage and hysterical.

And now they have pushed the Whites into the sea. The Black Sea. He smiles at the contrasting colours. The beginning of a fresh decade, a new Russia. There remains the Crimea, and the Caucasus. Not till every White is off Russian soil will the job be done. After that, call on neighbours, such as the Turks, not that he has any wish to return to the land of the old enemy, but he won't have any say. No private thoughts.

She's taking a long time. He drops the spent cigarette on the floor, moves his buttocks. In spite of the freezing room, there is a line of perspiration on her upper lip. He touches a jigging breast, rubs the nipple between thumb and forefinger. Yes …

On all fours, still astride him, the woman hangs her head, exhausted. He eases her away; she's as good as any he's had these last months. She indicates a tin basin of water and grubby-looking cloth next to the dead stove. He wipes himself, pulls up and buttons his trousers. When he turns round, she is fastening her blouse. There's a wariness about her. He's seen it before: happy to service a bolshevik commissar, even one with a scarred face, in the hope of better rations or accommodation, but now comes the moment of reckoning. He feels in his pockets for coins and gives them to her.

'Thank you, Commissar.' He can see determination, desperation, competing with guardedness ingrained in all Russians in the presence of authority. Romanovs, Whites, Reds, whoever is in power makes little difference to the daily struggle. 'There's also for the firewood, Commissar,' she ventures.

With a stub of pencil, he scribbles a few words on a crumpled piece of paper and gives the message to the woman. 'Take this when you collect your ration.'

'Thank you, Commissar.' He smells her fear, of him and what he represents.

Like small stones on a roof, the rat-tat-tat of a machinegun sounds in the street. He picks up his cap and Mauser pistol, opens the door, starts down the splintered staircase. Fedya will have begun searches, each building, for food and property.

TWELVE

Teheran, Persia, February 1920

If only she could sleep for days, not wake and the truth still be here. Had the house remained, she could always have nursed the possibility that life as it was might eventually be put back together.

She does not expect to see Captain Kemal Bey again, yet the morning after he gave her the news from Baku he is standing on the corner outside the bank as she leaves the legation.

The months she and Lev spent with Papa in Paris when they were eight years old, Papa's uncle, *dyadia* Pavel, used to delight in showing them his butterfly collection: beautiful, helpless creatures pinned to a board mounted under glass, wings never to close or flutter in flight, open to the admiration of all.

She feels like one of them now. The way to escape the captain is to pretend she has not seen him, cross the road, go down to the bazaars. But he walks towards her.

'Esther Yefimovna.' There is concern in his eyes.

'Captain Kemal Bey.' She does not smile and realises her reluctance to speak to him is, as much as anything, because he has witnessed her tears. The roofs and cupolas of Teheran shine like shattered crystal under a lapis-coloured sky. She shivers and tightens her shawls, stamps her feet on snow.

'Forgive me if I alarmed you,' he says, 'but there are matters to discuss. I am able to help you and your family. I might have spoken of this yesterday but … it was not the moment. I would what I had to tell you had been different.'

'I do not wish to talk about it.'

He nods in acknowledgement. 'My contact also mentioned conditions in Baku under the Azeri administration. Prices are high, there are shortages of everything.'

'The same as here.'

'Popular unrest is increasing. There is the impression that when the Red Army arrives, as it surely must before long, the citizens of Baku will welcome it on the grounds that nothing can be worse than the situation they're already in.'

'Azeri or bolshevik, my family and I have decided we shall not be returning. We may go to England. Members of the legation are leaving. We could join them.'

'What route will you take?'

She repeats the names she has memorised.

'Who will lead you through the mountains of Kurdistan?'

'I have no idea. Somebody familiar with the way, I suppose.'

'Esther Yefimovna, have you any grasp of how things are there? It is a lawless place. Each tribe protects its own and ignores the Teheran government, indeed any authority. Unless you have a guide who is known, you could all be massacred or, at least, your father killed, and you and your stepmother and brothers sold by bandits.'

Like Anahid.

'These are desperate times,' the captain pursues. 'The whole world has been in ferment. Empires have broken up, old habits and certainties scattered, dust in the wind. New countries are forming but not without struggle, bloodshed, flexing of muscles strengthened by seizure of power.'

People glance at them, edge past.

'You're making difficulties,' she says. 'Why is it your business?' She crosses the road. He follows her.

They arrive in the square of cannons and sit on the same seat as yesterday.

'I have made several journeys to Anatolia during the last year,' he reminds her. 'As soon as the thaw begins, I can take you all as far as the Black Sea; from there, a boat to Constantinople. You once told me you wished to play the piano. You will be able to in the capital. It is a city of culture.'

And also a port. Ships leave there for Europe.

'You need help, which I can provide. The tribal chiefs will not be surprised to see me with a group of … we can say, pilgrims. They will treat us respectfully, especially if I tell them it is my wife and her relatives.'

'Your wife?'

'I'm asking you to marry me, Esther Yefimovna.'

Her heart bellows as if it would be rid of her. She stares at his face. 'Why?'

He smiles. 'I did not expect my suggestion to be greeted with that word. Esther Yefimovna, you are stateless.'

'Papa has a passport and the deed signed by Tsar Alexander the Second leasing oil-bearing land to my grandfather. We shall always be Russian.'

'Such documents will carry no weight in the mountains. But

as my wife, you – and naturally your family – will be entitled to protection.'

Wife. Twice he has said it. He really is proposing to her. She can't. She hardly knows him. And he comes from a country with different traditions, where men have more than one woman. She imagines herself veiled, living like Anahid. One question in a public square, and a lifetime guarded and controlled. It's ridiculous. In any case, she doesn't love him. That's what marriage means, Nadia and Papa, trust, sustaining each other.

She looks at black eyes, soft skin around them and the temples, and a tremor darts through her as she remembers Moszhuhin's films: flashing eyes and prolonged kissing. No. Impossible. 'I can never marry somebody I do not love.'

'What do you understand by that, Esther Yefimovna?'

She blushes, and Moszhuhin's painted features stay in her mind. 'A feeling. Like my father and stepmother.'

'I do not request that of you, only to trust me.'

'A secluded life? Veiled?'

'You will not have to. Already in Constantinople, younger women have rejected this, although their elders may disapprove. It will take another generation, perhaps two, for the tradition to disappear altogether. And in the countryside, faces are never covered. When we arrive in the capital, I will not hold you to the marriage if that is what you wish.'

A contract of convenience, as often happens in royal and aristocratic circles, securing property or money; in this case, a few weeks' duration to facilitate a journey. 'If it means the tribal chiefs treating us better, can't we just *say* I'm your wife?'

The captain blinks in surprise. 'That is hardly honourable, Esther Yefimovna. Do you have such objection to being married?'

'It is not how I imagined it would be. I'm not certain I have the right to at all if I'm to be a serious pianist.' She stands up, and he does the same. 'I must go for my brothers. Thank you for trying to help us, Captain Kemal Bey, but I really can't accept.'

She walks away. He knows where to meet her. He will be there tomorrow. She is trapped, pinned, like one of *dyadia* Pavel's butterflies.

Nadia is speaking English, imitating somebody. 'My dear Madame Markovitch, I could not possibly ask this of a lady of your class.' Nadia giggles, reverts to French with Papa. 'He's such a pet, Doctor McClusky. I think he's forgotten I nursed countless people in Baku and Enzeli. There's nothing I haven't seen or can't deal with.'

A rumble of amusement from Papa.

She pushes her bread round her bowl rather than eat it, and glances up. Nadia has her hand over Papa's, and they are smiling at each other, Papa's eyes animated for a few moments. This is love. You just know when you're with them that things are right, the feeling they have. She wants to go on looking at them. They are the only man and woman she sees together in this city.

Papa stands. 'Come on, boys. Time to visit Madame Lavirotte.'

He takes them with him when he pays the rent. The landlady always asks Jacob and Anton what they've been learning.

She and Nadia stay at the table.

'You seem troubled,' Nadia says.

She grimaces, shakes her head.

'Is there something?' Nadia pursues, 'I mean … apart from this,' Nadia gestures at the room, 'and the lack of everything.' A pause. 'Esther?'

She bites her lip, blurts out, 'I've had a proposal.'

Nadia smiles in exclamation. 'What's been happening? At the legation?'

'No. It's silly. Out of the question. And in Europe, my life will be the piano. On the concert platform. That won't leave space for husband and children, will it? You gave up your medical studies to marry Papa.'

'I had to because I returned to Baku with him. Anyway, tell me, who is your beau?'

'He's not. It would be a marriage of convenience to get us out of here.'

She explains to Nadia about encounters with the captain but doesn't mention his nationality. And nothing of sitting in the garden or wandering through the bazaars. That she chooses what she recounts irritates her, makes things private between herself and him.

'What is his name?' Nadia asks.

As she replies, her stepmother's brows draw together.

'A Turk. We've never trusted them.' Nadia glances around the four walls that are the extent of their world. 'Constantinople. And from there a ship to Europe. France.'

'You're warming to the idea.'

Nadia sighs. 'We were happy in Paris.'

'I have a horror of being stuck in a harem in Constantinople. Like Anahid. I'd die. He says he'll release me, but how do I know he will?'

'When the boys are in bed, I think we should tell your father.'

Papa frowns. 'So,' he begins when Nadia has finished speaking. 'A Turk seeks my daughter's hand and offers to take us all on the first stretch of a journey to Europe. Have Turks and Russians ever believed each other?'

'I told him I couldn't marry him, Papa.'

'It would be a way of leaving here,' Nadia says. 'We can't do it on our own.'

'And marriage to Esther is included in the agreement,' Papa repeats. 'This is what concerns me. You have been seeing him, Esther, without our knowledge.' There is not anger but seriousness in Papa's tone; the old Papa who, perhaps investigating some misdemeanour or infringement of regulations among his employees, needs to ascertain the facts before deciding on action.

'I have not, Papa, in the sense of a rendezvous. He knows the boys study at the legation each morning –'

'How does he?' Papa interrupts.

'I told him. I saw him by chance. He enquired after Jacob. He assumed Jacob was my son. Sometimes our paths have crossed, on the corner by the bank or in the square of cannons.'

'You have not discouraged him, Esther, and so have compromised yourself. He is not used to women alone in the street. If he was wrong, or at least ill-advised, to speak to you, it was most foolish of you to respond.' Papa sits back in his chair, but his eyes do not leave her face. 'If, the first time he addressed you, you had made it clear you were unwilling to reply, he would, if he were honourable, have ceased to bother you. But you have not done that. I see no alternative for you to marry him if we are to accept his help. You must ask him to come here so I can assess him.'

She stands up. 'He has behaved with extreme politeness, Papa, and,' she fumbles with frustration at appearing to take the captain's side, '… and respect. I can't possibly be his wife. I'm not sure I can commit to anyone if I want to be a concert pianist, but certainly not somebody from such an alien way of life. I don't have any feelings for him. When you married, it was for love. Mama. Nadia.'

'You have no choice.' Papa's voice reminds her of how he spoke when he refused to let her travel to the conservatoire. 'What was there to be gained from any conversation when your background, expectations, were so different? What were you thinking of, Esther?'

There is nothing she can say without further prejudicing herself.

'You would never have been free to walk unchaperoned in the old days,' Papa comments.

'I would have gone to the conservatoire. I might even have been a concert pianist by now. Instead, my future is to be sacrificed.'

'Unless you prefer England. I feel maybe you should be married, Esther. Perhaps a husband will have better control over you than I have done.'

Next morning, water drips from roofs. She sloshes along the street with the boys. Departure needs no longer be delayed.

As she leaves the legation, the captain strides towards her. 'Good morning, Esther Yefimovna.'

She breathes the masculine smell she has become used to. Will he really release her? Or will his attitude change? Will she disappear into the women's quarters of his household?

'My father wishes to see you.'

'Good. We must make arrangements now the thaw has begun.'

There might be another snowfall. Yet, it would only be a temporary reprieve and not alter the overall plan, which will unfold as surely as seasons. Everything is beyond her grasp.

She does not want to spend time with him, bereft of anything to say as if this is a first meeting.

'Captain Kemal Bey, if you don't mind, there are things I have to do, one or two items in the bazaar …'

'Of course.' He bows. 'Shall I join you here in an hour when you collect your brothers? I could return with you to your father.'

'Yes.'

'Until then.' He turns, walks back the way he came.

She watches him. Why didn't she pretend that the first time?

When she opens the door to their room and ushers the boys in, Nadia and Papa stand up. The captain is behind her. She makes the introductions.

He clicks his heels. 'Monsieur.' He bows to Nadia. 'Madame.'

Everybody sits down, Jacob and Anton perched on the same chair so the captain can be seated, his uniformed presence imbuing even Jacob with solemnity.

Papa takes charge, the old Papa, used to negotiation, dealing with people. 'You find us in reduced circumstances, Captain. My daughter tells me you are in a position to aid us.' He pauses so she can translate.

She does not look at the captain as she speaks. That she is the only means of communication gives her the small comfort of some control. While waiting outside the legation, she mentioned to him her maid, Ana, who helps the landlady in the kitchen. Life has become successive expediencies, clutching at straws. Secrets. Lies.

The captain replies to Papa. 'I have matters to attend to in Anatolia. As my wife's family, you – especially the ladies and children – would have my protection in these wild and lawless times which is why, with your permission, I would marry your daughter.'

The last words refer to her yet sound unreal as she voices them, like some legal arrangement concerning a distant person in a bygone age.

'You have my consent,' Papa says. 'Regarding remuneration, we have just enough for our everyday needs.'

'I do not ask for or expect reimbursement. And my brother is in Trebizond, where you will be welcome. He has boats going to Constantinople.'

From inside his jacket, Papa produces a leather wallet she has not seen before. 'I have my daughter's birth certificate, also that of my marriage to her late mother.'

The captain takes the documents from Papa. 'Thank you. The contract can be drawn up at our embassy. I will provide two witnesses. You may wish to accompany your daughter.'

Papa stands.

A business deal. I am the payment.

'Lallah is with child,' Anahid tells her in the courtyard. Tight yellow buds cover the rosebush.

'Good. If the baby is a boy, Mirza Khan will be content.'

'She may miscarry or have a girl.'

'In which case, he will still want a son from you. We shall be leaving soon. And you're coming, too.'

Anahid puts a hand over her mouth and shakes her head.

'Anahid, yes!' she persists. 'Someone is taking us across

the mountains into Anatolia, to the Black Sea and a boat to Constantinople.'

'Anatolia,' Anahid repeats. 'My country.'

'All the more reason for you to be with us.'

'Maybe I would see some of my people. Who knows the way?' She swallows, braces herself, tells Anahid.

Anahid frowns. 'A Turk. No, Esther.'

She grabs Anahid's arms. 'Yes! You said yourself, not all Turks are bad. Remember Achmet Bey, your father's friend.'

'That was before.'

'I won't hear no! Turks killed many Russians, don't forget. But the captain was on the European Front. He is not in favour of the sultan's advisers and the policies that led to war. I can tell him you're fearful, lost your brother on the Turkish Front in the Caucasus; we can make up some story so you're Russian not Armenian. You don't have to say anything. You will be my maid.'

'You seem well acquainted with this captain, Esther.'

Is this the moment to admit to his proposal? Only if Anahid will be more likely to go with them. She regards the blue eyes of Van, plunges on. 'I need you.'

Anahid's face relaxes. 'I will be able to help you for you know nothing of men, do you?'

Three days later, she paces the courtyard, glances every few seconds at the door, wills it not to open. She looks for the last time at the rosebush, vine, oleander. How long shall I be without a piano?

Yesterday, the captain accompanied her to Papa and Nadia: preparations were almost complete; there were no reports of flooding or avalanches. They will be leaving by car tomorrow at sunrise when the city gates open. At six o'clock this evening, she is to be married; no love, flowers, kisses, things she might have expected or those of which she is ignorant.

She gasps. Anahid stands at the top of the steps, twice as heavy, wrapping herself into an indigo cloak, over which she attaches a veil, and a half-moon-shaped scarf which she winds round her forehead, chin and shoulders.

'I've put on two of everything,' Anahid explains. 'I do not want to be cold. The bundle I've tied to my waist. But ... Esther ...'

'What?'

'Kiki.'

'Lallah will care for him.'

'Unless she eats him. She's sick, suddenly recovers, sends Seyed Ali to the bazaar demanding all kinds of food he can no longer find. It's probably where he is now.'

She grabs Anahid's hand in case her friend decides to return for the bird. She unlatches the door into the street, looks right, left, pulls Anahid to the tramway and the European Quarter, each breath taking her further from the bazaars.

At the lodgings, she runs up the stairs, tugging Anahid, yanks her into the room. Anahid is trembling, eyes darting like a trapped animal. She sits Anahid at the table. 'I have to fetch my brothers.'

'No. Don't leave me alone. Please.'

'I'll only be a few minutes. You're quite safe. Nobody knows you're here.'

Anahid hugs herself as if she would stop shaking. 'Seyed Ali used to give me a special drink. How am I going to be without it?'

'Just a little for your lips,' Anahid insists. 'It is your wedding day.'

Papa and Nadia are with Madame Lavirotte. Jacob and Anton pause from the tin soldiers. 'Is Esther getting married?' Jacob asks.

'We're all leaving in the morning,' she tells him.

She glances at the pot of red cream Anahid is holding. 'It's not that sort of occasion.'

'Where are we going?'

'Across the mountains, Jacob.' With fumbling fingers, she dresses in the grey blouse and black skirt.

Anahid retrieves a jar from her bundle. 'A dab of rouge on your cheeks.'

'I'm not an actress to be painted. Why did you bring these with you?'

'Ah, Esther,' Anahid sighs. 'Some perfume, at least. You should make an effort for your husband.'

'Can we take the fort, Esther?'

'No.' She combs and twists up her hair, pins it at the nape of her neck. 'We can build another.' She puts on her hat, her Europeanness, for the last time: from tomorrow, she and Nadia will manage with scarves. 'Isn't that what the Russian army did when it went to a new place?'

'Yes,' Anton chips in. 'Vitaly Ivanovich told us about the Cossacks. They used to read and study the stars when there was no fighting.'

'And have horse races,' Jacob adds, 'and hunt foxes and rabbits.'

'And deer, pheasants, partridges,' Anton continues.

'What's a partridge, Esther?'

'We'll ask Papa. Pack the soldiers carefully. Ana can help you till I come back.'

At the embassy, she and Papa are shown into a room. Flowers and Arabic script embellish part of each wall and above the doorway. Brightly coloured, embroidered cushions are scattered on a *divan*.

The captain greets Papa with a handshake; for her, a nod of acknowledgement. She catches a whiff of lemon cologne. 'The imam will be here soon,' he says. 'As well as the witnesses, there will be an interpreter as you will respond in German. Your father is welcome to observe.'

The green-turbaned imam and his retinue come in, a flapping of black robes, odour of strong tobacco, and muttering in a language she has never heard, to which the captain replies. The imam sits on the floor.

The captain faces the imam at a distance of a few paces.

The interpreter is at her side. 'Go next to him.'

The imam waits, strokes his greying beard. When everyone is in position to his satisfaction, he takes from his belt a brass inkpot inscribed in flowing lettering, and a pen that looks like bamboo. He unfolds a sheet of parchment, rests it against his left palm and wrist, dips the pen into the ink, and writes in flourishes across the top, right to left.

The interpreter murmurs to her, 'He is writing, *In the Name of God, the All-Merciful.*'

The imam questions the captain and records his answers. The only other sound is the scratch of the pen.

The imam finishes, pauses. Sighs.

Her stomach feels as if it's contending with brawlers.

The imam draws in his breath, speaks, eyes on what he has written.

The interpreter says, 'What is your name?'

She turns to Papa, but his gaze is fixed at some point beyond anybody in the room. She straightens her shoulders and stares at one of the blue flowers which ornament the wall. She is Russian and not ashamed. 'I am Esther Yefimovna Markovitch.'

The interpreter translates. The imam writes. She does not glance at what he is doing but imagines syllables transliterated into liquid script.

'What is your religion?'

'I am a Jewess.'

'What is your desire?'

The piano. The interpreter advises, 'Say: to make public my wish to take this man for my husband.'

Perspiration pricks her, even the end of her nose, but she continues to look at the blue flower and repeats what the interpreter said.

'Do you want to retain your religion or change it to that of your husband?'

'To retain my religion.' To remain who I am.

The parchment slides over the imam's palm as he covers it with words.

The captain signs the page. For the first time, he turns to her.

'Now you,' the interpreter prompts.

'Esther *Hanum*,' the captain informs her. 'It means Frau Esther.'

With as steady a hand as she can manage and the unfamiliar pen, she writes. The witnesses add their signatures. From another part of his belt, the imam brings out a seal and presses it to the certificate.

'It has his name on it,' the interpreter tells her, 'Hafis – a man who knows the Koran by heart – Mirza Mohammed Shirazi, because he comes from Shiraz; also the inscription, *Slave to the Lord of the World.*'

The imam stands up, gives the captain the document, mutters as he did when he entered the room. The captain replies. The imam and his party leave.

The captain takes from his pocket some papers and a small packet. 'These you gave me,' he says to Papa; to her, 'I would like you to have this.'

A gift? 'No. Not in these circumstances.'

His eyebrows arch. 'It is the custom.'

Papa frowns at her.

'There is nothing usual about this situation,' she insists, 'no singing, dancing, banquet, beautiful clothes.' Nor being together afterwards.

'The times we live in prevent it,' the captain points out. 'All the more reason.'

'Thank you, Captain,' Papa intervenes in German, rescuing the packet and placing it in her hands. He continues in French, 'Of course my daughter accepts. She is just a little overcome.'

How dare Papa side with him against her! She looks away; embarrassment burns her face. The captain and Papa walk towards the door. She follows them.

The captain says to her, 'I shall see you tomorrow at sunrise. There are final preparations to make.'

She is dismissed.

She and Papa step into the street.

She is married.

Esther *Hanum.*

THIRTEEN

'It was not gracious of you to refuse his present,' Papa begins as they walk back.

'There's no need for one. It's not a usual marriage.'

'We are dependent on his goodwill, Esther. To react as you did was tactless.'

'Does that mean I have to do everything he says? I'm not a servant.'

'Where there is reason and understanding on both sides, neither husband nor wife will make demands with which the other cannot comply.'

'Papa, it's not like when you married Nadia.'

'It is a legal settlement to which you gave your consent.'

'Why do you support him against me? Who is wed in her everyday clothes and returns to her lodgings? I have no trousseau nor anything Nadia and I have sewn and embroidered. Even Livvy and – what was his name? – Peter, in Baku, had a meal after their wedding, and we all sang.'

They reach the turning to Madame Lavirotte's lane. Across the road, she sees an old man in a long robe tied at the waist, and a close-fitting cap. He reminds her of Seyed Ali.

She takes Papa's arm. 'Can we go straight on? We could spend a few minutes in the square of cannons.' If it is Seyed Ali, is he looking for Anahid? He might simply be on an errand for Mirza Khan or Lallah.

They sit on the opposite side from where she used to talk to the captain. While she explains to Papa about her suspicions, she eases open the packet's stiff wrapping. Nestling in the parchment on two layers of lawn cotton is the filigree necklace she and the captain saw when they walked through the bazaars late last year.

For the first time, she considers him as a man who has just married. Not for him, either, is it what he might have expected, and to a woman who is unveiled, unafraid to say no. Is the gift an attempt to bridge their backgrounds, to make the best of the situation?

She will not wear this jewellery, but thank him and try to be a little more what Papa calls gracious.

She and Papa find Anahid hunched on the pallet, shaking, hugging herself.

'Poor girl must have been drugged,' Nadia comments. 'And that perfume cost a bit. She's been describing a partridge to the boys.'

Her brothers are asleep. Nadia and Papa go to the other room.

She puts her arm round Anahid, breathes in attar of roses.

'I miss the drink Seyed Ali used to give me.' The spasm subsides. 'I am used to being awake at night,' Anahid adds.

'I always had to be ready. Esther, you must understand these things before your husband comes to you.'

'You don't need to tell me anything. It isn't that way.'

'Meaning?'

'What I think you're going to say, lying with ...' Embarrassment heats her cheeks, stifles the rest of the sentence. 'There's no love.'

'Ah, what is that? A man must marry preferably a woman he likes, but she need not reciprocate. Do you?'

Does she? They have talked more than she is prepared to admit to Anahid or Papa. His appearance and manners are without reproach. Is that enough?

'Is he concerned how you feel about him?' Anahid pursues.

No. Although there is the necklace.

'You see, Esther, a wise man does not court a woman. She is just the field he sows, his shadow, her place in the inner part of the house.'

'Anahid, you've left all that behind. In any case, Mirza Khan spent a lot of money on you and wanted you to be happy.'

'That was because he desired a son. This Kemal has to do what is right for you, look after you, but generally men do not consider it good to adore anyone. It makes them weak. They crave their homeland, or war, beautiful carpets, rare weapons, but not a person. Of course, there are exceptions. The devotion of Leila and Madjnoun is celebrated in song. But mostly, apart from things a husband does at night or time he allows for his wife, he doesn't really know what to do with her, whether to treat her as if she were a child or a lady; scold her if she's clumsy or forgive everything and spoil her.'

'What nonsense! They are two human beings. There should be trust, respect, co-operation. Anyway, none of this has to do with the captain.'

She closes her eyes, thinks of Nadia's hand on Papa's at the table, fondness in their expression, and Moszhuhin's prolonged kissing in films. How can one lead to the other? It's a mystery.

The dawn air has unique freshness, unsullied before the new day's heat, smells, and rubbish-heaps tamper with it. In grey, sleepy silence, men scoop yesterday's muck out of the gutter and fling water over the rough, dusty street. Others deliver to homes from casks strapped across spindly-legged ponies.

She walks with her arm round Anahid's trembling shoulder. Anahid's head is bowed, face half-covered as they follow the captain. His military fez has been replaced by fur. He has scuffed leather boots and a double-breasted khaki greatcoat free of army insignia. His moustache is unwaxed. He little resembles the man she used to talk to.

Fixed to an old Benz tourer are canvas bags, blankets, and a bucket containing bottles. The captain has left the engine running; it splutters, judders. Papa sits in front, Jacob on his lap; the rest of them squash in the back with the bundles.

The captain eases the car down the road and alongside the square of cannons. He turns right onto the tramway, past clay walls, flat roofs and cupolas, and blue smoke of morning fires. When they reach the lane to Mirza Khan's house, a glance assures her it is empty. Anahid is leaning against her, eyes shut.

The sky pinks behind the mountains. As the sun comes up, it tinges snow on summits like a blush. At the end of the tramway, they pass sycamore and other trees' spring green. Ahead is the

Kasvin Gate, large and heavy-looking, already open, through which she and the family entered the city with Mr MacDonell nearly two years ago. Tiles glazed in many azure shades adorn the gate under a black archway – inscribed with writing she can't read – and four towers. She wonders if Mirza Khan has alerted those on duty at the twelve gates to check the identities of people leaving, but when the captain speaks, the guard puts up his hand in what could be a salute.

Beggars with terrible sores lie in the dust, singing in mournful voices, palms outstretched. With no straggling outposts, unlike Baku or cities she has been to, Teheran appears to rise from the desert enclosed by its wide ditch and sand-coloured mud rampart.

The car noses along the road, a serpent, a line drawn, neither climbing nor descending. All around is space, distant mountains, and light, infinite shades of colour slipping over the earth in waves.

I am squeezed in the corner with Esther, warm, safe. The shaking has stopped. Esther probably assumes I'm asleep, but every so often I open an eye and see Elburz' great white backbone above bare foothills; Demavend, lonely snowcap soaring into the sky, dwelling-place of spirits which Seyed Ali used to say had to be placated. With every breath, I am further from Teheran and the harem walls, free as a bird ... I hope Lallah remembers to feed Kiki ... floating on this plateau at the top of the world.

This is an ancient country, savage and desolating, in the shape of a startled cat with ears pricked and back arched, Seyed Ali told me. Man has made little impression here; we pass where he has scraped the surface, scattered some grain; an oasis of trees, a stream, a village and a few animals, but it is as if he is a temporary visitor.

Is Esther aware her face flushes when I talk about men or this Kemal? It suits her. If she's like that in front of him, he will want her. I have kept myself covered and acted the part of frightened maid to please her, but have taken a look at him. He is handsome, strong. Esther is foolish describing this marriage as convenience, by which I suppose she thinks they will not be together as man and wife. As her husband, he has the right. Why not? I shall have to teach her what to do. She knows more of him than she admits although she has confided how he told her about the house in Baku.

She is carrying such a burden, keeping the destruction from her parents rather than add to their distress. They have accepted me; her brothers, too, as children anywhere will when they have not been taught to hate or distrust. Her father bears marks of suffering, with his turkey neck and threadbare collar; Nadia is the stronger. Esther is so brave. I love her. She is my heart's true friend. I will do anything for her.

'A wagon!' Jacob exclaims.

She shivers in dawn light and wonders what has happened to the car. They have slept in a mud house in Kasvin. The town is as dusty and dilapidated as when she delivered the letter to General Dunsterville, but there are no British soldiers, bits of weapons or vehicles abandoned in the street. After they arrived, the captain left them without a word, six in one room, floor thick with rugs laid across each other, fabulously woven in bright colours, flowers, and arabesques. She wrapped herself in her blanket and relief that he was not there.

The conveyance is pulled by four horses hitched abreast. It is lined with carpets, corners curling, more of which drape over the top of arched, wooden ribs, protection from the sun. The sides are open. There is space to lie down.

The captain offers his hand as she climbs up. 'There has been snow in the foothills,' he says, 'so we may encounter drifts or, more likely, floods, for it will melt at this time of year as quickly as it came. We are making for Tabriz, capital of Persian Azerbaijan. There is unrest in the area. There is greater safety in numbers than I on my own can give you so we are joining a caravan.'

His hand is rough, warm. As soon as she is in place, he releases her, helps Anahid up, passes the boys to them. She tells the family what he explained. She looks at her pianist's fingers; it is the first time any man, apart from Papa, has clasped them.

The captain takes the reins. His touch stays with her, a quiet, private feeling separate from creaking wood and the clop of horses' hooves.

'When I'm big, I'm going to be a camel-driver,' Jacob announces.

'You can't do that and be a soldier,' she points out.

Jacob considers this, eyes ranging from here to there, gaze not broad enough to encompass all he sees while they wait in the wagon at the caravanserai where the animals and men have spent the night.

At home, she once read about the great caravans that follow trade routes such as the Silk Road from one end of a country to the border of another, and on, with jade, amber, silks, spices. This one consists of six brown, woolly-coated Bactrians. Between each double hump is perched a striped, stuffed, canvas saddle held together by thick branches and bound with ropes.

The drivers, in ragged turbans, sheepskin overshirts, and baggy blue breeches, secure the cargo, yell to each other and at the camels until every one is piled high and loaded down both sides.

Anahid hunches, shivering. 'Smelly people,' she whispers. 'Like those who took me to Teheran.'

She puts her arms round her friend. There is a jingling of bells, swaying of heads and ugly, pendulous mouths as if the beasts are anxious to be on the move, nudging, whinnying, pawing the ground while they are pushed into single file. With a shout, the leader and his animal set the pace, long, sad, measured steps, the captain bringing up the rear.

She loses count of the days, a monotonous jangling, jolting west, between and towards mountains, camels strong and tense on soft-padded feet, a forest of legs, knobbly with great knees. The beasts' languorous movements give them an air of stateliness, majesty, even wading into snowmelt up to their ankles. Vultures flap away from some meal. The drivers forever call out; sometimes it has the sound of singing. The only stops are for bartered food or silty-tasting water, and for the men to pray.

In the distance, mountains are blue and white across the upper parts where they merge into the sky, but never seem nearer. Foothills are tawny in the curious, intense light which renders them painted, artificial, every shade from yellow to ochre to burnt umber. Patches of blue-green rock appear, as if worked by an artist, and she remembers the patina on ornamental copper plates at home and a malachite necklace she sold in the Teheran bazaar. A blood-red ridge seams through the greens and browns.

Every night as shadows lengthen and merge, they halt at a caravanserai, sufficient journey for a camel from the previous one. With the animals, they stay in the wagon in the courtyard, a high, dried-mud enclosure roofed with tree-trunks and packed earth, doors locked. The captain brings dubious-looking lumps floating in thick sauce in a small pot, with hard, dark bread. Eat, he urged the first time, a foul, smoky smell about him; her stomach turned, but she dipped and sucked her bread, forced herself to swallow, broke a piece and dunked it for Jacob.

She falls asleep to the camels' melancholy groans and barks, horses neighing, a distant jackal howling. The captain and the drivers are inside a hovel, twenty or thirty paces square.

They rest by a rushing river which is swollen after snow. 'I want to see.' Jacob kneels, peers.

The captain jumps from his seat. 'The boys can come with me,' he says, stretches out his arms, lifts Jacob followed by Anton. 'Your father, too.' He points to a mud hut across the road. 'It is a tea house.'

Why can't he look at me when he speaks? she wonders.

Papa climbs down to Anton. Jacob has gone with the captain. She watches her brother slip his hand into the captain's, treating each moment as an adventure. Does he remember anything of Baku, of Teheran even? Or is he able to slough off what happens like an old skin and enjoy now? She hopes he never changes. He will suffer less.

The drivers have unloaded the packs, and lead the camels to the water, push them in up to their knees. The animals drink, nodding, bells jingling; they throw up their heads and give a solemn roar before dipping again and more, enough for days.

The men shout, cajole, slapping, pulling at the reins, a splutter of invective and singing. They make the beasts kneel, tip pailfuls over them, and force them under.

She wrinkles her nose at the sour, rotten smell of herself. Her mouth tastes stale.

'We could wash our clothes,' Nadia says. 'You and Ana go, further along.' Nadia begins to unbutton her blouse.

Anahid does the same, removes a double row of emeralds secured at the front by two large, vertical ones. 'Mirza Khan gave it to me. I can sell it.'

'If bandits don't get us first,' Nadia observes. 'Hide it beneath the carpet.'

The sun has slid from its height. She holds onto a side rib of the wagon, uses a wheel as a step, lowers herself to the ground, offers a hand to Anahid, who has put the cloak on over clean garments.

'We have to cover part of our faces, Esther.'

'Why?'

'It is what they are used to.' Anahid indicates the drivers. 'Otherwise, you will draw attention. They will stare. It could be difficult. Your husband will not be pleased.'

Esther *Hanum*.

Anahid extends the dark-blue muslin over her head, nose, mouth, and secures the cloth at the back of her neck. 'Go on.'

With her scarf, she copies Anahid.

At the river, she suggests they wash their hair.

'No,' Anahid emphasises.

'Why not?'

'There isn't time. It must always be beautiful for your husband. Only he should see it and never witness you looking like a drowned rat. You need to learn these matters, Esther.' They rub collars, cuffs, squeezing. A dozen paces away, Nadia is rinsing her monthly rags.

'There are things I can say to you, just the two of us,' Anahid pursues. 'He will come to you one night.'

'With everybody there? Don't be silly.'

'There will be an opportunity, I'm sure. You must know what to expect. The brown mark on your shoulder is considered a sign of great beauty.'

'He isn't aware of that.'

'Not now, no. But he will see it and be aroused.'

'How will he?'

'Esther, listen! While we're alone. When he comes to you, accept him, be ready, open yourself to him.'

'What *are* you talking about?'

'Sh! Don't shrink from him or turn him away, for that might make him take you by force, and you will forever associate him with that horrible moment, and it will spoil everything.'

'Take me? Where?'

Anahid regards her. 'You haven't any idea, have you? I didn't know anything, either, before Mirza Khan, but his wives told me what would happen and what to do. Under the veil, oriental women are very enterprising; they help each other, pass on their experience. They perfumed and greased me, arrayed me like a bride.'

'Greased you?'

'Between my legs. To make it easier. It will hurt at first.' Anahid pauses. 'That's how he will enter you, Esther. You had a brother, the same as me. Did your mama or nurse wash you together when you were small? You must have seen.'

Yes. *Nyana* used to bath her and Lev. She recalls the tiny thing, less than a finger, and being jealous and where was hers? and *nyana* saying it was his little boy's pack. Just as hands, feet, toes grow bigger, does that, too? But as for what Anahid calls entering her, how so? Perhaps it's some Persian custom favoured by Mirza Khan. It doesn't bear any relation to Moszhuhin's films.

Anahid hasn't finished. 'So lie on your back, splayed. Draw your knees up.' Anahid glances in the direction of the tea house. 'The men are returning. Time to stop. Remember what I have said. There may not be another chance to talk.' Anahid bundles the garments she has squeezed out, covers her face, sets off.

She collects the rest and follows Anahid, the dutiful Persian wife. The camels are cropping grass, chewing as if pondering. Near her, one of them looks up, stares into the distance with a doleful expression that has learnt patience; eyes which have glimpsed beyond horizons, framed with long lashes, giving them a childish, affectionate quality.

The captain stands by the wagon, a glass of dark, steaming liquid in each hand; brows meet in a frown. 'Do not go away from us again,' he says. 'There could be danger.'

'We needed to do our laundry,' she tells him.

'Are we now to have it flapping like a spectacle? It is not the way.'

Inside her, a giggle mounts; under the weight of his ill-humour, it is no more than a flicker when it reaches her mouth. She stands facing him, not bothering to hide her irritation. 'Why have we come this way so have to wear our clothes till we stink? At least in Teheran we could wash them and ourselves. The animals have had a good clean. Why not us?'

There is a bellowing from the camels, rubbery lips pulled back from yellowed teeth and thick tongues in a savage snarl as the drivers load the packs. Voice shrill above the noise, she adds, 'We're cooped up like pigeons in a cage, hardly room to turn round, every bone in our bodies aching.'

'Which route would you have chosen?' the captain demands. When she does not answer, he continues, 'No matter which direction from Teheran, there are open spaces, mountains to cross.'

Anger lurks in his expression. Fear quivers through her, yet he cannot harm her in front of everybody. She stays looking at him: dishevelled, unshaven, that smoky, sweaty smell. She wrinkles her nose. He grips her hand. 'You will get in the wagon.'

Anahid, already there, whispers, 'Do as he says, Esther. Calm yourself.'

She climbs up, retrieves herself from him.

'The tea,' Anahid prompts.

She takes one of the glasses. The temptation to hurl the liquid at him overwhelms her, but she feels Anahid draw her arm away. 'Quieten yourself,' Anahid urges.

She relents, not wanting to bring attention to Anahid.

The captain has moved. 'Esther,' Anahid says, 'never quarrel with him in front of others. Differences of opinion are to be kept between the two of you.'

'Oh, stuff and nonsense!' She tosses the glass's contents, splattering the dust short of the captain. Anton starts to cry.

Guilt that she is the cause expels her annoyance. She rocks her brother, soothes him, kisses the top of his head. 'Did you have tea?'

Anton nods, sniffs.

'It was strong and smelt smoky, same as the room,' Jacob tells her. 'The samovar wasn't clean and shiny like ours. There's a brazier which makes your eyes smart and it pongs. Not as nice as Madame Lavirotte's. There are shelves, and people sleep there in their clothes.'

She hugs Anton. Papa returns and with him earthy, tea house fumes. The only camel she can see lifts its head, stretches rear legs, throwing the packs forward. It gets up, sending the cargo into place. The drivers yell, prod the animals into line. The captain settles onto his seat behind the horses. Her view is of his back, broad khaki greatcoat straining across.

She stands by the wagon, breathes early-morning air rather than foul sheepskins and shouting. She looks at snow-capped mountains. One rises separate from the rest, much nearer.

'Esther. It has not been easy for you.'

She jumps, turns to find the captain at her side. Embarrassment spreads in a flush from her neck to her cheeks. It is his first use of just her given name. He doesn't realise that in Russia this is a mark of intimacy between family, close friends. 'No,' she says after a moment, 'not at all.'

His face is stubbled, dusty, streaked with grime; greatcoat crumpled, a tear in the bottom corner. She wants to ask, why did we have to be married for this journey? but decides against it. She doesn't wish to speak to him any more than necessary so that in Constantinople she can leave him and pretend it never happened.

'This evening, we should be in Tabriz,' he says. 'This ridge,' he adds, pointing, 'nearer than the others, is Sahand.' His hand slopes to the western horizon. 'Those are the highlands of eastern Anatolia. We are making progress.' He speaks as if the mountains are comrades.

'And Constantinople?'

'Some way yet. We shall stay with the caravan beyond Tabriz until Erzerum.'

She must tell Anahid; Erzerum, she is sure, is her town.

The captain takes her fingers. He raises them to his lips and is gone.

For hours, they lurch through foothills of flowering thorn as the road sweeps around Mount Sahand, the plain to the left packed with orchards as far as she can see. She plays scales, his touch still there; nails chipped, dirty, nothing about them, or her, sweet-smelling. Yet, he did it.

The sun is edging from its height as they pass banks cultivated in terraces of rich earth, covered in branches cascading with blossom, pink and lemon. They come into Tabriz, once famous as the terminus of the Silk Road from China, now with a half-destroyed blue mosque veneered in ancient mosaic; tombs and archways as old as time, and broken piers and vanished glory.

The captain delivers them to a mud-brick house and goes to dine with a chieftain who has declared Persian Azerbaijan separate from the rest of Persia.

In whitewashed walls are niches holding oil-lamps, pewter mugs, and rose-leaves and herbs in dishes. She lies alongside Anahid on a black and red carpet; listens to the river which runs through the town. Papa, Nadia, and the boys are in an adjoining room. Soon after their arrival, they were all given chicken and onion, rice, and platters of melon, grapes, and sweets; brackish-tasting water was in separate containers for drinking and washing; to a third had been added a couple of ambergris pellets for them to rinse their clothes.

Sleep eludes her as she feels the captain's lips on her fingers. He will enter you, Anahid said. No, he will not. Yet, there is a strange tingling in her lower stomach and between her legs. There, on coarse hair, she rests the hand he kissed, parts her limbs a fraction. Everything is closed up, and she thinks of Mirza Khan's courtyard in Teheran and the spring buds when she last saw them, petals tightly layered, protecting the ones beneath.

'I remember Gaspar when he was that age,' Anahid says in the morning, holding the picture of Lev. 'I used to brush his curls. Stop it, Nanni, he would insist. That was his name for me.'

She takes the photograph from Anahid, places it with her clean skirt and blouse.

'We've both lost brothers,' Anahid comments. 'We may find them again.'

'I shall hate to lose you if any of your family is in Erzerum.'

Anahid hugs her. 'We can write to each other. I might go to Constantinople.'

She lets Anahid secure the bundles and wanders to the unglazed window, the taste of curdled milk – the real mountain drink, Anahid said – and warm, freshly baked bread, still on her tongue.

In the street below, people are assembling. Standing apart from the crowd is a tall man in a fur longcoat draped with pistols, daggers, gold chains. Rounds of ammunition are slung over his shoulders and in belts circling his waist. He has a stick almost his height, the thickness of his wrist. The chief, she decides. Among those near him is the captain.

In front of the silent throng, someone is dragged on his back, bare feet in the air and tied between a pair of rifles. They are lifted and beaten on the soles. With each hit, the onlookers murmur as one.

'No!' she gasps.

Anahid enfolds her, turns her away. 'It is tribal law. He's probably stolen something.'

'Why is the captain watching?'

'He is the chief's guest. He cannot skulk in a corner.'

'Surely we should be on our way?'

'It would be discourteous to leave before the punishment. There must have been penalties in your country, too, Esther.'

'Yes. The tsar had secret police, but we never knew what they did or saw anything like this.'

She trembles, fearful of the unknown, of the husband who kissed her hand.

FOURTEEN

Eastern Anatolia, spring 1920

Dread of what may have happened to Baba and my brothers, or to the house in Erzerum, takes hold more every day. We have passed Ararat, cone of magnificence and majesty, crest enveloped in a white pall illumining space. We are in the heart of the Garden of Eden, paradise on earth where man, through disobedience, separated himself from God. There is nothing in this desolate, arid land. Perhaps we are already in Anatolia, the boundary by Little Ararat just a small rock at the side of the track. It is here that Persia, Russia, and Anatolia meet. Borders change, the business of emperors and treaties. Those who travel this route, however, as have generations before them with camels, oxen, donkeys, surrounded by tawny mountains, have no care for such formalities.

I cannot ignore that this Captain Kemal has helped Esther and her family, for they could never have done the journey on their own. I must regard him as a good Turk, like Baba's friend, Achmet Bey. There has been no opportunity for him to come to Esther. I thought he might the night we stayed in Tabriz, but no doubt that murderous-looking chieftain kept him feasting – he probably killed a sheep – and discussing for hours. Esther only talks to him if he addresses her first, but I have caught her glancing at him. I have no idea what she is thinking, feeling. I should explain to her that he will not appear familiar or even speak, except something for her to translate, as that is the way in the East. An Oriental gives certain times to his wife but will not laugh with her or show affection in the presence of others. So what she may interpret as coldness is, in fact, respect.

She is lovely, her skin a warm, creamy colour. She is modest when we undress and turns away, but I have seen her breasts: they are beautiful, the roundness of pomegranates, tilting upwards just the right amount, full but not too big, with large, very brown nipples. Mirza Khan would have adored them. There, I'm like an oriental first wife at the bath-house, assessing a prospective bride for her husband. I want you to be happy, Esther. I shan't enjoy leaving you. I must make good use of time that remains. Tell you things.

Tell you things, tell you things. Erzerum, Erzerum. It fits the creak of the wheels. One week, maybe, until my city, beneath these darkling stars.

'Esther,' Anahid touches her arm. 'Look at the hyacinths.'

She turns to see a swathe affirming life, the spring, fragrance wafting on air amid sun-baked, rocky heights.

Earlier, in a dusty town crouching under the gaze of broad-shouldered Ararat, scarlet Turkish fezzes with blue tassel the only spot of colour, the captain exchanged the wagon for a native cart, an araba, pulled by two ponies.

They labour uphill behind the caravan, along great flat stretches, past woods and fir-forests, more open spaces, and a church of black basalt. By a stream, a heron is fishing, a solemn, pale-grey creature with the surprised, bashful eyes of a girl caught unawares.

They pass villages of wooden houses, fruit-trees, and a water pump. They stop to buy yogurt and rice. Women in headscarves, with shy, wild, staring children, hoe dry land among tender vines. A shepherd waves to them from his hut. A cowherd leads away his animals. A pattern of ordered simplicity, renouncing the outside world and things engulfed in time: war, revolution, the future.

On every horizon, purple mountains undulate. Light dazzles, blurs vision. The day is as still as eternity, tinkle of sheepbells floating, suspended, grass dotted with flowers, yellow, white, magenta; hidden glades appear as the road twists. She hears another sound, nearby: the captain is humming; some boyhood tune?

The road slopes into a valley of afternoon shadows and the scent of blue, wavering dungsmoke. They cross a wooden bridge with no handrails, over a foaming river. A woman is washing clothes, beating them against a boulder. Children from a mud-hut village play in a clearing. Ancient trees stand with crowns together, arrayed in spring's bright green, roots curled in and out of cracked earth like arthritic fingers.

Away from the track, she sees a lake; forests reach to the shore. The camels turn towards a stone caravanserai alongside which boats have been drawn up. The two ponies follow, picking their way.

'The air is warmer,' the captain says to her. 'We can put up the tents. Everybody will be more comfortable.'

A chance to do the laundry again.

She walks with Nadia and Anahid to the other side of the water, which is about a verst long. In the centre, separating them from view of anyone opposite, is an island with a ruined church.

They wade past their waists and soak their hair. 'I can't remember feeling so clean,' she sighs. 'Let's go in as far as we can.'

A yell stops her.

'Jacob!' shouts Nadia.

They scramble to the bank and into their boots, bundle wet garments, cover their heads, hurry back. Papa is sitting on a rock. On his knee is Jacob, crying, holding out a hand from which blood trickles. Anton is with them, arms round Jacob.

'I was helping,' Jacob whimpers, 'and the peg slipped.'

Nadia examines the wound. 'Where's the captain?'

He is walking towards them and unwraps a grubby cloth. 'The drivers keep dried camel-dung for medicine or barter.' He seats himself next to Papa and takes Jacob, soothes him.

She watches the captain wipe her brother's cut and put on it some of the stuff, which has crumbled. 'There now,' the captain says. 'As brave as any soldier.' He glances up at her and smiles. Her heart catches between beats; she blushes.

Jacob gazes at the captain. She tells Jacob what he said. 'Thank him,' she prompts.

'Merci, monsieur.'

The captain nods and sets Jacob on his feet.

Nadia ruffles her son's hair. 'Always enthusiastic. You must be more careful.'

Jacob stands looking at what the captain has done as if he can't believe it is part of him.

The captain indicates the houses by the boats. 'I will see if there is any fish to sell, or it will have to be what I can snare. We need wood to make a fire.' He points to Jacob. 'One hand only, young man.'

She repeats this to Jacob. The captain strides away until, in fading light, he is just a shape. His gentleness with Jacob lingers, a glow within her.

She finds Anahid inside the smaller tent, hugging herself to stop shaking. She embraces her friend. 'I thought it had finished.'

After a minute, Anahid eases her away. 'I will sleep on the far side, and you here, near the entrance. He will come to you. I know it.'

'I shouldn't think he's given a second thought to that marriage ceremony. He certainly doesn't pay me any attention. He only speaks to me to pass on information. I'm no more than a courier.'

Anahid laughs, a tinkling sound. There has been too little merriment. 'He's showing restraint, respect for you, Esther. It is the way in the East, I've told you. I'll be rolled into my blanket so ignore me. He's a kind man. It's a very important quality.'

'We're supposed to be gathering wood and making sure Jacob doesn't open that cut.'

The captain returns with bread and three trout. While he makes the fire and cooks the fish, she helps Nadia and Anahid arrange the washing by the araba.

They sit, drawn by light, warmth, the sweet catch of woodsmoke. 'You'll eat with us, Captain?' Nadia offers.

'Madame,' he acknowledges the invitation.

Nadia asks him about his family and work as if she were interviewing a suitor for her stepdaughter.

Anahid goes into the tent.

She wishes she could, too, although she does not feel tired.

They throw the skeletons into the embers. 'Thank you, Captain,' Nadia says. 'It is the best meal we have had in some time.'

Jacob is picking at his wound. 'Leave it,' Nadia tells him.

'The muck's fallen off,' Jacob laments. 'It hurts. It's going boom, boom, inside my skin like a drum.'

'Let me see.' Nadia turns his hand over.

Jacob winces. 'Ayee!'

Nadia frowns. 'I'm worried it's becoming infected.'

'One of the fishermen's wives should have something,' the captain suggests. 'Can Jacob go with me?'

Jacob stands up, puts his other hand in the captain's.

Papa and Anton have gone. She stays with Nadia by the fire.

'I would never have thought a Turk could be so presentable,' Nadia says. 'And kind.'

Yes, he is. What do I do if he ... as Anahid insists he will, not to talk but to ... the prospect terrifies me. Men and women make babies. I mustn't have one if he is to release me from the marriage.

But none of this can she admit to Nadia, who was her big sister when she was a child, hugged her the day of her first monthly bleed, and showed her how to fold and pin the squares and roll them into a bag for Sonia to wash. The mystery remains, the divide between those who know what happens when a man and woman lie together, and those who don't. Livvy did, but she only saw Livvy once after the wedding; her face had a luminous quality as though part of her were elsewhere.

She gets to her feet.

'I'll wait for them,' Nadia tells her. 'Won't you keep me company?'

'I'll check Ana's all right.' The captain and Jacob will return. Nadia will take Jacob, which will leave her and the captain by the fire. No.

She lifts the flap. 'Anahid?' she whispers. She crawls inside, sees Anahid's back. She curls into her blanket, hopes to be lulled by lakewater lapping the shore, pine-trees murmuring, a bird's sudden squawk.

She hears Nadia's voice and Jacob's, and Nadia shushing him.

'*Bonne nuit, madame,*' the captain says to Nadia.

Her stomach thumps. She sits up.

'Esther?' Is it her imagination; the breeze in the trees? 'Esther?'

She opens the flap.

He is a few paces away. 'I did not want to wake you.'

'I was not asleep.' She stands outside and catches the aromatic smell of tobacco.

'A fisherman's wife has wrapped Jacob's cut in cloths perfumed with herbs, a traditional remedy. Also, a small dish of black honey to prevent fever. She thought he was my son. Ours.'

Why didn't I stay inside?

'We have had little chance to talk,' he adds. 'Shall we walk or are you tired?'

Any fatigue is hidden by nerves strung out. She follows him to the lakeside. In Teheran, he was always in front of her. Here, it's because the track is narrow. The island with the ruined church conceals the fishermen's houses on the other shore. Fragrance from pine needles under their feet suffuses the air. The moon has risen and shines on the water's rim. She feels her limbs loosen.

'It has not been easy for you these weeks.' He stops, takes her hand. 'You and your family have been very uncomplaining.'

His fingers are warm against hers. 'Except for that time by the river when we did our laundry.'

He smiles. 'It was not the marriage you or your parents expected. When my eldest brother was married, he first saw her face after seven days' feasting and celebration when she raised her veil. It has been the way for centuries, arranged in the hope the young people will get along. If I ever thought of it, I assumed it would be the same for me.'

'Did your mother and father have someone in mind for you?'

'Perhaps they talked about it to each other. There is always a cousin.'

One waiting for him?

'I think that's what they're for,' he adds; 'family fortunes are not broken up. But war alters things. As you have found. In the Ottoman Empire, old ways are breaking down. There will be more changes.'

'But not revolution such as we have had.'

Moments pass before he answers. He looks at her as if he would memorise every detail. 'I hope not.' He puts his arm across her shoulders, draws her to him. His greatcoat is unfastened, and she trembles as he holds her against his shirt. 'You are cold.' He places the coat as far round her as it will go.

She wonders why she doesn't shrug it off, step away, and why she feels content next to him and his tobacco smell.

He smoothes stray hair off her forehead, caresses the side of her face. She closes her eyes. His lips are gentle, those that touched her fingers weeks ago soft against her own, moving to her neck where the pulse is. She is warming, opening as petals unfold in the sun, like the roses in the Teheran courtyard.

With one finger, he traces the shape of her cheek, her eyebrows; holds her for a moment. 'Shall we walk back?' He sets off, and she follows. Separated from his warmth, she shivers.

When they reach the tent, he takes her hand, kisses it. 'I will see you at daybreak.'

She watches him until he's at the houses.

She goes inside. She lies down, wraps herself into the blanket, but the memory of him on her skin, of his arms around her, will not leave. Tingling, waiting for the return of his touch, she sighs, irritated by emotions she hasn't asked for, cannot understand, least of all control. She rolls onto her right. Maybe she dozes, is awake again, body seeming no longer to belong to her but that of a stranger, taunting: why are you lying alone?

She opens the flap. Some of the fishermen sit by the lakeside; voices rise, fall. She sets off along the path.

She passes where she and the captain stood. The track winds up a pine ridge. Another church stands on the hillside, grown about with trees and shrubs. Branches push through the roof. Lilies glow silver in moonlight, and she stops, breathes their perfume.

A cloud hides the moon, throws building and flowers into gloom, and she quivers. How much further to exhaust herself, expel from her body feelings that have invaded it?

It isn't that she hears a sound on the track behind her: perhaps a new shadow, a change in the others, makes her turn. 'Captain Kemal Bey!' How often did she greet him thus in Teheran? and he used to bow, say her name, suggest they walk. Now, there is only anger she saw weeks ago when she had washed clothes in the river.

'What are you doing?' he demands.

'I can't sleep.'

His face softens. 'You must not come into the forest. There could be wild animals, unseen danger.'

'I'm not conscious of any threat. It's such a lovely place. How did you know I was here? You followed me?'

'I was with the fishermen. I could see the tents, ensure all was well.'

'With no sleep?'

'There were important matters to discuss, things happening in this country. I could be on guard, too. I wish you to be safe.' He puts his arms round her.

She wants to push him away, stop the feelings returning, the warmth, tingling, sensation of herself unfolding, but his mouth is on hers, with urgency.

He kisses her face, her neck, and she clings to him for to do otherwise would be to cut herself off from oxygen. 'Esther, Esther,' he whispers into her hair until his lips find hers; his hand moves over her breast, and she moulds herself against him, gasping. He carries her a few paces to a clearing and lowers her onto pine needles as if she were some rare porcelain. He unfastens her blouse, caresses the mark on her shoulder, moves down her skin. As he discards his coat, she is aware of a flash of metal, and he lays a gun on the ground, but its significance floats into the rest of reality.

The woods and ravines smell sweet and heavy like honey. She kisses his cheeks, his eyes, suspended in time. A recollection flutters across her mind, insubstantial, from another existence, Anahid: lie on your back, splayed; draw your knees up. She has no need of Anahid, of rituals, preparations, advice of wise women; this body, this Esther she did not know existed nor seek to bring to life, opens to welcome him.

'But I cannot swim,' she repeats.

His voice is teasing. 'You grew up a stone's throw from the great Caspian Sea?'

'It's very salty.'

'I will hold you.'

She cannot say how long they have lain together, slept. They walk to the far end of the lake. The dark water is chill, ripples silver under the moon, and she hesitates, but he guides her in, floats, arms around her strong, securing her on top of him. Precious, a treasured possession, protected, she rests the lean length of him and gazes at a velvet sky.

'When I was a cadet at the Military Academy in Constantinople, we had to swim every morning in the Bosphorus,' he recalls. 'I went there when I was twelve and stayed with an uncle. Very proud of myself, I was, in my uniform.'

Constantinople: a name, an image, and as with so many thoughts this night, fleeting, separated from her by time and distance. She is content to drift, smears of blood on her thighs gone with her maidenhood forever.

They return to the shallows, her hand in his until they are on the track. As they reclaim their clothes, amber dawn glimmers on the horizon.

'He came to you,' Anahid says as they bundle their belongings.

She remembers Livvy, forty-eight hours after the wedding in Baku, and realises that same luminous expression must be on her own face; proclaiming, now I know what it is, what happens. She can look at Anahid with the fresh eyes of shared knowledge.

'I can tell,' Anahid pursues. 'You have the appearance of a girl who has been plucked, which means you are one no longer. He will return to you. You are his field, he will plough you and sow, and you will learn how to please him, to keep him homing as does the bee to the flower for honey.'

'What poetic language! Actually, he did not come to me.' Is she expected to tell Anahid everything? Isn't it just for her and Kemal, not to be chewed over, compared? To gossip about this, to let the daylight in, will surely destroy the magic. But that was what Anahid was used to with Mirza Khan's wives in Teheran, perhaps because they had nothing else to do. And what do you have to do today, Esther?

'Down by the lake?' asks Anahid. 'On pine needles?'

Nadia emerges from the other tent. 'Goodness, Esther.'

Her silence is eloquent.

'Not such a marriage of convenience,' Nadia adds. 'What will you do in Constantinople?'

'Play the piano. He knows that.'

As he gives her his hand to help her into the araba, his eyes meet and hold hers; infinite tenderness, fathomless pools in which she has lost herself and will again.

She stretches her fingers, moves them in the opening bars of Beethoven's Moonlight sonata, the night's passion reaching the tips. For the first time, she wears under her blouse the necklace he gave her in Teheran. The filigree lies on her like a caress.

So now it has happened. Esther is no longer a virgin and truly married to her Kemal. I woke up. Had something disturbed me? I was not aware of sound, certainly not of Esther. I sat up, realised she was not there, and guessed they were together; her face this morning confirms it. She has a beauty, radiance. I missed the feel of Mirza Khan, anticipation, excitement, and cried myself to sleep, holding the piece of silk I embroidered when I was in Teheran; silly, when I didn't love him, but at least I'd had a function.

Esther would not talk about men when she was a virgin, and even now she isn't she won't. She is my friend, I love her but cannot understand her. What am I for?

They cross a fertile plain, pass a ruined fortress, rattle down to a wide river valley, climb again to a ridge. Waking hours vary little, bound by rising and setting sun, punctuated by needs – human and animal – of food and water.

Each night, Kemal comes to her. She learns the textures of his skin, around his eyes, on his neck, back, arms; the coarse hair that curls on his chest, lower limbs, that on the upper parts finer. She traces with her finger the scar which sits uneasily where flesh was gouged from his shoulder during the war.

'*Moya dusha*,' she whispers, 'my soul.'

They camp on a carpet of rich grass and wild flowers surrounded by trees.

'Est-her,' he murmurs in the tone she loves, two syllables drawn out as if he doesn't want to let go of her name, her. 'My *lale* ... my tulip.' They move together under the blanket, stifling their joy, the river outside a raging torrent still swollen after the thaw, dawn light creeping into the new day.

FIFTEEN

Erzerum, eastern Anatolia, spring 1920

*O*ur *teachers used to tell us of the Ottomans' eastern campaigns: armies set off from this fortress city, thousands of metres above sea level, on a ridge which divides the Euphrates and Aras valleys.*

We are approaching the elaborate, grey ramparts in the best season, when air is clean and cool, and pastures vibrant green. For nearly six months, snow swirls out of the sky like feathers, winds rage, cold pierces, thirty degrees below freezing. This and hunger drive wolves from the rocky mountains to roam the streets. We would stay indoors except to go to school or work. If the sun was shining, we had to be careful it did not burn our faces. In summer, we spread cushions on the roof to sleep.

Ferida and Nevart, what has become of you since we used to meet by the river? I expect you are married. Nevart, you always had eyes for Vartan Saroyan. Did he return intact to wed and bed you? We shall have new experiences to share.

I am coming home, Baba. *In Persia, I have done and seen things you will never know about. I have not been the good Armenian girl you brought me up to be. But inside, she is still there. Anahid. We will start again, put behind us all the separation. I will look after you, and Edouard and Gaspar, and see if I can remember how to make* lokum: *starch, rosewater, lemon juice, sugar ...*

Where is he taking us, this Kemal? Past ruined buildings, poor people scurrying. What has happened while I have been away? I cannot recognise where I am. Who has done this? Tears trickle, soak into my shawl. My heart is breaking. Esther slips her hand into mine, clasps it.

They arrive at mud-brick lodgings. 'Esther, it is not advisable to admit you are Russian,' Kemal warns her. 'Tsarist troops were here for more than a year in what had been the headquarters of the Turkish Third Army. The memory is too recent. You could be imprisoned. We shall say you are French but have lived in Persia for some time. It will distance you from the war.'

She looks at troubled, brooding eyes.

'I have matters to attend to,' he adds. 'Sometimes, I shall not be able to return.' He rests a finger under her chin, tilts it, his expression she knows, memorising every detail of her face.

'Can we build another fort?' Jacob asks.

Kemal rumples her brother's hair, and the first smile she's seen since their arrival spreads across his mouth. 'We shan't be here long,' he predicts and is gone.

'Is he getting wood, Esther?'

'We'll have to see.'

I have found our road. I think it is, but there are no markers to show where I am. So many buildings have been destroyed. I have counted from the end the space each house would take, until I arrived at ours. Just a heap of bricks and stone. I have done the calculation the opposite way, but the result is the same pile. Our rubble. Different from any other. Mine and Baba's, *Edouard's and Gaspar's. And Mama's because her memory stayed with us, and photographs of her when she was young, and Edouard and Gaspar and I were children, and her and* Baba *on their wedding day.*

Nothing.

I stand on the edge of the debris. It moves beneath my weight, settles. I steady myself, spot marble paving-pieces the size of my palm; put together, they would make our entrance-hall. Glass fragments are scattered among them: the partition beyond which was the garden. There are two chunks of step, part of the outside staircase which took us to the roof. Storks used to nest on the chimney. Where will they go this summer? Cindered, timber lengths are abandoned at the back – from the table in the kitchen, or the salon? Or the chairs?

I am treading on my home.

And Baba, *Edouard, Gaspar? Have they seen what has happened? Have they, like me, returned, witnessed this but gone away again? Or did they die? Are their ghosts among the stones and glass? Are my feet on their spirits? And Achmet Bey, Bedia* Hanum, *and their children? Their ruins are next to ours; perhaps they got mixed up, and it is their house and them I am standing on.*

I move back.

What is that, there? Wedged between two blackened lumps, a piece of pink material or part of a doll. Yet, I didn't have any; I gave them to Achmet Bey's daughters. I lean across, pull, and it loosens. A slipper, the front where the toes would have fitted scorched open yet recognisable to the person who used to wear it. Anahid Touryan. Phantoms are everywhere, pressing in. I tuck it inside my robe and run; sobs try to break out, and here are Turkish soldiers, and I do not want to look at them or have to speak so I cover my face and walk until I find the street where we have been brought to lodge, and I scuttle up the stairs and sit and cry, fearful I haven't enough tears to drown all the memories, but still they come.

'Il y a eu un massacre, madame,' Madame Karavolias volunteers in languid French, glances round in case someone is listening.

Yet, they are alone in the hall.

Widow of a Greek, offspring of a Greek father and Turkish mother, Madame Karavolias lived in Constantinople as a child and picked up some French, according to Kemal. At first, she was not forthcoming, coal eyes wary, like a bird of prey and framed by hennaed hair, darting over new lodgers, assessing; she and a young woman – hardly more than a girl, whom the landlady refers to as her niece – keep to rooms at the rear, emerge occasionally to peer from behind a lattice screen, miss nothing, say little except to acknowledge the time of day.

Until she mentions the ruined buildings to the landlady.

'A massacre,' Madame Karavolias repeats. 'After the Russians left three years ago.' Lips curl in distaste at the word Russians.

An ache of alienation, displacement, weighs inside her chest at being forced to keep secret her nationality.

'You see, the Armenians and the Russians were,' – Madame Karavolias links the smallest fingers of both hands – 'but the Russians had to defend their country against revolution. So when they'd gone …' She pauses. Shrugs. Gestures in despair. 'A vendetta. Turks, and any Armenians who'd managed to return. Not one Armenian family remained, all butchered or fled. Only the school survived, though why, heaven knows, with no pupils and nobody to teach in it.'

... any Armenians who'd managed to return. Anahid's father and his sons?

'Of course,' Madame Karavolias continues, 'monsieur, your husband, was in Erzerum last summer for the congress so is aware of these things.'

As her eyes meet the landlady's stare, something prompts her not to admit ignorance. 'Yes,' she replies. 'I did not expect so much devastation.'

Congress? About which Kemal has no need to tell his wife, and she no business to ask.

She finds Anahid on the pallet, crying, hair limp and tangled. She strokes it, recalls its lustre when threaded with gold in Teheran.

The weeping subsides, but Anahid does not turn round. When she does, it is sudden, defensive, an animal sensing danger; her eyes are red, swollen, wild, face ravaged.

She enfolds Anahid. 'Will you have something to eat? There is some bread.'

Anahid shakes her head.

'You will become weak, sick. We still have a long way to travel.'

'I belong in Erzerum. I will die and be buried near Mama. Will she and I be the only Touryans laid to rest here?' Anahid raises herself onto one elbow. 'It's the not knowing, Esther. Did *Baba*, Edouard, Gaspar, perish with the house? Or have they never been back? And my friends. Ferida. Nevart.'

'You will come with us,' she says to Anahid. 'We are your family now.'

She tightens her embrace of Anahid, who kisses her cheek, neck, mouth.

'Nobody but you can understand,' Anahid sobs.

Their tears mingle until Anahid sleeps.

Forty-eight hours pass without Kemal. She helps Anahid and Nadia with sewing Madame Karavolias takes in: the niece is ill, but hemming blouses, collars, cuffs has to be finished on time.

The third night, she wakes with a start like the slice of a blade. She sits up. Kemal stands by the door. She gasps, holds out her arms. She gets to her feet, and he pulls her to him, that same smoky, musty smell about him; hands push down the straps of her chemise, move over her breasts to her waist, throw off his greatcoat and shirt. She trembles at his haste, his readiness, clasps him to her, matches his need as he lowers her onto the pallet.

'Esther, Esther,' he murmurs, and endearments in German and Turkish. It is over in moments.

They lie, limbs entwined. Slumber drags at her eyelids, but she forces them apart.

He looks at her, eyes serious.

'You are busy,' she ventures.

He nods. 'Mustafa Kemal – his is a name we shall hear a lot of – he has convened a National Assembly in Angora.'

'We are going there?'

He smiles, shakes his head. 'It is days out of our way. But there are things I must do in this area. The sultan is in Constantinople, virtually a prisoner of the British. Their forces have entered the Turkish Quarter and deported some of our people. British officers in Anatolia are being held in reprisal. The sultan has dissolved parliament. Mustafa Kemal's Nationalist

Party had a majority after the elections; we hoped to influence policy. We are still loyal to the sultan, want to free him from foreigners and make our land – Anatolia, not the empire of old – great again. You are safe with Madame Karavolias. She can be trusted. I have already stayed here.'

For the congress. She waits. And?

She tries, against tiredness pulling at all senses, to understand what he has told her. He kisses her once more. Her body sloughs off sleep that would claim it, and embraces him.

Her last conscious thought is that he might be in danger.

They probably assumed I was asleep, curled under the sheet, my back to the room. I cannot rest, can find no peace except when Esther and I lay together the other afternoon.

I heard the door open, close. No talking but in the silence and darkness of night, any movement, disturbance of air, has its own sound. And after, they were whispering. So much they had to say. Mirza Khan often used to speak very little. How different for Esther, no preparation for her husband or time to make herself beautiful. Was she expecting him, even? She never mentions him. When I think of the hours I would spend readying myself for Mirza Khan; yet, in the end, the result is the same.

By morning, he had gone. Esther said nothing, but her face had that special beauty. She is quite lovely.

Now, demons are swirling.

For days, Anahid tosses from one side of the pallet to the other, shivers, murmurs, mostly in Armenian, sometimes calls out or cries before subsiding into restless slumber.

Madame Karavolias brings broth to the door. 'And the blouses, madame?' Eyebrows questioning.

'They will be finished tomorrow,' she tells the landlady. 'I am working as fast as I can.' She takes the earthenware bowl. 'How is your niece?'

Madame Karavolias spreads both palms upwards in resignation. 'It is the malaria. Every year as the weather becomes hotter. But today she has had a tiny nourishment. See if mademoiselle will try some.'

'Thank you, madame.'

Later, Papa's thin, sunken face gleams with sweat as he sits at the table, arms tightened round himself to stop warmth escaping and keep himself together. Nadia stands by him, hand against his cheek not to ascertain feverishness but the tenderness of love. Nadia's features are lined, ageing. Papa begins to shake; shoulders shudder.

They shift the pallets so he and Anahid are in the same room. Day and night, Nadia sits with them, sponges burning skin, snatches sleep.

Except to deliver the sewing, an errand she offers to run for Madame Karavolias, she stays indoors, away from heat and street smells. The freshness in the air when they arrived has been replaced by a miasma.

Kemal is back one afternoon. She rises to greet him. He kisses her forehead; beard-growth prickles her cheeks. His greatcoat is stained, boots dusty.

'Papa and Ana are sick,' Jacob tells him.

Kemal releases her hands, strokes both boys on the head while she explains.

'We could depart tomorrow,' he says.

'They are not well enough to be moved. Nadia is exhausted.'

He sighs with frustration. 'A caravan will be starting for the coast at first light. We could join them. You have been here too long already.'

'We have been waiting for you,' she points out.

He regards her, unsmiling, brows drawn together.

There is a knock at the door. Madame Karavolias has a tray covered by a wire mesh. 'For Captain Kemal Bey.'

'Thank you.'

He is seated at the table. She sets down bread, soup, and a jug of iced *gazoz*.

He eats several mouthfuls before speaking. 'Esther, I cannot stay in Erzerum.'

'Why not?'

He ignores her. 'Neither should I leave you alone much.'

'Another forty-eight hours?' she suggests. 'Perhaps they will be able to travel. How many days' journey?'

'Ten. Would it be any more dangerous for the invalids than remaining here?'

'They can be kept separate from us.'

He pushes away uneaten food, stands up, chair falling to the floor. 'I will return after tomorrow.'

She goes to him, touches his arm, chest hurting with his visit's sparseness, lack of privacy, affection; unanswered, unspoken questions. He looks at her face. She searches his eyes for love but finds none. Throat constricting, she asks, 'Why can't you be in Erzerum?'

He puts his hand over hers. Her heart lifts. 'There are those unwilling to accept that we who would rescue the sultan from foreign – enemy – clutches are still loyal to him. We do not wish to depose him, but others believe we do.' He eases her from his sleeve. 'Two days,' he says. He opens the door and bounds down the stairs.

She turns to her brothers. They are scoffing the bread he has left.

This morning a lot of people are in the street; some have pocket-sized, red flags. Disquiet gnaws at her. Crowds mean trouble. In Russia, the tsar's police would move you on if you loitered in a group.

Head lowered, she cradles completed sewing. She arrives at the crossroads in the town centre. The population gathers on all four corners, air thick with garlic, armpits, expectation. She listens to voices around her and thinks how a language not understood sounds urgent, even angry.

She follows the populace's stare the way she has come. Soldiers, five abreast and too many to count behind, are marching, Ottoman banner – white crescent and star on a blood-coloured background – held aloft. She shivers, imagines such a parade through Baku nearly two years ago. She steps back, lets the citizens close around her, with no desire to witness troops wearing the uniform of those who occupied her city and did nothing to prevent the destruction of her home.

She wants to stop her ears to cheering, clapping, chattering. 'Bolshevik,' she hears. Did she imagine it, or is it a Turkish word like bolshevik? Others repeat it, and she glances up. At walking pace are a couple of cars, tops down so the occupants – three in front and to the rear – can see and be seen, although nobody acknowledges the reception. She inhales the smell of gasoline, Baku. The dozen men are dressed in black leather jackets and tall-necked, Russian shirts. Her first *bolsheviki* since Baku.

Her tongue feels dry, too big for her mouth. She is incapable of speech or uttering even the slightest sound of shock. She is being pushed by those demanding a better view; their odours stick in her nostrils. She looks at the man nearest her in the vehicle behind, at his eyes, the same colour as hers; at the ruined left side of his face, no longer livid, purple, as it was when last she saw it, but taut, settled into the skin. For a few seconds – the time it takes for the car to pass but it could be hours, all her life up to now – his gaze holds hers, says, you? here?

Her shawl has slipped. She corrects it, tries to steady her breathing and the pounding of her heart. It cannot be her brother. Heat, fumes, dismay at seeing *bolsheviki*, are playing with her mind … yet, that scar … Lev, who was handsome. Lyova. But many soldiers must be disfigured, not just him. It can't have been him.

Can it?

Of course not.

The crowd disperses. She crosses the road, not meeting anybody's expression as if she were anonymous, invisible.

She has been to the house before. She lets herself through the wrought iron gate set in a high wall, and walks across the garden between hardy plants tough enough to withstand extremes of summer and winter temperatures.

She is shivering. At the doorway, hands shaking, she gives the sewing, aware of eyes like currants in fleshy dough scrutinising her. The woman leaves her, returns with three more blouses, sufficient lengths of coloured thread, and some coins.

'Thank you, *Hanum*.' She puts the money in her pocket, lowers her face. Afraid. Of unknown threats, of being discovered. Of fear itself.

Once the door is closed, she turns towards the gate. Kemal is right. They must make for the coast, away from this unhealthy place which is affecting her brain. It cannot have been Lev. For the men in those vehicles were *bolsheviki*. Images chase each other: Kemal; *bolsheviki* in Erzerum, far from Russia; people welcoming them. All she wants is to get back to her family, the two rooms that have become a refuge, and leave Erzerum for good, tonight if possible. But Kemal said tomorrow –

'So, sister! It *was* you! Thinner, though.'

The harsh, Russian voice hits her as if its owner has punched her, jerking mind and body away from thoughts. She stops, regards the man who called her sister: his scrutiny of her from the car less than an hour ago now blazes beneath wide forehead and thick, bushy brows; full mouth, scar pulling down the left corner; hair cropped under a cap with a five-pointed star at the front; unshaven, leathered face that looks to have been exposed to every weather; stumps of teeth she remembers as whole and white. What have six years done to him?

In spite of his fierce study of her, fear and tension drain, allow sound to a smile bubbling up through her chest to her throat. Lev! He's alive as she always hoped.

Laughter escapes, and words. 'But you're not dead! That's wonderful.'

Eyes narrow in incomprehension. 'Should I be?'

'We had no news of you. Papa and Nadia were convinced you'd perished at Tannenburg with Sasha. I wanted to believe …' She has to let the family know. Take him with her.

'I was never there. The Turkish Front, yes.' He flicks the shawl from around her chin. 'What's this?' he snaps.

The gesture and what he has just told her halt euphoria as surely as a rifle-shot or douse of water from a mountain stream.

'Lost your tongue, have you? Tell me, sister, before I die of curiosity, what you are doing here and why you are covered up like a crow although not as much as the native women. You stood out in the crowd, face open to the morning air.'

Had she heard his voice but not seen him, she would not have known him: rasping, used to being listened to and giving orders but no part of the quiet, studious brother of her memory. Until those arguments with Papa the summer the war began. Was that the beginning of … this?

'So I have to guess, do I?' he continues. 'You were captured and now spend your days fetching and carrying, and … oh no, surely not …' Something amuses him; the mouth distorts further. 'You're not in a harem, are you? How are the mighty fallen.'

'Stop it! You and I have both had a shock. I only arrived a couple of weeks ago. We're leaving tomorrow for the coast.'

He raises his eyebrows. 'Some sort of tour?'

'We're refugees, Lev, for goodness' sake. We have nothing but a bundle each.' She points to the sewing, explains.

'The mighty are indeed fallen. Quite right, too. And,' he adds, 'it's not Lev. It's Leon Alexeevich Kovansky. Commissar Kovansky.'

'You … you changed your name?' she stutters. 'Disowned us? You were forced into it?'

'Not at all,' he emphasises.

'What are *you* doing here?'

'We're on our way to Mustafa Kemal in Angora. Two peoples throwing off the imperialist yoke; we should have a lot to talk about, show him how it's done. Now we have Russia under control, we look outwards to encourage others to reach for what we have achieved.' He speaks with passion, conviction, as if used to saying these things. The stuff of haranguing public meetings.

'Russia is isolated,' he continues, 'misunderstood by the rest of the world. They say they don't want to interfere in our affairs, but blockade and starve the country. They're planting dragon's teeth which some day will grow into bayonets and be turned in directions they least desire.' The words tumble from his tongue. 'So we must seize every opportunity to make contacts abroad.'

Her legs are not supporting her. She takes deep breaths to stave off panic; clutches the blouses, her only hold on a reality that is crumbling in front of her. Did Kemal lie about Mustafa Kemal's loyalty to the sultan and not wishing to depose him? Is anybody trustworthy, anything certain? 'Bolshevik,' she whispers.

'Yes, sister. Admit it. Come on. Get used to it. The dictatorship of the proletariat oppresses the oppressors. Your time is over.' Evangelistic ardour glares from his eyes.

She steps away, from contamination, all he represents and this terrible knowledge of her twin-brother. She struggles with speech. 'Traitor! No!' Her mind cannot encompass what she has learnt and will have to live with forever.

He grabs her shoulder. 'Yes, sister. Yes.'

She winces, tenses. His hand is rough. 'Don't touch me!'

He grips her arm. 'Why not? You're not precious, proud any more, are you?'

'Have you any idea what the *bolsheviki* have done to your family, to thousands like us?' Her voice rises. 'Papa is broken, old too soon. Jacob and Anton are rootless, without the schooling or settled life you had. We have no home, business, land.'

'My heart bleeds for you. It had to happen. Things could not have continued as they were. Nicholas Romanov entangled the country in alliances and wars with no concern for how the mass of his people was living.'

'You killed him. And his wife and children. It was unforgivable.'

'He was the cause of millions going to their deaths.' His hold on her loosens.

'I must go,' she breathes.

'We may meet again, sister, after the revolution here.'

'No. Kemal insists they do not want to depose the sultan, just advise him, protect him from foreigners.' Appalled at what she has revealed, she moves away, but Lev has her arm once more.

'Kemal?'

'My husband.'

'A Turk? So now it's coming out,' he stretches the words. There is menace in his voice. 'My sister married to an Ottoman, eh?' He clenches her. 'Eh?'

She stiffens at the vice of his fingers.

'I'll tell you about them. Six months I spent in the mountains. Entire units froze. I lost half my toes to frostbite, lived off a few scraps of bread a day and soup from boiled flesh and bones: donkeys, dogs, cats. The revolution set us free. But you weren't to know that, were you? You marry the enemy to suit yourself. Or were you made to?' Madness lurks in his eyes. 'Eh? Pregnant?'

Fear of him claws at her belly. 'How dare you!' She outlines how the wedding happened.

He pushes her, and she retches with pain and relief. 'Foolish women,' he says with disgust. He snatches her left hand. 'No wedding band? What sort of marriage is this? Isn't it a bourgeois symbol for the woman to wear a ring?' He drops it as if it were worthless. 'You've changed, too, sister, although you won't admit it. That is what uprisings are for. So you needn't act full of moral outrage. Whether your husband survives the revolution here, time will tell.'

Confused, tongue paralysed, she wonders if Kemal is with those waiting to receive the bolshevik mission. He, like Lev, hates foreign interference in his country. Are they on the same side?

She has to escape. Her feet find the will to move. She backs away before he can grab her. 'No,' is all she can repeat. 'No to everything you have said and are.'

'Yes, sister. Yes,' he taunts.

She is running. 'Yes,' she hears again. She looks round to see if he is following, but he is standing where they were talking. She turns down an alley towards Madame Karavolias's house, panting, tears blurring vision.

She climbs the stairs, loosens her shawl, wipes a sleeve across her eyes, bites her lip. She opens the door. Papa is sitting at the table, dressed, spooning soup into his mouth. She leaves the blouses and goes to him, places an arm round his shoulder. 'Papa,' she says and kisses the top of his head where white, wispy hair just covers the scalp.

He takes her hand.

'How do you feel?' she asks.

'Better,' he nods. 'It's slow, but good. I'll do for a while longer. God doesn't want me yet.' There is still a yellowish tinge to his skin. His gaze of weariness focuses on her face. 'You are sad, Esther.'

'I was hurrying,' she says. 'Nearly tripped. There was a parade through town which delayed me.'

SIXTEEN

Erzerum, eastern Anatolia, May 1920

The fever has gone and with it tortured dreams, demons, ghosts. If I am not to die here and be buried with Mama, I want to get away, for there is nothing I can do. I don't wish to walk again down our street and see that pile of rubble. Memories are burnt into my mind as surely as if I had been branded on forehead or arm, sign of possession; they have me in their grasp and will never let go. Now it is afternoon, Esther's pallet is once more with mine, and we are supposed to be resting.

'Esther? What is it?'

She is sobbing, tearing at some paper. I cannot bear her to be upset; it is like a knife, twisting, wrenching my insides. I sit beside her. She is ripping the photograph of her brother. I take a few pieces from her. 'Esther, what do you think you're up to?'

She snatches them back, makes smaller bits. I put my hands over hers. Two fingers are bleeding. 'Your lovely skin.'

She throws what she has destroyed on the floor, grinds it under her sandal, pulls herself from me. 'Leave me alone.'

'I can't. I hate you to be unhappy.'

Her eyes are red and puffed, mouth swollen, cheeks streaked with tears. Oh, my dear, dear Esther. She shakes her head. 'I couldn't tell them.' Words falter. 'It would kill Papa, and I cannot expect Nadia to carry such a secret. Jacob used to idolise him but hasn't mentioned him for a while. It's better they remember him as he was.'

'Why?'

She stares; fear smoulders. Her breathing quickens. Her mouth opens as if for speech but closes again. She swallows, shuts her eyes in a grimace.

'Esther?'

'I have to trust you.'

'I owe my freedom to you.'

She nods. Words form, line up – you go first; no, after you – if only she will release them. She passes her tongue over her lips. 'Lev,' she whispers. As she explains, I am crushed by how a brother can change, become brutalised.

Tears trickle down her cheeks along tracks left by others. She cannot speak more. I lie her with me on the pallet, take her in my arms. She must cry, as I did, until all hurt, sudden discovery, new knowledge, drain from her, take with them energy, leave just a body.

She weeps, the two-year-old boy with dark hair curling onto his shoulders unrecognisable among the pulp on the floor. I hold her.

Dmitry Grigoryevich sent him here from Novorossiisk, where they'd fought their way since Odessa; thousands of Whites had already escaped on French and British ships; unlucky types screamed by the harbour when the Red Army arrived, unless they'd thrown themselves into the icy water or blown their brains out; Cossacks shot horses and tore at them for food.

You're the best one for this job, Leon Alexeevich, DG said and scratched the wart at the end of his nose; good at putting the message across. Better than DG, that's for sure. And so – teeth clenched at the prospect of talking to Turks – a boat to Trebizond, to step again on Anatolian soil, three years after the ragged, frostbitten remnant of Nicholas Romanov's army had demobilised itself and left.

The important meeting with Mustafa Kemal in Angora is still to come: shake hands, encourage him to ditch the sultan, promise arms, money ... DG was a bit vague on what he should say about weapons and roubles: invading Poland had used a lot of the Party's resources.

Here, cheering, speeches of welcome, spiced rice and meat like that produced by the Armenian cook at home when he was a boy. More eulogies, handclasps, atmosphere heavy with Turkish tobacco and maudlin sentiments for these Russians who had overthrown the Romanovs, traditional enemy.

Now he is out of doors, although the evening air is almost as foul as that inside. He wanders along empty streets when he should be talking to his hosts, making an ally of a neighbour, an emerging country as he said to his sister.

His sister. He remembers her a dreamy girl, full of herself and the piano which resounded through the house every day, except when she was with the prim, German governess. He'd be at school or doing homework; apart from mealtimes, they saw little of each other. How she shrieked and wept at his injured face on her return from the capital, English Livvy in tow. By next morning, she had recovered and told him of her place at the conservatoire. He wondered how much his father had had to slip the jury to overlook her being a Jewess; realised how quiet it would be without her and he'd missed her music while she'd been away.

Sasha Adamov took to sniffing around, officially to see him but really to catch a glimpse of Esther. So he was felled at Tannenburg, was he?

No private thoughts.

How dare she marry a Turkish officer! Does a hand he shook just now belong to her husband? Is one that clapped him on the arm, the back, familiar with her? Marriage of convenience, my foot! Slut!

He saunters on, past anonymous clay and stone walls, ransacked and devastated buildings. Ah, Tanyushka! For some bread and a handful of rice, you embraced me with such abandon, skirt up round your waist against the barracks perimeter in Baku, until I clamped my palm over your mouth so you wouldn't give us away. The girl was among several often hanging about the gates. He hadn't been the first.

The Party, especially Lenin's wife, Krupskaya, expects its commissars to settle down to family life. No more trysts. After this mission, he'll try and return to Baku; since the end of last month, the Red Army has been there, welcomed by the people. Who knows, if Tanya hasn't already married, he might do just that. Comrade Kovanskaya.

Tanya, however, is for the future, and he wants a woman this moment. How, in this blighted town, when you never see one in the street on her own?

He reaches the crossroads where he spotted his sister this morning. He pauses, habit, for there's no traffic, nobody.

He takes out a cigarette they gave him, lights it, draws on it, grimaces. Disgusting stuff. Memory, cruel phantom, lays before him the liquorice whiff of Turkish tobacco through the house in Baku when his father was home in the evenings.

Somebody is walking his way.

Baba *always said the Russians were our friends, the bear across the mountains. Christian like us rather than the Turk. He did not say what sort of Russian. Any. The Bolsheviks are in Erzerum. They are Russian and therefore allies to Armenians.*

I must have slept. When I surfaced, Esther was asleep. I let her. It is the beginning of healing. When she wakes, she will cry again, but recovery will have started. So I have left her and come outside. I will not need to tell her I went to the barracks to find the Bolsheviks and inform them that Armenians here have suffered at Turks' hands. They should know the truth. Who else is to speak for my people if I do not?

A red smudge on the horizon is all that remains of today's sun. The night sky is clear, and stars appear. Soon, the moon will rise. A man is at the crossroads; smoke from his cigarette wisps into darkness, smell of liquorice drifts towards me, and I remember Baba *and Achmet Bey sitting together on an evening such as this, smoking. The man wears a black leather jacket and long boots. Whoever he is, I have no wish for conversation so will veil myself with my shawl ...*

She is only a few paces from him. Not big. Young, he guesses from what is not concealed by the thing she has over her head, and in the moonlight he realises it is his sister. What is she doing? Going to meet her husband? Alone? Unprotected?

Slut! Jealousy, fury erupt, stoked by sexual need with no likelihood of release. His twin. Can he … ? Why not? He wants to hurt her – and her bourgeois, old-fashioned language – teach her a lesson she will not forget, perhaps expel Ottoman seed from her …

Baba and Achmet Bey … in the salon or the garden, years ago. How many? A lifetime.
There now, I am past him …

She does not look at him as she walks within reach. He lets her pass, grabs her from behind, covers her mouth. 'Don't struggle, sister,' he breathes.

His hand is a vice, so I cannot bite him. His speech I do not understand, voice harsh, angry. His breath is foul: tobacco, garlic, gasping. He has pushed me into an alley, face against a wall that still has the day's warmth, and I can feel his prodding. He lifts my skirt, fumbles, and I scratch at the stone, a scream deep inside me unable to escape. Never try to stop him, Lallah in Teheran advised once in a moment of kindness … if he comes to you unexpectedly, or you're not prepared, don't tussle, it will make it easier. I can't move. His other arm is round my waist, and all the time he talks, neither Turkish nor Armenian, but such rage there is in him …

'So, sister, you thought to open your legs to the Ottoman, ally yourself with the enemy, did you? Don't touch me, you said this morning as if you were of value. Well I'm going to, for you're nothing but cheap. I'll show you how it is with a Russian, a man of the people, so you will remember and compare, like this …'

It will be over in a minute.

In the final thrust, he gasps, 'Esther.'
Esther? Oh, Esther, no.
My dear, dearest Esther.
No.
He has to know, this beast who would violate his own sister. He is spent now, grip on me loosened. I turn to him.

He fastens his trousers. As his glare meets my face, I push back my shawl so he can see my eyes, not yours, Esther, but my mother's, the blue of Van. His scowl widens into shock; ruined features contort further.

He disappears into the night.
I lean against the wall. Warm liquid trickles down me.
Oh, Mama.

If I hadn't slept for so long, she reproaches herself, Anahid would not have gone out. Anahid has come in, eyes red from crying.

'Why, when the devastation upsets you?' she asks Anahid. 'You said you wouldn't look again.'

'What would you have done if we were in *your* town?'

She doesn't have one. There will be no going back to Russia while Lev and his kind are in power. The memory of their meeting several hours ago has settled like a fungus, a growth that cannot be excised. She imagines days passing, weeks, months, years: no obliterating sleep but truth always there on waking; her whole life yoked to a few minutes.

They are all at supper when Kemal walks in. Unease

clenches her chest. She stands. Papa too; he sways, holds onto the table.

Kemal goes over to him. 'Please, do not get up.' They shake hands.

She translates. Papa sits.

Kemal kisses her forehead, greets Nadia, pats the boys' hair, glances at Anahid. He addresses himself to Papa. 'You are well enough to travel?'

Papa nods.

'It is good,' Kemal says, 'for in any case we must go. We have been here too long. We set off at dawn.'

There is a knock at the door. She opens it and returns with a tray from Madame Karavolias. She puts it down in front of Kemal. He picks at rice protecting half a dozen beans as if his mind is elsewhere.

'With another caravan?' Papa asks.

Kemal shakes his head. 'Too laborious, over the pass and down to Trebizond. I've hired an araba. There is a short cut which will bring us out along the coast. The track should be navigable. Three or four days. It will not be difficult to get a boat to Trebizond.'

Papa's shoulders rise, fall, a silent sigh that acknowledges demands still to be made on a weakened, ageing body. He turns to her. 'Perhaps I should rest. Sleep while I can.'

'Yes.'

'Thank you,' he says to Kemal.

Nadia and the boys accompany Papa to the other room. Anahid stacks the family's plates.

She sits near Kemal. If he is a Bolshevik, nectar she has tasted with him will become poison. But she has to know. Her heart thuds as desperation propels words from her mouth. 'Were you there to meet the mission?' She tells him about the crowd.

He finishes the food, pushes the dish away. Anahid adds it to the pile and takes them downstairs.

Her eyes search his face. Is he considering how to explain or conceal his sympathies?

'The Bolsheviks mean nothing to me, Esther.' Her lips part in a smile. 'They are upstarts calling on their neighbours, anxious for acceptance. I am not sure the Bolsheviks are important to people here, either. But after years of war, suffering – and remember, we are the losers – a parade, national pride, self-respect, are reasons to cheer. And no, I was not there. In Erzerum, it's best I keep out the way.'

She closes her eyes with relief. 'I didn't know ... you're busy ... hardly here ...' Words stumble.

He puts a hand on hers. 'The Bolsheviks will go to Angora, talk to Mustafa Kemal, leave feeling they have an ally. But for us who support Mustafa Kemal, there are more urgent things. The war's victors, who determine our fate, have made their decision. The Ottoman Empire, for a century derided as the sick man of Europe, is to stay forever on his bed. Large areas of eastern Anatolia are to be given to Armenians; territory to Greeks, to Syria – that is, the French – and the sultan allows this as the path to peace, his empire's dismantlement, the foreigner's permanent presence and influence. We must persuade him such domination is not a price we can or need pay.'

She listens to his passion. When he pauses, they look at each other. He trusts her. Her heart opens in reciprocation, and her voice catches as she tells him about Lev. She falters, bites her lip, presses on.

He stands up, lifts her to her feet, holds her in the circle of his arms. They remain like that for several minutes. When he says, 'There are a few hours before dawn,' she misses his warmth against her, until they are lying on her pallet, and she is able to lose herself in him.

I have washed away all trace of him, as much as I can, yet still his smell is in my nostrils, lingers around me, inseparable from that rabid speech, bitter, twisted face filled with hatred. Will time fade the memory?

Esther is with her Kemal. I am anonymous to them. Their loving is soundless like my tears. Love him, Esther. There are many ways, circumstances, of coupling. I have just known the most horrible. May you only experience your husband's, that brings a bloom to you which I shall behold in the morning.

'I have never seen the sea, Esther,' Anahid says.

The Black Sea, so named because of its sudden storms and high waves, is flat, calm, as if waiting for them. On the far side is Russia, although she cannot see land.

When they first saw the water, they shouted: *Thalassa!* as had people for more than two thousand years, ever since Xenophon, the Greek who defeated Cyrus the Persian in battle. Kemal told them of Xenophon's exhausted mercenaries making for the coast, driven mad by hunger, thirst, and a surfeit of honey. Jolting in the araba through banks of white and violet rhododendrons, and ferns, and yellow azaleas whose delicious scent invites wild bees, the story distracted her from sheepdogs wearing spiked iron collars as protection from wolves, ears clipped against frostbite.

The terrain is flat, vegetation luscious, rows of tobacco, and she wonders if Bagdanof's is still in Petersburg, where Papa bought boxes of Turkish cigars. Pomegranates, hazelnuts, and cucumbers grow in lines, and tea in squares of land divided by small hedges.

The araba rattles to a halt. The track diminishes to a few red-roofed, white houses, a mosque and minaret, and some fishing-boats. Kemal jumps down. 'I will see if one of them can take us to Trebizond.'

Lowering sun brushes the mountain-tops pink. She inhales deep breaths of sea air. Last night, she and Kemal slept under a purple silk marriage-quilt in a village headman's home; jackals howled in the distance. This morning there were hard-boiled eggs, and a spoonful of honey which tasted like wine. Soon, they will be on their way to Constantinople, a new life. And she will be able to play the piano.

The sky is brilliant with shades of red and orange. Kemal returns, helps her from the araba, eyes meeting hers. He assists Nadia and Anahid; calls across to a boatman, rough speech. Seven of them and bundles fill the boat. The man, in brown jacket and trousers, smiles, makes soft, hissing noises.

They pass settlements huddling in the dusk around a small bay or stretch of beach, from which craft set off. Men shout, and the boatman replies. She runs her fingers through green water; it is warm. Dying sun lights the sky silvery-grey with touches of crimson, beneath which jungle surrenders to darkness.

'I shall escort you to the house of my brother, Yashar,' Kemal tells her. 'He speaks a little French, learnt in Constantinople before the war. You will be safe. In the capital, you can stay with my parents.' From inside his greatcoat, he draws out a piece of paper folded twice. 'I have written to them to explain. You will be welcomed. If my father is not at home, my sister also can read.'

'You're not coming with us?' A breeze ruffles the water, and she shivers. 'Why? Please don't leave ... not now.'

He puts his hand on hers; she clutches it as if she would detain him. 'These are difficult times for this country, Esther. A lot is unresolved. The next few months will be crucial.' There is a pause between each sentence, as though he is selecting words. 'It is important I be elsewhere. I have to ask you still to trust me. I will come to you in Constantinople.'

... my sister also can read ... But not his mother? Fear of the harem, of seclusion, disappearing forever, chills her. She takes the letter from him. Dread grips her. 'It's not safety that matters now,' she protests. 'I never imagined you would abandon me.' When he doesn't reply, she looks at what he has given her. 'There's no address.'

'It is not our custom in the European way. Go to the Turkish enclave of Pera. It's down a hill off the Grande Rue de Pera. The property of Irfan Bey, my father, is the third on the right.'

'Irfan Bey,' she repeats. How ridiculous is this? There must be dozens, maybe hundreds of Irfan Beys in a city the size of Constantinople. 'When did you write this?'

'Before we left Erzerum.'

That he really is going away, that forces are at work of which she knows nothing, and he could be in danger, dig further into her heart. In the darkness, she looks into his eyes, realises she will have to rely on memory: his eyebrows, the shape of hair curling from forehead and temples; moustache, and the indentation between lower lip and chin.

'We are almost there,' he says.

Edging around several boats, they are into a broad bay across which tumble small, shaggy waves. She stares at great Trebizond, old Byzantine capital, where the tsar came to inspect troops during the war, and all trade from Persia and Asia Minor flows in by ship and caravan. There is no pier or harbour just the furthest ripple of wine-coloured sea, and the beach.

They climb out with their bundles. Kemal and the boatman exchange a few words. She sees the glint of coins her husband presses into the other man's hand; he will wait for Kemal.

Strips of uneven pavement border narrow streets, an occasional cat the only life. Houses are shuttered, silent, enclosed with their gardens by walls which front the road. The shock of what Kemal has told her pulls at her feet. She has to trust him yet wonders how she is going to bear being without him.

He turns a handle on a blue door and leads them along a path through trees, and roses whose perfume fills the air. No more than seconds after he knocks, someone is holding a lantern, his features an amber glow. The two men embrace, their speech exclamations, staccato. She and her family are ushered inside. Kemal's brother greets each one in French.

They stand in a hall which smells of flowers and old leather. Several women appear, carrying lights, and a dog noses the arrivals' legs, tail banging against them. Kemal does not enter but speaks all the while, embraces Yashar, steps away.

She pushes past Papa, Nadia, the hound, to the threshold. Kemal brushes her forehead with his lips. She cups his face, and he hers as if they are as fragile as mother-of-pearl. She must remember every skin texture, the softness of his eyelids and around his eyes and temples, and beneath his ears.

'I will come to you in Constantinople,' he repeats. 'Wait for me there.'

He is down the path. He turns, raises an arm in farewell, joins the road. She remains in the doorway, strains for his footsteps, calculates how many paces and how long for him to reach the beach; wonders if she can hear the boatman cast off. But a breeze rustles the trees, catches at her skirt, shivers her, and hands are round her shoulders, drawing her into the house, and someone closes the door.

PART TWO

The Armenians are caught between the hammer and the anvil. If the hammer falls often enough, you end up with a diamond.

Armenian expression

It takes three Greeks to get the better of a Jew, but three Jews to get the better of an Armenian.

Oriental adage

The woman without her husband is like a bird with one wing.

Arab proverb

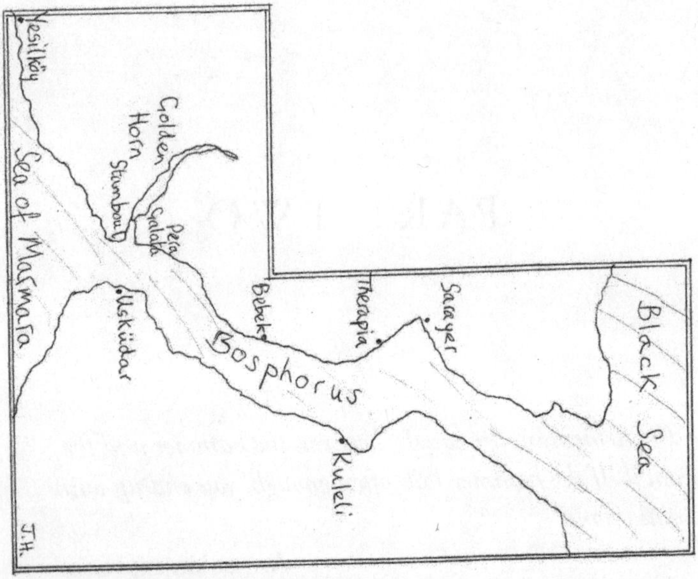

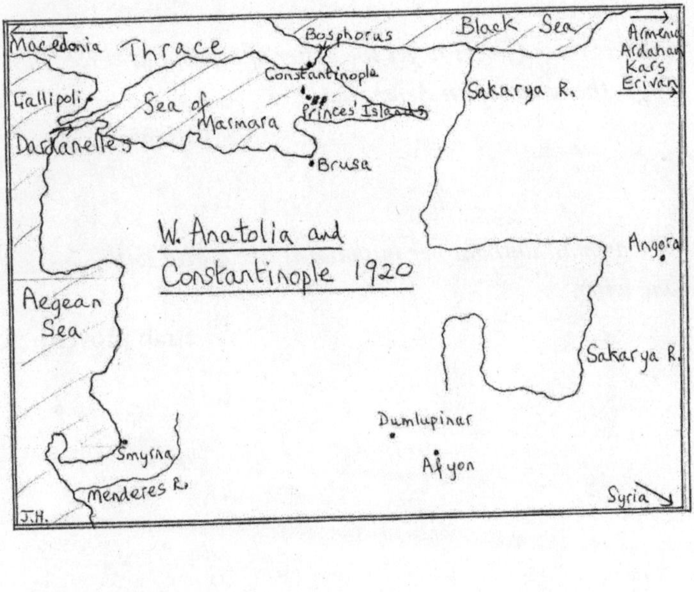

W. Anatolia and Constantinople 1920

SEVENTEEN

Trebizond, May 1920

If she opens one eye, she can see through tangled shrub the sweep of green forested bay; beyond it, a long way down, slate-blue water, broad and shining, where strangely rigged ships rest at anchor. But she shuts out the view and lies listening to sea sighing on the beach. In the distance, someone is singing, tuneless meandering. Trebizond at the end of the afternoon is stirring from sleep.

They have been here three days; for the first time, she and Anahid have left the garden. 'Should we?' Anahid hesitated after lunch.

'Why not? I want to look at something different, escape Abla *Hanum*'s scrutiny.' An expression that asks: are you a good wife for Kemal, as I am for his brother?

'I expect she's curious,' Anahid said. 'She's probably never met a European woman.'

By the shore, cargos, bales, boxes, were being shifted. She and Anahid climbed between ferns, oleander, toadstools, along a cooling hillside stream. At the top, they lay in the shade, languorous siesta hours.

Nadia and Papa have gone to the American relief agency: there is always news, however old. The only message she hungers for is from Kemal. Is this love, a sickness of heart, physical ache? She rehearses their every moment – by the lake, in the tent, in Erzerum – unable to assuage yearning.

'You're frowning, Esther.' Anahid's fingers are on her forehead.

'He says I have to trust him, yet tells me so little.'

'Yashar Bey thinks he may be in hiding.'

She pushes Anahid's hand away, sits up. 'What do you mean?'

'I overheard him talking to Abla *Hanum*.'

'And?'

'His words were: there'll be a price on his head if he couldn't even stay with us until morning. There was irritation in Yashar Bey's voice: young brother in a scrape.'

Yashar, courteous, tall, black-bearded, white already streaking hair at his temples. He runs the family business, trading carpets from Anatolia, Persia, and further east.

A jagged edge nudges her craving for Kemal. She did not love Lev enough to accept change in him. Her passion for Kemal is recent, unsought. Can it withstand whatever he is involved in? Fear that it might not begins to seep under her skin.

Anahid raises herself, kneels. 'True love transcends everything, according to the poets. If you really care for him –'

'You had no feeling for Mirza Khan. What do you know?'

Anahid stands up. 'Probably more than you think. Shall we go? Yashar Bey may have news of a ship for Constantinople.'

'I'm sorry. Don't let's quarrel.' As she gets to her feet, weariness clings to her limbs so that she has to force herself upright. Her stomach seems to be rebelling against quantities and varieties of fish and fruit prepared for them since they arrived.

Thought of the walk down the ravine and back to the house demands energy she does not possess. Anahid takes her hand, and she clutches it, picks each step over mossy stones.

Warm liquid trickles along the inside of her right leg. It reaches the curve of her knee, stops, sweeps to her ankle; left one the same. She lifts her skirt, grimaces. 'Anahid, look!' Blood smudges her sandals.

'Your monthly?'

'I suppose so. It feels as if my whole inside is coming out.'

Anahid grasps her. 'We must get back. Walk as fast as you can.'

Anahid pulls her, but she resists, stares at crimson in the dust. 'I can't. It's heavier. I daren't move.'

Anahid yanks off her shawl. 'Use this; yours as well. Come on, Esther, try!'

'I don't remember where the house is.'

'I'll ask.' Anahid drags her. 'Esther!'

She manages, wedges Anahid's shawl under her skirt and tears off her own. She gasps, scowls, hates the sight of blood, *her*, as it spreads through thin fabric, smears her fingers.

They reach the shore. 'What's their father's name?' Anahid wants to know.

'Irfan.'

In clipped, confident speech, Anahid starts talking to a man who backs away as he replies; bare-headed, fearless, dearest Anahid.

Anahid leads her along steep, white-walled streets and squares, past mosques and red-roofed, wooden homes bleached by sun and sea air; edges around donkeys, tall, golden camels with matted fur hanging from their legs, among smells of frying, hot peppers, onions, spices, to the blue door.

Nadia is in the hall. 'Esther, they said at the relief agency the Red Army ... oh, my poor girl!' Nadia shouts in French for help, towels, water.

Several women guide her to the room she shares with Anahid, lie her down, firm practised hands taking charge.

She can let go, give herself to waves of nausea and blackness rolling towards her. The last thing she sees is Abla *Hanum*'s face close to hers. There is sadness in the woman's eyes, and infinite understanding. Abla *Hanum* strokes her forehead with a cool hand, and murmurs something soothing.

She is drifting, up, up, a long way from the bottom where she has been floating. Words lap at her consciousness. '... it's probably just as well ... she always said it was never meant to be a real marriage ...' Nadia?

She's lying between sheets that are soft and perfumed with lavender. Her body feels quiet. If it could speak, it would beg: leave me, don't ask me to do anything. She places her palm on her stomach. She must be wearing a nightgown, for the material is thinner than her shift.

She's there, at the surface. In the distance, children sing. She turns her head. The curtains are closed. A lamp burns in the corner, and a sweet-smelling pastille. Nadia is sitting at one side of the bed, near her face, Anahid the other. Waiting. For her? She moves her mouth to try a smile.

Nadia lays backs of fingers against her cheek, an unaccustomed gesture of tenderness which catches her breath. 'Ana says Abla *Hanum* was recalling when it happened to her. And you know I was the same. Twice. Maybe you don't remember. You were only a child.'

She has the impression of intruding on a conversation started without her which seems to involve her. She frowns. 'What are you talking about?' Her voice sounds as if it, like all of her, does not want any demands made.

'You've miscarried, Esther, lost a lot of blood. It's stopped, but you must rest.'

Through parched lips, she whispers, 'I've what?' She looks from Nadia to Anahid. 'A baby?' Conceived during those nights in Anatolia, perhaps the first, and now gone, as are they, forever.

She closes her eyes, can't think, needs to sink once more into the softness that beckons, draws her down with welcoming arms.

Three days have passed, and Esther has yet to cry. I sit with her as much as I can for I do not want her to feel alone. The mornings quickly become hot and oppressive, but our room is on the shaded side. I can watch through the open window, around curtains made from Smyrna cloth, fishing-boats lying in deep-crimson sea for the noon rest.

The household is quiet, children instructed not to make a noise, as if somebody has died, the baby that would have been nephew and cousin here. Poor, dear Esther. I should not have told her what I heard Yashar Bey saying. I don't know how to comfort her. She sleeps a lot. When she wakes, she eats a little tuna, a few grapes or an apple or purple orange, drinks wine mixed with water. She lies staring at a hanging tapestry: blue satin with stitched red roses.

There is an air of faded quality about this house, ancient weapons on the walls, and engraved copper plates, and choice bits of pottery in niches; everywhere, painted verses from the Koran interspersed with flowers; embroidered cushions scattered on bolstered divans. *There is courtesy between Yashar Bey and Abla Hanum, no tension or sign of discord. And no other wife. The eldest child is a fuzzy-faced youth no doubt born a year after the marriage. His six or seven siblings include Jacob and Anton in their games with the ease of youngsters; language and nationality in themselves are no barrier.*

Nadia has been again to the American relief agency: their colleagues are helping Armenians in Kars and Erivan, where many have suffered at the Turks' hands. I wonder if Baba, Edouard, and Gaspar are in the new republic of Armenia? Baba always believed we would be independent.

I don't know whether to talk to you, dearest Esther, about what has happened to you. Or what to do. You have built a wall and retreated behind it.

Every time she surfaces, her first thought is how, and how soon, can she sink again into that dreamless, healing slumber where she doesn't have to think. Nadia washes her with rosewater. There has been no further bleeding. A pastille still smoulders on a copper tray.

Where is Anahid? She was horrid to Anahid concerning love.

Abla *Hanum* is here; she often comes, with a plate of figs, bowl of olives, or a pomegranate. Abla *Hanum* is holding a dish of cherries.

She turns onto her side and takes one. She's hungry. 'Thank you,' she responds in Turkish.

Abla *Hanum* cradles her hand, kisses her forehead, smiles at her with sad understanding as if to say: we are indeed sisters now, siblings in sorrow; I lost a baby, and so have you; I have had more, and there will be for you.

She wishes she and Abla *Hanum* could speak to each other.

She closes her eyes but cannot find peace. When she opens them, Abla *Hanum* has gone. She buries her face in the pillow and sobs scalding tears of anguish, until sleep reclaims her.

This morning is going to be different. She sits up, pushes back the sheet, eases her legs round, settles her feet on the silkiness of the Persian rug.

Anahid runs across and embraces her. 'Oh, Esther! You're feeling better!'

She rests in Anahid's warmth before standing. She wiggles her toes, walks a few paces to the dark, heavy, embossed cupboard. On one shelf is the contents of her bundle, all she possesses in the world. She lifts the clean blouse. Beneath it, on her skirt, is the letter Kemal gave her.

She delights in stiff paper written on by him, as if he is here with her. Yet, she has to be sure, and this might tell her.

There are several lines of Arabic script. 'Can you read Turkish?' she asks Anahid.

'It's how we learnt our lessons at school.'

She holds out the missive, explains. 'I want you to translate it.'

'Is that the right thing to do?'

'It will give me something of him. I don't think it's meant to be secret, or he would have made it secure.'

'And this will answer your question?'

'It might.'

Anahid's hands remain in her lap.

'Will you?'

'Nothing in it can change the feelings of your heart.'

'I'd still like to know.'

Anahid takes it, glances at the writing, folds it again.

'Anahid, should not a husband and wife be frank with each other?' She sits on the bed. 'You exhaust me. Is it such a big request?'

'Esther, where he is, what he is doing, are not your concern if he chooses not to tell you. When he is ready, he will come to you, and you will continue your lives. How he is with you is the way you will know him.'

'Anahid!'

Anahid looks at the script.

'Exactly as it is.'

Anahid mumbles.

'What are you saying?'

'I'm asking my mother and father to forgive me this dishonesty.' Anahid pauses as if she is studying the message. 'Are you ready?'

She nods. Apprehension ripples through her.

'He begins with the traditional salutation to *Baba* and *An-ne*.' Anahid's voice catches. 'Papa and Mama.'

'Go on.'

'*Please welcome my wife, Esther. She is with her parents, brothers, and maid …*'

There follow a few lines about what they lost in Russia, and their journey to Trebizond.

'*… As soon as I am able, I will join you …*'

So he really does plan to be with me. The ache which has lodged in her chest since he left, moves towards her throat.

'*… I hope you are in good health. Esther speaks French, Halidé. My dearest sister, do you remember what you used to practise with Yashar? …*'

She is shivering; her breath snags.

'... *I kiss your hands, dear* Baba *and* An-ne, *and embrace* Halidé. *Your son, Kemal.*'

She thinks of Lev's bitterness, lack of concern for his family, and she is crying, a shaking, shuddering, rending in two; where the split is, taking part of her with it forever. Anahid is on the bed beside her; cradles her, strokes her hair. The letter lies on the floor. The top third has folded over; she can just see one word alone at the bottom. It must be his name.

EIGHTEEN

Central Anatolia, June 1920

Like a leaden ball of fire, the sun sinks towards the horizon. Kemal pushes once more at the hay secured with ropes on the back of the araba, climbs up, and takes the reins. Some time ago, probably weeks, he exchanged the two ponies for a bullock, who seemed perplexed and yet delighted at the lightness of the task compared with the usual long carts.

'God willing, effendi, you will be in Angora by dawn.'

He nods, reaches down to clasp in farewell the hand of the man who gave him shelter through daylight's scorching hours. He flicks the reins, and the conveyance lumbers forward; another night, he hopes the last, with the weapons he dug from their hiding-place near the beach where the boatman returned him from Trebizond. Each daybreak when he stopped to rest, the cargo had to be unpacked, buried, and retrieved before he continued west.

The moon has risen. A cloud passes in front of it, and a tetchy wind. He is glad to have his greatcoat. He glances behind. The load looks steady.

The arid plain stretches ahead, and he begins to hum an old Rumeli folk-song his nurse used to croon when he was small. It blends with the rhythm of the beast pulling the araba. But he curses himself for thoughts the tune recalls: home, comfort, women and children, as the lovely face of the Russian girl he took to wife in Teheran rises unbidden in his consciousness. Esther. A name unlike any other, a whisper, sigh of a breeze in trees.

Moya dusha ... my soul. Never would he have imagined such language in her rich, velvety voice.

Time and again he has asked, why did he do it, involve himself, instead of letting her family leave Teheran with others from their legation? Was it genuine concern for their – her – safety or simply refusal to allow her to have the last word, this European girl, face uncovered, unafraid to argue with him?

Yes, there had been lasses before, Christian and Jewish, Italians, Circassians, and the exotica of the Levant in Constantinople's cafés when he was a cadet at the Military Academy. He, who had never seen an ankle or a woman's figure, would go with his friends, and for a few *para* play backgammon or dominoes, drink beer, smoke – something he would not have dared do in front of his father – and watch females dance, anklets jingling; wenches who might come and sit at his table, who were amusing, intriguing, and ready. When, proud of his manhood, he told Yashar, his brother's brows drew together in a frown; serious Yashar, married at eighteen to fifteen-year-old Abla; they'll give you diseases, Kemal, Yashar cautioned.

And there was Hannelore, an Austrian nurse from whom he learnt not only to speak German but also spend hours making love, those summer weeks his shoulder was healing during the European War. They would meet in the forest behind the hospital when she was off-duty. Hannelore, with thick blond hair which she released from its pins and plait as he unfastened her dress from throat to waist. Her fiancé had been killed at Lemburg on the Russian Front. Write to me, Kemal? she suggested when he left. He said he would. Yet, he had no knowledge of European script, and she would not have been able to read Turkish. Her melon-shaped breasts, apple-smell on her skin, became as remote as flowers in wooden boxes under the houses' windows in the village. He was not the first to enter Hannelore. He hopes she has met somebody else.

Esther ... European yet not available; passionate, when she spoke of her country or the piano, but distant. Had she walked with a young man in Baku as she did with him in Teheran? he used to wonder. Did she know how lovely she looked when she smiled? Not like the ones in Constantinople who smirked in imitation.

He was economical with what he said to her about her home's destruction in Baku. It hadn't actually been demolished; several in the street had, and number twelve would probably be next. The lieutenant who reported it to him – whom he'd extricated from a gambling debt – had lost a brother at Ardahan and harboured no love for the traditional enemy. He listened, tight-lipped: outside door hacked in pieces, marble hall littered with mud and glass, blood-spattered, smoke-blackened walls, stink of a year's decay; at the foot of the stairs – this recounted with particular glee – the tsar and tsarina's portraits, faces trampled, and at the top, charred piano, keys and strings dangling over the side.

When he sat with her in Teheran's square of cannons, her sobbing cut into him, produced a need, not just a wish but a longing, to comfort, protect her from anything that might so distress her again, a feeling none other had provoked in him.

As days passed after they left the city, and he observed her, spoke to her, he had the impression of something waiting to be discovered, unlocked. That night by the lake, hope sparked that nobody before him had seen, touched, the creamy softness of her skin, the mark on her shoulder; until the certainty he was the first, her virginal fluid staining not a marriage sheet she and her mother had embroidered but pine needles and earth.

A line of blue light creeps across the horizon as if an invisible hand is pulling away deep-purple sky. In the violet and amber dawn, Angora's twin hills rise like breasts from the plateau, followed by ruined battlements and lofty minarets; everywhere, red dust agitated by that fretful wind, on his greatcoat, boots, and when he runs his tongue along his mouth, a dry, bitter taste.

NINETEEN

The Black Sea, June 1920

The boat reeks of old carpets, paint, tobacco, sour grease, strange cooking; saw service for years before the war. The sea is as still as glass, dark-blue-grey, shading to light-green near the beach. She puts up her parasol, stands by the rail with a tin mug of hot water and Abla *Hanum*'s tea. She watches passengers accustomed to no harbours on this southern coast or at best a rickety, wooden jetty; they let down pieces of cotton or canvas attached to strings, for food from men on skiffs rowed out against the wake when the vessel stopped offshore. Hampers are transferred the length of a rope-ladder. A man struggles up with a couple of live fowl in a cage, reaches for a sheep and goat which he tethers to a post.

The tinkle of the engine-room bell signals departure; gulls follow, practise their mournful cry. They pass a village framed by trees. The shore sweeps back in ever higher ridges; broken cliffs fissure forest-covered mountains.

Like a capricious girl, weather is no two mornings the same. Sometimes, sun illuminates pink and white buildings hugging lower slopes. Or a coastline: exactly as the Argonauts must have seen it, Anahid tells Jacob and Anton while she divides olives Abla *Hanum* wrapped in waxed paper, and explains to the boys Jason's search for the Golden Fleece to placate his uncle because of a family quarrel about land.

When the Crimea looms on the far side, sailors point and mutter, and turn to Anatolia, while she recalls childhood summer holidays: oleander clumps and an arbour of vines outside a cool, colonnaded villa; laughter, sand between the toes, and the sweetness of a sea that has barely any salt. The following day, the Crimea has gone, the last she will ever see of Russia.

Another time, the mountains seem to frown, and she thinks of the lost baby; tears mingle with fine drizzle that thickens the air, blurs, clings damp on head and shoulders. The space inside her where the child would have grown is a void, expanding each dawn without Kemal.

Or a cold wind springs up. Silver-backed waves thrust beneath a heavy sky. Rain lashes the vessel, and she wonders where he is and what he's doing, and remembers his expression when he was displeased.

On the fifth afternoon, the boat veers through a break in the cliffs, the entrance to the Bosphorus – which means throat, Kemal said – a sinuous channel separating Constantinople from Anatolia, guarded by two forts, hills around them wild and rocky.

Anahid leaves Nadia and Papa eating the last of Abla *Hanum*'s cheese and smoked meat under an awning rigged up by sailors, and joins her at the rail overlooking the European side. They share the remaining hard-boiled egg.

The Bosphorus sweeps to the left. The shore is lined with villages – gardens shaded by mulberry-trees – and ruins; pine-groves rise behind. Crushed thyme, honeysuckle, Judas-blossom, waft in hot silence. Woodsmoke spirals. Smells of cypress and frying butter float; lilac, and pungent, burning sage, and an open drain's rank odour.

A barrel-organ clatters, shatters the peace. Music soars, buoyant, triumphant. She turns to Anahid, smiles. On and on the tune whirls, cuts into the heat. Jacob jumps from one foot to the other, sways with the melody.

'Look! Big fish!' points Anton.

'Porpoises to welcome us,' Anahid tells him.

They pass palaces, pictures in a fairytale, and the glint of a marble fountain; castles, mosques, mirrored in calm the deepest blue of a peacock's feathers or a precious stone, turquoises she sold in the Teheran bazaar. Gilded craft glide, a lantern and velvet cushions in the stern. Two men are greasing rowlocks with a stick in a little tin pot. They glance up.

'Cover your face, Esther,' Anahid says.

'This is Europe.'

'It's both. Do as I say. They might call out.' Anahid veils herself.

Jacob and Anton wave. The greeting is returned.

The Bosphorus twists with banks and bays, past tumbledown, wooden houses rising in three untidy tiers. The first storeys project above square, grated, ground-floor windows; the tops push balconies on wide struts over water lapping against stone quays. Platforms totter on rotting piles.

She looks to her left, the way the boat is going, towards a fretted skyline; mosques and minarets reach into vivid heavens, a panorama of domes, golden in the fading day, radiant Asia in Europe, fragile, immortal beauty.

'It is indeed a crown of jewels set upon seven hills, as we always heard it to be,' Anahid says.

Old, narrow properties with high, iron-grilled windows rise to green brooding forests. Is this where she'll find Kemal's parents? He's probably already there, for the stay in Trebizond was longer than expected. Warmth of excitement spreads through her. When she told Nadia about his letter, her stepmother insisted on independence: I refuse to be a guest in somebody's home, especially where I don't speak the language; you will have to decide what you're going to do, Esther.

Marble buildings, like decorations on a wedding cake, are surrounded by parkland. 'I think the sultan must live here,' Anahid murmurs, as if not to disturb him.

His palace is as splendid on the outside as was the tsar's in Petersburg.

The boat turns right into an inlet, a gleaming, blue hook. Ferry-steamers puff from one landing-stage to another, the clank of paddle-wheels just discernible, dodging naval launches, sailing-, rowing-, fishing-craft. A tall, white-masted ship lies at anchor. Several large warships wait.

Two of the crew throw a thick, looped rope which men fit round a bollard as the vessel nudges the quayside. The dripping cable strains, slacks, and the boat steadies. As soon as the gangway is run out, people rush down. Nadia and Papa stand behind the last passengers. She and Anahid pick up their bundles, take the boys' hands.

Ferry horns, music, hawkers' shrieks, water sellers' bells; priests in lofty head-gear and dingy gowns from under which protrude dirty, shabby boots. She repeats to herself Kemal's parents' address: a Turkish enclave off the Grande Rue de Pera. She must ask the way, in spite of Nadia, but everybody elbows, pushes, shouts, trades, butts the unwary off the pavement.

Nadia and Papa have stopped in front of a lady carrying a pink parasol; she is short and wears a wide-brimmed hat decorated with artificial fruit and flowers. 'You'll be refugees,' she begins in French.

Papa introduces them all.

'Eliza Grinling. Miss. I'm helping with arrivals. There are hundreds. Odessa? Sevastopol?'

Papa summarises their journey.

'That makes a change,' the Englishwoman's tone suggests she is beyond surprises, 'and explains why you've docked in Stamboul, on the Turkish side of the Golden Horn. We need to cross to the European Quarters, Galata and Pera.' She indicates a thronged bridge. 'Galata is your better option. The prices in the few hotels in Pera are exorbitant. The western embassies are there, and banks, bars, shops. There's a Russian restaurant, the Doré; the waitresses are *baryshnii*, well-brought-up girls.'

'I have directions to a house off the Grande Rue de Pera –'

'Best left until tomorrow,' Nadia interrupts. 'We need somewhere to wash, eat, sleep.'

'We can do all that there.'

'Follow me,' Miss Eliza Grinling says. 'Do not let yourselves be distracted by noise, beggars, or anybody. You have to be firm. Ready?'

Along a series of pontoons floating on barges stands a line of robed individuals holding canvas containers; people in kaftans, fezzes, the occasional black coat or straw hat, shove and drop money in, golden dust rising from their feet. From between gloved thumb and forefinger, the Englishwoman releases a coin, uses her parasol to ward off interception.

She grips her brothers' hands, manoeuvres them past men with open sores and mutilated limbs. Small boys clutch at her skirt. Drivers shout their fares, thrust out brown fingers in twos and threes to indicate how much. For a few moments, the crush on the swaying construction is so great that she has to stop, but she's being pushed by smells of sweat, garlic, tobacco, and concentrates on keeping up.

They're over. She's on European soil. Car horns blare. Cabs jerk and rattle across the cobbles, a din of wheels and hooves racing through narrow thoroughfares. Like a galleon, Miss Eliza Grinling steers a course into clamour, faces, flapping garments, an occasional horse-drawn barouche with the hood up.

They wait on the pavement edge as a yellow electric tram hisses round a corner; she has not seen one since the spring in Petersburg the year the war began. Passengers are on wooden seats behind a dark-blue glass partition. She has a sudden feeling of safety. She is in a city where you can go about everyday business.

The Englishwoman leads them up steep streets which have fine stucco edifices, although others are in ruins. Some of the pavements are lined with stilted trees, and the air smells of tar and petrol. Shops are lit by electricity, which also shows in a few houses. Many men are in uniform: white, khaki, navy; among the women, hardly a veil.

Down an alley, Miss Eliza Grinling comes to a halt outside a four-storey building with the sad, faded notice: *Hotel*. Up uncovered stairs, they follow a thin boy whose torn shirt is held together by twine. On the first floor is a copper brazier with an iron tripod over it. 'You can cook on that,' the Englishwoman says. 'You'll have to share it. You'll soon find your compatriots. There are some along the corridor, I believe.'

She stares, wonders what you have to do to produce something you can eat.

Miss Eliza Grinling ushers them into a room furnished with a table, large bed, chairs, the legs in bowls of water. 'To stop bugs,' she explains. 'Next door's empty, too.'

Nadia goes to inspect but is back within moments. 'We can't stay here. The bedding's not clean.'

The Englishwoman looks uncomfortable; she speaks to the lad, who shifts from left foot to right, shrugs, protests, spreads both hands. 'He insists it's spotless and has only been slept in by three people.'

She walks over to the blinds, lifts them. Sunset glints reddish-orange on windows; the Bosphorus shimmers amethyst in the afterglow, Golden Horn as still as a sheet. Pencilled against a green evening sky, the silhouette of Stamboul turns purple as the sun slips away. Shadowy domes soar one behind the other, high as the slender crescent moon. Tomorrow, in daylight, she will find Kemal's home and be reunited with him. She can return to fetch her family; Nadia will have had enough.

She straightens the bed she has shared with Anahid and Jacob, itching, scratching. Through the night, people banged on the outside door. Nadia and Papa have left to look for a hospital, always a source of news and possibly work.

A black dot scurries across her arm. 'Anahid, I can't go like this.'

'They won't see your limbs.'

She puts on her clean skirt and blouse, hears talking on the landing. Russian. When she looks out, a sour, rank smell fills her nostrils.

A woman is stirring something on the brazier, from which steam rises; she glances up. Dark, grey-threaded hair has been swept back; wisps have escaped around a delicate face with a small rosebud mouth.

She greets this neighbour, '*Dobrayeootra.*'

A smile transforms sad blue eyes and hints at former beauty. 'Ah, a familiar voice. When did you get here?' Her dress, probably originally yellow, has the appearance of a dried plum. It gapes between waist and armpits, fastenings redundant; the hem meets brown socks which reach past her ankles. The hand outstretched in welcome suggests that those addressed should bow over it or curtsey. 'Lydia Toumanova.'

She introduces herself.

'Odessa?'

She shakes her head, outlines their journey.

'When we docked, they disinfected us because of typhus in Odessa. Stripped us and put the clothes through hot steam.' Lydia Toumanova flaps her fingers into the sides of the garment.

She grimaces in sympathy at such loss of dignity.

'Did the knocking disturb you, Esther Yefimovna?'

'We wondered who it was.'

'It seems the previous tenants were, shall we say, ladies of the street waiting for clients: sailors. They've been thrown out for us, who are quieter, less trouble. I suppose some men don't know. Their ship comes in, they rush here, find the door locked …' Lydia Toumanova stirs the contents of the pot. 'We've asked downstairs for more charcoal. How many are you?'

'Six. But we shan't stay long.' She stops, cannot admit to this Russian aristocrat that she has married a Turk. Is this how it will always be? How can something so glorious also be shameful?

'Getting away isn't simple.'

'When did you arrive?'

Lydia Toumanova lifts her head as though the answer might be in the air in front of her. 'Hah!' escapes her mouth, followed by, 'Months ago. Every day, queues at embassies. Visas. Transits;' she shrugs as if such details are not her concern, and with 'wait a minute,' goes into the room next to Papa and Nadia's. She returns with a brown paper parcel, greasy patches on the outside like a map sketched by whatever is inside; she offers it. 'I remember our first day. I expect you've nothing for dinner. I go early, buy two lots.'

'We can't take your food.'

'Another time, you can help us.'

She shows Lydia Toumanova's gift to Anahid. 'What do you think?'

Anahid unwraps it.

She wrinkles her nose. 'They're just bones.' Scraps of meat and gristle cling to some. 'We can't eat those.'

'Not like that, we can't,' Anahid says. 'But they'll make a nice broth. That's probably what she was doing.'

'How do you do that?'

'Esther!' Anahid sighs, shakes her head. 'You boil them in water. Better with a few herbs and spices. All we need is bread to soak it up.'

'What would we do without you?'

'You'd have to find a way. Now, cover your face except for your eyes. The first impression of you is important.'

'Where's Esther going?' Jacob wants to know.

Anahid explains. 'And we can call on our neighbours, can't we?'

She picks up Kemal's letter, goes down to the street, and begins to climb the hill towards Pera.

She turns into the wide, cobbled road which must be the Grande Rue de Pera: six-storey buildings of light-coloured stone designed in the European style. People throng the pavement. Others dance, wave to the sound of invisible music alongside and behind a man, and rotate a handle to produce tunes from a keyboard strapped to his back. She's in Paris, visiting a fair with Nadia, who is betrothed to Papa and delights in taking young Esther and Lev; holds both by hands gloved in softest leather.

Lev. She pushes the memory away.

After the dancers comes a parade of masks and costume. Around her, clapping and exclamations.

'... *regarde, qu'elle est belle! C'est Marguerite Dufour* ...'

'... awfully good turnout this time ...'

The carnival passes, and everybody disperses. She starts walking but slows as she reaches the Pera Palas Hotel. Passengers step from curtained cabs, and she catches a whiff of eau-de-cologne. Uniformed valets pile brown luggage that matches.

'... I thought that little man in Vienna would never get us to the station. The Orient Express doesn't wait. At least in Paris they rush ...'

She gazes at Englishwomen who were in the Austrian capital perhaps yesterday; pencil-slim in outfits several hands'-width above silk ankles and high-heeled shoes. How daring to dress like that. Porters carry trunks and valises inside. She peers beyond the entrance and sees chandeliers – which suggest electricity – stained glass, gilded plaster; remembers staying in Petersburg's Astoria with Papa.

'… they say there are thousands of refugees … Russians …'

People look at her. She retreats, ashamed of her much-washed, unironed clothes, skirt down to her feet, and her shawl which has slipped back from her head. She pulls it into place. This is Europe. This is life, efficiency. This is elegance, grandeur, gaiety. She does not belong.

Past the hotel, a warm wind stirs dust. If she shuts her eyes, this and the heat make her feel she's in Baku. But here is no smell of oil, just myrtle and lilac, and fruit sellers' cries sound different. The sun burns through her blouse. She passes a butcher's stall. Meat is covered in muslin. Flies settle on it, and a boy waves at them with a whisk of dry yellow grass.

Down a hill, Kemal said. She turns along a slope. Clangour and bustle recede as if somebody has drawn a veil behind her. At the bottom, wisteria droops from a roof, a profusion of sagging blossoms like tiny blue bells, leaves blackening against the sky. Round the corner, silence envelops her.

She slows on narrow, uneven paving stones, between which tufts of wild oats burst. Buildings are dark-grey, reddish-brown, a wooden village, a self-sown seedling strayed over the Golden Horn from Stamboul. Cats lie blinking; one raises its head, eyes her, returns to rest on its paws. Ensconced in the shade, a youth with a tray of sweets plays a wistful, lilting refrain on an *oud* similar to Anahid's in Teheran. Out of sight, a pedlar's call echoes, and a donkey brays.

The third house on the right. That of Irfan Bey. A high, mossy wall, pierced by small gratings, lines that side of the street.

Nearby, a man with a white beard and skullcap sits in his doorway, fingers on a string of beads. His lips move, and she realises he is praying.

He looks at her. Holding her shawl in place, she indicates across the road. 'Irfan Bey?'

He nods, replies, and points diagonally.

'Thank you.'

She comes to a tall, wrought iron gate, lower half covered. On the left is a rope. She pulls it twice and hears ding, ding. Nerves and desire kick inside her.

An old lady, bareheaded and dressed in black, shuffles towards her.

She offers Kemal's letter through a gap and enunciates Turkish words she rehearsed with Anahid. 'I am Esther *Hanum*.'

The servant acknowledges her and fumbles with bolts for her to enter; she secures them while speaking, hobbles down a terracotta tiled path.

Unsure, she stays where she is. The garden is terraced, shaded by fruit-trees, evergreens, planes. Along the bottom is a water cistern. Roses wilt against a wall. In front of them, bamboo stakes support purple lilies. A magnolia is in bloom, thick, creamy, with glossy leaves; ilex and a magenta-coloured Judas, and tangled briars and tobacco plants, hot scent hurting her nostrils. Parched grass circles a dry fountain.

She looks up at the house: red-roofed, old, bleaching wood. Latticed shutters shroud the windows. Three women sit on the terrace in the shadow of a vine. The retainer gives Kemal's missive, indicates the gate. A woman unfolds it, shares it with the one next to her, who reads aloud. They drop it on the table, jump to their feet, clap, cry out for joy. Their companion also stands but says nothing.

The other two come towards her. They are dressed in blues, pinks, lilacs, silks that smell of lavender-water. They wear gold chain necklaces twisted several times: Kemal's slender sister, Halidé, and his rounded mother, grey curls coiled into a topknot.

Arms open in welcome, the older woman embraces her on both cheeks, holds her away, scrutinises, exclaims.

Halidé hugs her, still talking; she has a pale, oval face with uptilted, humorous mouth and melancholy black eyes, jewels when she smiles; shining raven hair is tied into a loose net.

She feels uncomfortable under such examination and display of affection from strangers. Did these women suffer during the war? she wonders and glances at their manicured fingers.

Where is he?

A pause in the chatter. Halidé tries, 'You speak French.' A flush of self-consciousness suffuses her.

'Yes.'

Halidé gasps. 'You understand?'

'Yes.'

Halidé introduces herself. 'And this is Besmé *Hanum*.'

Besmé *Hanum* embraces her once more as Halidé says, 'You are welcome, Esther. This is your home. We are your family.'

He can't be here. Perhaps he is visiting. Disappointment drags at her heart as she walks with Halidé and Besmé *Hanum* to where they were sitting. A man in a wide-brimmed hat is working in the garden. A boy sweeps the path around the fountain as if he'd rather be doing something else. Jasmine fragrance hangs in the air. She nears the house and notices white and yellow flowers, stars trailing through shutters and over walls. Each cluster of grapes on the vine is tied in a muslin bag.

The woman who has remained on the terrace is about Halidé's age.

'Esther, this is my cousin, Ayesha.'

She bends towards Ayesha but is offered a hand in greeting. As she touches it, she looks at Ayesha, who is unsmiling. Besmé *Hanum* snaps a few words, and Ayesha disappears indoors.

Halidé plumps up embroidered cushions on an iron chair. 'Sit down, Esther.'

She does. On the table are sewing and petit point of flowers and arabesques. She peeps again at the women's white languid fingers and keeps hers in her lap.

Ayesha returns, eyes red and puffed, suggesting she has been crying. Besmé *Hanum*'s voice sounds like a rap across the palm, and the girl takes up her stitching. The servant who opened the gate brings a tray of four glasses and a jug.

Halidé asks, 'Rose sherbet, Esther?'

Unwilling to admit never having tasted it, and as a change from 'yes', she replies, 'Lovely. Thank you.'

She savours the sharpness of the iced drink on her lips and tongue, and regards the boy who was sweeping. He is watering rows of fruit and vegetables, glancing in her direction. Beyond him is an orchard. How soon will Kemal be back?

Besmé *Hanum* is talking. 'Esther,' Halidé begins, 'to *An-ne* … you are a daughter. She is your mother. I am your sister. Come your family here.'

She turns, smiles at Halidé's efforts. Besmé *Hanum* nods, satisfied.

'There are six of us,' she reminds Halidé, Nadia's refusal in her mind.

When Halidé translates, Besmé *Hanum* shrugs. 'You are welcome,' Halidé says, using the plural.

'Your French is doing well.'

'Yashar ... and I learnt a little at school, with the Koran, and writing and numbers, and some geography. But *An-ne* maintains it is better I know how to sew and sing, draw, choose the right clothes, and move and sit correctly.'

Besmé Hanum scrutinises Halidé, who blushes and switches to Turkish. Besmé *Hanum* shouts at Ayesha; her niece does not look up but cuts a length of red thread.

'It is wonderful ... news of Kemal,' Halidé continues.

So he hasn't arrived yet. She feels a cold grip crush breath from her. Where is he? 'Is it a long time since you saw him?'

'Last year.'

'I have to get back, Halidé. Thank you both for your kindness.'

Halidé repeats this to Besmé *Hanum*. 'So soon?'

Besmé *Hanum* calls to the gardener, who is checking the grapes. He approaches on bowed legs to hear what she wants. His eyes are like black dots, face weather-worn.

She stands. Besmé *Hanum* does the same, holds her to look at her.

'*An-ne* fears you have suffered much, your home, your country.'

'Yes.'

With her palm, Besmé *Hanum* bangs on the table in front of Ayesha. The girl gets up, extends a hand in farewell, expression still of sadness. Confusion? Is Ayesha retarded, unable to join in conversation?

The gardener arrives with a bag of fruit and vegetables. He offers it to Besmé *Hanum* and returns to his work. Besmé *Hanum* gives her the produce.

'Thank you. You are very kind.'

Besmé *Hanum* answers, brow furrowed.

'It's normal,' Halidé explains. 'We are yours.'

Besmé *Hanum* embraces her once more and lets her go. She walks down the path with Halidé.

'Esther, is Kemal really well?'

'Very.'

'Kemal and *Baba*,' Halidé knocks together the knuckles of both hands –

'– disagree?' she helps the girl.

'Yes. *Baba* does deals with the British and French; he is a businessman not a politician. There was an … argument last time Kemal was here, he and *Baba*, not *An-ne*. Kemal is her favourite. Yashar is away, and my other two brothers were killed. That is why she is pleased to meet you; anything Kemal does is right. She will hope for … grandchildren? Whom she can see, not in Trebizond.'

And influence? she wonders, recalling the change of tone in Besmé *Hanum*'s voice; Ayesha, although no longer a child, has to be told what to do. 'Ayesha,' she says.

'She's had a shock.'

'What happened?'

'There has been an … understanding between our families … she and Kemal will marry. I suppose she thought she would be the only one … or, at least, the first.'

She stares at Halidé; replays the conversation with Kemal the momentous night they camped by the lake. He was telling her of Yashar's arranged marriage. Did your parents have someone in mind for you? she asked him, and he smiled ... perhaps they talked about it ... there is always a cousin ... I think that's what they are for.

She remembers soft skin around his eyes; the way they searched as if he would possess her soul ... *moya dusha*. Tears prickle her lids.

'I imagined Ayesha was,' she puts a finger against her temple, 'slow.'

'No, no. She's normal. *An-ne* is cross because she shows not a very nice personality. *An-ne* insists she accepts Kemal's will. He may still wed her if he is able to support two wives.'

Her heart clamours. 'Does she live with you?'

'No. Her family are on the other side of the Bosphorus. She comes for a few days, until one of her brothers fetches her home.' Halidé smiles. '*An-ne* already treats her like a daughter-in-law.'

As she will me – if I settle here – after the euphoria of news of her favourite son has worn off. 'Goodbye, Halidé. Thank you.'

Halidé clasps her. 'I shall see you again soon. My French will improve.'

TWENTY

By the time she gets back, Anahid has borrowed Lydia Toumanova's pot and started an aromatic broth simmering on the brazier.

'She gave me a couple of coriander leaves, Esther. Her husband is a prince. Anton taught their son to count to five while Jacob helped me with the water.'

Nadia and Papa return with bread. They have found work in a hospital run by the French but staffed mainly by local people. 'Crowded waiting-rooms,' Nadia sighs; 'most patients sitting on the floor. The porters and attendants seemed indifferent. The doctors welcomed me and pushed me towards a festering chest-wound. I couldn't ask him how it had happened but swabbed it, sprinkled some disinfectant on a cloth to pin round him, and sent him off with a parcel of lint and dressing. Heaven knows how long it'll stay clean. Your father, meanwhile, was fetching and carrying.'

'Another pair of hands is always useful,' Papa adds. 'And we were paid.'

Nadia wipes her bowl. 'This is good, Ana. You can teach Esther to cook, keep her from spitting at the ceiling.'

'We learnt that the British are in charge of the city,' Papa explains. 'Their forces took over a while ago: subversives – Kemalists, they're called – had raided arms depots here and sent the booty to Anatolia. The British went into the Turkish district and deported dozens to Malta. The sultan was pleased for somebody to impose law and order.'

Where she was this morning; old men and boys.

... we must persuade him such domination is not a price we can or need pay, Kemal said in Erzerum, of the sultan. Did Kemal know of the thefts?

'Kemalists?' Anahid repeats.

'Not our Kemal,' Papa replies. 'It's evidently a common name.'

'Yefim, who was the leader?' Nadia tries to remember.

'Mustafa Kemal.'

... us, by which I mean those who support Mustafa Kemal ...

'There's a price on his head,' Papa adds. 'And all his henchmen. Courtmartialled in their absence.'

She feels Anahid looking at her. Their eyes meet for a few seconds, and she turns away, recalls what Anahid heard Kemal's brother say in Trebizond.

Papa continues, 'The Kemalists don't have a lot of popular favour. The sultan is still venerated.'

'The Refuge of the World,' confirms Anahid.

For the moment, but will there eventually be revolution, the sultan removed from power? Kemal will not, cannot, return to Constantinople unless there is.

'Time to work,' Nadia decides. 'There's disinfectant and two brushes from the hospital.'

She scrubs floors, not caring about her hands or afternoon heat, as if to erase the realisation that Kemal must be an outlaw. But it has found her bones, set up a dull ache in her chest and stomach. She washes bedding and clothes until, exhausted, she slumps asleep on a chair.

They share with the Toumanovs the vegetables from Kemal's family. Later, they crowd into the prince and princess's room. People perch or sit on the furniture and threadbare rug. She lets accounts of dramatic escapes whirl about her: travelling in darkness, chance encounters, and selling valuables to peasants.

Nadia describes their journey with 'a very presentable Turk'.

Somebody sniggers, 'Can't be choosy, these days.'

The talk switches to queues at embassies, and unco-operative staff.

'The sooner our names are on a list, the better,' Papa agrees.

'You need a visa,' Prince Toumanov warns. He is tall, with light hair, blue eyes, unhurried gestures, an air of former elegance.

'Boats will take you to Bizerta,' someone adds.

'... a French colony on the north African coast ...'

'... they come from factories to hire you ...'

'... it's a way of getting into France ...'

'... unless you're returned to Odessa and handed over to the *bolsheviki* ...'

'... depends how much you can pay ...'

'They charged us five roubles for a glass of water on the voyage from Odessa,' the prince recalls.

'And twenty-five for me to have a cabin where I could wash,' his wife throws in.

'... and bazaar merchants grow rich as we exchange the last of our jewels, even our wedding rings and crosses round our necks, for a day's bread ...'

Back in their own room, she watches the lights of the city go out. Stamboul's outline is etched in bluish tints against the stars and night sky. She starts at a sudden movement and turns to see Jacob at her side peering through the window.

He snuggles up. 'I like this place. Are we going to stay here by the sea?'

'For the time being.'

'Can we explore all the buildings?'

'Perhaps.'

'Soon,' he stipulates.

How easily he slips into new surroundings, she thinks, while she is flotsam wedged into the sand of Europe but still lapped by the tide of Asia.

I have left Esther with her brothers. If they were at school, I said to her, we could have jobs. She repeated the word as if the idea of work for payment were some strange notion, beneath her. No more degrading than living as we are in what used to be a bordello.

I have covered my head and the lower part of my face, am going to cross the bridge and go into Stamboul, which glimmers white in the sun. I can listen, find out about Armenians; maybe meet some.

I never thought to see for myself the celestial city I learnt of from my teachers, so distant were we in the Anatolian mountains. Constantinople was not real, just a name, a gallery of riches and possessions. But now the sea is oily. Men in three barges empty dustbins on the water; screaming gulls wheel, flap, fight for floating garbage. Even a jewel makes rubbish, which has to be put somewhere.

I climb the cobbled streets of Stamboul, squeeze into a doorway to avoid a fearsome hamal, load piled on his back – perhaps a carcass or furniture – to earn a few para. *People seem in less of a hurry than on the European side. An orange camel lumbers down the hill, taller than the Bactrians in the caravan we travelled with, expression disdainful above the crowd. Vendors lead lazy mules – enormous baskets strapped either side – cry their wares, shout insults at each other.*

Stamboul's walls are in ruins. This is not the place of my girlish imaginings. Does nobody sweep? Is muck abandoned in gutters and corners, foul smell to mingle with that of cooking, and hang in clouds? Mangy dogs roam, cats in their hundreds leap across rubble-heaps and chase rats from sewers. Some houses are no more than hovels; unpainted shutters and doors swing off rotting frames; every so often, a window carving or lintel suggests original splendour, watched over by mulberry-trees, their purple the only colour. Grass sprouts from stonework, among which pigeons murmur and a lizard disappears.

A marble fountain stands dry, taps stolen; two boys throw stones into the basin. Tough-looking children, no older then Esther's brothers, dirty-nosed, underfed, play or roll, or stare. At me. In Erzerum, I would ask them why so many buildings are like this. Now, I do not wish to attract attention. The accent is rough, not the way people speak where I come from.

It's years since I bought anything. What am I doing in this place? Women draw water from a pump, or haggle. I can feel them eyeing me: she's new, they're thinking, a shapeless figure among the rest of us, but different. I mustn't give up. I am Anahid Touryan, an Armenian subject of his imperial majesty and as good as any here. I can't return empty-handed; neither can I let these wives, with their cold, appraising scrutiny, see what I purchase and how much I am foolish enough to pay for it. Turn away, Anahid.

This street is better. Some houses have windows covered in kafes, *shutters of latticed ash; we had them in Erzerum. The far end opens into a market. Men push barrows.*

The vegetable seller grins, teeth stained, blackened, one missing. I point to the beans. 'How much?'

'Fifteen the kilo.'

'Already? Not ten?'

'Not ten.'

'Twelve. Twenty-five the two kilos.'

No reply but he weighs them out. I buy aubergines, tomatoes, grapes, onions. He looks at my money, at me, counts the change, unsmiling.

An urchin stands watching, brown eyes too big for a face sunken by hunger. Why is he not at school?

'You want to earn a few para*?'*

The lad nods, steps forward, takes my shopping.

The man is talking to somebody. I hear, 'Ermeni,' *and they spit. Why do Turks so dislike Armenians? I glance round. He wants me to be embarrassed, ashamed. I hold his glare long enough to show I am not afraid. Just sad. Is this how it has been for Baba, Edouard, Gaspar? Are they somewhere they are fearful to be Armenian?*

Are they looking for me?

I tell the boy to go to the bridge. He has not yet learnt to hate.

Anahid often crosses to Stamboul; one morning, she returns with three white tunics.

'I met an Armenian stallholder, Esther. I'm to embroider the collars,' Anahid recounts. 'Mama taught me the patterns from Lake Van. If he likes what I do, he'll pay me and give me others. Also, he says on the second Tuesday in the month, the relief fund distributes quilts and blankets, and bread or flour, to refugees. Next time, I'll see if there's news of *Baba* and my brothers. It's good they left Erzerum when they did.' Anahid folds the garments with thin fingers, work-reddened hands; puts tomatoes and aubergines on the table. 'He told me there are rumours Armenians in the east, my area, were moved south. When I pointed out that was towards Syria and the desert, he nodded.' Her face crumples as if she has rotten food in her mouth.

'What's the matter? He's upset you.'

Anahid shrugs, shakes her head. 'Perhaps what I've eaten. I feel a bit ... not right.' She takes a deep breath. 'The sewing will distract me.'

'We all eat the same. Nobody complains. I'll ask Nadia for some medicine from the hospital.'

'It'll pass. There are hundreds more in need of help than me.' Anahid unwraps from damp muslin what remains of yesterday's bread. 'So, when are you going to your husband's family?'

'He won't be there.'

'It doesn't matter. Get to know them.'

'Nearly every morning you mention it!' she rounds on Anahid. 'Leave me alone, can't you?'

She goes over to the window, lifts the shutters, squints against the glare. Black-coated people troop to Galata Bridge; straw hats, fezzes bob in the queue for lunch-time steamers up the Bosphorus or out across the Marmara to the islands. They have lives. Where is hers? And with whom? Love can be cradled in the palm of a hand until something happens to scatter it into recollection. Is that why poets and writers seek to express its memory, its loss? It is ephemeral, insubstantial, and the mind, cruel guardian, will bring a kiss, a touch, at any time of day or wakeful night. ... my *lale* ... my tulip ... wait for me in Constantinople ... your eyes reflect the beauty of your soul ...

Lucky are Papa and Nadia who have not suffered and been forced into remembering.

Anahid is by her side. 'Esther?'

'I'm so afraid.' She turns and sees Anahid's incomprehension. 'That I don't adore him enough to be his wife as he's a revolutionary.' Her voice catches. 'I can't live with his mother. How soon before what I do or say displeases her?'

'That would be true whoever you married.'

'And as for Ayesha –'

'– I've told you, that is her problem. Not yours or his. He has married you.'

She is twisting her fingers. 'Nadia never asks me what I plan. It's as if he doesn't exist. What if the price on his head has already been exacted? What if he's dead? I shouldn't have lain with him and allowed it to develop the way it did.'

'Because he may have perished? What sort of love is that?'

'I can't stand the waiting, the not knowing, the thought that things might change. I want it to be as it was.' Beneath her collar, she touches the necklace Kemal gave her in Teheran. It no longer lies like a caress but a shackle's chain.

Fifteen minutes Anahid has been gone.

She knocks on the wooden door of the toilet in the yard, wrinkles her nose at the sourness that always hangs there. 'Anahid, are you all right?'

'Esther?' A creaking hinge; Anahid emerges, face wan with dark rings under the eyes.

'You're not well. We must tell Nadia.'

'No. I'll be fine.'

'You said that yesterday.'

They climb the stairs back to the room. The boys are examining each other's toes, sitting on the floorboards in a shaft of sunlight. 'Mine are bigger than yours,' Jacob boasts.

Anahid cuts a sprouting onion.

She lets her friend rearrange her shawl; the vegetable's smell pierces her nostrils.

'Now, you two put your boots on,' Anahid instructs Jacob and Anton, 'and eat these green bits. They'll make you strong. Esther's going to Kemal's family. You're coming with me to look at the doves and arcades in the bazaar.'

She pulls the rope by the gate.

Halidé runs down the path; she wears an emerald tunic and trousers. 'We have waited for you every day, Esther,' she greets her as she clatters the bolts; she kisses her on both cheeks, regards her, sniffs. 'Onions.'

'The shoots are nourishing for my brothers.'

Halidé takes her hand, leads her to the terrace, where Ayesha sits alone.

She straightens her shoulders. I am Kemal's wife, not you.

'There is no news of Kemal,' Halidé says.

She does not expect any, confirming her fear he's outside the law. 'There are so many things to do,' she dissembles. 'I need to study music, and my maid is not well.'

Concern puckers Halidé's brow. 'What is the matter?'

'Her stomach.'

'We must give you some medicine for her. It is good you are here, for soon, maybe tomorrow, we go to our *yali* on the shore of the Bosphorus at Üsküdar. The air is pure, and the house and gardens restful. You can join us. It's going to get even hotter.'

Many shuttered afternoons, lying on the bed, smells of the last meal or Lydia Toumanova's cooking hanging in each breath, she has imagined sitting in the shade of this vine, drinking iced sherbet, the gardener hoeing, the boy sweeping. 'Who would look after my brothers?'

'Come them too. All your family. We don't have a piano there but we do upstairs. You can play it today.'

As they reach the terrace, Ayesha stands up; she is dressed in pale blue, worked with silver round the neck and cuffs.

She feels the chill of hostility so does not smile but offers a hand in greeting. Ayesha does not take it but speaks, lips twisting. Halidé answers, a slap in her voice.

She follows Halidé into the house.

'Don't let Ayesha keep you away,' Halidé says. 'She's jealous. We wait for news of Kemal. When she sees you, she … blows out anxiety because she knows you don't understand. It is not kind. We should be sisters, friends. I shall not tell *An-ne*; she will be angry, and Ayesha will …' Halidé lowers her head, purses her mouth.

'Sulk?' she suggests.

'Later, I will impress on her she's bad.'

'Your mother is not here?'

'I think she's with the cook.'

Like at home in Baku, enough space for people to be unaware of what others are doing. She has grown used to lack of privacy.

She climbs stone stairs to the first floor. Halidé ushers her into a room. Green kilims hang on the walls. A carved, inlaid, upright piano stands in one corner. The stool has bevelled legs and a cushioned seat the same blood-red as the *divan*.

'Do you play, Halidé?'

The girl shakes her head. 'The *oud*,' she replies, sitting, arms around her knees. '*An-ne* says it is more suitable.'

She raises the lid. Inscribed in gold Gothic lettering are the words *Steinway. Brunswick and New York*; like hers in Baku. She wonders if Kemal asked his father to buy it; perhaps he planned, ever since meeting her last year, that she would live here. This is the trouble with separation, absence of news: imagination fills the gaps.

She settles on the stool, wiggles her fingers. The keys are a dirty cream, discoloured teeth. She starts with scales, bites her lip, thinks of the instrument at the legation in Teheran. This one hasn't been tuned, either. She continues with some arpeggios, begins a Mozart sonata, but the tone is so flat, grating on her ears, she cannot go on. She stands up.

Halidé claps. 'Good, Esther! More.'

'It needs tuning.'

'Excuse me?'

'The sound is not right. Too low.'

'It is quality,' Halidé comments as she gets to her feet. '*Baba* will have paid a lot of money for it. He does not buy cheap things.'

'I'm sure he doesn't. Thank you for giving me the opportunity. All pianos, even the best, have to be tuned, particularly if they haven't been used for a while.' Halidé is frowning. She takes the girl's hand, not wanting to upset her, feels the squeeze of Halidé's response.

'Come to the terrace and have some sherbet. It's pomegranate today.'

'I don't know how to talk to Ayesha.'

'If *An-ne* is there, Ayesha will not … dare be unkind. If *An-ne*'s elsewhere, I shall tell Ayesha to remember her manners.'

'What did she say when I arrived?'

Halidé's face reddens. 'That she loves Kemal, will wait for him for ever, sunrise and sunset, until he is with her.'

'How much time has she spent with him?'

'Not much, and with *An-ne* in the room. We came to this house the year before the war. Kemal has been away a lot. There was never an … arrangement between him and Ayesha.'

They are at the bottom of the stairs. In a recess is a framed photograph of Kemal in uniform. She picks it up. It has been coloured and mounted on black cardboard. Booted feet slightly apart, he stands in front of a desert landscape, eyes fixed on some point beyond the photographer. His right-hand fingers are closed over a gold jacket-button, thumb tucked inside. The left arm, bent at the elbow, rests behind his back.

'When he completed at the Military Academy,' Halidé explains.

She tries to connect this man, a statue, with the lover she said goodbye to in Trebizond, but cannot. None of what happened with Kemal belongs here but where they were together. The possibility they might never see each other again, or that she cannot love him enough to live with what he believes in, strikes renewed fear into her. She reaches for the sound of his voice. It has gone.

She returns the photograph to its place. 'Do you have a fiancé, Halidé?'

In spite of shuttered light, she cannot miss a blush suffusing the girl's cheeks. 'The brother of my sister-in-law, Abla, has visited several times.'

Another cousin ... there is always a cousin ... 'So you're betrothed.'

'There is no arrangement, but he has spoken to *Baba*; it would not be correct for us to sit and talk even with *An-ne*.'

'And Kemal spoke to Ayesha's father?'

'Oh, no, I'm certain not. He and Ayesha may have sat with *An-ne* on a couple of occasions.'

'Do you want to marry?'

Halidé's face becomes red as the evening sky over Stamboul. 'I am eighteen, Esther. I am ready. But we know nothing, Ayesha and I.' Halidé hesitates until words tumble after each other, 'What is it like?'

'It is ... you can't imagine ... unforgettable ... I must go now, Halidé.'

They turn towards the terrace. 'Where are you living? For when Kemal comes back.'

A rundown hotel once used by prostitutes? 'Just two rooms. I haven't seen a name.'

She is almost there when she realises Halidé forgot the medicine for Anahid.

She finds Jacob and Anton on the shady side of the cobbles. Jacob throws a stone. 'Let's try and pee further than that,' he says to Anton as he unfastens his trousers.

Anton sees her. 'Hello, Esther.'

'What are you doing, boys?'

'P –'

'– practising,' Anton cuts across Jacob.

'Come inside.' She hustles them through the door. 'In the autumn, you're going to school.' Nadia and Papa have learnt of a Russian junior high.

'Turkish lads play in the street,' Jacob insists. 'We saw them in Stamboul, with Ana.'

'Where is she now?'

'She said to leave her for half an hour while she did the sewing.'

I could tell them it is Mirza Khan's. For I am with child, I am certain. This sickness, tenderness in my breasts and lower belly, every part of me alive, even hair-tips and tingling finger-ends. All the years I lived in Mirza Khan's house, and so much he wanted a son from me; the performance we had in Hamadan, kissing the lion; the bracelets, anklets, amulets he arrayed me in; the trouble and longing, and talk of consulting doctors in Europe, to no avail. For this is not Mirza Khan's. It cannot be: we left Teheran five months ago at least, and he had not lain with me the previous days. And I have bled. Twice. But not since Erzerum.

Even so, I could maintain it is Mirza Khan's. Except that Nadia, who is a medical person, will wonder what is happening when there is no birth at term. This infant is from Erzerum. From Esther's brother. None of the silks and perfumes and scented water, and the lengthy preparations I was allowed in Mirza Khan's home. Just a few brutal, anonymous, life-creating moments.

I cannot admit to Esther who the father is, and upset her more than she has been. He appals me. It is Esther who is important. If she is in ignorance, she has the chance to be happy again. But I have to say something. Soon. Before it shows and some story dragged from me. I cannot go on pretending I feel unwell because of what I have eaten. I must make a decision. For ever. No-one will know the truth.

Oh, Baba. Your Anahid hopes to find you, to at least have news of you, but will you want to see her, belly big with child and no ring on her wedding finger, no certificate of marriage? What have all of us endured since last we saw each other? How much room is there for understanding, forgiveness? Or will you lower your eyes, turn me from your sight?

Will Esther's family do the same?

'What do you mean, somebody attacked you?'

'Violated me, Esther,' Anahid whispers, sitting beside her at the table. Jacob is asleep. 'Forced me.' Anahid's solemn expression holds hers, voice stumbling on to a conclusion.

No! Her mind cannot encompass the injustice: Anahid obliged to carry a baby; she, Esther, losing that of the man she loves. 'He simply set on you?'

'Took me from behind, the matter of a moment.'

'He didn't say anything?'

Anahid looks at her lap.

Deep inside, a scream forms, gathers strength, a wave that will engulf her. As if it were her face against the wall, fingernails dragging on warm clay. 'Because you were Armenian?'

Anahid doesn't move.

'No!' she shrieks. 'It can't happen like that! Life created or lost in such a random way.' Her eyes fill with tears.

'Ssh! You'll wake Jacob.' Anahid holds her close. 'We have to tell Nadia and your father.'

She feels Anahid trembling.

'We mark squares on paper, eight across and down,' Papa explains to the boys, 'and we'll draw and cut out pawns, knights, bishops ...'

She and Anahid sit with Nadia, repairing sheets from the hospital. She pauses in her sewing; how could Anahid have survived what happened? She finds words, clusters them into sentences to Nadia.

Nadia puts down her mending, rests her hand on Anahid's cheek. 'How this poor girl has suffered.' Nadia thinks for a minute, adds, 'We'll stay till after the birth, by which time there may be news of our families. People keep arriving. Lev might even find us.'

A prickle of fear, revulsion; a crushing sadness that this is how it will always be at the mention of her brother's name.

'What if he did come through the war,' Nadia suggests, 'fought with Denikin and ends up here?' Nadia sighs, strokes Anahid's cheek. 'We'll care for you.'

'Thank you.' Anahid's lips are thin, pinched; fingers grip rumpled cotton. The needle hangs poised, flashes and plunges into the material.

TWENTY-ONE

Western Anatolia, July 1920

He cracks his wedge of cornbread in half and dips it in watery broth. If he eats, flies will cluster on his soup. If he uses it as a swat, he will go hungry. His neck and backs of hands are rough, reddened, scaly; ulcers tear at the inside of his mouth. He snorts, disgusted with himself that he has no more pressing preoccupation when Greeks are advancing into Anatolia.

At least the wind has died for a while, settling dunes of soft golden sand. Cicadas thrum their desperate messages. Soon, he will light the two lamps, which will bring out mosquitoes. Hopefully, they will sizzle before finding human skin. Ach! Enough! This is Anatolia, the land he is committed to fighting for and freeing from every foreign adventurer. Where is the star student of mathematics, veteran of Gallipoli and Syria, that he should moon like an old woman?

He gets to his feet, sways. Shirt and trousers hang on him, rags blown round a stick. He runs his fingers over the beard which protects his face from the sun. He looks at the camp:

fifty men chew on their ration, scratching, and he is responsible for them.

The eight rifles he brought from the Black Sea across the plateau to Angora are all they have. From Angora, he and his comrades set off west towards the Aegean to meet the Greek invader: sons and brothers of brigands who drove his father from Macedonia seven years ago, threatened workers, extorted money, ambushed wagons. Irfan Bey has done well in Constantinople; he will anywhere, but the captain of the gendarmerie who advised him to leave Macedonia didn't know that.

When news came that the Greeks had captured Brusa earlier this month, former Ottoman capital, emerald city of silk plantations, he called a halt. The Greeks will press inland but find deserted villages, burnt crops, as his and other units retreat, draw the Greeks further from the sea and their supplies, broaden the Front and lengthen the enemy's communication line; a classic strategy since the Parthians against the Romans. It was an early lesson he learnt at the Military Academy. Once the Anatolian winter sets in, the Greeks might feel less satisfied with themselves.

The boy he posted as lookout runs, kicking the sand. 'Effendi ...'

The child stands panting, recovers his breath; told them he was ten, but appears younger. Not much older than Esther's brothers.

He grasps the lad's shoulder. 'Easy now,' he says.

'More refugees,' a pause to gasp, 'dozens, women and children.'

Along the track, the wail and creak of solid, wooden wheels. He goes to meet the carts, past bleached bones of birds and probably a camel.

The aged *baba* at the head of the procession waits a few paces away, hand on heart in greeting, too exhausted to speak now that he has found sanctuary.

He will tell them later they move off tomorrow, to cast the invisible net ever wider, trail the Greek after them. Like a starving, thirsty man is pulled to a mirage.

TWENTY-TWO

Constantinople, late summer 1920

'There are black flags in Stamboul,' Anahid reports one lunch-time; she straightens on the hard chair, hand against her lower back. Every day, she leaves early, returns with fruit, vegetables, bread, an occasional lamb scrag, chicken feet or wings. 'People mourn land the sultan has given up.'

'They say at the hospital he has signed a peace treaty with England, France, and Italy,' Papa contributes. 'He and his advisers are to remain in Constantinople, but an international commission is to control the city, the Bosphorus, and the Sea of Marmara. We're safe.'

She pauses, a spoonful of soup halfway to her mouth. Is this the signal for Kemal and others to rally to Mustafa Kemal? She repeats to herself Kemal's longing to rid the country of foreign influence. She remembers when Baku learnt of revolution in Petersburg: Papa assembled his household in the salon and read aloud from the newspaper *Kaspii*; outside, crowds were cheering, singing, dancing. Is the same to happen here?

She glances at her brothers. They are chewing, eyes on their parents.

'You should go to your husband's family,' Anahid tells her later as they walk down to the blue-green water. Heat of the dying sun still oozes from cobblestones and walls. The sea shimmers like washed silk.

'They're at their *yali*.'

'That's no reason not to.'

When she recalls Kemal's face, all that comes to her is the photograph at his home. Lovemaking has become blurred into a memory of passion forever out of reach.

'Just by your presence, you would be supporting them,' Anahid adds. 'You should be there when he returns or to receive news of him, share it with his family, rejoice, cry. Whose side are you on?'

'I can't leave you and the boys.'

'I am not your responsibility. You married him. What do you have here, Esther,' Anahid thumps her own chest, 'a heart? Where is it?'

'Don't lecture me about husbands. You have one in Teheran, and I freed you from him. Perhaps you should have stayed there.'

Anahid blanches.

She turns, makes her way back at a pace she knows Anahid can't manage.

'Esther?' Anahid is calling.

She ignores Anahid. In every dark-haired man she passes, she sees Kemal, feels the softness of his lips. But it is fear that hurts: what she would say if it were him, what they would do, how they would be with each other. I should not go on considering myself his wife. He said he would release me from the marriage if I wished. Well, I liberate him. He can wed Ayesha, and everything will be as it should. Anahid wonders where my heart is. It is with the piano: years waiting for the conservatoire, months without playing, nothing can stop the yearning.

The room is empty. They must be with the Toumanovs. She sits at the table, spreads her fingers in the opening chords of Chopin's étude, the 'revolutionary'. She presses on the wood; music shouts in her head.

Half an hour later, Anahid appears, panting after climbing the stairs.

She stands up, faces her friend.

'I was hasty in what I said, Esther.'

'There's some truth in it, though. I have to make a decision and so I have decided.'

'What?'

She moves round the table to Anahid. 'To free Kemal from the marriage, as he promised he would me.' She unfastens the necklace, closes it over Anahid's palm. 'You can sell it.'

'Wait until you've seen him and are sure.' Anahid embraces her. 'We are a pair. I have a baby on the way and no husband; you have a husband …'

'… *had*, Anahid …'

'… and no child. You can share this one when he's born.'

'The Volga is the largest river in Europe,' Jacob stands and recites before school, arms straight as he has been taught. 'It is five thousand versts long.'

'Five thousand five hundred,' Anton corrects.

She doesn't know. Every day, the boys have to repeat to the class ten facts about their homeland from the previous lesson.

When she has delivered her brothers, she sometimes goes to the wharf, breathes sea air. Cats sit, stare, wait for fishermen. Gulls squat on the domes of Stamboul and call to each other. Anahid says there are pictures of Mustafa Kemal in the bazaar; has come back shocked to hear people accuse the sultan of being degenerate, only interested in his throne and himself, with advisers who are as bad and agree to anything that protects themselves. From the hospital, Papa and Nadia have brought news of what is now the Turks' war of independence: Mustafa Kemal is the terror of the Franks – foreigners – with a lightning army spreading across Anatolia.

The birds' melancholy music carries perhaps to where the Bosphorus opens into the Marmara, and she dreams of boarding a ship for France.

But many mornings, fog rolls off the water, blurs domes and minarets as autumn slips into winter. Prince and Princess Toumanov have gone; after months of queues and haranguing, they obtained visas for France.

Anahid has let out her skirt as far as the material will allow; from the Armenian stallholder's offcuts, she makes vests for the baby, embroiders edges with flowers, grapes, bees.

In the evenings, a couple of logs burn in the chipped white porcelain stove in the corner; beside it is a third which has to last until bedtime.

'Check!' exclaims Papa. 'Well done, Anton!'

She pauses from repairing a sheet. Again, Anton has beaten Jacob. At the clatter of footsteps on the stairs, and raised Russian voices, she puts down her mending.

She opens the door, peers out, greets two women and a man

who are on the landing. Their bags are made from pieces of carpet. His greatcoat, bare of insignia or epaulettes, is caked with mud.

'Where's the toilet?' one of the women gasps, panic in her expression.

'Downstairs.'

The other woman is panting. 'They said there was a room.' Tied under her chin, a frayed shawl covers her hair.

'Yes.' She points to where the Toumanovs lived.

'Valentina Maksimovna. You came from Sevastopol, too?'

She shakes her head.

'We stayed till the last moment.' Valentina Maksimovna bites her lip. 'They hammered my brother-in-law's shoulder board into his flesh and rolled him in a barrel encrusted with nails.'

Her tongue, suddenly too big, sticks to the roof of her dry mouth. 'They?' she whispers.

'Cheka, bolshevik secret police; said they didn't want justice, simply to settle accounts. Which? All he'd ever done was fight for his country.'

A memory, flickering summer fragment, strolling along the promenade in Sevastopol with a pink parasol, string orchestra playing Mozart, figs clustering on silvery branches … but it is Lev's twisted face she sees. Is he capable of this, the worst a human can do to another? The wound from Erzerum tugs, scar tissue hurting. 'Let me make you some tea,' she offers. 'Come and join us.'

The boys sit on the bed, and Papa remains standing so the new arrivals can have their chairs. Valentina Maksimovna's sister is silent, mouth moving as if in prayer or recounting something; her eyes, red-rimmed from crying, keep darting to the door. When Jacob gets up – throws himself – boots hard on the floorboards, to help with the tea, the woman starts, hands flying to her cheeks.

She gives a glass to Valentina Maksimovna, whose fingers feel like splintered wood.

'You're lucky, Esther Yefimovna,' Valentina Maksimovna comments, holding hers and looking at them. 'We soaked ours in alcohol to crack the skin, and rubbed dirt in. If they stopped you at a checkpoint and you'd got soft hands, they'd shoot you.'

She shivers, aware of a palpable, terrible evil which still clings to these people and fills the room.

'We joined the Don Cossacks in '18,' Valentina Maksimovna's husband says, 'not that we had much in common with them. All they were concerned about were their own territories rather than a united Mother Russia. But every one of us wanted to defeat the *bolsheviki* and for a while we did the following year: Kursk, Orel.'

Papa produces a half-full bottle of vodka from Prince Toumanov.

Valentina Maksimovna's husband pauses to drink, raises it in a toast. 'We were short of ordinary soldiers: too many junior officers with no-one to command; generals in charge of nothing more than a battalion. If they'd put the cavalry there,' he sets the bottle on the table, 'and the guns there …' he places his glass diagonally. 'But they always thought they knew best, those top brass, obsessed with rank, uniforms, salutes, as if we were in the time of the great Tsar Pyotr; hearts of lions, brains of sheep. The Reds pushed us back. We made a brief stand behind the Don last January, but they drove us on to the coast. English and French got thousands of us out, sick, wounded, as well as Baron Wrangel's army. We hung onto the ship's side. There are no White forces in Russia now.'

'The beast has awakened in man,' says Papa.

There are other evenings, shawls huddled round shabby shoulders, air blurred with cigarette smoke; crying until grey morning seeps through the shutters; stories of posters showing a peasant twirl a toad goggling at the end of a rope; of neighbours skinned and scalped; disembowelling, crucifixion, burying alive. Wild-eyed children join the school, sores on faces and limbs, heads shaved against lice. They wear ill-fitting clothes from Red Cross parcels or diplomatic-mission handouts.

Not all refugee-ships dock in Constantinople. Some continue to the Marmara, even as far as the Gallipoli peninsula or islands and ports in the Aegean, the flotsam of history washing up on any shore that does not reject them, to find sanctuary in crowded, dingy camps, and fill hospitals with cases of typhus and dysentery.

'Esther, can you persuade your father to stay at home?' Nadia tries. 'He insists on going with me.'

'If he's here, he'll sit and brood. It isn't good for him. And they won't pay him if he doesn't work.'

'So we're to risk his health – his life, even – for money,' Nadia retorts. 'You are fitter than him. You could put in a few hours as a waitress at the Doré or play the piano.'

'And who would look after the boys, fetch and carry? Ana can't do everything.'

'You always say that.'

'You never give me an answer.'

'The old are most vulnerable to fever.'

'Papa's not yet fifty.'

'He's run down, debilitated. He hasn't any fight in him.'

Nadia brings back disinfectant; its smell permeates the rooms. She watches dark curls litter the floor as Nadia uses the razor on Jacob and Anton.

'Ayee! I don't like it,' Jacob protests.

She remembers Lev's close-cropped hair in Erzerum; her heart wobbles. 'That's enough, Nadia.'

'What do you mean? Have you seen typhus: bleeding spots, congested eyes?'

The fierce bar of sunset settles behind Stamboul. She draws the faded curtains, against revolution, war, horror: two lengths of fraying calico.

She stands at the window; apprehension gnaws at her. Anahid is late from returning the sewing, unconcerned about being out alone.

'With my face mostly covered and cloak round me, nobody'll look at me twice, Esther,' Anahid said.

'You were not safe in Erzerum.'

'You take and collect the boys from school along rain-sodden pavements.'

Today, however, has been dry and cold; the old year has given way to the new. The sun crouches, casts shadows over Stamboul's outline, while lights on this side of the Golden Horn string like jewels. And here is Anahid, preceded by a lad carrying something. Only when he enters the building, does she realise he is with Anahid.

She opens the door. Footsteps sound on the stairs, and Anahid's commanding voice.

Anahid's porter has a samovar, which he places in the corner opposite the stove. He wears two pairs of trousers, maybe more, holes in the top one compensated for by layers beneath. Anahid gives him some coins. 'Thank you, *Hanum*.' He is away, clatters down to the street.

'There,' Anahid says. 'The room waiting for it all these months.'

'A little bit of home, Ana?'

'I paid for it with the necklace from Mirza Khan; I wanted to detach the big emerald at the front, but the man said leave it, and gave me some tea as well.'

She puts her arms round Anahid, leans in to kiss her friend. 'Don't forget mine. Buy something for the baby.'

Anahid moves as if underwater; lowers herself on and off bed or chair as though afraid of damage to herself or whatever she might be about to sit on.

'You take the sewing, Esther.' Anahid wraps in brown paper a pile of folded blouses.

Papa offers to accompany her. The chess has been abandoned until the boys have copied out a poem by Pushkin, which they must learn by heart. 'I'll hear you when we come back,' she tells them as she settles inside her cloak.

She and Papa walk towards Galata Bridge. Icy, late-afternoon mist descends in a fine drizzle. She holds Anahid's work against her chest, tugs her shawl around head and shoulders.

Papa points to the fuzzy skyline of Stamboul. 'To think Russia dreamed she would own Constantinople,' he says. 'Tsaregrad. What vain hopes, foolish ambitions!'

'With hindsight, yes, Papa. We were not to know it would end as it did.'

'Should I have fought?'

Inside her, a spark kindles at Papa's unaccustomed way of talking, as if a spring has been released in him. She turns to him, but he is looking at the ground as they walk. 'No. You were older than many who did and had a young family. And the *bolsheviki* weren't going to last, were they?'

'Yes, but should I have helped defeat them?'

'No, Papa.'

'Should I have enlisted in honour of Lev, for our motherland?'

Sick of secrecy, of her stomach cramping, bile rising to her throat whenever her brother's name is mentioned, she almost tells Papa about Lev. But she remembers Papa's comment that the beast has awakened in man, and cannot break his heart. 'You made the right decision, Papa.'

'Dear girl, trying to make her ageing father feel good. I loved him, Esther, wanted to shape him according to my ideals, my belief that hard work, success, was the route to integration for our people. He was to be better than me: I'm sure I've told you, to gain a residence permit in Petersburg so I could sit my examinations at the Technical Institute as an extern, after studying in Paris –'

Yes, she has heard this before.

'– I'd had to register as a butler because I was a Jew. How proud I was that Lev was fighting for Russia. It is the greatest thing anyone can do, die for his country.'

How is she to answer?

As they cross the bridge, Papa asks, 'Do you still long for the piano?'

'All the time. There is nowhere here. But when we get to France –'

'Do you reproach me for your marriage to Kemal?'

'No.'

'What has become of him?'

She explains what he must be doing and what she has decided.

'There grew a fondness between you.'

'Yes.'

'I hope you haven't been hurt. Mustafa Kemal, eh? Another Lenin? We shall see the pictures of him Ana talks about. Esther, Nadia appears strong but she is still young and would not be the same on her own. If anything happens to me, she will need taking care of.'

'Papa! You and Nadia will grow old together.'

'Who can tell?'

Morning air nips at cheeks and fingers, wreaths of soot rise from stovepipes, but the sun shines in a cobalt sky. Perhaps this will be my last walk with sewing before the birth. He kicks, weighs inside me. I am sure it is he. I am not afraid. Nadia will help me. Esther will fetch her.

'Some Russians have opened another restaurant,' I said to Esther. 'The Turquoise. You could offer to play the piano there.'

'I'm going to be a concert pianist.'

'You have to start somewhere.'

I have bartered her necklace for lengths of muslin, which I've cut into squares for the newborn. I do want her to love him. I cannot have anything but disgust for her brother, but the infant is part of me as well, has grown within me until his time, and I wish him to be cherished. By everybody but especially Esther. She was sobbing in the night, away from me, into the pillow. She has lost so much. If she can devote herself to this baby, it will make these months worthwhile.

Each day when Nadia comes in, I regard her face, her eyes, for news of my family, in case they are not in Armenia. But she busies herself, embraces her children, asks them what they've been doing.

Yet still refugees arrive, not just Russians but Kurds, Armenians, Arabs, Albanians, from all corners of the sultan's empire. To ward off hunger-pangs, everyone finds something to sell, even if it is only the ability to carry from here to there through a sea of mud after the rain.

In Stamboul, Mustafa Kemal surveys the scene as if he would see into your soul, discover your every secret. Some basket-workers squat under the bazaar's arcades and skeins of coloured wool drying on the parapets beneath his portrait. I recognise my people's hard, guttural consonants and throaty laughs, music to my ears.

We greet each other 'good light,' as is our way. I waste no time on pleasantries or their surprise. 'Do you know anyone by the name of Touryan? My father, Stepan; brothers, Edouard and Gaspar?'

One of the women is unpicking a piece of basket. Tendrils of hair have escaped from her scarf. She pauses, looks at her friend, at me, shakes her head.

'From Erzerum,' I persist.

'Whole communities were transported.'

My stallholder has used that word. Ferida? Nevart? Where were they taken? Why?

'Where are you from?' I ask.

'Atadagh, a small place. We spent years in the mountains, forced there by the Turks. They took men of fighting age, drove us from our homes, stole anything we carried.' The woman's teeth are broken or missing; she hawks, spits into a cloth. 'Months ago, we heard they were burning fields and villages, leading people to safety so the

Greeks would have nothing. We could see the smoke. We walked at night to the coast and a boat. We'll wait here until Mustafa Kemal's pushed the Greeks into the sea although, heaven knows, we've no quarrel with them, Christian like us. The world's gone mad.'

The woman nods towards my belly. 'You on your own? You can join us.'

I tell them about Esther and her family.

I hope Baba, Edouard, and Gaspar have found such friends.

Papa wakes coughing, with aching head, back, limbs.

'I told him to stay in bed, Esther,' Nadia says. 'He insisted on getting up but hasn't the strength.' Nadia twists her hands in agitation. 'How much money is there? Have we saved anything?'

'Thanks to Anahid, yes. She's a good housekeeper.'

'So if I don't work for a while, we can manage. I'll nurse him. I'll just go to the hospital to explain.'

Before setting out for school with the boys, she eases open the door to Nadia and Papa's room. Short, steady breaths: Papa is asleep.

Nadia returns with two brown paper packages. 'Chlorodyne.' She puts a bottle on the table. 'It can affect the heart, but we'll use a soupçon.' Nadia unwraps the other parcel. 'Ammonia. Awful smell. One drop in water. I'll sponge him with it twice a day.'

Nadia sits with him; dozes on a chair when he sleeps, his palm against hers; talks to him when he wakes, feeds him broth or tea, dabs his skin.

'My turn, Nadia?' she offers.

'Those could be the crucial moments.'

'Let me at least keep you company.' She holds out her arms. Nadia takes them, and they clasp each other.

'If we can get him through this first week,' Nadia says into her shoulder, 'bring the crisis on, he'll start to recover.'

A scented pastille goes only a small way to dispel the reek of chemicals. Papa's eyes are congested; he stares in the direction of the curtains, thin fingers on the worn, mended sheet. The spots on his face are mottled, dusky. A few have been bleeding.

'Rachel,' he murmurs Mama's name. He peers towards Nadia. '*Ma petite Nadia.*'

'*Mon chéri,*' Nadia tells him through sobs. '*Mon adoré.*'

Her throat catches. Papa knows what it is to love: Mama, Nadia, all his children. And she herself? Capable of devotion simply to the piano? No. She cherishes Papa.

'*Moya dusha ...*' His voice becomes indistinct.

Her heart aches as if it will crack.

Nadia wipes round Papa's eyes. 'Is that better, *mon chou-chou*?'

His lips try a smile.

A few minutes later, pain carves into his expression. His body jerks as if attached to strings at the whim of invisible hands, before resting.

'Yefim?' Nadia whispers, mouth close to his.

Tears already trickle down her cheeks, for Papa has gone; the death he was expecting has found him.

Hospital staff take him away and fumigate the room. They explain the convulsion at the end was a heart attack. He is buried in a cemetery alongside other typhus victims.

Jacob climbs onto her lap. 'Esther, will Papa really not come back?'

She hugs him. 'No, poppet. He's died.'

'What does that mean?'

'He's with God.' But she is little comforted by what she tells him. God is a stranger, not part of their lives, He of her ancestors, who led His people from slavery in Egypt, recounted every year at Passover when they were in Baku.

'I hate to see Mama sad,' Jacob says. 'She cries in her sleep. I can feel her shaking.'

'Papa's in heaven,' Anton adds.

She looks at the child's large eyes, certainty in his voice reflected on his solemn face. Are the annual repeating of a story and donations to the synagogue enough to sustain them through heartbreak?

'God must want him very much to take him when we need him, too,' Jacob falters. His body trembles. She cradles his head against her shoulder; wishes thick curls were there to ruffle instead of stubble.

She weeps at night; rain and wind rattle the window. Her chest hurts with longing for Papa, to hear him, talk to him. Like a wave breaking on the shore, pain threatens to submerge her.

Anahid heaves herself up and sits on the edge of the bed.

She snuggles to Anahid's massive front. 'I can't imagine life without Papa,' she sobs.

'I know.' Anahid's lips are on her hair.

'He made decisions ... I didn't always agree ... but he was there, our rock.'

'I know.'

'So much lost ... the house, Lev, the baby, Kemal ...'

'Kemal will be back.'

'I can't live with him. I've told you.'

'You have music, and soon there will be this newborn.'

'Where can I play the piano?'

'Something will happen.'

'What are we going to do? Who will decide?'

'You and Nadia.'

She eases herself from Anahid and goes onto the landing. She pauses outside Nadia and Papa's room, pushes open the door. Nadia is asleep. Jacob and Anton lie either side of their mother, holding hands across her.

Nadia returns to the hospital. Anahid stays indoors lest, clumsy of movement, she should slip.

She wraps herself against the February wind that blows down from the Black Sea. The Bosphorus writhes, changes colour as clouds push across the sky. She buys cabbage, carrots, celery in Galata. Anahid cooks them.

She takes Anahid's sewing, brings more, averts her eyes from Mustafa Kemal's stare. Evenings are heavy, empty, without Papa's voice to encourage the boys at chess or tell them stories; just the simmering of the samovar.

One morning when she comes in, Nadia is still there.

She stops in the doorway. Anahid is on the bed, biting on a wad of material; her head flails on the pillow. Nadia leans over her, holds her hand.

Nadia turns. 'The baby's started. Won't be long.'

Apprehension and excitement beset her. She should help but doesn't know what to do. When she lost her child in Trebizond, there was blood, mess, pain. It must be the same with a birth.

'You can boil water,' Nadia says, 'and borrow towels. You don't have to watch.'

She steps towards Anahid, a mound that rises, falls, with breathing and grunting.

Nadia wipes Anahid's brow. 'Good girl,' she soothes. 'Bear down ...'

She loses sense of time as she fetches, carries, chops and slices vegetables. She stands by the window, rubs away a patch of condensation. It has been snowing, giving Stamboul yet another beauty, domes and minarets suspended above a white carpet against a vivid sky.

Later, on the stairs, she hears a baby's cry, lusty, outraged. She leaves the bucket, rushes through the door. Anahid sobs, exclaims in Armenian.

'A boy!' Nadia gives him to Anahid. 'And healthy by the sound of him.' Anahid puts him to her breast. The yelling stops. Anahid murmurs to him.

She hovers outside a circle of love.

Anahid looks up, cheeks wet with tears. 'He's a Theo, Esther. Don't you think he's a Theo?'

Her eyes encompass life brutally conceived yet brought into the world whole, perfect, a covering of dark fluff over his head, tiny fingers on Anahid's enormous, vein-mottled breast. Her legs feel as if they will not support her. Beads of exhilaration, shock, spill onto her face.

Theo. He is a miracle.

TWENTY-THREE

Western Anatolia, summer 1921

Like wicked eyes, station-lamps glare, beacon for any Greek plane, but a risk he has to take, and soon the train will be away. He stands on the platform, draws on the butt of a cigarette, face masking exhaustion. Women sit in open trucks, nurse babies, surrounded by bundles and kitchen utensils; look at the sky, or stare at him with bitterness and yet the quiet, unfailing patience that belongs to Anatolians. It's for them I'm fighting this war. Their land. Their freedom. Others arrive, trail household goods, grip hands of bewildered children. His soldiers find room for them, speak only when necessary.

Pride glows beneath his desperation. Gone are the men's wild songs, their jokes and repartee as they fired simply to display marksmanship. Months of instruction, and a battle against the Greeks in the spring, have imbued them with discipline, purpose. They left Greek dead in their white ballet-skirts and upturned, pompommed shoes, cockaded kepis trampled in mud; took their weapons, deaf to groans and gurgles of the wounded, and different kinds of screams.

The wagons are full. He watches them trundle eastwards. The families who found his unit last summer were eventually put on a transport; no doubt they have been uprooted again. He wonders how many weeks will pass before these people can return home. Greeks continue to push from the south.

On the rare occasion he glimpses himself, on a piece of polished metal, malarial eyes query him from a face now host to a map of creases and topped by a shaved head. Would Esther recognise him? He hardly does so himself. Only a flicker tells him he is still Kemal, son of Irfan Bey, and one day Anatolia will be liberated, and he will rejoin Esther. He repeats her name, mouth not moving. The memory of her lovely expression never leaves him; reminds him who he is.

They ride through the night, he in the high-collared, khaki tunic and astrakhan hat of the private soldier, with brass buttons and no badges of rank for he is no longer in the Ottoman army, but at the front of the men as they defer to him. They are making for the Sakarya valley. The river carves its way across the Anatolian plateau into the Black Sea but throws out a loop near Angora, coils suddenly northwards until it turns west. There, they will wait for the Greeks.

Shortly before dawn, they dismount in a village square. Several long carts are drawn up alongside each other, pulled by buffalo rather than the usual oxen. A dozen women, jacketed and pantalooned, feet in brightly coloured, knitted cloth secured with rope, stand by the conveyances.

A baby lashed to her back, a woman clears aside the hay that covers the top of her cart, to reveal piles of shirts, socks, shoes. 'For you, effendi,' she says between cracked lips.

He has a momentary recollection of gifts when he graduated

from the Military Academy. 'Where are you from?' he asks.

'Beyond Erzerum.'

Her comrade has guns, rope-bound boxes of ammunition. The smell of armpits rolls towards him. 'From Trebizond; the Russians.'

'You've travelled all this way,' he says. Buffalo will have been quicker than oxen, but they must still have been on the road for weeks.

There are tunics made from carpets, petrol tins full of medicines; daggers, swords with heavy, curved blades and engraved handles, or fashioned from ploughshares.

'They told us from the minaret everything was needed, for Mustafa Kemal, to save our country.'

Relief softens the edge of his tiredness, at people's response to the Treaty of Sèvres, death-blow dealt to the sultan's empire by Britain, France, and Italy. 'I will tell Mustafa Kemal,' he assures the women. 'You've done well. Turkey is proud of you.'

Emboldened by such support, he wonders if he and the men might lie down, sleep for a few hours, but no, they must press on. He has become used to napping on horseback. He turns away to light another cigarette butt. Too late, he realises he is near his mount, a chestnut gelding, white ankles coated in the yellow dust of the plain. At the flash of the match, the animal rears, knocks him to the ground. Pain like a weapon-thrust sears his side. Blackness envelops him, her dear, beloved face hovering, insubstantial, until that, too, is extinguished.

TWENTY-FOUR

Constantinople, summer 1921

He has captured my heart, enslaved me as surely as when I lived in Mirza Khan's house. Theo. Not for him such gifts friends offered before the war: when Gaspar was born, neighbours called in with coffee, lokum, spices; somebody pressed a gold coin into my three-year-old palm. It is a miracle that in the midst of suffering and death, rumours and hated memories, this new life can be the source of so much love.

Why should I cleave to this scrap of yelling humanity who never lets me have more than a few hours' sleep, who needs to be washed and wiped and changed many times a day, so that there are always damp muslin squares hanging in the room? Esther has an aversion to mess. She wrinkles her elegant, Jewish nose. 'You do it, Anahid.' And so I clean his bottom, and his penis, the size of half my little finger. He has a mark at the top of his right thigh, on the inside, the same thumb-nail shape as Esther's on her shoulder. I wonder whether her brother has one; if he has, whether she knows.

There is no logic to this adoration. My head could tell me I should loathe or at best disown him. But my heart has flooded my whole being with feelings I can't put into words, for as soon as I do – happy, joyful – they are fastened down, become finite, bound by my understanding of them, when the emotions I would try to describe are like the sea, the desert, endless. It is as if the passion I would have given my husband – not Mirza Khan, but if I had been married in the normal way to an Armenian boy – and the devotion I can no longer show my family, are concentrated on Theo.

When I lift him from his cradle – Nadia brought it from the hospital – I nuzzle his neck's softness, the tips of shell-like ears, inhale warmth, slumber, our prized sliver of olive-oil soap, my own milk. When I have settled him to sleep, I yearn to take him out and rest my face against his, and have to force myself to leave him. I wait until he wakes, as does a lover for a beloved.

This does not mean I do not wish Esther to care for him, or Theo for her. There cannot be too much affection. He is fatherless but can have two mothers. Yet, I don't want to keep her from Kemal, for she did cherish him. They had so little time together. Is there a future for them? She insists not but has yet to tell his family.

She puts the blouses on the table, and money from the previous sewing in the purse in the drawer. Anahid is supporting Theo under the arms of his yellow dress; gazes at his face, murmurs to him in Armenian.

When Anahid becomes aware of her, she changes to French. 'You are a good boy, aren't you?' Anahid holds Theo out to her – 'You have him, Esther,' – and turns to him. 'Go to Mama Esther.'

It is the moment she aches for. She has no right to this baby. She is forever tired as Anahid feeds him in the night. So is it because she has known desire and carried a child inside her, if only for a few weeks, that her sensations are engaged on a level she would never have imagined possible? For Theo, as surely as if he found a spade and staked out territory, has laid claim to and won her love.

What shall I do with you? she thought when she was first alone with him; Anahid was downstairs. She didn't dare place him on the floor, yet was afraid of dropping him. Sit with him, Esther, Anahid said when she came back.

She takes Theo from Anahid now, and contentment's warmth spreads through her. It is tactile, this fondness: the feel of his limbs, soft but strengthening; touching the end of his nose with hers. She smoothes the dress's red frill across his chest and shoulders. 'You're getting heavier,' she says and lowers herself onto the chair. He looks at her with large, dark, widely spaced eyes.

He wriggles in her grasp, body taut. His face flushes, and he begins to cry. 'I think he'd prefer you, Anahid.'

'No,' Anahid coos but reaches for him, soothing. He falls asleep.

She watches; emptiness pushes warmth away.

Days pass without Nadia paying attention to Theo until, putting aside the sheet she's mending, she says, 'Come to Mama, Theo.'

Anahid is dangling his legs on her lap, his favourite position; he stares at her, chuckles, dribbles. Anahid regards Nadia. '*Grand-maman*,' she corrects, hands Theo to Nadia.

Nadia cradles Theo. 'My little Jacob. Mama's Jacob.'

'Nadia, he's Theo,' she tells her stepmother. 'Not Jacob.'

'Theo,' Nadia repeats.

'Esther, why don't we go to Yesilköy one afternoon?' Nadia suggests.

'Where's that?' She is lengthening Jacob's brown knickerbockers.

'Oh, not far.' Nadia concentrates on threading a needle. 'Somebody mentioned it at the hospital. It means green village. There are different trees, acacia like in Baku, and flowers, and we can walk up the hill for a view of the Marmara. We can take a cab, or hire a boat if the water's not too rough.'

'We can't afford it.'

'There are lots of places we could visit: up the Bosphor to Sarayer or Therapia where families and embassies have summer residences, luxurious villas, or even across to the islands, although they are a bit further. It would get us out of the city and the heat.' Nadia appears pleased with herself.

'We've bought boots for the boys. We've nothing to spare.'

Nadia sighs. 'Esther, you're becoming quite dull sometimes.'

There are moments when Nadia pauses from sewing and focuses on anything. She takes an interest in her nails, files them, rubs with a piece of cloth, bends her fingers to consider the result.

'You know Yefim and I met in Paris?' Nadia volunteers. Lamplight catches her hair, now sprinkled with grey. 'Did we tell you? Handsome he was and so gallant. Papa knew his uncle; Yefim was staying there for a few months. Mama and Papa invited them to dinner. Perhaps they felt sorry for Yefim: he was a widower with two small children.'

I was one of them, Nadia. She says, 'Would you like to go to Paris when we have our visas? I'll see where we are on the list.'

'Paris? What for? Yefim won't be there. He returned to Baku.'

Nadia picks up her stitching. In a corner of the sheet, she has embroidered the letter M; around this, she is entwining a G for Ginsberg, her family name.

'The first Romanov tsar was Mikhail, 1613-1640,' Jacob stands beside her and recites as she darns socks.

'1645,' Anton corrects on her other side.

Jacob ignores him. 'The next tsar was Alexei Mikhailovich.' He stops, drops his shoulders on a snort. 'Why do we have to learn this, Esther?'

'Because it's about our country.'

'But we don't live there.'

She runs her eyes over her brother, a shaven-headed stick in knickerbockers which are dark where she let them down. 'You're still Russian.'

Nadia is mending. 'They say at the hospital Turkish nationalists have signed an agreement with the *bolsheviki* and have a supply of arms and money. So revolution will come here, too. The *bolsheviki* will show them the way.'

Kemal has sold his soul to them. Bitterness has insinuated itself under her skin and numbed her. Fresh news no longer hurts.

'I wish I could fight,' Jacob asserts.

'It's not our war,' she tells him. 'Or our country.'

'I want a uniform like those boys we saw.' Cadets, older than Jacob, from the Military Academy at Kuleli, the other side the Bosphorus, on leave in Galata, smart in green, and fezes with moon and stars on the front. 'Where do we belong?' he adds.

'France.'

'Where's that?'

'In the west.'

'Where's that?'

Where life is elegant, and all will be well. 'Where the sun sets.'

'Paris is a beautiful city,' Nadia confides to Anahid. 'Yefim and I met there. What a good-looking man he was!'

'And you were very young,' Anahid comments, attaching a blue frill to the bottom of Theo's yellow dress. 'How romantic!'

Anahid is so patient, she thinks.

Nadia is sewing a button onto her blouse. 'Nineteen, I was. Just a girl. Studying medicine. Can you imagine? Someone of that age learning to be a doctor?'

'Did you go for walks?' Anahid asks.

A smile nudges Nadia's lips. 'We were never alone. Mama invited him to bring his children. We all used to stroll in the Bois de Boulogne. Do you know it?'

She catches Anahid's glance in her direction. Anahid says to Nadia, 'I haven't been to Paris.'

'Yefim and I were wed there. I had a dress by Vionnet.'

'There was a photograph of you in the drawing-room at home in Baku, wasn't there, Nadia?'

'We had heartbreak, too. A couple of miscarriages and a daughter stillborn. Nina, we called her. Ninochka. And at last, my two bundles of joy, my babies.' Nadia drops her work, peers at Theo asleep in his cradle.

'That's our Theo, Nadia, not Jacob or Anton,' Anahid warns. 'Don't wake him.'

Nadia sits down. Sighs.

'Concentrate, Jacob,' Anton tells him.

Jacob keeps glancing at the door. He always has a guarded expression, making him seem older than his nine years. Nadia is not back from the hospital.

Jacob moves a pawn.

'That wasn't the best,' Anton reproaches him. 'You could have gone to K4.'

Jacob stands up; his chair clatters to the floor. 'Esther, I'm going to search for Mama. She needs care.'

'No, Jacob. Where will you? We don't want to lose you as well.'

Nadia immersed in memories, wandering the streets.

The windows shake; rain splatters them, the first gale of autumn. 'Where's Mama?' Jacob demands.

She joins her brother, watches through the glass the downpour whip round ankles, lift hats, throw itself against buildings. It pelts in squalls, races over cobbles, chases the unwary, laps into puddles the dust of summer, bounces off the road in mist. People run, coats pulled onto heads, shoulders bent, women slowed by damp skirts.

Footsteps bang on the stairs, and she hears Nadia's voice. Was that Nadia sprinting?

Nadia exclaiming? Nadia laughing?

The door opens. Nadia comes in, and with her a draught of cold air and the smell of sodden clothes.

'Well!' Nadia removes her shawl and hat, shakes them. 'How silly! Such a sudden storm!' She speaks with excitement; her cheeks are pink. She turns to the doorway. 'Captain Boileau, meet my family.'

A tableau has formed: Jacob, legs apart, arms folded across his chest, stands by his sister; Anton behind; Anahid holds Theo.

'This is Captain Boileau of the French army,' Nadia completes.

He shakes hands with each of them and puts his sky-blue kepi on the table. He is tall. Although his black hair is not yet grey, a sallow skin and khaki uniform give him an appearance of age, perhaps suffering. He is clean-shaven except for a small moustache.

Nadia drapes her coat on a chair. 'Captain Boileau. Your jacket? We can dry it.'

'Thank you, madame, but it is all right. Really.'

'You must have tea. Esther, is the samovar ready?'

She busies herself, glad of something to do; senses the captain's reluctance to be in shirtsleeves.

Anahid turns her back on the room, occupies herself with Theo.

'Captain Boileau and I have been talking about Paris,' Nadia chatters. 'It's some time since he was there, like me. Absence makes the heart grow fonder, doesn't it?'

She glances up from the samovar. Jacob and Anton are looking at the captain, who is regarding the shabby furniture and stove. Nadia hasn't told him, she realises; that we're refugees with nothing but what he can see and most of that not ours. Did he think Nadia was French?

'Do take a seat, Captain,' Nadia urges. 'I'm afraid our husbands are dead or abroad with their regiments, but my sons can entertain you. Jacob, Anton, have the same chair so the captain can sit down.' Papa's, along with his bowl, glass, and cutlery, was given to new arrivals upstairs.

Nadia settles at the table. 'Well! Captain Boileau saved me ... indeed rescued would not be putting it too strongly, from a silly situation the other side the bridge.' Nadia waves towards the Golden Horn.

She stands up from the samovar. 'You went across to Stamboul?'

'I had a look round the bazaar, and the big mosque with its ancient tombs. It was very restful in there, the blue and green.'

'Ayia Sophia,' the captain adds. He watches Nadia while she talks. A smile animates his mouth, relaxes him.

Nadia continues, 'How was I to know it was Friday, and I shouldn't have been there, on my own, face uncovered. I mean, really! These people get so excited, all jabbering at once and gesticulating. Captain Boileau came to my aid.'

She can't decide whether to laugh or show annoyance that Nadia made a spectacle of herself. The captain did the gallant thing and now cannot politely extricate himself. Best give the poor man some tea and let him go.

She takes it to the table. 'Have you been long in Constantinople, Captain?'

'About twelve months. We've had a military mission here for a couple of years. I expect you have heard of General Franchet d'Espérey, who rode into Constantinople on a white horse, a gift from local Greeks. The Turks, naturally, call us the occupying force.'

'A white horse!' Nadia exclaims. 'How amazing! Beautiful!' She dips a lump of sugar in her drink and puts it in her mouth.

Blue eyes rest once more on Nadia, the captain's expression that of someone looking for the first time at a great painting.

The next afternoon, a bang at the door startles her. She glances up from patching elbows on Jacob's pullover. The only person who knocks is their neighbour, Valentina Maksimovna, who opens with, 'Esther Yefimovna, do you have … ?'

A second rap.

Anahid is tying herbs into a bunch; she raises her eyebrows. She stands up. Has Kemal discovered where she is? Her heart thumps.

'Captain Boileau!' The sadness of relief.

He holds a bouquet of chrysanthemums in gloved hands. He bows from the shoulders. 'Madame.' He does not offer her the flowers but adds, 'Is madame your stepmother at home? She has no bad effects, I trust, from her experience in Ayia Sophia yesterday and her soaking in the storm?'

'None at all, Captain. She is very well. She is at the hospital.'

'Hospital?' There is concern in his voice.

What exactly has Nadia told him? 'She helps there. A year's medical training is worth a lot with so much suffering in the city.'

'Indeed.'

'Please come in, Captain.'

He removes his kepi, follows her into the room, still clutching the chrysanthemums.

'Shall I take those from you?'

He relinquishes them with, 'Thank you, madame.'

Anahid is hanging the herbs to dry at the window; she turns to look at the captain. 'Madame,' he greets her with a tilt of the head.

'I'm not sure how long my stepmother will be. Probably the rest of the afternoon. Can I offer you tea?'

She can see him weighing in his mind whether or not to stay and what the implications of either might be.

'You are very kind, madame, but perhaps not. My respects to madame.'

'Markovitch,' she tells him.

She closes the door behind him.

There is no vase. She has to cut the stems and put the flowers in an ordinary glass, which means her brothers will have to share one.

Later, Nadia comes in and says, 'They should go in something else, Esther.'

She recounts the captain's visit to Nadia.

Nadia's brow furrows; she repeats his name – her voice doesn't show whether she recalls who it belongs to – and comments, 'Constantinople is full of French officers.'

The days shorten. Mist clings on hair like dew, leaves miniscule droplets on the edge of shawl or sleeve. The captain does not call again. There is no reason, she tells herself, why he should involve himself with a family of exiled women and children.

'Come on, Theo!' Jacob and Anton encourage, crouched in a corner.

Anahid has placed Theo on his back on the floor; he wears knickerbockers she made for him from bits of material in different shades of yellow. He manoeuvres himself onto all fours and crawls to the boys, talking in his own baby-language. When he reaches them, he rolls, laughing, onto his padded bottom; pulls himself to sitting.

Jacob kneels with him. 'Race Uncle Jacob!'

Theo sets off to another corner. Jacob keeps behind him.

'Mind the stove,' Anahid cautions.

Anton stands in front of it. 'Theo's won!' he proclaims. 'Bravo, Theo!'

Theo chuckles. Anahid picks him up, perches on the bed, unfastens her blouse.

Jacob and Anton lay out chess on the table. She looks at Anahid murmuring to Theo as he sucks at a blue-veined, pendulous breast. His hair is thickening, darkening, with promise of a curl. His hands open and close, and she senses a well of pleasure.

When Jacob and Anton were born, she was absorbed with herself and the piano. The babies were part of Nadia and Papa, their happiness. She might occasionally play with them, but doesn't recall tingling nerve-ends, this longing, as if her heart is expanding. She wonders if Mama felt like this about her. A memory surfaces: she is on Mama's lap; Mama strokes her cheek, kisses her forehead, says: my beautiful doll.

She waits for Theo to finish, the moment she can caress him, feel on her shoulder his fingers, dimpled where knuckles and joints will later show.

Next morning as Anahid leaves for Stamboul, she tells Theo, 'Be good with Mama Esther.'

He grips chair and table legs, attempts to pull himself to his feet, falls back on his bottom, giggles, tries again. Was she as persistent as this at Theo's age? Or Jacob and Anton? Where they are concerned, she can't remember, was not interested in such mundanity as managing to stand up. There were photographs of herself as a baby in a flounced, frilled dress, hair decorated with a ribbon too large for the amount it needed to contain; Mama's beautiful doll, to be petted, who must at some stage have stood. Did she or Lev achieve this first?

She fends off thoughts of Lev. Theo is across the room, ready for a foray. She kneels, holds out her hands to him. 'Come to

Mama … Esther.' She hesitates between the two words, the miracle of them.

Theo sets off. She reaches out to help him up but stops. He clutches her, prattles. She waits as he clings, pushes himself onto feet that may be surprised at what is being requested of them but do not resist. His bottom wobbles, and he turns to her, mouth opening in a smile, with grunts and gurgles of glee. He steadies himself against her shoulder and gazes at her. I know you, he seems to say.

Her heart skids, and she hugs him. 'Well done, my young man! We must tell Mama, Mama Ana.'

Chubby arms are round her neck. Still on the floor, she closes her eyes, sways with him, breathes him in, suspended above time. He tugs at her hair, and a strand loosens. He puts it to his cheek, coos, wriggles to free himself from her embrace. She lowers him and herself; he buries his face in her waves and curls. She plucks out the pins, releasing a cascade; drifts with love and the feel of his fingers.

They've gone. He sits regarding her.

She lifts him. There is a sour smell, and the padding is damp. 'I think I'll have to change you. Mama Ana might not be back for another hour.'

She lies him on the table, unfastens the knickerbockers and soggy fabric. She wipes the softness of his little boy's kit, as the *nyana* called it when bathing her and Lev. 'There, that's better.'

Theo smiles at her, catches her hair.

She stops, stares. Inside his right thigh, at the top, is a mark. She touches it. A sign of great beauty, Anahid said about hers on her shoulder. But it is the *nyana*'s words that stay with her:

the good Lord gave you one each so neither should be jealous of the other. Lev's is in the same place as Theo's.

A fresh square fastened, she lifts Theo to the floor. Could it have been … ? No. Yet, it may have been … Anahid's assailant in Erzerum. Would Lev have done that? Her heart tells her, no, never, and in any case lots of people have marks. Her head says, yes, he was no longer her quiet brother but a man who had been brutalised. She washes, pounds, the muslin in the bucket, as if to erase the suspicion from her mind, until she realises it will not go away but the material is clean.

Theo grasps her, pulls himself to his feet. She bends down, scoops him into her arms. His eyes – Lev's? – survey her. She clasps him to crush anything that might come between them.

The door opens. She turns. Anahid is carrying a metal cage for the stove.

Anahid pauses when she sees her. 'Are you unwell, Esther?'

Her hair, all of her, is in disarray. She forms a question, but it sticks in her throat.

'Esther? Is Theo – ?'

'He has a mark. At the top of his right thigh.'

Imagination, or do Anahid's eyes flicker?

Anahid passes her tongue over her lips; she has a guarded look. 'Yes. It's not uncommon.'

She forces words through her mouth. 'My brother has one. In the same place.'

Anahid puts the cage round the stove – 'An exact fit! I wasn't sure,' – undoes her shawl.

She has to know. She will prise it out of Anahid, even if it means hurting her, breaking open the wound from more than a year ago. 'Anahid!' she flashes. 'Answer me.'

Anahid's expression is now of fear, an animal cornered.

She sets Theo on the floor, grabs Anahid's wrist. 'Speak! Who was it that night in Erzerum? You'll tell me. However much it pains you.'

'What?'

'Was it Lev who attacked you?'

Silence.

'Admit it! Why are you protecting him?'

'I'm not.' Anahid works herself free, massages her arm. 'Your fingers are strong, Esther. Those of a pianist.'

She is not to be deflected. 'Anahid. Was it Lev?'

'We had no conversation.'

'Did he say anything?'

Anahid shrugs, nods.

'In Russian?'

'I suppose so.'

'Was there a scar on the left side of his face?' Yet, Anahid said her violater had taken her from behind.

Anahid closes her eyes; weeping moves up her body, ripples shoulders, pushes tears between eyelids and down cheeks. She whispers, 'He gasped your name at the end. I was meant to be you. He was stoked with anger. So I turned round, let him see me and realise his mistake.'

She gags, bends double, at the rim of another world, one without Theo, life shoved onto an alien axis. Like something scabrous, what she has learnt begins to crawl over her skin, and she must live with it for as long as she draws breath. Her lips are parched. 'How did you bear it and say nothing?' But she knows the answer. Anahid didn't want to shatter her, or Papa, Nadia, the boys. Such love.

'Don't reject Theo, Esther.'

She steps back from Anahid's haunted expression.

'You might never have known,' Anahid adds. 'Just that small mark.'

Theo pulls at her legs. She sits down, lifts him onto her lap. Tears batter her, scalding, primeval; wet her hair and the top of his head, Anahid's arms round them both.

TWENTY-FIVE

Angora, autumn 1921

'Ah, Monsieur Kemal! Good evening.'

The meal of pilav and beans over for another day, Madame Fernande Bertrand has established herself at a table in an adjoining room. A single light bulb burns from the ceiling. Near the stove in the far corner, a couple of men scrape violins and sing pining, Rumeli folk-songs, conjuring visions of lost Macedonian mountains.

Madame Bertrand extends her hand in greeting; several silver bangles tinkle.

'*Bonsoir, madame.*' He bows from the shoulders, clenches his teeth against twinges like hot needles.

'How are your ribs?' She indicates he should sit opposite her.

This is always her first enquiry. 'They are ...' He tries to recall the reply he gives, the French words; settles for, 'They are well.' He carries shame that the injury after the gelding knocked him to the ground in the summer was not gained in battle, when so many have been killed.

Her forehead creases above thick, charcoal brows. 'I think you have some *douleur*?'

He nods.

'You have some pain.'

'I have some pain.'

'Good.'

This, not due to his broken ribs still hurting but because he is speaking French. In a black tunic, Madame Bertrand is a journalist, about his mother's age. Her dark hair is short, *à la Franga*; eyes, jet markers in a sculpted face, miss nothing. She talks to everybody – in French, German, even some Turkish – the contents recorded, he imagines, in the notebook she has with her.

As a result of the campaign at the Sakarya river in the summer, Italy and France abandoned their scheme to partition Anatolia and withdrew their forces. Madame Bertrand arrived in Angora following the treaty signed by her government and that of Mustafa Kemal – francophile and admirer of Napoleon Bonaparte – who has never been to France but is steeped in French philosophy.

So, Monsieur Kemal, she said, we must improve your French so you and your wife can converse – it had not taken her long to discover that Esther was in Constantinople – I am sure it will be preferable to German. We will have half an hour's conversation every evening.

The confrontation with the Greeks had lasted twenty-two days; the invaders stormed Turkish positions on a series of arid heights. The Greeks retreated but are still on Anatolian soil, the western fist, along a Front from the Marmara in the north to the Menderes valley in the south. Mustafa Kemal, known since the battle as the ghazi – warrior against the infidels

– proposes a final attack after the winter, which will give time to restock arms. The French have already supplied Creusot guns and ammunition.

The ghazi is installed in his home in Angora, a dusty city built on red clay, with a population of white long-haired cats, and goats covered with shaggy, silken ringlets. And people whose speech is not easy to understand. The ghazi remains loyal to those who fought but do not aspire to compete with him, and encourages them to settle their wives and families in mud-brick chalets and villas in the vineyards around his property; Madame Bertrand is staying in a guest-house at the bottom of the garden.

'When do you plan to bring your wife here?' she asks.

'I plan ...'

She smiles with a nod of encouragement.

'... to bring my wife here ...' Can he? Of course. Esther will be an example to the other women. Those sitting with an air of unease beside their husbands, are unveiled. The ghazi has stipulated a woman's place is at her man's side. There is to be an end to the harem. '... when I have a house, and,' he taps the table...

'... furniture,' Madame Bertrand supplies.

'Furniture. And a piano.'

'The ghazi has one.'

There is no water except for spring rains and scattered wells. But Esther is used to managing without; things will improve once the war is over, and they can return to Constantinople. Her rich, velvety voice still sings in his head. 'After the ...' He wraps his arms round himself as if to ward off cold but grimaces with pain.

'... the winter,' says Madame Bertrand.

When the thaw begins. He'll keep away from Greek lines, follow the Sakarya valley to the coast, find a boat to Constantinople. The thought will keep him warm inside the cocoon of snow which will protect Angora. As he looks through the window, the first flakes fall.

TWENTY-SIX

Constantinople, March 1922

She laces her boots to take the boys to school. She lifts Theo onto her lap in his yellow jacket and trousers, inhales his skin's unique scent. He chuckles, eyes squeezed into slits, and puts his arms on her shoulders.

She rocks with him, admission of love, liberation from fear and her brother's grossness, brutishness, washing her again. Every day, as many times as he wants to, she has let Theo push himself to his feet holding her legs, and swung him up; Erzerum's horror and Anahid's revelation months ago submerged by layer upon layer of trifles – cuddles, laughter, dribbles, senseless chatter – reinforcing bonds that anchor her to him.

She sets him on the floor. He gazes at her, an expression that is his alone. 'Be good,' she says, swaddling herself with her shawl.

Jacob already has the door open. 'Come on, Esther,' he urges. 'Tsar Alexander Pavlovich made peace with Napoleon at Tilsit in 1807.'

'That's it,' encourages Anton.

She hurries down the worn staircase to deliver Jacob to his lessons before he forgets what he has learnt; or there is another snowfall. Anahid was scornful of the squall earlier: people here know nothing of snow, Esther. It is thin compared to that in Erzerum. And for just a few hours each winter? Huh!

He pulls up the collar of his greatcoat beneath his fur hat; doesn't look at anyone. The French might have signed an agreement with the ghazi, but the British have not, and the sultan is still in his palace along the Bosphorus. Wind blustering from the south makes the morning as hot as June. Almond-trees are in blossom. The Bosphorus shimmers green, beautiful, enticing. Dock-hands singing and calling to each other, the clank of derricks, bales' soft thud, tightening ropes' screech on mussel-encrusted barges: the sounds of his youth.

He pauses on a corner as a tram clatters round. The boatman will wait for him until sunset. In Angora, he has prepared a two-roomed house for Esther and himself. Finding furniture took all winter: the Armenians who used to manufacture it are no longer there. Water is in a copper pitcher, brought from a well five minutes away. He has not slept in the bed. It is to be for their marriage. So accustomed has he become to lying down in hills and plains, sheets and quilts only pain his joints. He has continued to stretch out on the floor, greatcoat covering him; murmuring Esther, to remember the feel of her name on his tongue.

Bring her, Kemal, bring her, the ghazi enthused, when he broached the subject of returning to Constantinople. The ghazi regarded him with eyes the colour of the Bosphorus: she will be a breath of European air and can play the piano in my home; it's good enough, even though it arrived in a couple of parts on mules.

The ghazi seemed in no hurry to begin the spring campaign, preferring to let the Greeks struggle with decreasing supplies, and guerrilla raids on their transport and railway.

The tram has passed. He has a few *para* in his pocket and gives some for a bunch of little closed tulips ... my *lale* ... my tulip ... The man selling them, and narcissi, nods thanks, propped against a wall, crutch to one side, trouser leg pinned up.

In a neighbouring doorway, he puts the remaining coins among matches, artificial flowers, medals, silver thimbles, buckles, on a tray held by an old *baba*.

After leaving her brothers at school, she climbs the hill of Pera; sun blazes until the wind cools and becomes keen, invigorating. Low, dark, greyish-purple obscures the sky. There are vegetables to buy, but she pauses outside the Pera Palas Hotel. She stands at the foot of marble steps, gazes at chandeliers, thinks of Europe, comfort, better things. The doorman has seen her and is approaching.

From the pavement, a man calls, 'Madame!' An officer in khaki. 'Madame, excuse me. Yes ... it is you.'

'Captain Boileau!'

He turns his back on handsome, double doorways and the rowdy, European city, down towards the Turkish enclave. A hodja passes him, a turbaned schoolmaster such as the one who used to beat him; next, a Kalmuck from Mongolia. Sudden clouds smother the sun. Flecks of snow fall on him and the flowers. He has forgotten how capricious March weather can be here.

Abeddin, the gardener, hobbles over to open the gate, across his chest a hand gnarled like a pruned sycamore as he says, 'Good morning, effendi. Welcome to your return.'

He greets the retainer. 'Is Irfan Bey at home?'

'Tomorrow, effendi.'

He looks along the path, which is still wet from snow. Years ago, the house was painted red and green. There is an air of decay about it now. His heart stutters, that behind a latticed window Esther might be asleep. He rehearses in his mind the French words he will speak to her when she wakes and he gives her the tulips ... *ma chérie ... mon amour*.

'Kemal!'

It is not a cry, more a long outtake of breath, his sister Halidé running, holding a pink shawl around herself, hair flying. He catches her. How thin she is.

'Kemal,' she sobs against his shoulder.

He eases her away, ribs aching. In spite of her loss of weight, she is beautiful. Tears cluster like pearls along her lower lashes. The wrap loosens, and he sees a necklace with a locket in the centre. He rests it on his fingertips.

'Mustafa Kemal,' she tells him. 'All the girls have them. People say those he meets shine with some of his glory for ever afterwards.'

'He will do great things for our country.'

Halidé smoothes the side of his face. His heart contracts at her softness, tenderness. 'Are you hurt, Kemal? You're frowning.'

'It is nothing; there was some injury last summer, but it is healed.'

'Is the fighting finished?'

'There will be a final battle soon.'

'We have waited for you. Every day.' Halidé has taken his arm and walks with him towards the house. '*An-ne* is asleep. Ayesha is here, too.'

'And Esther? She is well?'

'Madame, please excuse me. I fear I startled you.' Captain Boileau steadies his breath. 'How are your family?'

'As you remember us.'

'And *le petit?*'

'Theo,' she says, joy gathering within her. 'He's just turned one year old.' She wonders if the captain has any children.

He smiles. 'Can I offer you tea? It is not the weather to stand talking in the street.'

She precedes him up the hotel steps. No flicker of recognition, or any emotion, crosses the cleanshaven face of the doorman who saw her loitering. This is Europe. This is how people live. Nevertheless, she feels uncomfortable at her clothes' shabbiness, and that in his eyes she had an assignation with the captain.

She allows herself to be guided around rectangular marble columns which reach past a wrought iron, first-floor balcony. The captain settles her in a corner at a table for two. Chairs are red plush with short, wooden legs. Antique mirrors hang on crimson flocked wallpaper, giving the room an illusion of even greater space. Across from her are a brazier and a samovar. A Turkish carpet absorbs footsteps, adding to the atmosphere of warmth. String musicians play Mozart but not loudly enough to muffle a clanking, descending lift and the sliding of the birdcage door.

'I'm sorry not to have been in contact,' the captain begins as soon as the waiter has taken the order.

'There is no obligation.'

'I was sent to Adana, in the south-west, after the treaty with Turkey last autumn. This has meant re-drawing their border with Syria, for which we hold mandate since the peace settlement in Europe. It involves movement of populations but hopefully, as a tolerant outcome, will endure. I fear any agreement between Turks and Greeks will not be so easily reached. How they dislike and distrust each other.'

Turkey. The new country Kemal wanted. She asks, 'Are your family here?'

The waiter brings tea and sticky, sugared pastries.

'I am alone, madame. My wife died during the *grippe* of 1919, having received all my letters through the war. I am a licensed pilot and started work in Morocco. I was in the first battle of the Marne and commanded scout planes. And later …' the captain pauses. *J'ai fait Verdun.*'

She has not heard of Verdun. Her eyes meet his: blue, shrouded by sadness, declining further query.

'And so I am here, which enables me to indulge my interest in Ottoman architecture,' he gestures across the room, 'and enjoy some of its opulence.'

'Which explains why you were at the mosque that day Nadia was there.'

'It was originally a Byzantine church. Tell me, madame, would it be improper for me to pay my respects to your stepmother? Of course, she may have no recollection of our encounter or, at least, not one she wishes to revisit.'

'I'm sure she'd be delighted.'

Should she mention Paris, their wait for visas? He might be able to hurry things along. Would he be offended by such a suggestion? Papa would have known what to do. Dear Papa. But if Papa had been with them, they would not have met the captain.

Tears trickle down Halidé's face. She flicks them away.

Foreboding, like a dagger, pierces him. He stops on the path. 'What has happened?'

'We have not seen Esther for more than twelve months.'

'Didn't you ask her to live with you? Where is she?'

'She did not say. Just, two rooms somewhere. We welcomed her, said all we had was hers, invited her to bring her family. There was a strangeness about her, Kemal, as though she were fearful. She played the piano and insisted there was something wrong with it. She smelt of onions, told me the shoots were nourishing for her brothers.'

He imagines Esther finding fault; she was not afraid to take issue with him in Teheran. Can he spend the few hours he has searching for her? A week and he might not succeed … two rooms … or she could be in one of the camps or already have left the city. He is on the edge of an abyss, a shell of the husband who arrived at the gate, a wisp and scrap of a man, heart cut from him. Esther does not want to be found. Why?

Halidé's hand is on his. 'Come and see *An-ne*.'

He removes his hat, forces himself to enter his father's home, breathes in gulps; feet, whole body, heavy with exhaustion.

Where is she? Why didn't she wait for him?

His mother is in the hall, in a mauve robe tied at the waist, hair now grey. She enfolds him in the smell of lavender-water he remembers. She eases him to arm's length, tears on her cheeks as she puts her fingers against his shaven head.

He kisses her hand. '*An-ne.*'

Standing in the archway at the far end is Ayesha. How many years is it since he saw her? She walks towards him. She wears a pale-blue dress worked with silver at the throat. The folds of the skirt ripple as she moves.

An-ne takes the flowers.

'Kemal.' Ayesha's voice is quiet without being timid. She offers her hand; he holds it, warm and soft, untouched by a harsh world. When her eyes meet his, she lets them linger. Lustrous hair is rolled at the back of her neck into a net that sparkles with filigree. He breathes in a subtle aura of roses.

'Ayesha,' *An-ne* says, 'go and prepare food for Kemal.'

Finger by finger, Ayesha releases herself.

The following lunch-time when she brings Jacob and Anton from school, Anahid hands her an envelope.

Before even unfastening her coat, she reads writing slanting to the right: *Madame Nadia Markovitch*. There is a feel of quality about the paper. It can only be from the captain; nobody else knows where they are.

'Who brought it?' she asks Anahid.

'An urchin.' Anahid slices cucumber and tomatoes, scatters them on yesterday's bread soaked in olive-oil. 'I had to give him a few *para*.'

She puts it on the table at Nadia's place. When she mentioned to Nadia the encounter with the captain, Nadia frowned: Boileau? and added: Yefim and I met in France.

As soon as Nadia returns, they all sit down. Anahid ladles potato soup.

'A letter!' Nadia exclaims, turns it over, eases it open with her finger; a smile forms, expands, as she reads.

'Philippe Boileau.' Nadia beams at everybody, picks up her spoon. 'You remember the French captain who escorted me here in the rain last year? He proposes an excursion with me to Yesilköy.' Nadia's eyes sparkle. 'I always said we should go somewhere like that. How charming. Do we have any stationery, Anahid?'

'My hat has seen better days,' Nadia laments that evening. 'We can't afford a new one, can we?'

'I'll do something with it.' Anahid looks in the table drawer where she keeps money. Alongside the purse is a small pair of scissors, bits of lace, silk, calico, and the yellow ribbons Anahid used to wear in her hair in Teheran. 'Any ideas, Esther?'

From the back, she retrieves a piece of silk embroidered with vine-leaves and tulips. 'You did this in Teheran.' It is wrapped round … 'Oh!' … a girl's pink slipper, the end where the toes would have fitted scorched open.

Anahid reclaims it. 'From my home,' she explains as if not wanting to disturb someone; she folds the silk around it. 'All that was left.'

She feels as if a door has been closed; that she was trespassing.

'A blouse,' Anahid tells Nadia. 'I can cut down a tunic from Teheran. It'll be nice with your skirt. The right colours.'

Each Sunday afternoon, Captain Boileau and Nadia go out together. Nadia always returns with a box of Turkish delight from Hadji Bekir, face flushed, eyes shining.

'What did you do?' she asks Nadia, licking soft sugar from her fingers, savouring sweet jelly in her mouth.

Nadia regards her as if she hasn't understood. 'We walked.'

Another time, 'We took a cab, went for a ride.'

'Does he mention France?'

'I don't think so. I can't recall every conversation.'

'Do come in, Captain,' Nadia says.

He leaves the packet he is carrying and shakes hands with everyone.

Nadia removes her hat and coat. 'We've been up the Bosphor to Bebek; saw the most glorious sweep of the bay, and still blue waters just lapping the shore, and a few quiet houses above a pretty cove. Such fragile beauty, wasn't it?' Nadia turns to the captain, smiles. His enjoyment meets hers.

Her heart stumbles. Two people happy visiting, talking.

'An artist's inspiration,' he replies, 'old, narrow properties rising to forests that are green all year round.' He puts a hand on Jacob's shoulder; Jacob's eyes have remained on him from the moment he arrived. 'Were you aware of that, Jacob? Some trees are green all year round?'

Perched on the same chair as Anton, Jacob shakes his head.

'Do you paint, Captain?' she asks.

'Not recently. Nadia has been encouraging me to take up my brushes again.'

Nadia. She looks at her stepmother, who has been watching the captain.

'Is the samovar ready?' Nadia wants to know. 'Well done, Anahid. I'll pour the tea. We've brought some cakes.'

Anahid fetches plates. There are six syrupy doughnuts.

Anahid opens hers; she has Theo on her lap, is weaning him, sharing her food. She dips the tip of her little finger in the confection and offers it to Theo. He sucks, turns to gaze at everybody.

Her heart tumbles.

'Would you like to go out on a boat to the islands?' the captain suggests.

'Yes!' Jacob and Anton chorus.

'Yes please,' Nadia corrects.

'Yes please.'

'How many are there?' Jacob asks.

'Nine,' the captain says, 'but only four are inhabited. We'd better make a day of it, hadn't we?'

They board the ferry at Galata Bridge. The captain has exchanged his uniform for a beige suit and wide-brimmed straw hat. Jacob and Anton stand with him at the rail, opposite big ships. 'That's the Union Jack,' he points. 'And this is the French tricolour.'

She looks at the vessel, grey and uninteresting. Might it be the one to carry the family to a new life?

The captain tells the boys about Io who, according to Greek legend, swam the Bosphorus as a cow. 'Which is why, in Greek, it is the Ford of the Cow.'

Jacob's eyes never leave the captain's face.

The boat steams into the glittering expanse of the Marmara, plays of light between receding domes and minarets on the skyline until they disappear through a veil of heat. Dolphins frisk in milky blueness. Strung out along the misty Anatolian coast, cliffs dropping into the sea, the islands sit squat and whale-backed.

'Local people call them 'red' because of their rocks' tinge,' the captain explains. 'Deposed or disgraced members of the imperial family used to be exiled there.'

'What does that mean?' Jacob wants to know.

The captain answers; Jacob considers.

The ferry takes them to Buyuk Ada, the Great Island also known as Prinkipo, the largest of the nine. They wander past old houses, grand but pretty in pastel colours; among olive-trees, spring sun filtering onto winter faces. Wind sighs through pine-groves; needles lattice the ground; the smell – and that of thyme, bracing, pungent – infuses every breath. Nadia and the captain walk together with the grace and ease of two people used to each other. Anton is alongside his mother.

Jacob picks up a pine-cone, prods the ends. He keeps it, runs to catch up.

The captain puts a hand on Jacob's shoulder. 'Look,' he whispers.

A large, slim, long-tailed, sooty-brown bird has perched on a branch. 'A falcon,' the captain murmurs. 'Eleonora's falcon.'

With a shriek – *kak-kak* – the creature soars.

They find a wooden seat above a sandy bay. Nadia unpacks the picnic-hamper the captain has brought.

Jacob and Anton sit cross-legged. 'Captain Boileau knows a lot of things,' Jacob observes, breaking off a piece of bread. 'It's better than school.'

She shares a hard-boiled egg with Anahid and Theo.

'We had a lesson about Eleonora's falcon,' Anahid recalls, 'named after the queen who granted protection to their nests. I never thought I'd see one. We were too far east.'

'You were lucky with your teacher,' Jacob comments.

Anahid gestures towards the water. 'And we learnt of Leander, who swam across the Dardanelles every night to meet his love, Hero.'

'Ughh!' Jacob responds.

Except for a few, like Papa and Nadia, such devotion does not endure. She gazes at the Marmara, malachite where it touches shallows at the foot of the cliffs, blue as a lapis pavement to the land on the horizon.

Theo battens onto Anton, pulls himself to his feet.

Jacob crawls, turns. He sits back on his heels, leans forward, slaps his knees. 'Come on, Theo.'

Everybody stops talking. Anton holds Theo's hand. Theo takes several steps and, when Anton eases away, continues alone into Jacob's outstretched arms.

'Well done! Bravo, Theo!'

Anton kneels; Theo totters to him, returns to Jacob.

She crouches, calls, 'Theo.'

Jacob manoeuvres him to face her. 'Go to Mama Esther.'

He wobbles to her, and she clasps him – warm, padded, smelling of sea and pine-scented breeze – clings to his babyhood, his dependence on her. He wriggles from her, and she watches him toddle to Anahid.

'I wonder if she ever thinks of Papa?'

Anahid is peeling potatoes. 'I'm sure she does.'

'Why?'

'Because they had years together and two children. One does not cut off such an important part of life.' Without glancing up, Anahid adds, 'What will you do if she marries him?'

'You mean he'll propose to her?'

'They're both alone. They enjoy each other's company. The boys like him.'

'But ... love? And if that is her feeling, what about Papa?'

Anahid shakes her head. 'Oh, Esther. Love has many forms.'

'It isn't so much what will *I* do as what will *we* do? You, me, Theo.'

'I shall expect to find you asleep,' Nadia tells Jacob and Anton as they go along to their room. Nadia closes the door and sits at the table; she picks up some socks to darn, spends time threading the needle. It is Sunday evening, a week after the excursion to the islands.

Nadia looks across at her and Anahid. 'Philippe has asked me to marry him. I have accepted.'

She passes her tongue over dry lips. She must say something. 'I'm glad you're happy.'

Nadia smiles. Her eyes are eloquent; dark ones Papa must have fallen for in Paris. 'He is a good, kind man, and I have become very fond of him. I believe we can be content together. We shall have an embassy apartment. Philippe thinks the Turkish war will finish soon, when he will probably have to return to France; his parents live in the south, although he has a sister in Paris. Constantinople may not be for foreigners. It will belong to Turks, the reason they've been fighting. If you want to stay with us, Esther, you are welcome. But you may have your own ideas.'

Her heart thuds; words chase each other from her mouth. 'Do you think of Papa?'

'Every day. He was my first love. There is something special about that; there can only ever be one. But there are different sorts of feeling, Esther. Nobody can take from me what I had with your father. He, too, remember, lost his first *adorée*, your mother. Philippe is in the same situation. Those who are left can rediscover happiness.'

'My future is with the piano, Anahid. I'm better with just you and Theo.'

Anahid is stitching a green jacket for Theo. 'It is not right that Kemal should find you gone. Love is eternal, Esther. If *Baba* and my brothers have not perished, they are perhaps in Syria, Palestine, Lebanon, the republic of Armenia, or further afield.' With her teeth, Anahid severs cotton. 'Seven years we have been separated. Yet, if I knew where they were, I would go now. Immediately.'

'And abandon me?'

'You could come with me. It is the difference between choosing people or things.'

'It's a chance I can't miss. Paris. My old teacher may still be there. And *dyadia* Pavel in the boulevard Malesherbes. He can give me her address. Kemal can never be part of that. I have chosen you and Theo instead of him; you preferred me and my family – whom you hadn't met – to Mirza Khan, and disappeared without a word.'

'Won't you tell Kemal's mother and sister?'

She shakes her head.

'I would say, Esther, that when you let your feelings for him die, a fraction of you did, too.'

PART THREE

I will start over again, and change my life's pattern,
Will put my naiveté to shame.
   Yevgeny Yevtushenko – *The Snow Will Begin Again*

For centuries the Turks have always walked from the East in the direction of the West.
                                        Mustafa Kemal Atatürk

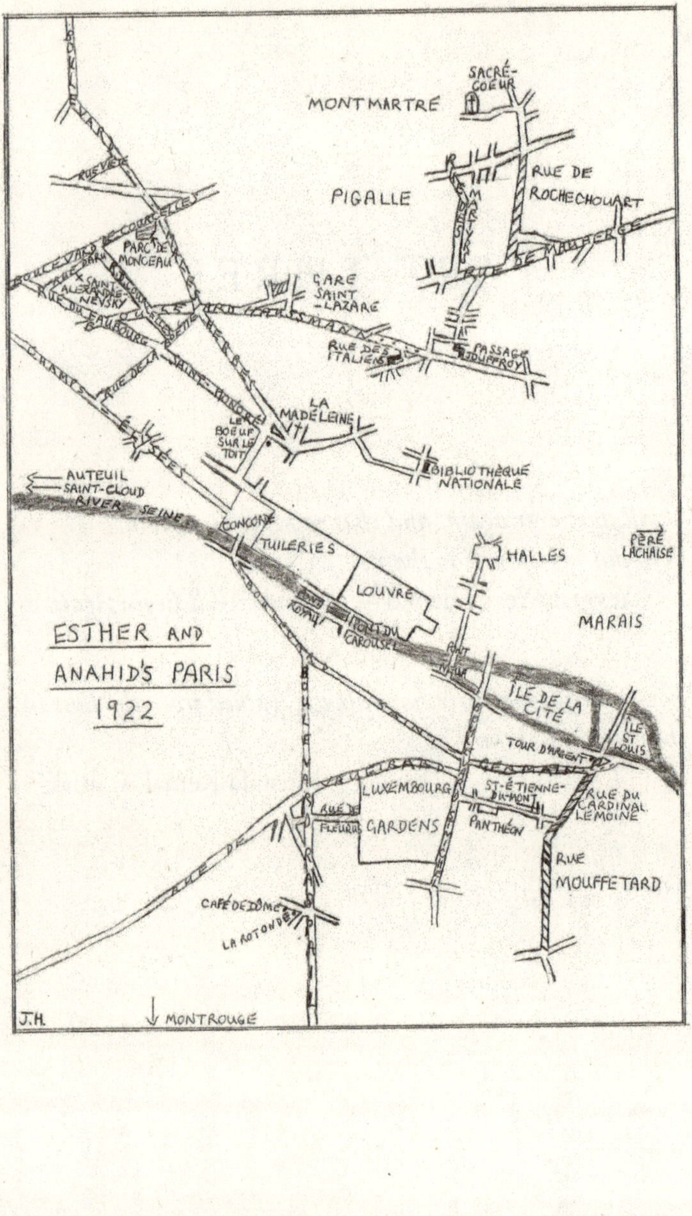
SACRÉ-COEUR
MONTMARTRE
PIGALLE
RUE DE ROCHECHOUART
PARC DE MONCEAU
SAINT-ALEXANDRE-NEVSKY
GARE SAINT-LAZARE
RUE DES ITALIENS
PASSAGE JOUFFROY
LA MADELEINE
LE BOEUF SUR LE TOIT
BIBLIOTHÈQUE NATIONALE
AUTEUIL
SAINT-CLOUD
RIVER SEINE
CONCORDE
TUILERIES
LOUVRE
HALLES
PÈRE LACHAISE
MARAIS
PONT ROYAL
PONT DU CAROUSEL
PONT NEUF
ÎLE DE LA CITÉ
ÎLE ST LOUIS
TOUR D'ARGENT
ESTHER AND ANAHID'S PARIS 1922
LUXEMBOURG GARDENS
ST-ÉTIENNE-DU-MONT
PANTHÉON
RUE DU CARDINAL LEMOINE
RUE DE FLEURUS
RUE MOUFFETARD
CAFÉ DE DÔME
LA ROTONDE
J.H.
MONTROUGE

TWENTY-SEVEN

Paris, June 1922

Liliane Boileau is gracious, she decides; chattering, gesticulating, rather than silence be construed as annoyance at being disturbed in the late afternoon.

'... of course, how foolish of me ... dear Philippe wrote ... he was getting married again ... how lovely ... so lonely for him to be widowed at thirty-four ... men don't like to be alone, do they? ... where did I put the letter? Oh, you are in the way, Delphine.'

Delphine? Ah, a typewriter under its leather cover at the end of a mahogany table.

'Delphine's very useful but she does take up space.' Liliane pats the machine, riffles through, re-arranges, piles of papers, concedes defeat with, 'You can tell me all about yourselves. You must think of this as your home and stay as long as you wish.'

She looks at the room of this woman who has made her own life. A piano! A gas lamp is fixed above it, and a painting of a narrow, cobbled street. Excitement flutters: how soon can she play? Leave it till the morning: she is weary and doesn't want the disappointment of an untuned instrument like in Teheran or the one Kemal's father bought.

Oriental carpets conceal most of the floor; lace curtains and crimson velvet drapes hang at the two windows. On the walls are portraits, landscapes. Canvases are stacked in a corner near a cast-iron stove. Chairs are scattered: upholstered, embroidered, spindly legged, some with wooden arms. There is a smell of lavender, coffee, contentment. *I could live here.* She imagines fifteen, twenty years ahead: she and Anahid will be Liliane's age now, and Theo a young man.

In appearance, Liliane makes little concession to style or the expectations of others: Philippe's height; not fat or thin but solid, imposing. Her face is strong, a few wrinkles around the mouth, every muscle in use when she speaks. Thick, springy dark hair is pinned up. She has on an orange homespun blouse, and a skirt the same colour which reaches almost to her ankles, below which peep black stockings and flat cloth sandals. Round her neck are beige wooden beads.

Liliane indicates a man who has just arrived in the doorway. 'This is Antoine.'

After standing still for a moment, he comes in as though each part of him has grown used to moving independently of the rest. He has unruly raven curls, and a scarf thrown across his shoulders.

'Madame,' he greets her first, with a handshake and bow. Coal eyes linger, appraise, as if dragged from one focus of interest to the next.

Anahid is holding Theo. They are dressed in blue.

Antoine pats Theo's head. 'Isn't he beautiful! Both of them. Madonna and child.'

'He'll be wanting to paint you,' Liliane says to Anahid. Liliane touches Antoine's arm, a delicate, tender, gesture. 'Let them settle in, Tou-tou. They've come all the way from Constantinople by train.'

Upstairs is a bathroom. Cold brown water trickles into the basin; she cups it in her hands, splashes her face and Theo's. After four days rattling through Europe and years of no taps, this is luxury.

In Liliane's guest-room, she opens the leather suitcase bought from the allowance Philippe gave her and Anahid. It contains their few clothes – they wear their wedding ones – Anahid's bits of material saved in Constantinople, and the chipped tin soldiers. Theo can have them now, Jacob said, grown-up in new knickerbockers and shirt, but there were tears in his eyes when he hugged her goodbye.

'Esther, the bed's not big enough for us and Theo,' Anahid remarks.

The cover is riotous shades of red and yellow matching the wallpaper. 'We'll take it in turns to sleep with him. Liliane can give us extra bedding.' She regards the floorboards; sun shafts onto them and a rug of flowers and birds entwined on an ivory background.

The mahogany chest has eight drawers. She opens the deep top one, releasing a whiff of perfume. She places Papa's leather pouch of sand *dedushka* dug from the oilfield; you have it, Esther, was all Nadia said on the wedding morning.

She wonders what happened to the land deed Papa had with him when they left Baku.

'What is Tou-tou?' Anahid asks. 'She called him Tou-tou.'

'A diminutive?' She is holding her Nansen passport, available to Russian and Armenian exiles; Philippe obtained it for her, and another for Anahid and Theo. It is stamped with a profile of Doctor Nansen – the League of Nations high commissioner for refugees – and the words *Société des Nations*. The world's nations are to consider themselves a family. No more fighting or war. 'We shan't need these again.' She leaves hers next to her tiny piece of Baku, and her hat, almond-green, close-fitting.

She shuts the drawer, lion's-head handles rattling.

'She reminds me of an Anatolian peasant, capable-looking,' Anahid comments. 'Should we change? Keep these for best?'

'Best?' she echoes. 'What is better than this? We are going to have tea with Liliane. We are in Paris.' She smoothes the skirt of her dark-green satin dress which stops a hand's-width above her ankles. There is a panel of pleats back and front. The neck is square; sleeves finish between shoulder and elbow. It is the most revealing thing she has ever worn and makes her feel she belongs in Europe.

She glances round. 'Where's Theo?' She darts out. The unvarnished door to Liliane's bedroom is closed. She clatters down the wooden staircase. 'Theo?' she calls. She enters the living-room. He is stroking a Siamese cat which is reclining on the carpet, head on paws, purring.

'He's with Claude,' Liliane says.

Liliane indicates they should sit at the table; she pours pale liquid from a brass pot. *Thé à l'anglaise.* There is a sense of occasion in her voice.

Antoine lounges on a chair pushed back, stirs his tea in both directions, for something to do, she decides, as he refused sugar. He passes a plate of galettes; eyes move along the women opposite him, and Theo on Anahid's lap, while Liliane fills the silence.

'And how is my little brother?'

'Philippe? He is well.' She tells Liliane about the wedding at the French Embassy in Constantinople and the meal at the Pera Palas Hotel. 'He and Nadia, and the boys, are having a holiday by the Bosphorus, where the embassy has summer quarters. Philippe's hired a car.'

'He was still at school when I first came to Paris,' Liliane recalls. 'I was a student at the École des Beaux Arts, copying masterpieces in the Louvre.'

She gestures around the paintings on the walls. 'Are these yours?'

Liliane smiles; a laugh escapes. 'You are too kind, Esther. A few. In the furthest corners. But most of my time now is spent discovering those who have far more talent than I, and making their work available to anyone who would possess it.' With her eyes, Liliane seeks Antoine's until they meet and hold hers. 'I found Antoine,' she says. 'Didn't I, Tou-tou?'

Downstairs next morning, in an aroma of coffee, she hears Liliane pottering about the stone-flagged kitchen across the passage. In the living-room, Claude sits on the windowsill in the sun, looks out at the courtyard, from where comes the thwack of the concierge beating rugs.

She lifts the piano lid, touches some white keys. The sound is good. She tries a few scales, relaxes into the warmth of relief.

Liliane appears and after greeting her asks, 'You play?'

'Yes.'

'Go ahead. It doesn't have much use these days.'

She practises arpeggios. Her body sways as her hands move along the keyboard. She starts a Chopin mazurka. When Anahid and Theo arrive, she stops.

Liliane offers them warm rolls and a dish of green-gold jam. 'Mirabelle. It's a bumper year. You can help me make some more.'

'Antoine left early?' she asks.

Liliane allows a laugh. 'Or late, depending how you look at it. Not long after you retired, in fact. He does not live here but is welcome, as are all my protégés. You will find I keep open house. Antoine I picked up out of the gutter, dead drunk. He had barged into an exhibition I had organised, carrying an armful of pastels, etchings, drawings. The gallery owner chased him out, but I could see the work was brilliant.'

Liliane stands up, pulls a couple of canvases from those near the stove; street scenes: cobbles, shopfronts, a church in the background. 'People know these places,' Liliane says, 'feel comfortable with them, can relate to them, not like the weird, childlike, dream-stuff of the Fauves and Cubists.'

Liliane sits down. 'He set up a stall under the archway outside the gallery, with a sign: *Exhibition and Sale of Paintings. Five francs cheaper than you'll pay inside.* He shouted at critics and visitors. I should have ignored him or at least been angry, but when did common sense feature in art, in its widest meaning?'

Liliane's gaze pierces her.

'Instead, I felt sorry for him, gave him my business card, bought one of his watercolours, and took it upon myself to sell others for him at a more interesting price than he was getting. Until then, he'd been hawking his work around when it was hardly dry; he should have had a licence, but shrewd

Montmartre traders – the butcher, junk dealer – would let him use the pavement outside their premises for a cut of the profit, and the rest barely touched his pocket but went straight on absinthe.'

Liliane passes the jam to Anahid; Theo enjoys it from the tip of a spoon and bangs on the table. 'I installed him in a studio in Montmartre. This was last year. He is welcome here any time but knows better than to cross the threshold drunk.'

Liliane offers her another roll. 'You must play again, Esther.'

Anahid tells Liliane about the place at the Petersburg Conservatoire.

Liliane's eyebrows arch. 'We must find a teacher.'

'I'll ask *dyadia* Pavel if Madame Giraud is still in Paris.'

From a bridge, she looks down on an island which ends in a point like a ship's bow. Men sit fishing with long, jointed, wooden poles. The water flows fast, surface pushing before swelling smooth against log-driven piles. In a park at the edge of the river, people walk in the shade of spreading chestnut-trees. You could spend a whole morning standing, watching. Nobody pays you any attention.

She wears her wedding clothes and is on her way back from the bank in the ninth arrondissement, where Papa kept an account during that visit in 1906.

In the cavernous, wood-panelled interior, she presented a letter written by Nadia requesting the account be closed; don't give the impression of being desperate, she remembered Nadia saying in Teheran. She held her head up. The cashier, wing collar protruding into a skinny neck, recalled Papa: there was the felicitous occasion of his marriage, was there not, madame?

Over the gulf of sixteen years, the cashier peered at her with rheumy eyes. A glow of happiness spread through her that Papa should not have been forgotten. She emerged with five hundred francs; not worth as much as before the war but, when you had been living from day to day, it seemed a lot.

She purchased notepaper and envelopes from a stall by the Seine, where there were books in English for sale. She also bought cream cakes in a box wrapped with red ribbon.

On the bridge, she closes her eyes, breathes tranquillity after the noise and bustle of the Bosphorus and Constantinople. She lifts her face to the sun, draws in its warmth, a different heat from the stranglehold she has been used to.

She has borrowed Liliane's bicycle; just let it take you, Liliane said; you'll soon get the idea. She remounts. The pleats in her dress fan out. She tucks them under her thighs, cycles in a straight line until the Luxembourg Gardens. Past the palace at the entrance, she wheels the bicycle through an avenue of chestnut-trees along a recently watered gravel path. Children play – Theo will – only these are supervised by nurses who know each other and sit on iron benches or chairs. In the branches, woodpigeons chatter, too.

A woman pushes a squeaking perambulator towards her: Anahid, wearing clothes she made in Constantinople, and the blue wide-brimmed wedding hat. Theo is on faded green upholstery, legs covered by a blanket the same colour. Liliane was taking Anahid and Theo to see what they could find for him.

'She's very kind,' Anahid says, 'but we can't continue accepting her charity.'

'I don't think she regards it like that. We're family, connected to her brother.'

'You may be. How did you go on at the bank?'
She explains.
Anahid frowns at the parcel from the patisserie. 'We must save, Esther. One of us must look for a job.'

Two letters: half a page to Nadia and Philippe; the second has less distance to travel – a few kilometres the other side the river – but requires more thought. Her memories of *dyadia* Pavel are the butterflies, lofty rooms, and muslin-shrouded windows of the apartment on the boulevard Malesherbes; the housekeeper, always in black, iron-grey hair scraped into a coil at the nape of the neck.

She writes on the envelope:
Monsieur Pavel Markovitch,
Bd Malesherbes

She can't remember the house number; neither could Nadia. She puts her name and Liliane's address on the back.

A couple of days later, it returns. The number 123 has been scrawled on the front and, underneath, *décédé.*

TWENTY-EIGHT

Angora, summer 1922

He stands by the window, inhales from a cigarette, looks out at the sun-baked lane winding up to the wall which marks the boundary of the ghazi's garden. Mud-brick dwellings huddle lattice to lattice and roof upon thatched roof in afternoon heat.

Again, he has hurt her, has done every time, and he hates himself because it is his fault. A traditional wedding – such as when his brother Yashar married Abla, with days of feasting and dancing, and his sister and other women preparing Ayesha for him, painting her with henna, perfuming her, dressing her in beautiful clothes, the wives whispering in her ear – would perhaps have made a difference. These matters are important to girls. But not to Esther, a voice reminds him, and he thinks of easing a worn, faded blouse off exquisite shoulders in pine-woods, Esther reaching for him, the joy of their first coupling.

He pushes Esther from his mind. Ayesha is his and she is not happy.

Come to Angora with me, he begged all those weeks ago in Constantinople. We'll be wed before sunset. We'll be together. He saw in her eyes what he took to be love, battling shock, apprehension. He could not return to Angora without a wife, and the only way to forget Esther was to replace her.

And so they left, embracing Halidé and *An-ne*, who wept. The boatman was waiting for him, Stamboul a dead silhouette looming above the Golden Horn, the lights of Pera beckoning like a siren. Late into the night, they stepped onto Anatolian soil, far enough along the Black Sea to be away from Greek lines. They stayed in a low-ceilinged cottage, a safe house he had used before; there, under a crimson marriage-quilt retrieved from a chest, they consummated their union, his hand over her mouth to stifle her cries as he forced into this sheltered, unprepared girl two years of yearning for Esther. He should have waited till they were in Angora and had had time to get to know each other.

He stubs out what remains of the cigarette in a brass dish and returns to the bed. He sits at the bottom. Ayesha lies on her side. She has tucked under herself the hair he loosened and ran his fingers through. One of her veils covers her face. She wears a white cotton gown, hand-stitched in blue around the collar. If she would only peel it off – even encourage him to – open her arms to him if not her legs.

'Ayesha.' He tries to keep irritation out of his voice. 'Ayesha, look at me.'

She does as he says until her gaze flickers above the muslin to another part of the room.

'Ayesha, what is this? No woman is modest in front of her husband.' He restrains himself from leaping up and tearing the material away. Or perhaps he should, and have her again, and again; eventually, she will accept his feel, that this is the married way, instead of a body tensing beneath him, fingernails digging into his flesh. In Constantinople, there could be a child, a second, a third, the unpromising start forgotten in the intimacy of family life.

Ayesha allows the gauze to slip. He pulls it from her. She does not move. He senses a shrinking from him in her mind. Her cheeks and eyelids are puffed after crying. There is fear in her expression, like that of a trapped animal.

'Ayesha, you are still not happy.'

'I am your wife.'

'But I want you to be glad.'

'Was *she*?'

'We will not talk about Esther. She belongs to the past. She is not mine. You are, and we have our future.' The words sound empty as Esther's embraces invade him, coil round his neck, soft lips on his, time upon time, and in the moments between, lying skin to skin ... *moya dusha*.

In the lull before the final campaign against the Greeks, the ghazi has established as near-normal life as conditions allow, with little furniture and intermittent electricity; he has already invited the lovebirds, as he referred to them: she can play the piano, Kemal, enliven our evenings.

It is some while since she touched a piano, ghazi. I fear she is fatigued by the journey, he apologised.

The ghazi regarded him.

It is the custom not to enquire about a man's wife. On

another occasion, he volunteered to the ghazi: she has a chill. A few days later: I hope, perhaps tomorrow, she will be well enough to walk from the house.

You enjoy her maiden's bloom before showing her to us, eh?

A ripple of amusement from those who heard, sufficient for the ghazi to feel his riposte was appreciated, yet without upsetting the new husband.

The ghazi, a glass of raki between slender fingers, slapped him on the back. So; a game of billiards, I think, Kemal.

'I cannot continue to make excuses for you to the ghazi,' he says to Ayesha.

'And I cannot go into the stinking street to meet women with uncovered hair and faces, and men looking at me.' She has refused to see the wives who have called.

'Soon, I shall have to leave for the Front.' Abandoning her here. It's madness. Even Madame Fernande Bertrand has returned to France. 'Do you want me to take you home? I will come to you after the battle.'

Relief edges into her eyes. She nods, voice no more than a whisper, 'Yes.'

TWENTY-NINE

Paris, summer 1922

Theo cries, piercing the night, face as red as his sore gums. She turns in bed and cuddles him.

Anahid gets up from the floor, 'Ssh,' and gives Theo her little finger to gnaw.

'He is not settled, *le petit*,' Liliane observes in the morning as she pours coffee. 'There must be something we can do for him.' She shrugs. 'I know nothing of babies.'

'It'll pass,' Anahid says.

When Liliane has gone out, Anahid insists, 'We ought to find somewhere else to live, Esther. It isn't right she should be disturbed.'

'You just said it won't last.'

'You could still play the piano here.'

She practises when Liliane is out and Anahid shopping; Liliane entrusts Anahid with a few francs, having learnt they will not all be spent. Chopin preludes, études, polkas, mazurkas, Beethoven and Mozart sonatas, bring joy to her soul, despite no teacher, money, music, nor prospect of them.

On her return, Liliane might stand in the doorway, watching, removing her straw hat decorated with flowers and fruit: I heard you from the street, Esther; you must meet Pascal; he calls in for tea sometimes.

With Liliane, things happen not by planning or invitation but of their own volition, particularly her teas. They come and they go! Liliane exclaims; and this one I don't see again because he has found a job waiting at table, or that one is away for some while as she's needed at home to care for *maman*.

There might be two or three days with nobody in the afternoon. At other times, she and Anahid arrive from pushing Theo in the perambulator in the Luxembourg Gardens, and half a dozen people are talking at once: long-haired men; crop-haired women in skirts way above their ankles, and short socks or uncovered legs.

When Antoine is there, he sketches, suddenly shouts: don't move! Everybody stares at him, conversation suspended, and he laughs at their not knowing who he means.

'Antoine has asked me to sit for him,' Anahid reveals as they stroll in the gardens and nod the time of day to nurses with their charges.

'And will you?'

'Yes. He'll pay me. I'm to go to his studio.'

'I'm surprised he hasn't already drawn you at teatime.'

'He does that to amuse himself, he says, if he's bored.'

'He doesn't have to be there, surely?'

She finds Liliane's teas exhausting, everyone expounding on different subjects, and the Parisian accent still strange compared with the modulated Russianness of the French she spoke with her family. She misses Jacob and Anton more than she thought possible. Even now, she thinks: I must tell Jacob … remind Anton …

Anahid appears unbothered by the chatter; if she doesn't understand or has nothing to contribute, will smile or fix a wistful gaze at the wall, or occupy herself with Theo, speaking to him in Armenian.

She and Anahid are never questioned about their families or what happened. Many of Liliane's friends are too young to have fought in the war. The few who did may have no obvious physical wound but seem old beyond their years. She feels they look at her without seeing her, with eyes that have observed too much, things no human being should have to witness. She recalls Philippe's *j'ai fait Verdun*, in which must have been trapped memories he would carry for the rest of his life.

'*Elle est juive,*' she understood once, concerning herself.

Somebody countered, 'It doesn't matter … the Jews, it's not a problem.'

'Dreyfus,' another added, and there followed a long discussion, everybody with an opinion, which meant little to her.

'Who is Dreyfus?' she asked Liliane when they'd gone.

'An army officer. There was some scandal in the 1890s, and a trial. He was imprisoned for spying; falsely, it was found much later. He was rehabilitated.' Liliane said as an afterthought, 'He was a Jew.'

She leaves Anahid and Theo in the gardens, turns along the path to the rue de Fleurus; Babette, Liliane's battered Model T Ford, is parked in her usual spot towards the end. She recalls the Model Ts that final summer in Baku: the British gave them to the *bolsheviki* in exchange for petrol.

Prim, shuttered, tall stone houses line both sides of this short, narrow street. Who lives in them? she wonders. What do they do and where do they go each day?

She steps through the outer doorway; the concierge will be having a siesta. She crosses the courtyard and lets herself into Liliane's passage. No sound of voices. A good afternoon for piano practice, unless Liliane is working on the catalogue of the Austrian painter Schiele, who died a few years ago.

She opens the living-room door. Stands still. On the floor, eyes closed in rapture, Liliane lies naked. Splayed legs are drawn up at the knees – large, those of a peasant – and in the ample space between, Antoine, with the beauty, symmetry, perfection, of a Michelangelo sculpture, moves in a rhythm that is theirs alone.

She permits them their privacy, leans against a wall, heart pounding, cheeks and neck burning, blouse sticking to her back; around her belly and thighs ... this is what shocks her most, her arousal, not that Liliane and Antoine – of an age to be mother and son – are lovers, that it is the afternoon, the door is unlocked, they aren't in the bedroom, but remembering Kemal when she lay as Liliane does now. The recollection attacks her, demands an answer, and for a moment the weight of wanting is too much to bear; forget what he is fighting for, what he may or may not have done, just the feel of him, his shape, skin on mine.

If I'm confronted with others' desire, will I always be reminded of him?

Minutes pass. In the living-room, murmurs gather volume. She regains the courtyard, into the street, along to the gardens.

Is my solution to discount love, replace Kemal, find another man to cause gasps and cries of joy?

Anahid is pushing the squeaking perambulator towards her. 'What's the matter?'

'We'd better walk for a while.' She tells Anahid what she saw.

'That is their business. Not ours. We will prepare tea in the kitchen. I've found juicy cakes and saved Liliane some centimes.' Anahid pats the parcel in the corner of the perambulator; there is a patisserie in the place de l'Odeon, beyond the gardens. 'Liliane and Antoine will hear us and finish. And the day will continue. Even Antoine can't keep at it the whole afternoon.'

She bites her lower lip at this harem-talk.

Whenever she returns, she will wonder what she is going to see. Anahid is right: they must live elsewhere. One of them will have to work. It is not good for Theo to be in this environment.

'Esther, I'm to earn some money!' exclaims Anahid.

'You already do.' Several mornings, Anahid has borrowed Liliane's bicycle and cycled to Antoine's studio the other side the river. He pays her five francs to sit for him for an hour. Anahid gives a couple to Liliane and puts the rest in a purse under the mattress.

'Antoine's nearly completed the picture. I don't suppose he'll want me after that. I can make ten francs as a figurante in a film. Somebody he knows is looking for extras. I just have to stand around being decorative. I'm to report at seven o'clock on Monday with a ball-dress and long white gloves. Do you think Liliane might have something?'

Liliane brings gowns from a chest in the cellar. 'When I was a student. How grand we thought we were. Will ivory gloves do?'

The faint perfume of lavender opens as Anahid tries them on. 'Yes, with this.' Anahid holds pale-pink taffeta the length of herself. 'Would you mind if I cut back the shoulders?'

'Go ahead,' Liliane encourages. 'It's lain there for twenty-five years and is likely to for another twenty-five. I should have some thread somewhere.'

Anahid works until the garment is to her satisfaction. 'Ten francs,' she says and twirls in front of them.

For three days, Anahid spends hours in the dress; waltzes, waits, takes the floor again. '… with Anatole, Eugène, François … we'll probably only be on screen for about two minutes.'

Anahid is offered fifteen francs to dance a minuet. 'So, of course, I said yes. Fifteen francs, Esther!'

'Can you do a minuet?'

'I can now. They put me in an eighteenth-century costume, and a tall, powdered wig with a couple of enormous ostrich-feathers on top. It was hot and heavy, and everybody became cross. There's a shop off the Champs-Elysées, one of the girls mentioned, where they make the clothes. I'll call there tomorrow. I could sew for them.' Anahid picks up Theo and carries him round in waltz time. 'Paris is a wonderful city, Esther! You can go anywhere, speak to anybody, do anything!'

Claude is incapable of inelegant movement; an aloof, imperial creature. He passes much of his day stretched out on a window ledge. He allows Theo to stroke and prattle to him; when he tires of this, he rouses himself, sways elsewhere. One morning, Theo catches up with him and grasps his tail. A growl escapes Claude's Siamese throat.

'Theo, leave him,' she cautions from the piano.

He ignores her and attempts to restrain Claude by the back of his neck. Claude whirls with a nimbleness not shown before and scratches him.

He is crying on her lap, little soothed by biscuits and caresses, a trail of red pricks puncturing his arm, when Liliane comes in.

'Claude's getting old,' Liliane declares. 'I've had him I can't remember how long. He's no use any more, never brings a victim to the door. What's the point of a cat that doesn't mouse?' Liliane shrugs as if irritated by her own softness. 'But I keep him. He's a dear. What can I do? Where would be his home otherwise?'

Later, in their room, she tells Anahid about Claude; Anahid has started working at the dress-shop, La Topaze, in the afternoons and goes straight there from Antoine – who still wants her to sit for him – as it is the same side of the river. 'Liliane wasn't in the least concerned for Theo.'

Anahid settles in bed beside him. 'We must walk the streets until we find somewhere to live.'

She crosses the courtyard and hears music she doesn't know, meandering, not very tuneful.

'Ah!' Liliane greets her.

Liliane is in an oriental peignoir patterned in lapis lazuli and coral. Antoine is bare to the waist.

A young man turns from the piano and stands up.

'This is Pascal,' Liliane says, 'a student at the conservatoire.'

He offers a limp, clammy handshake. She breathes in unwashed body. Blond waves just touch his collar. His eyes are violet, skin smooth. Beautiful, rather than handsome. Envy bolts through her that he should be at the conservatoire.

'Tea,' Liliane decides, 'and Esther can play for us.'

Antoine puts on his shirt, rescued from a chair. He doesn't fasten it, airing whorls of dark hair across his breastbone.

She looks elsewhere, meets Pascal's glance. 'Russia,' he says. 'Igor Stravinsky is in Paris.'

She tells him about her conservatoire place. Liliane brings in a tray. They sit at the table.

She takes Theo on her lap.

'Entry to the conservatoire here is difficult,' Pascal explains. 'By competitive exam. There are bursaries but …' He shrugs. 'You know Monsieur Debussy, Monsieur Ravel?'

'No.'

Pascal smiles. His teeth are very white and even. 'There is a move now, Monsieur Debussy began, and Monsieur Ravel and Monsieur Satie are among the vanguard, away from the romantic, an experiment with new forms. Monsieur Ravel has been much influenced by Gershwin, the American.' He leaps up and embarks on more of the music she heard from the courtyard.

He stops. 'Mozart would have expressed it this way.' He repeats the bars but in strict time. 'And Beethoven, in his later years,' the same, in variation, tune still discernible but in the left hand. 'So you see, it is a logical progression. To push back the boundaries.' He laughs, sounding like a girl. '*Voilà!* Months of study reduced to two or three sentences and a minute's demonstration.'

'So you're saying I'm stuck in the past.'

'I am not.' He stands up, indicates the piano with a theatrical bow.

Her heart hammers against her ribs, that she should perform for a conservatoire student who knows important people. She sits Theo on the floor with the tin soldiers.

Oblivious to the room, Liliane and Antoine, the conversation with Pascal, she plunges into Chopin's étude, the 'revolutionary', that she used to play for Anahid in Teheran. This is her inheritance, the flame she must keep alive, all the more because great Russia that captured Chopin's Warsaw has herself fallen, to *bolshevik* scum.

She finishes, snatches her fingers away as if they have been burnt.

Theo imitates clapping. Liliane and Pascal look at her. Antoine glances up from sketching.

'You have remembered everything.' There is admiration in Pascal's voice.

'I need music. I have to study again the big pieces I learnt in Russia, not commit them to memory the wrong way.'

'Which?'

She holds Theo's hand while the concierge – tired dark eyes sparking with interest and scrutiny – gives Anahid a key. Anahid came to Liliane's an hour ago full of the two rooms she'd found in the rue du Cardinal Lemoine by asking anyone in the street where there was somewhere to rent.

She lags behind Anahid up a winding, splintered staircase so Theo can negotiate each step. She steers him round a one-armed doll and a broken, wooden train. There is an odour of stale garlic, urine, poverty.

Anahid has unlocked a door that was once painted brown. There is a table, a couple of chairs, a stove, gas ring, and the smell of a place closed up for too long. Anahid unfastens narrow shutters. Dust dances in the strip of sunlight between window and floorboards. Beyond, an iron-framed double bed allows enough space for a chest of drawers.

'And the toilet?'

'Along the landing, past the cold tap.'

There, she recoils from the stink of ancient drains. On either side of the aperture is a cement shoe-shape. She thinks of the privacy of Liliane's bathroom and filling the washbasin with water.

She goes back to Anahid.

'I'll make some curtains,' Anahid says. 'And there's a bath-house at the end of the street, by the river.' Anahid stops. 'You don't like it.'

She shrugs. 'It's not what we're used to.'

'But we can't stay there forever, can we? Should we?'

No. Yesterday, Theo climbed onto a chair and played with the typewriter. Next to it was an open book. *Nude on her stomach: gouache and black crayon, 1917* the caption informed her. She flicked over the pages: *Reclining Woman* ... *Lovers* – two women, these ... *The Embrace*; all by Schiele. This morning Theo moved some canvases, placed them as though they were pieces in a board-game, to the left, right, this way, that, talking to himself. You mustn't, she told him; they're not yours. He looked at her as if expecting her to explain. He began to put them back but dropped one. She helped him, hoped they were in the correct order.

Anahid locks up.

It's only minutes to the gardens, she consoles herself, and the rue de Fleurus and the piano.

At the foot of the staircase, they stand aside for an old woman dressed in black, with thick, wrinkled stockings, and flat, worn shoes. Grey hair has loosened from its pins and flops above her collar. The hand which clasps the banister is gnarled, joints swollen, skin around the nails dirt-ingrained.

'*Mesdames*,' the woman mutters through toothless gums yet a flash of gold. Blue eyes rest on Theo, and a light comes into them, like a rekindling; she touches his head, submits to the stairs.

She manoeuvres the perambulator from the doorway, the pavement of the rue du Cardinal Lemoine just wide enough; up past grim, flaking exteriors which reach three and four storeys high, a further one, sometimes two, built into the roof.

At the market of the adjoining rue Mouffetard, she jostles over the cobbles. With an air of detachment and trying not to look as if she has done very little shopping, she feels tomatoes, carrots, turnips. Should they be soft or hard? They are piled in wicker baskets on wooden stools and upturned boxes; hand-written cards announce *1F50* or *1F80 le kilo*. Stallholders bawl them to be the best and fresh.

She watches what other women do, in their faded cotton pinafores. She has the few francs Anahid put in the purse. Determination in her voice, she demands, 'A kilo of tomatoes.' It seems a lot.

Theo beams at everybody including the umbrella man shouting his wares.

'*Bonjour, mon petit*,' people coo over him.

'*C'est un beau bébé*.'

'He's the treasure of *maman*.'

She begins to see the same faces. At her weekly visit to the bath-house, neighbours nod: *Bonjour, madame.*

The old lady they saw that first day pronounces her name Ka-treen. Her husband was killed at Verdun, she confides on the stairs. 'And my son,' *mère* Catherine shrugs, sighs, 'he joined the Foreign Legion.' She pats Theo's head. When he smiles at her, she croons, 'They're adorable when they're young.'

Only then? Unbidden, the photograph of Lev she kept until Erzerum, his dark shoulder-length curls, fixes in her mind; a monster who would violate his sister. She stares, wills *mère* Catherine to say something fond of the lad in the Foreign Legion. Is there ever any news from him?

'If you want me to look after Theo, you simply have to ask.'

'Thank you.'

But she does not wish to leave him with anybody. He is all she has. And she is all he has, she and Anahid, all there is in a cruel world.

Liliane rescues more evening-gowns from the cellar: I shall never wear them, Esther. They've been waiting for somebody like Anahid.

She takes them back to the rue du Cardinal Lemoine one at a time, folded in the perambulator. The outsize leaves of chestnuts in the gardens are crisp, red, golden; those that have not fallen, fragile and defiant in the sunlight of what Liliane always insists might be the last warm day.

Anahid brings bits of velvet, taffeta, and other offcuts from the dress-shop; she puts them in a drawer with the ruined slipper and silk cloth; makes shirts and trousers for Theo, and exclaims, 'He'll be the most brightly dressed child in the quartier, Esther!' She embroiders collars and cuffs as she did in Constantinople, patterns her mother taught her; cuts strips of material, ties some around her hair or winds both together, secures them at the nape of her neck. With perfect hand-stitches, she produces skirts, blouses, close-fitting to achieve the pencil shape that is la mode.

'You're growing thin, Anahid.' The breasts that suckled Theo in Constantinople have shrunk and sagged.

Anahid shrugs and when she has removed pins from between her teeth, replies, 'Nobody has big bosoms these days, Esther. Anyway, Theo is the most important. We can manage without if necessary: if you don't see or smell food, it's easier. Walk in the gardens or into the museum.'

'Is that what you do?'

Anahid laughs. 'I have done. Paintings are even more beautiful when you're hungry. Perhaps the artists did them when they were starving.' She still sits for Antoine in the mornings.

Liliane let her keep her key. She is happiest when Liliane isn't there; just her, Theo, and the piano. A world of wonder where she can close her eyes and escape for hours into the Liszt B minor sonata, which she learnt in Baku. Pascal left her the music.

Theo plays with the tin soldiers. When she finishes one afternoon, he climbs onto her lap. She reaches for him. Chubby arms around her, he prods her nose and mouth. She kisses his fingers, clasps him to her.

Dark curls are on his collar, tumble over his forehead, and make her think of Lev at Theo's age. 'Time to cut your hair,' she says. He looks at her, goes with her to the table, where she rummages in the drawer. Among buttons, old brushes, bits of paper, are some scissors. 'Stay there,' she murmurs to him. Heart thumping, she kneels by him and clips until his babyhood is strewn on the carpet.

The door opens. Liliane exclaims, 'Well! It suits him. He's a real little French boy now.'

'French boy,' beams Theo.

She tidies up and, when Liliane has gone into the kitchen, puts a lock of Theo's waves in her pocket.

Pascal works with her on the final prestissimo of the Liszt, releasing his unwashed odour.

'You're better than me, Esther. I don't practise as much as you.'

'What do you do?' How can somebody at the conservatoire be like that?

'Try different styles. Compose. I don't drive myself as you do.'

'I have to find *exactly*, not my own impression or what I would like it to be, but *precisely* what Liszt intended. Each time, I discover something new. He had the inspiration, wrote it down; we who come after must extract his spirit from the music and reproduce what he wanted. When I perform in public,' she turns the pages with a sharp snap, 'nothing less will do.'

THIRTY

Dumlupinar, western Anatolia, late summer 1922

Although the men have lanterns, his mount picks her way up the hill; he's grateful, for any jolt pains his ribs even after a year. He has lost the gelding that kicked him to the ground: a bullet in the head to relieve it from a broken leg. This mare suits him better. Pack-animals stumble behind. The artillery has already been dragged up.

Stars pit the velvet sky. He looks towards the east. It is as if the night, often friend and protector, is reluctant to leave. For many, Greek and Turk, it will be their last. Not that the Greeks are aware of this: spies report that they were out dancing in Afyon until an hour or so ago. He cannot remember when he danced. Perhaps as a boy of ten at Yashar's wedding. I never shall again.

He watches the sky discard the blanket of darkness. A red glow heralds sunrise above the Anatolian plateau. His heart pounds, and he breathes a plea. He pats the mare's flank, feels her tremble. Instead of a church bell tolling or the wail of the first call to prayer, the artillery barrage's roar thunders down the salient.

THE WEST IN HER EYES

Sometimes, he thinks he imagines it but, no, there in the distance, two weeks later, gleams the Aegean. Rivulets of sweat sting his vision and stick dust to his skin. He glances around: eyes glisten in emaciated faces; horses, equally spectral, force themselves forward.

'... they took my daughters, effendi, threw them from the window ...'

'... killed the beasts, tossed the innards into the well ...'

Shrivelled hands reach out to him, remnants of humanity crouching at the roadside by myrtle-shrubs.

'... used the mosque as a latrine ...'

The voices float behind him, lost in the foulness of unburied bodies, charred flesh, cindered remains of villages and lorries. The retreating Greeks who inflicted these horrors, their last revenge after four days' battle, will have no further to run when they arrive in Smyrna. They will be pushed off Anatolian soil into the sea.

He braces himself for a final effort as they enter Smyrna, scimitars drawn, baggage-camels lumbering at the rear. A lizard scuttles up a whitewashed villa. The horses' iron hooves deafen on the smooth, marble pavement, a wall of men and steel gleaming in the sun or curving like lightning flashes under the bazaars' arches. Exhausted, cracked cries of welcome struggle from thousands of throats as the procession turns past statues, domes, minarets, and latticed mansions to the waterfront.

Pink tamarisks dance; pale asphodels wave, apparitions of flowers, as if they, too, would add their greeting. Along the cliffs spring anemones: rose, mauve, blue. The length of the promenade, scrubby, knotted myrrh-trees stand sentinel above a turquoise Aegean. Smells of rotting plankton and salt waft towards him. This September, no ships line up to take away from the great Levantine port raisins, figs, apricots, and all the bounty of a fertile land. Only British and French men-o'-war wait in the bay to evacuate their people.

A knocking sound drags him from sleep. Rifle-shots? Very near. He sits up on his bed-roll. His legs ache, as do his arms, back, neck. He forces himself to his feet, realises that the banging is an unlatched shutter. The breeze has strengthened, Smyrna's *imbat* come calling.

He hobbles to the window. A cloud of crimson and black smoke tilts, and three lofty pinnacles flecked with bursts of orange, banners in the wind. He pulls on his boots, clatters down the staircase into the street, to shouts, wailing.

Firemen on horseback dig cisterns in search of water while others rush around with buckets. Citizens in nightclothes run from doorways carrying furniture, candelabra, bedding. Cinders and ash rain like a volcano spitting. Palm-trees have been transformed into unsteady, burning beacons in an inky sky which glows with a reddish light that seems to radiate from within. The sea shines flaming copper. Multicoloured furnaces rage, throw up jagged, writhing flares, silhouette Greek church towers, domes of mosques, houses' flat roofs, in some leering premonition of Judgement Day.

The stench of charred wood and flesh clings inside his mouth. He stops by the entrance to an alley to still the ache in his ribs. Latticework has been smashed, doors kicked in, but one remains intact. On it hangs a boy's naked body, arms and legs nailed there, a sticky cavity where the stomach was. Dark wavy hair trails in matted streaks across the child's forehead and down the face. A pink tongue lolls between unblemished baby-teeth.

He leans against the wall, retches, thinks of two Russian lads, Esther's brothers; of a son he and Esther might have had. It is good there wasn't one. This is not a world for children. He vomits again, heaves great sobs until pulled along, staggers with screaming masses towards the waterfront. Turkey, the new republic, is being birthed through the bowels of hell.

THIRTY-ONE

Paris, late 1922

*J**acob and Anton go to the French school,* Nadia writes from Constantinople. *Perhaps when we're in France – which will be soon – we shall be able to find a Russian tutor for them so they do not lose their heritage.*

The Turks' war of independence is over. According to Philippe, Mustafa Kemal – the fiery, nationalist leader we hear so much of – would have continued his struggle in European Turkey and driven the Greeks from Constantinople back through Thrace; that would have meant crossing the Dardanelles, which were still occupied by the French, Italians, and British. So an armistice has been agreed. A commission from Mustafa Kemal's government in Angora has entered Constantinople. The British have given the sultan safe passage to Malta, which was more than they did for our tsar and tsarina.

I cannot believe that after all these years there is finally peace everywhere and we can settle to family life. We shall travel by ship to Marseille, thence by train to Nice where Philippe's parents have a villa, but we shall be in our own home before long.

I will leave space for your brothers.

Jacob has written in French: *Lessons are boring, and the boys say my French sounds funny. The soldiers in the city are not very smart.*

In Russian, Anton has added: *We read about Pushkin, and I had to stand up and explain, and I recited a few lines from* The Tale of the Golden Cockerel, *only I got one or two bits wrong as it was a while since I had said it.*

She folds the sheet of quality stationery. Has Kemal returned to Constantinople and found me gone? Has he even survived? I shan't ever know.

Mama plays the piano, Theo says, and Mamana brings the bread.

And manages the money, for now there is also fuel. She learns that when the stove starts to pop, it needs feeding: twigs bought in clusters; wire-wrapped, split pine the size of a small pencil; half-dried hardwood lengths in bundles. She economises on fuel by piling layers of clothes under her coat. *Mère* Catherine has told her to search out *boulets*, egg-shaped lumps of coal dust.

Ice forms round parapets of bridges. Some cafés have braziers outside, so she lingers on terraces but not too long or waiters stare at her. She buys roasted chestnuts, hazelnuts. She spends time in a bookshop with a big stove, tables, and black and white rugs on wood; each day, she reads a page from Turgenev's *Fathers and Children* in English, old Russian life, the country-estate, tugging at her even though it wasn't her Russia; until the copy isn't there.

With the remaining centimes, she purchases three mandarins in a paper cone one afternoon. The barrow-boy is stamping his feet, and she warms herself at his brazier.

Back home, Anahid looks doubtful. 'We should save.'

'We have to have some treats.'

Anahid relents, puts an arm round her shoulders.

She doesn't tell Anahid that another day she stopped at a corner café adjoining a *grand boulevard* and ordered a *café crème*. She sat at a marble-topped iron table by the whitewashed wall and gazed at gaunt winter trees, and sunlight on a bronze statue of a military man with drawn sword. The coffee was very good. Not until the pink lowering sun did she drink the last of it cold, licking cream-flecks from around her mouth.

Anahid chews the fruit so as to savour it; smiles. Juice trickles over her lip, down her chin; she catches it with her tongue, wipes some from Theo's mouth, gives him her fingertip.

'Mamana,' he chuckles.

Theo's contraction of Mama Ana has passed without comment; she wonders if Anahid has noticed; or that she is simply Mama.

They spit the pips into the fire, throw in the skins and packet, and suck their fingers clean.

This bicycle of Liliane's now knows its way over the Seine and down the grands boulevards' *magnificent avenues of trees to Montmartre. I cross the river at the end of the rue du Cardinal Lemoine – which crowds to the water's edge – and traverse the* île *saint-Louis, which chokes the Seine into channels. Along cobbled quays sit fishermen. Up stone steps, cramped streets are lined with tall, honey-coloured houses, carved doorways, and ivory spring blossom.*

Antoine lives in an impasse *near the new basilica of the Sacré-Coeur. A church just built is strange to me for in Anatolia they went back centuries, frescoes blackened with incense and candle-grease;*

you felt you were part of a long tradition. This Sacré-Coeur's central dome reminds me of Constantinople. I have peeped inside. The atmosphere was peaceful, yet distant as it was many years since I'd been in a place of worship. This made me feel guilty, and I thought of Baba and Mama, and came away.

Antoine's studio is on the second floor, next to a flight of steps at the top of the alley. He has painted the view and others. He likes me to go in the mornings when the room has the sun and light is at its best.

He has done drawings and pastels of me, and an etching. I have become used to him working; to not moving till he gives me a few minutes' rest. He does not talk a lot. He asks if I'm well, and Theo; when I told him we were in the rue du Cardinal Lemoine, he wanted to know, for a while, how things were. Once, I enquired after his mother, remembering she had been sick. He said: she manages. I have yet to witness him drunk as Liliane described. He never mentions her. I wonder how long they have been lovers or whether they still are. An idle curiosity: as I told Esther, it is their business.

I leave the bicycle inside the hallway; no sign of the lad I slip some centimes to keep it safe for me. The odour of stale cooking lingers: garlic and cheap oil. I climb the wooden staircase. Antoine's door is never locked but, as always, I knock, he shouts, 'Yes', and I go in. The smell of paint hangs in the air. Canvases are propped against unpapered walls; he sells most of his work.

'Bonjour, Ana.'

'Bonjour, Antoine.'

He wears the same dark-green stained smock. His footsteps sound on the floorboards as he walks towards me. He shakes my hand.
'Ça va?'

Our usual exchange. I stand, wait for him to say what he wants to do. He lifts the lid of the oak chest which contains fabrics, different shades and textures; he may use them for background. He brings out blue silk, holds it to my shoulder, lets its length ripple to the ground. 'The colour of your eyes.' That rare, lazy smile.

Unease flutters me, or surprise, something in-between, for he hasn't made such a remark before. He drapes the divan and the two footstools with the material. He turns to me. 'I would like you without clothes.'

At the table, he sorts through what he needs among brushes, tubes, bottles, rags, jars of pencils and charcoal; this morning he has found room for a glass of fresh daisies. I pass my tongue over dry lips. Apart from the eunuch, Seyed Ali, only one man has beheld me naked: who paid a lot of money for me, housed me, provided everything for several years, and enjoyed my body. Antoine will give me a few francs. This is art. I must forget the past.

I unbutton my blouse. I sense he is ready and expecting me to be.

'You are cold, Ana?'

'No,' even though the stove in the corner is unlit. I push my camisole-straps off my shoulders, exposing my breasts. I unhook my skirt, step out of my shoes. My cheeks suffuse with a blush, nipples hardening. 'How do you wish me? On the divan?'

'Reclining. With your face towards me.'

I do as he asks, hand resting against my mount of Venus, its dark mass. At a large easel, he works without speaking, absorbed.

I could drift asleep.

'Keep your eyes open, Ana, but looking down.'

I regard this body. For three years, it has not been oiled or perfumed, nothing more than water, a little soap, and now the bath-house once a week. On my legs is less than on a newborn's head; in Teheran, I would have spent a morning removing it.

Antoine moves my left arm to my thigh. He returns to the easel. The softness of his touch stays on my skin, warms it, and my belly.

'You go to the shop this afternoon, Ana?'

'Yes.'

'But you will come again tomorrow?' There is a trace of uncertainty in his voice. Is he afraid I might not?

In Teheran, I grew used to doing a man's bidding, to being confined, restrained. Not to be here hasn't occurred to me. Antoine's hesitation, when previously I was always told what to do — yes, pampered, spoiled, but not given a choice, a decision to make — I find charming. 'I will,' I assure him.

She turns round on the piano-stool, drained. She has played the whole of the Liszt by heart, the bravura of the final prestissimo her best ever.

Pascal shakes his head, whooshes air through his teeth. '*Incroyable.* You have done all this, driven yourself, for an audience of one.'

'I must begin something else. I was to have started the Beethoven concerti at home.'

He grimaces. 'Needs an orchestra. Nobody wants to hear just the solo.' He thinks for a moment. 'What about Schumann, the *Fantasie*? That'll show off your talent. For this is what you must do; meet people.'

For days, we follow the same ritual, and the painting progresses. I regard his bent head, for he spends a while mixing reds, yellows, browns, white, to obtain exactly the right skin shades.

I do not examine what he has achieved at the end of each sitting. I did after the first, but it was splashes of colour, so I shall wait. He does not seek comment before a piece is completed.

'So! You may relax, Ana.'

I already have. He contemplates his work, as a lover might gaze at his beloved from whom he is to be parted. He turns to me. Again, that smile.

'So,' I repeat. 'It is concluded?'

He moves the easel for me to see; walks to the divan, crouches to observe from my level. Nothing has prepared me for the portrait. The details are spare, not in the manner of a photograph. Yet, it is Anahid.

His hand is on my arm, a touch that has become familiar. 'It pleases you?'

I look at him. 'Yes.' My voice is quiet, of one who does not wish to disturb a sleeping infant. The picture is an entity, another being in the room besides ourselves.

He raises my palm to his lips. 'I do perfect work when you are here. There will be more paintings. And better. You are my muse.' Against my face he rests fingers smudged with red and white. His mouth on mine is soft, tentative. 'You're ravishing,' he murmurs between kisses; strokes my breasts, lowers his head to them.

I open my legs, arch myself to him …

… he is sleeping, sated, silk drape creased and damp with our coupling. There will be no lunch today if I am not to be late at the shop. Ingrained in me is all I learnt in Mirza Khan's house: how to please a man, to satisfy without loving.

A tear trickles from the corner of my eye, down my cheek.

'Pascal proposes an evening out with you, Esther,' Liliane says. 'Probably Le Boeuf sur le Toit on Friday. It's near the place de la Concorde. He charged me to tell you.'

She unfastens Theo's coat. 'What an unusual name.'

'A ballet by Cocteau and Milhaud. Cocteau's often there. You might see him. The one time I visited, he was drumming with a negro jazz band.'

'Jazz? What is this?'

'Oh ...' Liliane moves her arms and shoulders up and down in a sort of shrug before laughing. 'Difficult to explain. Black musicians in America do it. I think they make it up as they go along. Ask Pascal. He'll play you some.'

It doesn't sound like somewhere she wants to be. 'Is it a restaurant?'

'More of a club. It only opened last year. It's *the* place: all the best people in Paris, poets, businessmen, publishers; the English Prince of Wales has been once or twice, I hear. Have a few hours off. You deserve a change. They'll love you. Somebody new. You never know who might be there and can help you.'

A pianist? But would such a person frequent that sort of establishment?

Again, the European use of the word love, offered as easily as tea or cake; how can they feel that way towards a stranger?

Anahid could be with Theo; she's always home by then.

We have a property outside Nice, Nadia writes, *a white stone house called the Blue Shutters, at the end of a sandy road, surrounded by oak- and pine-forests. At the back, our lawn is carpeted with hyacinths and bluebells, daffodils, tulips. Every month has its flowers; even December, so mild was the winter. In January, we had jasmine, and fragrant, cascading mimosa which reminded me of acacia in Baku. There are roses everywhere.*

A girl from town comes in most days. Philippe motors the boys to school in Nice each morning, but we may arrange for them to be weekly boarders at the pension. *After so much dislocation, some structure to their lives with others their age is good for them.*

Stay with us, Esther, as soon as you can …

How many hundreds of kilometres? She and Anahid will never have enough money for train fares.

She breathes in, remembers acacia.

'Esther, I found these,' Liliane announces on Friday, offering her an enamelled comb in greens, blues, reds, and a necklace of two or three dozen different-coloured beads. 'Have them if you wish.'

On the kitchen wall is a mirror the size of her face. She puts the comb in the side of her hair, fastens the beads. They give her an exotic appearance. She feels uncomfortable in fripperies. There has been no frivolity for ages.

'They match your clothes,' Liliane comments.

Over her green blouse, she has a multicoloured cotton bolero which Anahid cut from Liliane's ball-gowns. She would have worn her Constantinople outfit. Too formal, Anahid insisted; no-one dresses up these days.

Pascal arrives, much perfumed. He wears brown and beige shoes, a pale suit, and is holding a wide-brimmed hat the same shade.

'Show Esther some jazz,' Liliane suggests.

He plays unusual rhythms, a melancholy melody which pushes at her heart. It is not the way to treat the keyboard.

They walk down the boulevard Raspail, past hotels, impressive façades, and into the boulevard saint-Germain. The evening is warm, air heavy with sweetness of budding chestnuts and lilac. People are strolling, sitting outside cafés and bars. Men and women. She isn't used to this mixing, has never promenaded alongside a young man. Kemal always went ahead of her. In Baku, Sasha came to the house. The freedom she has grown used to, pushing Theo in the perambulator, is now edged with restraint, uncertainty about the next few hours.

Through the plain brown door of Le Boeuf sur le Toit, cigarette-smell hits her; talking, laughing, arguing, singing, dancing. She hears the piano before she sees it, a jerky tune. 'Is that jazz?' she asks Pascal.

'Yes.'

Girls in slim dresses that finish halfway up their legs, hold one another cheek to cheek in the crush between elegant, wrought iron tables. Shadows writhe on walls and ceiling in smoky light. She thinks of Schiele's *Lovers* in Liliane's book. Perhaps these women are together because there are so few men.

'Pascal!' someone calls.

'*Bonsoir, Pascal.*'

'*Ça va, Pascal?*'

He shakes several hands in greeting.

'And Esther!'

'… the Russian Jewess who lodges with Liliane …'

'… they don't live there any more …'

'… moved to the *cinquième*. …'

'… down in the world …'

'... she and the other, the Armenian, Anahid ...'
'... and *le petit* ...'
'... he's adorable ...'
'... she's the mother ...'
'... no, it's Anahid ...'
'... it's Esther, I assure you ...'
'... he goes to both ...'

Across the room, the chatter passes.

'... still see her at Liliane's, for the piano ...'
'... she plays? ...'

She is invisible.

A couple of women do wave to her. '*Bonsoir, Esther.*' They have bobbed hair and no bust, like boys. She returns their greetings.

On the nearest wall is painted a human eye. Writing surrounds it. People are adding contributions.

'*L'Oeil Cacodylate,*' Pascal explains.

'What is it?'

'It's nonsense. Open to everything, anything, nothing.'

It appears to follow her. She shudders.

Pascal finds an unoccupied table with two chairs. She sits down. Not everybody is young and loud. Some men are older and talking, oblivious to the din. She is aware of a stout, snub-nosed, middle-aged man, apple-cheeked as if from the countryside. He has a plate of food in front of him yet wears white gloves; he dabs his capacious forehead with a handkerchief; heavy chin wobbles. She wonders what he is doing here. He is probably thinking the same about her for he is looking at her, adjusting his monocle.

'Do you know who he is?' she asks Pascal.

'Monsieur Diaghilev, the impresario. He must have heard you were Russian. I could introduce you.'

'You are acquainted?'

'We were. I haven't seen him for some time.'

She allows a smile and turns from Monsieur Diaghilev's scrutiny.

Pascal indicates someone else, bearded, with a pince-nez, black suit, and stiff collar; wispy hair has retreated to cling around the base of his head. 'Monsieur Satie. He is an inspiration to my generation, yet nobody appreciates his work. He breaks all the rules and produces exquisite music. If I had a fraction of his talent ... you want vodka?'

She hesitates. 'I don't think so –'

'It can't be true.' Pascal asks people behind, 'Have you met a Russian who doesn't drink vodka? Let me present you one.'

They laugh, adding to her discomfort.

'How about a *fine à l'eau*?' he suggests. 'It's the nearest thing.' He catches a waiter's attention, hand on his arm; long, slim fingers ease along the black sleeve as the young man moves away.

The pianist has arrived at a halt. He stands up to acknowledge cheers, whistles, applause, and gives a mockery of a bow. The noise subsides. Her *fine à l'eau* is brought. She takes a sip of golden liquid. It is bitter, burns her throat, sends a flush to her cheeks. She puts the glass down, hears her name, looks round.

'... you haven't heard her?'

'... she's good ...'

'... Esther'll play for us ...'

No, she won't! Apprehension clutches her stomach. This isn't a serious place. She can't perform here.

'Esther!'

'Come on!'

'Esther!'

She turns to Pascal as if he'll wake her from a nightmare. 'I can't!' she says beneath the clamour.

'Why not?'

'But ... it's not a concert.'

'Doesn't matter. Go on! Not the Liszt. Nothing too long. Something to show you off. To dazzle.'

The Chopin étude. Part of her, embedded in her fingertips.

'Esther!'

'They won't stop till you do,' Pascal warns.

Like children demanding a diversion. She stands up: shut out the short hair and make-up and noise, and that awful eye. Just play.

She winds her way to the piano. People swivel round to her. Conversations cease mid-sentence. The room is quiet.

Imagine they've paid to hear you. Imagine ...

She sits on the stool, rests her hands on her knees for a few seconds. She hurls into the crashing chords of the 'revolutionary'. She isn't here ... she's at her Steinway in Baku ... in Mirza Khan's house with Anahid listening ... at Liliane's ... flying on wings of eagles as she unleashes frenzy from the keys until the passion is spent.

The applause is like a rifle-shot. Claps merge, grow, as if they are rain on a tin roof.

'Bravo!'

'Esther!'

'Encore!'

The whole room takes up the refrain.

She stands, inclines her head in acknowledgement. '*Merci*,' she mouths.

Faces blur as dozens of voices call, 'Encore!'

This is what happens on a concert platform. An encore. She brushes her fingers along the side of her skirt, pretends the worn cotton is silk, the rustle of an evening-dress.

She begins a song by Mikhail Glinka, *The Skylark*, arranged for piano by his protégé Balakirev; it soars above mountains, rivers, oceans, imbued with melancholy. Doctor Bagratuni bought the music in Moscow before the war.

This time, the reaction is more jocular.

'Bravo!'

'Long live Russia!'

Others are talking, scraping chairs back, moving about. Disorientated, she tries to spot Pascal. She has gone a few steps when somebody else starts playing, another clunky tune she supposes must be jazz with a thumping rhythm in the left hand, and singing ridiculous words that sound like 'eat chocolate, drink cow'.

She has to get away, outside in fresh air, free from din and smoke.

'Esther!'

This from behind but she ignores it, pushes her way to the door.

Stops.

A young couple stand chatting to people at the table nearest them. The woman glances around: Anahid, Antoine's arm across her shoulder. Anahid in a yellow skirt cut below the knee, showing long, strong legs.

She grasps Anahid's wrist. 'Where's Theo?'

Anahid starts. A smile is overtaken by eyes glittering in a frown; she releases herself. 'At home, of course. Asleep, as you left him.'

'But –'

'*Mère* Catherine is with him.'

'*Mère* Catherine? In our – ?'

'She's often offered. She adores him. He reminds her of when she had her son.'

Antoine turns to her. 'Bravo, Esther.'

'You were wonderful,' Anahid adds. 'We were in time for the last piece.'

'They've forgotten me already. On to the next thing. You've no right to leave Theo like that. What if something happens to him? Don't you care?'

'You know I do. Calm yourself, Esther. You must have a drink. Where's Pascal?'

'How can you?' Tears blur her vision.

'Esther!' Another voice from behind. She forces her way out.

The air is still warm. She's running. Into the place de la Concorde. Cross the river, cross the river. The words beat a rhythm with her footsteps. The tears overflow. At the club, she entertained, amused for a few minutes; supplied conversation-fodder. She has always wanted to play in public. Now she has. Is this all it's going to be? After hours of hard work? On the bridge, she stops to steady her breath; peeps at placid black water.

She presses on, down the boulevards, uncaring of glances she attracts from strolling couples. What if Theo wakes, calls, realises she and Anahid are not there? The ache pulls at her heart across the place du Panthéon – as ever, ruffled by a breeze – and into her street. Exhaustion enfolds her, slows her feet as she climbs the stairs. The gas-bracket on the wall is so dirt-encrusted it is not completely on.

She lets herself in. *Mère* Catherine is knitting. 'Already, Esther? The night is young, surely.'

'Theo?'

'Asleep.'

He is; in the same position, as Anahid said.

When she finally crawls into bed – *mère* Catherine was in no hurry to leave and revealed socks for Theo in the making – sleep eludes her.

Later, Anahid slips in beside her, smelling of tobacco. 'Pascal was concerned about you. Diaghilev was talking to him. They left together. Diaghilev was in a fur coat.' Anahid giggles. 'He looked like a bear.'

She keeps her back to Anahid.

She is up first in the morning.

Anahid stretches her arms above her head. 'Diaghilev likes young men. Antoine thinks Pascal may have been his lover.'

She grimaces as she fastens her blouse. 'Isn't that against the law?'

'Doesn't mean it doesn't happen.' Anahid gathers Theo, murmuring to him in Armenian.

'Mamana,' Theo gurgles.

'Vera at the shop has mentioned Diaghilev,' Anahid pursues. 'Her husband designs for him; she says he and Diaghilev were, for a while –'

'Anahid!'

'What?'

'Don't talk that way! And in front of Theo, too.'

Anahid hugs and kisses him.

She coils her hair.

Anahid puts Theo on the floor, pushes at the bedcovers, peels off her nightdress. 'No-one would guess you were once married, Esther, all buttoned-up as you are.'

The remark stings, an open razor. How thin Anahid is as she stands up, ribs and hip-bones showing; svelte, she calls it, or gamine, the fashionable shape.

'What were you and Antoine doing there?'

'I wanted to be there in case you played. I knew if I said so you wouldn't go and leave Theo.'

'So you're not just his model.'

'I inspire him to work.'

'In the evening? At that sort of place?'

Anahid hooks her skirt.

'Does he love you?'

'He desires me. Is that the same?' Anahid runs her hands down her bare front and cups sagging breasts. 'Pity about these. Not as much for him as Liliane, but he enjoys them, nevertheless.'

'Does he mention her?'

A clipped 'No. That's their business. I told you before.'

'Do you love him?'

'I'm able to please, satisfy. It's what I was used to, remember.'

She's had enough of this harem-talk. She takes Theo to the toilet. When they return, Anahid has gone.

She dresses Theo in the yellow jacket and trousers Anahid has let out; gives him the last of yesterday's bread softened in water, and eats what he leaves. She puts him in the perambulator, pushes him to the market, hopes to find solace in morning routine. She will not go to Liliane's again.

In the Luxembourg Gardens, she wheels Theo round the bandstand, the Statue of Liberty, the pond, hating life in Paris:

old rules don't apply, serious study counts for little, and music means rowdy dischords. How fickle people are; how transient acclaim. Inside her head chases the thought: if Anahid marries Antoine, will she want Theo?

Anahid will be with him now, posing, and the rest. She visualises the perfect body she saw on Liliane. Other memories nag: Anatolian mountains, breeze in pine-trees, the touch of her husband. She stares through tears at the gravel path.

THIRTY-TWO

Paris, spring 1923

The knowledge that a few minutes across the boulevard saint-Michel and the gardens waits a good piano, becomes too strong to resist. After three days, she inserts Liliane's key into its lock, resolved to ignore the evening at Le Boeuf sur le Toit.

'You made a big impression, I hear.' Liliane, in a peignoir patterned with palm-fronds and birds of paradise, kisses her on both cheeks.

'Huh!'

Somebody is moving about upstairs.

Liliane picks up an envelope from the table. 'This came for you yesterday. I set it aside so as not to lose it as I did dear Philippe's last year.'

She reads:

Madame Esther Yefimovna Markovitch

The writing is even, slopes to the right with flourishes on the E and Y. She draws out a sheet of paper. At the top is repeated her full name. Underneath:

Madame

My acquaintance Sergei Pavlovich Diaghilev was much taken with your performance at Le Boeuf sur le Toit the other evening and, as a fellow-Russian émigré, has recommended you to me. I shall be pleased to receive you any afternoon from fifteen hundred hours.

Respectfully yours,
Maurice Tournon

A royal summons. She hands the letter to Liliane. 'Who is he? Why should he want to see me?'

Liliane finds some spectacles. 'I don't know him. But if Diaghilev has advocated you, he must be a pianist, perhaps a teacher.' Liliane puts an arm round her. 'Well done! You have a chance! You will go prepared to play for him.'

She looks at the address at the bottom. 'Rue Viète. The seventeenth.'

'I will give you the fare for the autobus.'

She writes to Monsieur Tournon, thanking him and suggesting the following day at three-thirty.

In her Constantinople dress and hat, music held against her chest, she gets off the green bus on the boulevard Malesherbes, where she stayed with *dyadia* Pavel when she was eight. She remembers nothing of the area.

The rue Viète is a quiet street off the boulevard. The outside of the house appears well cared for, windows protected by wrought iron balconies and shrouded in lace. The concierge directs her to a cage-like lift which takes her to the first floor. The door of Monsieur Tournon's apartment is solid, handsome, with fresh blue paint. A polished brass plate informs her:

Maurice Tournon
professeur de piano

The housekeeper shows her to the salon and announces from the doorway, 'Madame Markovitch, monsieur.'

Her initial impression is of pungent tobacco. The man who stands up to meet her has dark, greying hair, moustache, and goatee beard. His shirt collar is high and stiff, trousers narrow, jacket buttoned, all of which accentuate his height.

'Madame Markovitch.' He offers a hand in greeting. The second and third fingers are stained brown. 'Please sit down.'

She does, on a thin chair. Sun filters between open crimson drapes and lights the room. White shepherds and shepherdesses gaze from green wallpaper. On the parquet is an oriental carpet. A clock ticks with caution inside a glass case on the carved mantelpiece, which is covered with trinkets. Where bookshelves leave space, pictures hang: snow, mountains, forests. On a table, music and other papers are strewn around a head-and-shoulders photograph of a woman in a blouse which fastens beneath her chin; her lips are slightly parted, eyes smiling, as if she were going to speak when the photographer captured the moment.

Along one wall is a straight-backed red damask sofa. And a grand piano, top raised, dark wood shining.

'What were you doing at Le Boeuf sur le Toit?' Monsieur Tournon begins. 'A somewhat racy establishment, I hear.'

As she answers, he regards her with a discerning but not unkind expression. 'I didn't like it,' she tells him.

'Why was that?'

'There seemed frivolity, dedication to shock rather than seriousness. It's not something I'm used to.'

'There is a fine line between high spirits and pushing at

artistic boundaries. The upheavals we have lived through must affect the creative mind. Are you familiar with Monsieur Stravinsky's work?'

'No.' She remembers Pascal mentioning him.

'Although he left Russia ahead of the revolution, he cannot be untouched by it. Yet even before the war, he and other composers were experimenting. I recall the first night here of his ballet *The Rite of Spring*, the story of a girl who dances herself to death to celebrate the season while the world looks on. There was a riot: many in the audience rushed onto the stage, cast about them with their umbrellas.'

Should she smile or show consternation?

'Your family are in Paris?'

She explains. He is the only person who has asked about them.

'And your husband?'

'I … we …'

'Forgive me, Madame Markovitch. I do not want to pry. But Sergei Pavlovich has contacted me before with his enthusiasms; some wilder ideas have come to nothing. However, he is an enabler and gathers around himself people of great talent. I have to admit that the reference to Le Boeuf sur le Toit was not in your favour, but Sergei Pavlovich was adamant I should see you and delighted to introduce you as a fellow-Russian. His passion can be infectious. Talking to you, I realise that – débâcles in your life notwithstanding – you are committed to serious study, know about the hours of practice, the loneliness.'

'It's only then that I'm really alive, never lonely.' She tells him of her place at the Petersburg Conservatoire. 'After I left Russia, when there was nowhere to practise, I used a dead keyboard.'

He smiles, nods. He retrieves from the table at the side of his chair a yellow packet; pulls out a cigarette, lights it, inhales. Pale-brown smoke drifts upwards. 'So. You have music. What have you been working on?'

'The Liszt B minor sonata. And now the Schumann *Fantasie*. And earlier things from memory.'

He indicates the piano. 'Take your time. Play what you wish.'

She sits at a Bechstein. Her hands are too warm. She begins with a few scales and a Chopin mazurka from her girlhood lessons. She opens her copy of the Lizst although she does not need it.

Her body sways with the rich range of inflection. At the end of the prestissimo, she waits before starting the benediction, an epilogue.

The final, solitary note. She looks up: Monsieur Tournon's salon, everything unchanged; the shepherds and shepherdesses on the wallpaper seem emphasised, as if they have been listening.

He walks over to her. 'Is it not sublime, that conclusion? And to think it was an afterthought: he had great difficulty, you know, finding effective resolutions to more flamboyant works. It's encouraging, isn't it, someone like Liszt having trouble?'

'The pause was too long.'

'No matter.'

She stands up in case he wishes to demonstrate, but he indicates she should come back to her chair.

'It is some while since I heard any of Chopin's mazurkas. The traditional dance of Poland, is it not? Rhythmically fascinating. You have a fondness for Chopin, for I hear you played one of the études the other evening.'

'My teacher in Baku was an exponent of him.'

'There is a symmetry in your choice of music: Chopin apparently envied Liszt's fiery performances of his études.' Monsieur Tournon lights another cigarette. 'I will give you a lesson. Shall we say, at your request? I shall be in Switzerland later in the summer. My wife is in a sanatorium.'

She glances at the photograph on the table.

'Do some more on the Schumann and write to me when you feel ready.'

He's not mentioning money but assuming I haven't any.

I must find a job.

Mère Catherine can be with Theo.

'Go away! Get lost! *Sale Russe!*' With a flick of the fingers and a grimace, the clerk dismisses the man she's standing behind in the queue. 'A work permit requires your passport *and* a letter from your prospective employer.'

The Russian turns to her, brow furrowed. She translates.

'Thank you, *barynya*.' His vodka-breath fills her nostrils. 'They say they need labour in the factories, and this is how they treat you. I've been to that counter and the far one.' He points along the room. 'Come back tomorrow, they insist. They seem to forget that when we advanced into enemy territory in the early weeks of the war, it was to lure troops from the western Front and save Paris from falling to the Germans as it had in 1870.'

'Next!' the Frenchman shouts.

The Russian hasn't finished. 'They have short memories, *barynya*, these people. Thousands died at Tannenburg for Paris.' He unbuttons his shirt. A scar runs the length of his breastbone. He prods it. 'Tannenburg. And this is the gratitude I get. I shall tell Wrangel. I was in his unit.' He slopes off; fumes linger.

The clerk snatches her documents from her. 'Another Russian!' he spits through gaps between teeth. 'Coming here!' Dirt clings beneath fingernails. Elbows and cuffs are stitched with worn leather. 'It's because of you we lost all our savings.'

'How so?'

'Your tsar received a big loan from the French government, on the strength of which many Frenchmen, my father included, bought Russian bonds. Russia never repaid the debt.' He snorts, stamps her passport, begins to copy details.

'Have you forgotten Tannenburg?' She repeats what the veteran told her; thinks of Sasha's death. 'You make us sound like leeches.' He glances up. Afraid he might refuse her, she adds, 'I'm sorry about your money. The tsar was murdered by vermin, and my family have nothing.' She outlines what happened. 'Are we better off than you?'

He does not answer but stands up, goes into a back room.

She turns, looks at the queue behind her and at the other two counters.

'… but they say they cannot engage me …' she hears in Russian-accented French.

'… they will not write a letter …'

The day after meeting Monsieur Tournon, she put on the Constantinople outfit again and found her way to the rue Daru, a street of elegant, six-storey buildings. She pushed open the cast-iron, cage-type door to the Hermitage restaurant, named after a great Moscow establishment of the 1860s. From Anahid, she'd learnt that – according to the Russian *patronne* of the dress-shop – the Hermitage had survived longer than any other émigré enterprise.

Vladimir Antonovich Bubnov, the *patron*, informed her he had escaped from Odessa in 1919 on the *Marlborough*, with Marie Feodorovna, the dowager empress. Perspiration gleamed on a scalp exposed by receding dark hair, and she caught a whiff of violet bonbons; his cheekbones' high slant suggested some Tartar blood. Could Esther Yefimovna work seven evenings a week? Of course, she assured him; looked at his tie-pin, wondered if the pearl was genuine. While the tsar and tsarina surveyed the scene from frames on a wall, Vladimir Antonovich regarded her with eyes the colour of the sea of Marmara. You must have a permit, he insisted: if papers are not in order, the authorities will close us down.

The clerk returns. Without a word, he pushes across her passport and a document marked *Permis de travail*.

Rumours abound: Vladimir Antonovich sold his wife's jewels, including the ruby necklace given by the dowager empress for sitting with her an entire stormy afternoon during the voyage to Marseille; make that his womenfolk, too, some throw in, else how could he have opened the restaurant? ... he has a mistress in Pigalle ... his eldest daughter is really his mistress ... he is a bolshevik spy.

She talks little, repeats nothing, and every spring and summer evening serves her countrypeople: vodka; zakuski, the hors d'oeuvres such as pirozhki – pastries of anything the harassed cook wants to use up – and blini, buckwheat pancakes filled with caviar and covered in sour cream.

To the Hermitage – famed for its breaded, chopped chicken

côtelettes Pozharski – come whole families, cousins, uncles, from along the river at saint-Cloud and Auteuil. How fortunate they are to be together, she thinks; to greet each other with a kiss on the mouth, chatter round a table – like the French – in the accents of Moscow, Petersburg, Kiev, flick through the latest edition of *Posledniye Novosti*, and imagine they are at home. In a corner, somebody plays the accordion or balalaika. Sputtering gas lamps cast a sallow light.

Vladimir Antonovich welcomes everybody by name, with patronymic and title; people who had money in France before the war – even property – and live off their gold and diamonds, their furniture, and one day, she supposes, will have to sell houses and land.

In a room at the back, old generals try to forget their woes with cheap vodka, eat at a reduced price, place ludicrous bets on games of bezique and canasta. Time and again as she passes the open doorway, she hears: if I'd put my cavalry *there* and my guns *there* … She remembers Valentina Maksimovna's husband in Constantinople and his contempt for such men.

'Mustafa Kemal, the renegade Turk,' someone yells from *Posledniye Novosti* one autumn evening, 'president of the new republic of Turkey.'

'Ha! Another upstart. What is he to us?'

As soon as everyone has gone, she retrieves the paper and, with shaking fingers, finds the column at the bottom of a page: restoration of Turkish sovereignty in Constantinople, the Dardanelles, and eastern Thrace; no mention of a bolshevik revolution.

That she misjudged Kemal weighs on her however much she

tries to dislodge it: he probably married Ayesha, any memory of me as insubstantial as leaves in sodden Paris streets trampled to a pulp.

She climbs into a juddering Babette alongside Liliane. Usually, she walks to the restaurant, only uses the bus if there's rain; less spent on fares, more saved for a piano lesson. Today, Liliane has an appointment in Courcelles and has offered her a lift.

Liliane settles her cloak round her shoulders to free her arms. A felt hat is crammed onto her hair. 'It'd be easier to move back here, Esther.' Liliane coaxes Babette through dark and drizzle to the end of the street.

'What about Theo? I can't expect *mère* Catherine to have him all day.'

'Bring him with you.'

'And separate him from Anahid, leaving her alone?'

'You're looking thin,' Liliane tuts. 'There are rings under your eyes.'

She's lucky if she's in bed by one. Anahid is up at seven-thirty.

'*Ça va?*' was Anahid's greeting this morning.

She forced herself to the edge of slumber that was not ready to let her go, screwed her face at the sound of neighbours' shutters being rolled up, the rumble of a cart, clip-clop of horses' hooves. '*Ça va,*' she replied.

'And the piano?'

What could she say?

She waited in the tunnel of dread for Anahid to announce she was going to marry Antoine and take Theo. But Anahid dressed, ate a tartine of yesterday's bread dunked in milk which was probably off.

Anahid kissed Theo's cheek. '*Au revoir, mon brave.* He's still asleep.' From the doorway, 'See you later.'

She had been holding her breath without realising; she sighed, expelling fear, allowing relief to flow into her. She put her arms round Theo, took up the space Anahid had left, and slept for another hour, his head on her chest, hands against one breast.

Liliane deposits her outside the restaurant at six. She has to set the tables with red- and white-checked cloths, and gobble whatever the chef, Ivan Ivanovich, gives her. There is never anything when she finishes work and is hungry.

'Holy Mother of our Lord!' she hears amid shattering crockery as she pushes open the kitchen door into the smell of garlic and, unusually, coriander.

Ivan Ivanovich is picking up the remains of several plates from the stone-flagged floor. 'He'll take them off my wages,' he laments, shoves the pieces in a corner. 'Now in Smolensk, they would say: you are overwrought, Ivan Ivanovich, you must have a day's rest, we shall survive on cold meats.' He used to be employed by a family, cooked French food as well as Russian. They adored my *oeufs en gelée*, Esther Yefimovna, he told her on her first evening; my pastry, he kissed his fingertips.

He is shorter than her. He sits her down. She eats a few lamb pirozhki. He brings a steaming pan, the smallest. 'A little bit of *dovta*? A taste of home?' He ladles some spiced casserole into a bowl. 'Just for you.'

She inhales the coriander; is in Baku where Elena used to prepare the dish in sour milk.

'You want to go back, Esther Yefimovna?' he asks. He watches her as might a cat its prey. Dark wavy hair crowns a perfect structure on which there is no spare flesh. A line of sweat gleams from his upper lip.

'Back, Ivan Ivanovich?'

'Yes, my sweet.' He lowers his voice. 'To Russia. I can arrange it.'

How? Unless he's in somebody's pay. Whose? 'What do you mean?'

'Anything can be bought if you have what the seller lacks, in this case information. Vladimir Antonovich, he's a tight-fisted old crow. Works you to the bone, does he? Heard him plotting, have you? You must know what goes on.' Brown eyes never leave her face, as if to see into her soul.

The nape of her neck prickles. She breathes in the *dovta*. Her accent must have given her away, for she hasn't told Ivan Ivanovich about herself. Maria Bagratuni's words that final summer in Baku break into her mind: by making sure opponents of the *bolsheviki* have what they need – supplies and information – ordinary people like us can help defeat this rabble. Here, it is the reverse.

Perspiration has stuck her blouse to her skin. She pushes the *dovta* towards him, stomach rebelling at the suggestion she should spy on the generals, men such as Papa, old before their time with nothing but dreams and regrets. She stands up, grips the edge of the table. 'My life is in Paris, Ivan Ivanovich.'

At the door, she turns. He is still watching her. 'Katya's late this evening,' she says.

Katerina Pavlova lives in two rooms in the Marais, with her brother, his wife and baby. A sultry, small-breasted girl from Kiev, her ambition is to be noticed by a fashionable artist.

Katya always walks some of the way home with her. Around midnight, they set off past shuttered *grands magasins* of the faubourg saint-Honoré. The drizzle has cleared. Frost has formed on ground-floor window grilles. 'You missed a drama earlier on.' Shaking from Ivan Ivanovich's proposition, she recounts to Katya about the smashed plates.

'Now in Smolensk, they would *increase* my wages,' Katya mimics his drawl.

She giggles, for Katya's sake; wonders if he has offered her the chance to return to Russia; if Katya is already aware of what he said; if he asked her to arrive late.

They part company at the Madeleine, beneath Chinese lanterns slung between trees. Musicians are putting away their violins. 'We could go on to the Dôme, Esther.'

'I haven't the strength.'

Women are strolling, furs wrapped round their shoulders. 'They say girls were given them by American soldiers in the war.' Katya sighs. 'I'd love a fur, wouldn't you?'

'One day. Bye, Katya.'

She crosses the river at the Concorde; tramps who sleep under the bridge rummage in dustbins, pull out scraps of food and newspapers. Another night, she will take the *pont* Royal; the next, the *pont* du Carousel, in case somebody is tracking her. She stops to inhale woodsmoke from an oven in a bakery cellar, and warm herself by the vents. She hears the hum of a car crawling into the further end of the road; hurries on, skirts the gardens, across the boulevard, and through the warren of streets. Is this to be her life, a perpetual wariness, inability to trust anybody? Familiar sounds – the snarl of a cat prowling its territory, a footstep on cobbles, voice raised in anger from a dark building – become a threat.

She runs down the rue du Cardinal Lemoine, impatient to clasp Theo.

The first movement of the Schumann *Fantasie* ebbs from her. When she lifts her head, Monsieur Tournon is looking at some point beyond her.

A smile plays on his lips, and he turns to her. 'Good,' he nods. He comes to sit beside her. 'Technically, I can find no fault. The result, I can see, of hours of practice. But ...' He hesitates. 'There's something missing. Some ... if I say commitment, I don't mean hard work, for that is evident in abundance. No, it's more the need to show the music's effect on you and what Schumann was trying to convey. This is a love-poem conceived in agony at his apparent loss of his great *adorée*, Clara.' He stands up. 'Can I ... ?'

Did she not insist to Pascal that she must get to the essence of what a composer intended? Hasn't she done that, or has she been merely concerned with technical correctness? Anahid's words before they left Constantinople return to her: when you let your feelings for him die, a fraction of you did, too. Can she rejuvenate what was?

Monsieur Tournon sits at the piano, unbuttons his jacket. His formality dissolves. Passion and anguish rise from the keys, impeccable control yet an impression of sudden inspiration which clenches her heart, fills her eyes with tears.

He glances at her. 'We must always move the listener. It was as if you were holding back.'

'Yes.'

'Try the opening theme again. Here is a man who believes he has lost the only woman he can love.'

She plays, remembers a moonlit Anatolian night and bed of pine-needles; saying goodbye at his brother's house in Trebizond; miscarrying his child; discovering Turkish nationalists had bolshevik support. Memories colour the music until she is sure she will shatter.

'A different person performing,' Monsieur Tournon comments. 'There is spontaneity, as if you have learnt something that breaks your heart, and are inventing the delicate interludes; they are so beautiful, reflective, as to catch the breath. Bring this to them every time. Their sweep is rapturous.'

The watery winter sun is lowering to the horizon when she takes her leave of him. The money is in an envelope on a table by the door.

'Do you have far to go?' he asks.

'The rue Daru. I shall enjoy the walk.' She needs fresh air and to regain her equilibrium before the restaurant, where she must be on her guard.

'You will contact me again.'

It is not a command. There is just sufficient inflection for her to feel he is not certain she will; that if she doesn't, he will be disappointed.

Rain starts as she turns into the rue Daru. Above the entrance to the Russian cathedral of saint-Alexandre-Nevsky, a semi-circle mosaic is flanked by two towers and crowned by a third.

Each is topped by a gold dome and cross which remind her of Christian churches in Baku and Constantinople, opulent compared with the synagogue's austere exterior. Her impression of Christianity has always been a celebratory religion – at Christmas, the Bagratunis' house was decorated with streamers and tin stars – and sheltering, as opposed to the Jewish faith's harshness and its constant threat of pogrom.

Water gushes down the cathedral gutters. She finds she has climbed the steps so pushes open the door.

She inhales incense, sweet, intoxicating, in the cool interior. A choir, invisible, intone rich, deep, phrases. Frescoes and ikons cover the walls. Candles flicker. Faint red glows at the far end.

An old woman clad in mourning is on her knees washing the floor; after a while, she struggles to her feet, faces a gilt and silver screen of ikons, strikes her forehead, right shoulder, left, and lastly her chest, before bending double. Is she Russian? If so, how and with whom did she come to Paris, and from which part of Russia? The woman straightens and with her bucket moves away.

She stands and lets a strange, unexpected peace surround her.

She doesn't return there every day. But if the weather is wet, or Liliane gives her a lift past the grey buildings on the boulevard de Courcelles, and she has minutes to spare, she goes inside; for the dry, the quiet, the Russianness – although previously unfamiliar – the only bit of Russia where she can ever be safe.

There are a few seats along a wall, where she sits one evening the following month. Her thoughts drift. Her head sags. She forces herself awake, aware of a shadow in front of her. She looks up. A man in a basin-shaped black hat, and a wide-sleeved, full-length robe the same colour, regards her with dark eyes. A bushy moustache and beard do not conceal his kindly expression.

'You are troubled,' he says to her in elegant Russian. An ikon on a chain hangs against his chest.

'I came for the solace.'

'So many seek God in these adverse times. We may be far from home and the motherland but do not have to be distant from God.'

'I am not of your faith.'

'We are all God's children, created in His image and loved by Him. He does not reject any who search for Him. When we crave that respite which the world has not, when we withdraw even for a few moments, God is there.'

Love again but spoken by a Russian, as if she could relate to God. This she cannot understand. 'I'm not very good at love.' The priest glances a question, and she tells this stranger about Lev, Kemal.

He nods, no trace of surprise or censure. 'You are welcome here,' he assures her.

'He's dead.'

'Lenin.'

'Vladimir Ilyich.' The syllables are stretched in mockery.

The talk eddies around her with tobacco smoke as she carries plates one January evening.

'Killed? I'd give whoever did it my jewels if I still had them.'

'No. In his bed. He'd had a stroke. More than one.'

'They tried to bump him off, though. Before. Fanya Kaplin shot him.'

'Pity she didn't make a better job of it.'

'Esther Yefimovna! It's a day to rejoice, isn't it? A glass for Esther Yefimovna!'

Vodka is thrust into her hand. 'To Russia!' someone proposes. 'The motherland. Russia without Lenin.'

'The motherland!' everybody shouts, as if the country they left will hear and know she has not been forgotten. They down their drinks in one gulp, heads thrown back.

She swallows hers, breathes out a rush of air to soften fiery fumes.

The balalaika-player starts a boisterous melody.

'If we could be there …'

'Others will take his place: Trotsky; Stalin, man of steel.'

'He's strong, they say. Even more than Lenin.'

'Too soon to return.'

'We shan't ever.'

'Don't! You'll have Boris Alexandrovich crying.'

'Dry your tears, Borya. Toast the motherland. Another vodka for Borya!'

The music becomes wilder.

An hour later than usual, she and Katya set off. Further along the street, Ivan Ivanovich is climbing into the rear of a black car. She recognises him by his *shapka*, fur cap with earflaps. Perhaps he is being pushed. Katya is silent.

'He's gone!' Vladimir Antonovich greets her at the door next evening. He is still wearing his dark, homburg hat, and coat with astrakhan collar.

'Who?'

'Ivan Ivanovich. I've been to his room. Nothing.' Vladimir

Antonovich stands aside to let her in. 'I treated him as my son, and that's what I get. Can you cook, Esther Yefimovna?'

'I can make soup from bones.'

Katya prepares pirozhki. The following day, a thin, pale-faced man is installed, who produces cakes dripping with honey.

She earns extra money that spring, sewing buttons and epaulettes onto uniform jackets Anahid brings from La Topaze, for *The Soldier's Tale*, a ballet by Monsieur Stravinsky. The weeks Paris hosts the Olympic Games, she works at the shop in the mornings as the *patronne*, Vera Davydovna Buchinskaya, needs another assistant. *Mère* Catherine looks after Theo and reads to him. He has given the tin soldiers names – Babou, Bébé – and doesn't shout at them as Jacob used to.

The world is hushed and still under the disarray of wars and revolutions. The only soldiering now is on a Paris stage. The *bolsheviki* have a new weapon: fear. At the restaurant, the chef never talks about himself. Ivan Ivanovich is not mentioned.

There are many images of me. Pastel. Watercolour. Oil. They have titles such as Nude Reclining; Girl on Blue Silk, *where I am seated, knees drawn up, arms resting on them, head bent.* Odalisque in Yellow Culottes *is after Henri Matisse, although I have not told Antoine of my life in Mirza Khan's house.*

Why do I continue with him when I have the job at La Topaze? Yes, the francs, or is it also that I cherish him? Yet, it is not something that provokes marriage, a home, children. I often return to him when I finish work; I remember commenting to Esther when she'd seen him and Liliane, that even he couldn't keep at it all afternoon. I was wrong. I do not always go back to the rue du Cardinal Lemoine, knowing that mère *Catherine will stay with*

Theo. Most times I do, though. Antoine holds me in the open doorway to change my mind; a kiss, and another, and I am gone into the night, leaving him anticipating more, as I learnt to do with Mirza Khan.

'You are agitated, Ana,' he says one summer evening.

Am I?

'It is not good for you. For me.' He sits next to me on the divan. From a small packet, he takes a pinch of white powder between thumb and first finger. He sniffs it, both nostrils in turn. 'You try some.'

I copy him. Cold shoots from my nose to my brain as if a needle has pierced my skull. I feel alive, alert. My tongue is numb. 'Mmm,' I manage. 'What is it?'

He shrugs. 'Coca.'

We embrace and pet. Naked, in the middle of the floor, he draws until he can wait no longer.

I think of the draught, as Seyed Ali called it, which he used to prepare for me in Teheran. I missed it very much when I left.

Only on some days do we have coca. I look forward to it.

THIRTY-THREE

Shishli, south-west Anatolia, autumn 1924

'You were in Europe, Kemal.'

Forests, flowers in window boxes. And Hannelore. 'Austria, Fikri.'

Fikri is an intense, bird-like man who spent eighteen months in a British prison on Malta and has come back full of democracy. But the other five, seated at the table in a low-ceilinged room lit by a lantern, have not needed to be prisoners of the British to long for democracy in their fledgling Turkey. 'We can learn from Europe,' Fikri says in his precise speech, 'especially the British.'

'The ghazi makes a show of his western attitudes,' he points out to Fikri, whose head is tilted, listening. 'He is proud of his unveiled Turkish wife who stays by her husband's side.'

Which is more than he can claim for himself. He returned to Constantinople after the armistice with the British and French a couple of years ago, not undercover this time but by steamer, welcomed by thousands of boats decked with Turkey's red flag as pearly domes and minarets soared from the Bosphorus through clearing mist. Young women lined the streets, faces greeting the morning. Girls crowned their newly cropped hair with jasmine and blossom, and joined citizens cheering and brandishing the ghazi's portrait framed in laurel and pine, as their hero paraded in an open-topped Daimler.

He went home to find that Ayesha was with her family. Halidé had married their cousin and was in Trebizond.

An-ne's expression was sad. We could move to Trebizond, Kemal, your father and I: Yashar's eldest is already betrothed; I don't know my grandchildren. But he won't go; insists he'll do business with the ghazi here. You will put in a word for him with the ghazi?

He assured her he would although for the moment the ghazi would be touring the country, seeing and being seen. I have to accompany him, *An-ne*.

She touched his face, and lines gouged by war and suffering; stroked his hair, now dark-steel-grey. A smile flickered in her eyes. It has grown. You are my Kemal again. She took his hands in hers, and he noticed the outline of veins protruding under her skin. *An-ne* alone and old. Has she been happy? he asked himself, something he had never thought to wonder.

Ayesha was always stubborn, *An-ne* said. And the Russian girl, she was haughty, of her own mind. You need a suitable wife, Kemal, but who is there? No more cousins.

He brought *An-ne*'s fingers to his lips, and with them the same whiff of lavender. He pictured her looking out on a world where women walk unaccompanied and unveiled; one in which she had no place.

He pulls his attention back to the men with him around the table; Fikri is disparaging the ghazi's spouse. 'She read aloud a poem by Byron which nobody understood. Ordinary people, those for whom we fought, will not be impressed by Byron. They require time to settle after ten years' conflict, to re-cultivate their land. They crave security from lawlessness. Social reform can be introduced gradually, by parliament. Let them have good government before giving them a choice of leader.'

Fikri's suggestion hangs in smoky air as every man weighs the implications, and the word treason passes between each glance.

'The ghazi assumes for himself the prerogative of caliph, successor to the Prophet Mohammed,' he adds to Fikri's comments; 'has us address him as pasha, the highest title from Ottoman days. The oriental despot in another guise.'

And callous, not the officer he idolised as a cadet: the ghazi dismissed the burning of Smyrna two years ago as a 'disagreeable incident', and moved his headquarters from the quayside to higher ground; Greeks, Armenians, Turks, all blamed the other for the fire, while some said it had been an accident worsened by the wind. He closes his eyes, winces at the image of the child nailed to the door. It never leaves him, drags him screaming from sleep. Esther's brothers: pray God, wherever they are they're safe.

'If the National Assembly is to function as a healthy body, it needs an organised opposition,' Fikri pursues.

Months they have spent touring Anatolia with the ghazi, listening to his speeches, promises, to people regarded as backward and temperamentally unsuited to democracy. 'One hint of rumour and your head will no longer belong to you,' he reminds Fikri.

'So we adopt the way of the East,' Fikri submits, rubs forefinger and thumb together as if crumbling something. 'A little intrigue, scheming, an informer or two. They say there is a constant stream of visitors toiling up the hillside to the ghazi's home. We must use our positions as deputies in the assembly to influence what happens.'

From the bottle in front of him, Fikri pours colourless liquid into six glasses and passes them round. Alcohol is forbidden except in the ghazi's house in Angora. Fikri has a vineyard and distils his own.

'To Angora and the new Party,' Fikri proposes. 'The Progressive Republican Party.'

They repeat the words, and drink.

The liquid sears his throat. He thinks of the cheerless room in the house he shares with four men in Angora, and the naked, treeless plain which soon after their return will be wrapped in snow.

THIRTY-FOUR

Paris, autumn 1924

Monsieur Tournon writes to her at the rue de Fleurus: *It has come to my notice that a piano and studio are available above the Pleyel factory in the rue de Rochechouart. They have been makers of pianos in Paris for a hundred years. Although some distance from your place of work, they are at least this side the river. Were you to be interested, I should be very happy to defray the rental ...*

'Lucky girl!' Liliane enthuses. 'He must believe in you.'

She folds the letter. 'No. It is charity.'

'Can you afford to be proud?'

'I can still practise here, can't I?'

'Of course. But I do not have the influence or connections in the musical world that Monsieur Tournon does, not to mention people you may meet at Pleyel.'

She has stayed working at La Topaze since the Olympic Games; Vera Davydovna is doing well. Perhaps her wages will be sufficient to pay her way.

In the end, she goes to Pleyel half the week, for Theo's sake. Up flights of wooden stairs, the faded mahogany grand takes most of the space and is hers for longer than she expected as there is a discount for Monsieur Tournon's pupils. The keys are stiffer than those of his Bechstein, and her Steinway in Baku. She perseveres, glories in the richer sound; recalls that Chopin was in Paris, became a friend of Pleyel, and played one of his instruments, maybe this.

The other afternoons, she fetches Theo from the rue du Cardinal Lemoine to be with her at Liliane's; he is bright, repeats after *mère* Catherine the words under each picture in his Brown Bear book. She remembers his Armenian grandfather was schoolmaster in Erzerum; when Anahid talks to Theo in Armenian, he replies in a mixture of Armenian and French. She wonders what she and Anahid are going to say to him about his parentage and heritage when he is old enough to ask.

I have tried everything I know coaxing Antoine to tell me where he gets coca; it reminds me of Delilah in the Old Testament wheedling from Samson the secret of his strength. Once, I called him Tou-tou in endearment. He stopped his caresses, looked at me as if I were a stranger; said it had been Liliane's name for him. We never discuss her. She is his business, not mine. His is not automatically mine, as I attempted to explain to Esther regarding Kemal. There is part of him – weeks, months, and Liliane did set him up in his studio – which belongs only to her.

Another time, 'Antoinou.'

That lazy smile, and he curled himself around me.

'Where do you buy coca?'

He shook his head. 'You do not need to know. A little with me sometimes is sufficient.'

It is not. I have money saved, wrapped with my scorched slipper in the embroidered silk. I put less in the purse for Esther and go without food.

This September evening I decide to walk a different way to Montmartre. It will not hurt Antoine if I arrive late. From Vera's shop in the rue de la Boëtie, quite a grand street, I wander down the boulevard Haussmann, linger in front of the Galeries Lafayette and Au Printemps. Here are shoes and dresses, blouses, hats, but nothing prettier than Vera sells. Paris! A name in a book, occasionally on a teacher's tongue when I was in school; a city even more distant and inaccessible – and therefore more fabulous – than was Constantinople to us who lived in the mountains of Anatolia.

I reach the end of the boulevard and wait for a motor car, bicycles, a carriage pulled by steaming horses. Across the road, I see Antoine. My lover. My Antoinou. Come to meet me? I stand on the kerb, raise my hand in greeting, which will become an embrace when he is with me and a caress when we are in his studio. I tremble, a shiver of readiness.

He has not seen me. I follow him. He is in a hurry: wherever he is going, he wants to be home before me. Curiosity pushes me on. He turns right, where there is nobody, just gaunt buildings. I smell cooking. Somebody is singing. From an open window erupt sounds of an argument, a man and a woman.

Antoine is at his destination, a door which might have been painted black. I quiver again because something tells me this is where he gets coca. I step back. If this is the place, he must not suspect that I know. I return to the main thoroughfare, cross to the Crédit Lyonnais from where I can spot him but he will not be aware of me. After several minutes, there he is.

As soon as he is out of sight, I go down the street; into a narrow passage with a few stools, chairs, tables, and a bar. In a haze of smoke and dim light, men are sitting, lounging. The nearest regards me but not in the sense of seeing me. I breathe the reek of sewage and degradation.

'You're looking for …?'
'She's lost.'
'Or she's mislaid her tongue.'
'This is no place for you, chérie.*'*
'The flics *come for us.' A snigger.*
'Perhaps she's here to buy.'
'Can't turn away trade.'

A man at the far end, clothes rumpled, ill-fitting, lurches towards me, brings with him the stink of vomit.

I'm through the door; slam it behind me.

And run.

'Monsieur Tournon!' Madame de Chelles greets him. 'Always on time! And this must be your little discovery.'

Monsieur Tournon introduces her.

Bracelets jangle, rings flash, as Madame de Chelles extends a hand, purrs, *'Enchantée;'* addresses herself to Monsieur Tournon once more, 'Russian, you said? There are so many. So sad. She's Jewish, no?'

'I believe so.'

'No matter.' Madame de Chelles dismisses the subject with her fingers.

Yet, you mentioned it, she thinks. As do other people. And

say it's not important. But it's bothersome enough to comment on. Irritation prods her, at this and the way Madame de Chelles talks over her head to Monsieur Tournon, as if she is too young or stupid to be included in conversation, or does not understand French, or is not even here.

Nothing, however, will she let spoil this debut public recital. At the shop, she is sure she has seen Madame de Chelles, a stout matron with blond hair and quantities of mauve cosmetics that match her clothes; a typical client of the *gratin*, the Paris upper crust, whom Vera Davydovna is keen to cultivate. Madame de Chelles lives in an apartment on the first floor of an expensive-looking house built in the last century off the Champs-Élysées; on the final Thursday of the month, she holds a musical soirée.

Vladimir Antonovich agreed to release her, Tartar eyes speculative: we did not know of this other life, Esther Yefimovna.

There is no payment, merely her supper and the experience. The piano has been placed between two rooms which have been opened into one. Siamese cats scamper around their mistress on Persian carpets. A tabby sits on a centuries-old chair, watches the twenty or so guests search for their names at half a dozen tables; orchids have been arranged in the centre of each, surrounded by a battery of silverware, white porcelain, and embroidered cream napkins.

She and Monsieur Tournon are seated at the side. She declines champagne from a black-coated waiter, asks for water. She accepts a morsel of salmon, pushes it around her plate, manages a mouthful. Too tense to eat more, she gives the rest to one of the cats; shakes her head when offered chicken and chopped vegetables. She looks at scrolled plaster patterns which edge the ceiling; at a wooden cross above both doors, gilt-framed mirrors on crimson- and gold-striped wallpaper, and portraits of eighteenth-century women in powdered wigs, swathes of chiffon just covering their breasts. Pine-logs crackle in both fireplaces. The room becomes warm.

She is aware of glances in her direction, of being appraised. She wears a blue dress of Liliane's which Anahid altered. Anahid wanted to cut it unevenly to below the knee and decorate it with beads. 'You will be a sensation,' Anahid assured her. 'It is la mode.'

'I couldn't possibly! Why should I draw attention to myself?'

'You have to be noticed if you're going to be someone.'

She allowed Anahid to raise the hem above the ankle. Anahid made a wrap from yellow cotton lawn she found among her bits of material.

'I'll arrange the beads in your hair,' Anahid improvised.

'They'll come out.'

'We'll string them with gossamer.'

'Beautiful Mama,' said Theo.

She hugged him. The beads didn't move.

After the dessert is served, Madame de Chelles shoos out all her pets except the tabby, which she holds as she introduces her first artiste. A young woman sings and is joined by a man of similar age for two duets. The next item is from a violinist.

She eats a few spoonfuls of meringue, lowers her wrap to her chairback, drifts with melodies.

'... a student at the conservatoire,' Monsieur Tournon is whispering to her.

She shakes with the realisation she is in danger of sleeping. She is unused to sitting in the evening, and is tired. People are clapping. Waiters are removing the plates and serving coffee.

'And now,' Madame de Chelles – the cat still in her arms – launches as if to herald an important announcement, 'we have a new guest, a pupil of Monsieur Tournon,' she smiles in his direction, 'Madame Esther Markovitch, who will play the piano for us.'

She stands up. Heads turn towards her, and there is polite applause. Faces blur and sway, and she wonders if her legs will support her.

The room is quiet. She forgets that all eyes are on her; everything except this much-awaited moment. She begins the Chopin 'revolutionary' étude. She is Russian and not ashamed, and – like Chopin – lost her city to the enemy. The agitated chords lift her through galaxies.

'Excellent,' she hears at the end. She acknowledges it with a bow.

She remembers a pine-forest and lake in Anatolia for the first movement of Schumann's *Fantasie*. The notes tear her heart, knowing as she now does when to let them surge forward, when to relax.

After she finishes, she keeps her head down, unable to return to the present.

Her audience are on their feet. 'Splendid!'

'Superb!'

'Encore!'

She forces herself to stand. It is as if everybody in the room longs for her to notice their own reaction.

'Encore!'

She sits again at the piano. Something short.

She is incapable.

She must.

A Schubert *Song Without Words* which she learnt when she was eleven.

It's done.

Monsieur Tournon is at her side. 'Wonderful,' he murmurs. 'They like you. They will want to hear the whole of the Schumann.'

The waiters bring trays of small glasses.

'Do you wish to stay?' Monsieur Tournon asks.

'No.'

The next thing she is aware of, they are in the red taxi; she is weeping.

'It was an exceptional debut, Esther,' he assures her. 'Madame de Chelles was delighted.'

Her pulse bumps at his use of her given name. She wipes her eyes. 'I don't know where he is. I didn't wait for him. I shall never find out.'

She receives several invitations that autumn and winter to salons in the eighth and seventeenth arrondissements. When Monsieur Tournon is not with her, she eats supper in her hostess's kitchen, manages more than the first occasion.

'Help yourself,' Madame de Chelles' butler says to her one evening.

She looks up from her salmon; this is the only time she has fish, savouring the pink flesh, garnering strength for the complete *Fantasie*, pushing everything else from her mind. He has put a black bowl on her table; inside is some white powder. 'What is it?' she asks. A garnish?

Straight-backed, he permits a ripple of surprise to crease his face above the wing collar. 'Cocaine. It'll do wonders for your playing.'

She bristles at the suggestion her performance should need help. She regards the cocaine. What is she supposed to do with it? She thinks of Ivan Ivanovich's pan of *dovta* at the restaurant. Nobody is who they seem. She finishes her food, goes to the room at her disposal where there is a flush toilet, washbasin, and chair. Soon, the butler will escort her to Madame de Chelles. She will sit in a corner of the salon until invited to the centre. Nothing must disrupt the routine. One day, these people will pay to hear her.

Whenever I return to the bar off the rue des Italiens for coca, I crumple my clothes, make sure some of my hair hangs loose. Instead of hovering in the doorway like a frightened rabbit and inviting comment, I go in and buy. Out, and along the dingy street. Away from prying eyes. I could be getting it for somebody else. When I was small, Mama might send me to the bazaar for eggs; I would hand over coins she had given me and go straight home.

Theo is asleep. Antoine has a car and has gone for a spring visit to his mother. The packet is in my pocket. Sufficient for today, tomorrow, a third if I ration it, yet why do that? Antoine may be back by then.

Left nostril. Right. A frozen butterfly takes flight between my eyes, flutters in the front of my mind. I inhale, a deep, steady breath not to waste any grain that might still be sticking to my skin.

'There's no money, Anahid.'
'You must be mistaken.' Anahid is fastening her blouse.
She holds up the empty purse.
'What do you need?'

'Vegetables for *mère* Catherine's soup, enough for all of us.'

'Will tomorrow do?' Anahid combs her hair.

'Why isn't there any?'

'It's been spent.' Anahid's face challenges: you have savings; use some.

She turns away. *Mère* Catherine would never steal cash. No? Perhaps she and Anahid are being careless, too trusting, wrapped as they are in their lives. Or did Theo move some coins to play with? She looks at him. He is standing, eyes solemn on his mamas and their raised voices.

As if seeing her line of thought, Anahid leaps to intercept it – 'You mustn't,' – hand on his shoulder.

'Why not? Did you put our centimes somewhere, Theo?'

He shakes his head.

'Don't destroy his innocence, Esther.'

She goes to the bed, lifts the mattress. Her francs are there. She takes one. 'What did you buy, Anahid?'

'I can't remember.' Anahid has sat down with Theo on her knee; she asks him, 'What did *grand-mère* Catherine read to you yesterday?'

'*Le Chat botté* about a cat in boots who makes his fortune.' Theo speaks as if it is an exciting thing to do. He snuggles against Anahid's breasts.

Were he younger, she thinks, and Anahid had milk, he would suck. A spasm of jealousy, like glass, cuts into her.

'But I'm sure *grand-mère* Catherine was telling me the story,' Theo adds, 'because she said a lot of words, and there were only a few under each picture.'

Anahid can't recall where the last centime went; you're lying, Anahid.

Maybe I should keep my money elsewhere.

She hates herself for the thoughts.

When are you coming to see us, sis? Jacob writes in June. *It's really good here, and when I'm not in school ... hurrah! ... I help on the boats. We get a lot of Americans, men who wear round blue caps and pretend to be sailors, although they don't know the first thing and are happy to give a local lad some francs to do messy jobs or fetch and carry. Mama does not approve of Americans – foreigners, she calls them – which is funny when you consider that's what we are, yet I feel French more than anything. Anton seems the most Russian of us. You never find him by the water.*

Love and everything, Jacob.

Anton's letter is in Russian. *How wonderful it is to inscribe the old language and roll the syllables around the tongue. Don't you think Russian is beautiful? Philippe paid for a Russian tutor the first couple of years. Jacob is impatient with the Cyrillic alphabet, but I practise it whenever I can. He is anxious to finish studying, hasty, but I love him dearly. We are two sides of a coin. One of us has to keep alive our Russian heritage, destroyed by the* bolsheviki.

Marvel! Pushkin's birthday, which was last week, is now a day of Russian culture among Russians everywhere, and there was a reading from Ruslan and Lyudmila *on the* Office Russe *steps in Nice. I would have gone if it hadn't been for lessons. I belong to a Russian youth movement – Jacob is supposed to but would rather be on the quay – and on Pushkin's birthday we recited poetry, and sang. Most are Christian. Mama is very interested in the faith and has been to the church in Nice. It was built by Russians before the war, gold domes, grey marble, no expense spared. Perhaps you can come down; we can speak Russian.*

Affectionately, Anton.

He and Jacob are thirteen. How tall are they?

Nadia's letter laments the *colonisation of the coastline* by artists, writers, actors. ... *the world has been coming here in the winter for the mild climate since the 1850s, and there are Russian-owned villas, although many have been sold to British or Americans. However, all year round we see moneyed American women from the hotel du Cap, hair as short as boys. Chattering old ladies, with huge diamonds and pearl earrings, clutch leashes of tiny dogs decked with equally miniature ribbons; on their arm, as often as not, a man young enough to be a son or grandson. I ask you!*

Madame Chanel, the dress designer, apparently stopped at Cannes with an urchin's crop and figure, brown as a cabin-boy after weeks cruising the Mediterranean. Surely, the last thing a woman needs is weathered skin like peasants or fishermen. I go out with my large-brimmed hat and sometimes parasol, too. I content myself with my garden and chickens ...

She reads the letters to Anahid.

'Antoine could take us in his car, Esther. In August. I think we deserve a holiday. Three years we've been here. I'll talk to him.'

A fortnight without practice or work? Would Vladimir Antonovich and Vera Davydovna keep her jobs for her?

She has started the first Beethoven concerto, studio door wedged open in the heat.

'You're soaking wet!' Nadia embraces her in the front yard by a semi-circular rosebed.

'We came through a thunderstorm and couldn't put up the roof. Hailstones as big as grapes.'

'And we lost the mudguard,' Anahid says.

'Did you get our telegrams, Nadia? Morning and evening we sent them. Four days! I thought we'd never arrive.'

'I expect they're somewhere.'

'Antoine nearly drove over a precipice.'

'He did very well,' Anahid defends him and goes to the Renault for the Constantinople suitcase.

Nadia bends down to Theo. She wears a battered straw hat, a faded blouse, and ankle-length skirt Anahid made for her in Constantinople. On her feet are workmanlike shoes with square heels. Her face is lined and has the glow of someone who spends time outside. 'Do you want to see the chickens?'

Theo nods.

Nadia straightens up. 'He reminds me of Lev.'

Her heart bumps. There's no resemblance, to the Lev she met in Erzerum.

'When I first knew you,' Nadia adds. 'You can't have been much older than …'

'Theo,' she supplies.

'How old is he?'

'Tell *grand-maman*, darling.'

'Four and a half. Where are the chickens?'

'Uncle Jacob will show you.'

A young man is walking across. 'Hi, sis!' he calls in a voice not quite an adult's.

'Jacob!' He's as tall as Papa.

He hugs her as if she's falling apart. He smells of sweat and the sea. They ease away, and she looks at him. He is in a creased shirt and trousers, handsome in an effortless way.

He crouches to Theo, kisses him on both cheeks. '*Bonjour.*' He holds Theo's hand. 'Better say hello to Ana. Who's the chap?'

She watches Jacob greet them, take the case from Anahid, easy manner.

'Here's the other half,' Nadia smiles.

Anton opens his arms, exclaims in Russian, 'It's lovely you've arrived! Do you speak Russian to Theo?'

'He's a little French boy.'

'Come indoors,' Nadia suggests. 'Would you like tea? Philippe will be back in time for an apéritif. We don't bother to change for dinner.'

The salon is comfortable and cluttered: heavy wallpapers, deep brocaded sofas heaped with cushions, worn rugs on the floor, an ikon in the corner; photographs of Nadia and Philippe on their wedding day, and Jacob and Anton within the last year. Chairs are covered in petit point. Reading-lamps have fringed shades. On a writing-table stands a vase of roses and lilac, perfumes mingling.

Paintings depict cart-tracks lined with wooden houses, a few people, a goat, a pig; as far as the horizon, rich brown earth. She turns to Nadia. 'They could be out of Turgenev.'

A chicken struts through the doorway, jerks its head in enquiry. 'Shoo, Eglantine!' Nadia claps her annoyance. 'You know you're not supposed to be in here.'

She wanders from the dining-room onto a stone path which surrounds the lawn, bound by palm- and olive-trees. On three sides are cloisters giving onto land which Nadia and Philippe have had terraced for cultivation. She breathes figs' sweet leaves and salt from sea she can hear: a gentle sigh like some great creature resting after the day's heat and exertions. Nightingales sing. Crickets thrum.

Dinner was late, without hurry, windows open. The maid had prepared bouillabaisse, the saffron-laced fish stew; salads from the garden – lettuce, tomato, beetroot, radish – with flavoured dressings; cheeses, fruit, pastries; tea, water boiled in Anahid's Constantinople samovar.

'Mama plays the piano,' Theo said. Everybody looked at him. As if aware of attention, he added, 'A lot.'

'Does she, dear?' Nadia answered.

She noticed fondness in Philippe's eyes as he watched Nadia.

'Yes. I listen to her.' Theo jumped his hands up and down on the table in imitation of her. There was a ripple of laughter; this little French boy sitting with adults during a Mediterranean summer's evening. A rush of love for him caught her. She wanted him to stay unhurt by life.

Nadia gazed at her. 'You used to when you were a girl. Just starting when I first knew you. In Paris. It's nice you've taken it up again. Must be something about that city.'

Like a pleasant way of passing the time? Hours of practice, two jobs to pay for lessons and facilities at Pleyel, described in letters to Nadia.

How she misses it.

Philippe has joined her on the path. 'The peace and stillness are delicious,' she tells him, inhaling as if she would store some.

'We think so.' He extracts a cigarette from a silver case. 'We can't change the past, Esther. But we can let it go.'

We have found a pension on the same side of Nice as Nadia and Philippe's house. We were lucky, the landlady told us, eyeing us: in August, there are few vacancies. It is wonderful here, sea air, flowers, a feeling of otherness so different from Paris. The light inspires Antoine. Early morning sun casts a golden glow, scarcely distinguishes water and earth steeped in purple haze.

We have tucked ourselves into an inlet on this wild, craggy coast, and lie naked in the shade of overhanging rock and arum lilies. He is asleep. He has been drawing and is going to paint. He wants me with him. Always.

He is waking. I bend to him, touch his mouth. He enfolds me. 'This lovely place.' I sigh. 'The tranquillity, compared with Paris.' 'One night, we will stay out here so I can capture the dawn.'

His lips are on mine, hungry, as if they would seal and devour me. I lean back, stroke his face. 'You said we would look for coca in town, chéri.'

'I did not, Ana. My words were: if I sold a picture, we might. It is not good to have it every day.'

But I need it. Now. He is kissing me again. Oh, Antoine.

Antoine and Anahid arrive after breakfast for an excursion in the car.

'Would either of the boys like to come?' Anahid asks. 'We can't get both in.'

'Jacob's off to the boats,' she says.

He walks into the hall. 'Room for one more?'

'I thought you were away to your rich Americans.'

'They can manage. They'll be delighted to see me tomorrow. Today I have wealthy Parisians to show around.'

'Huh!' she laughs. 'Which of us does that describe?'

Down towards Nice, they pass Nadia in her hat, carrying an equally worn basket; she waves in greeting, doesn't turn to look. They join the Moyenne Corniche, the middle coast route, past low olive-trees with silvery foliage, and cacti and palms, sun caught in protecting mountains from which brooks cascade. On the right lie kilometres of pale sea dotted with sail-boats. Each breath is of thyme and rosemary.

She wonders if Anahid is annoyed at having to sit with her and Theo because Jacob got in front. He watches Antoine driving. Anahid stares out of the window, eyes wide, dark circles under them; wrings her hands, rubs thin bare arms.

After an hour, they stop to stroll. Antoine stays near the road, sketching. 'I must return and paint,' he calls to Anahid. 'We must visit every summer. Eh, Ana?'

Anahid wiggles her fingers at him. Fragile alpine flowers, blue and white, line the path. 'We could take some back, Esther,' Anahid suggests. 'Grow them in Paris.'

'We haven't got a garden. In any case, they'd die before we arrived. They belong here.' She marvels that they should flourish in such arid soil.

'Do you think your mother would like some, *chéri*?' Anahid asks Antoine.

He doesn't answer, absorbed by work.

Theo touches the stems. 'No, darling, leave them,' she warns, but too late. He picks one, offers it to Anahid.

'No!' Anahid shouts. 'You mustn't do that.' She snatches it from Theo, lets it fall, tramples it with her canvas sandal.

Theo stands looking at Anahid.

He turns, runs. 'Mama, Mamana is angry.' He puts his arms round her legs, rests his head against her skirt.

She crouches to him. There are tears in those large black eyes. 'Mamana is tired.' She kisses him. They follow Jacob to the car.

He is in the driving seat, hands on the wheel. 'This is what I want, sis, so I can taxi Americans.'

'You're only thirteen!'

'Doesn't hurt to dream. You do, about the piano, don't you?'

Anahid takes Theo, lifts him up, presses her lips to his cheek. 'You're heavy.' She sets him down, keeps hold of him, stares as if at something she alone is aware of.

They drive on and stop in a valley near a torrent to open their picnic: cold chicken, potato salad, baby artichokes, cheese, pastries; purple figs and cherries from the garden; a bottle of red wine and one of water.

Afterwards, Anahid lies and sleeps. Antoine draws her.

Why didn't I think of it before? What if she's pregnant?

Anahid sits up, runs to the Renault, gets in, starts the engine. 'I'm flying! See you later.' The vehicle stutters towards the road.

Antoine jumps to his feet. 'Ana! No!'

The car bumbles to a halt. Anahid's hysterical laughter shatters the silence.

'Lev carried the eggs in, good boy,' Nadia announces at breakfast on their last morning.

She longs to be home, where Lev is never mentioned.

Anahid is buttering a tartine. 'His name is Theo.'

Nadia blinks. 'What did I say?'

'Lev.'

'He looks so like him, how I first remember him.'

Her cheeks are burning. 'We were older than Theo when you met us. We were eight.'

'We?'

'Lev and I.'

Anahid stirs sugar into a bowl of warm milk, a frown across her brow.

Jacob and Antoine have gone to where they stopped, for Antoine to paint.

She sets off on foot with Theo and Anahid up the road at the back of the house. A breeze ruffles the air as they arrive at the top. Below in the bay is Villefranche, where they were yesterday and walked past shops a few steps down from the street; strings of onions and peppers hung outside.

They sit on sandy ground, listen to the crickets, the sea, the peace.

'I've got a headache in my legs,' Theo says. She cradles him on her lap. He falls asleep.

Anahid draws her knees up and clasps them. 'Do you ever feel afraid, Esther? About the future? I suppose you have the piano, always something to work for.'

'You have Antoine. Your job. Theo. Me.'

Anahid smiles, but it doesn't reach her eyes.

'Are you pregnant?'

'He uses rubbers.'

'Are you going to marry him?'

Anahid shrugs.

'Has he asked you?'

'No.'

'Do you want him to?'

'Not really. We're all right as we are. It doesn't seem to matter in Paris.' Anahid lets sand run between her fingers. 'If you married, you could become a French citizen.'

'We both could in any case, after a few years in France. For me, marriage doesn't go with so many hours of practice. Only the piano and Theo are important.' She strokes his hair, bends to kiss it.

'And me.'

She regards her friend and the lovely blue eyes in a thin face. 'And you. If you need me.'

Anahid embraces her. 'I would not be here but for you.'

She holds Anahid, reluctant to leave another person's warmth. 'This week, even with none of the things that keep us apart in Paris, I've felt –'

Anahid pulls away. 'I am all right.' She emphasises each word.

THIRTY-FIVE

Angora, summer 1925

Violet and amber dawn seeps into the square through jagged torch-flares. Alone at one end, he closes his eyes, but the image of the child in Smyrna is still there. Concentrate! He breathes in several times, appreciates the air before the day's smells sully it.

People scurry in front of him, carrying he is not sure what, looking down, busy, perhaps so they will not be stopped, questioned, given a job to do, or taken away. Others have loaves and sweetmeats to sell on trays. Youngsters scamper around and between them. Long may their innocence last. When they are grown, may they not reproach their fathers and grandfathers for the Turkey that was allowed to develop.

To his left are four scaffolds, three opposite him, four to the right. From seven, men hang in death's twisted embrace. The crowd jostles, presses against barriers; eagerness rises like steam, women with heads covered. Is it for this spectacle that their sisters trundled hundreds of kilometres in carts years ago, to bring him food, supplies, clothing?

The remaining prisoners are led out. He stands erect, stares ahead.

'No, effendi! I beg you! I have done nothing wrong!'

'In the name of Allah, show mercy!'

White smocks are put on the condemned. On each is pinned the man's name and: *Journalist who has written disloyally of the ghazi*, although few here can read.

He fixes on some far point.

'Who is to care for my wife and children?'

'We have only published the truth!'

A soldier is at his side. 'All is ready, effendi.'

Without moving, he says, 'See to it.'

Through the shrieking, he counts in his mind: one, two, three, four, five …

At last, quiet, until cheers from the crowd, swelling as people get the idea.

The torches are extinguished.

He thinks of the climb to the ghazi's villa. Later, there might be western music, to which men will partner women in a foxtrot or waltz. If there are journalists or other visitors the ghazi wants to impress, there will be entertainment: the *zeybek*, the vigorous, masculine dance of the reclaimed Aegean coastlands. And in an adjoining room, yet another game of poker, over which the ghazi will ask, 'The traitors have been executed?'

He will reply, 'At dawn, pasha.'

'They were repentant?'

'They protested their innocence to the end, pasha.'

'They must be made an example. Those who have the power to write must use it for the good of Turkey.'

And the ghazi's cold blue Macedonian eyes will penetrate him with the stare he knows so well, and he will suppress bile rising from his stomach, and study the cards in his hand.

THIRTY-SIX

Paris, late 1925

'Anahid, there was money in the purse last evening. Where is it?'

Anahid's eyes glaze, pinpoints deep in their sockets, as if the blue has darkened with her effort of concentration. 'Let me see. Yes. Eighty centimes.'

'Anahid! It's empty. Don't be silly. Where's our cash?'

Anahid's face shows surprise. 'It's there.'

She grasps Anahid, shakes her, can feel her bones; so little flesh covers them under the cotton blouse. 'Don't say black is white.'

Anahid snatches herself free, puts her hands on her arms to protect them. 'You deceive yourself, Esther. Don't hurt me like that.' Anahid grabs her coat, rushes out.

She runs to the staircase. 'Anahid!'

Mère Catherine appears on the landing above, leans over the banister. '*Bonjour, Esther. Ça va?*'

'*Bonjour, mère Catherine.* Anahid has gone, without … she has forgotten …'

There were some, I swear it. Coins sparkling, winking, complicit. I am alone. Esther is rough with me. She is alarmed. I do not want to upset her. I will care for her. Dear Esther.

'Anahid, you must tell me what's going on. I had to abandon my lesson yesterday.' She played the opening of the first Beethoven concerto but led into the development with the wrong fingering. She began once more; instead of losing herself in the music, all she could feel at her fingertips was Anahid as her friend's face flickered in front of her.

Anahid finishes embroidering yellow the collar of a shirt she has made for Theo. 'What do you mean? There is nothing.'

'But you've been behaving in an odd way for weeks. And the money …'

'What? Try this on,' Anahid instructs Theo. 'Arms straight.'

'It wasn't there. You needed it for something.' She is twisting her hands; Anahid stills them.

'You delude yourself, Esther. You're working too hard. You'd better go. Vera doesn't like it if we're late.'

He is asleep. Exhausted. He keeps cash in the drawer, under papers. Yes! Here. He will not miss it; he's been commissioned to design scenery for a ballet.

Everything back. Undisturbed. Drawer closed.

'Has Anahid told you, Vera Davydovna … is she in trouble?'

The *patronne*, a few years older than her, raises pencilled eyebrows; there is no trace of natural ones. 'She seems all right. A bit twitchy, highly strung. Lack of sleep, if you ask me.' Vera Davydovna chuckles; peroxide hair glints. 'Can you take some sewing as you did before? It'll be after Christmas. For *The Firebird*.'

'Yes.' She must be careful not to prick her fingers or make them sore, as happened last time. More francs. More lessons. More for Pleyel. She'll have to find a new place for her earnings.

She winces, ashamed of the thought.

If I sit without moving, it is fine. But no, even now, they're there: notes, money, flying, tumbling as if they're snow. I must catch them, but they elude me, and I need them, must have them. For coca. Stop! Don't fall and disappear ...

'Mamana?' Theo stands in his nightshirt. He jumps, copies me.

'Here, Theo. Don't let them touch the floor because they will melt –'

'Anahid!! What are you doing?'

Esther has come in angry; maybe there is trouble at the restaurant. She has brought night-cold into the room. She leads me by the arm towards the chair.

'No, Esther. I have to pocket them. I must.' We struggle. She is stronger than I realised. I have less and less strength. Except after coca when I can do anything. She has won, has sat me down.

'Mamana was dancing. So I was, too.' Theo waves his limbs as if he were a rag-doll.

'Were you in bed?' Esther asks him. He nods. 'Go back, there's a good boy. I'll tell you a story.'

He goes. He does what Esther says; they are right with each other.

'What was it, Anahid?'

I look at her. How can she understand?

The next day, frost rimes railings, tingles her face and the tip of her nose. When she leaves La Topaze, instead of going to Pleyel she crosses the river to the rue de Fleurus.

'No Theo?' Liliane embraces her on both cheeks.

'Not this time.'

'What can I offer you? Tea? Coffee? Perhaps a trifle early for liqueur. Is he well?'

'Yes. Tea. Thank you.' She follows Liliane to the kitchen; her stomach flutters at what she must ask.

'How's it going, anyway?'

'Steady. A few soirées.'

Liliane pours boiling water into an earthenware pot.

'Liliane, I was wondering if you could give me Antoine's address?'

Liliane looks up; surprise stretches her features.

She recounts last evening to Liliane.

'You mean, he will know something Anahid's withholding from you?'

'Possibly.'

Antoine does little to conceal his amazement as he turns from his easel. 'So, Esther?' Unkempt hair almost reaches his shoulders.

'I mustn't keep you from your work.' Neither does she wish to stay any longer than necessary under Antoine's scrutiny in this room which smells of paint and has no heat. Dregs have congealed in the bottom of a tin mug. How does Anahid stand it?

Antoine indicates a chair. 'Wine?'

Canvases rest against each table-leg, of Anahid clothed and naked. She looks at the half-empty bottle on the top. Does he drink with Anahid? Is that the trouble?

'I've come about Anahid.'

Affection suffuses his expression, chased by alarm. 'She is all right?'

'Was she with you this morning?'

'Yes.'

'Was anything the matter?'

'She was as always. My Ana. I cannot imagine being, or working, without her. What is it, Esther?'

'I was hoping you could tell me. There's something wrong. Has been for some time.' She repeats last evening's episode.

Antoine's face turns as if it would shrink from what he is hearing. He picks up a rag, rubs at the handle of a brush, returns to his easel.

'What do you suggest, Antoine?'

'I will talk to her.'

'We have not had coca for a while, chéri. Antoinou.'

He is flourishing. He has sold the painting he did when we were in the south: mountains violet, stone house-walls almost blue, roof earth-red; a stream with bushes, pale-brown, rust, orange. To celebrate, he took me to the Tour d'Argent for caneton au sang and a magnificent view of the river. Even though we were round the corner from the rue du Cardinal Lemoine, I hurried back to the studio with him.

'It's for a special occasion, Ana.'

'Every day is, with you, Antoinou.'

He kisses me. I must exhaust him so that he sleeps and I can take money from the drawer. Have I the strength? I am so tired.

In the middle of the church, she lets peace, frescoed beauty, incense, enfold her; you can reach and reach in your search for something other than, outside of, yourself, and might find it here.

The same black-clad old lady is washing the floor; she finishes, gets up, faces the screen of ikons; head upright, eyes open, she touches her forehead as before, right shoulder, left, her chest, and bends double.

She realises it is the shape of the cross, the Christian symbol. She stares at the ikons. She has only a few moments if she is not to be late at the restaurant. How can I help Anahid?

There is no cash; just paper, stuff that is not important or interesting to me. He always keeps notes or coins here. They must be somewhere. Have to be.

I pull the drawer further out. Rubbish. A bit more ... and ... ah! It crashes to the floor. Letters, bills, everywhere. But no francs. Antoine is moving. I have woken him.

He raises himself onto an elbow. 'Ana?'

Like a goat we passed in the mountains last summer, transfixed by car lights in the dusk, I freeze in his gaze as he speaks my name.

He swings his legs off the divan, stands up, naked perfection. 'What were you doing, Ana?'

My voice sticks in my throat. I force a whisper. 'Looking ...'

'For?'

He is by me, eyes on mine. Those I have drowned in. Antoinou. Perhaps I do care for you.

'It was not there, was it?'

He knows. But doesn't say. Which is how he tells me.

'If there is anything you need, Ana, you can ask me.'

Except coca. And he is aware of that, too.

He turns from me. Picks up his clothes.

'Anahid wasn't here yesterday afternoon,' Vera Davydovna says; there is an edge to it. A pair of hands short and costumes started for *The Firebird*.

Anahid wasn't home last night, either. Or the one before. That in itself isn't unusual because she stays with Antoine.

'I can't pay her if she doesn't do the hours,' Vera Davydovna points out.

'I'll go to Antoine at lunch-time. He must know what's happened.'

There is no response when she knocks. Antoine is slumped at his table with two empty bottles, another open. The odour of unwashed body is in the air.

'Antoine!'

He lifts his head as if it is too much effort.

'Antoine! Please! Where is Anahid?'

He moves his chin onto his arms and peers in her direction. His eyes are red, hair tangled. He has not shaved for days. 'Her work is with me.' His voice catches in what could be a sob. 'I can do nothing without her.' He indicates the easel and crashes bottles to the floor.

I have found my own square of stone to sit against by the river and feel at home. The one Baba *and* Mama *made for their children was, in the end, a pile of rubble. Mine is under a bridge, and I can be with my special friend which never lets me down.*

There is a damp, muddy smell off the Seine, and a rhythm to the pushing and swelling of water; impossible to see the bottom. I can watch it, and walk along when I need money; night is better and not difficult to find somebody. I remember Esther's brother, my face rammed to the wall. There, I had no choice. Here, it's not bad because you don't have to look at who is doing it to you. When I have a few francs, I cross the gardens and up the streets to buy; pick rotten tomatoes and apples from the gutters of the Halles. I do not go to the rue du Cardinal Lemoine. It is too far.

I am safe. Nobody to bother me, to accuse me of what's not true; to say no.

For five February afternoons, she abandons the piano. She asks regular customers in the back room of La Rotonde, where Anahid went with Antoine in the summer; climbs six staircases above the wrought iron entrance to the Tour d'Argent. Waiters in long, starched white aprons regard her. She pushes open steam-fogged doors to bars on the *île* saint-Louis, Montmartre, Pigalle; ignores prostitutes smoking cigarettes. Everywhere, the same shrug, shake of the head.

A knot of fear lodges from her chest to her belly.

'Where's Mamana?'

'She's tired, darling, and resting somewhere else.' She hates herself for the lie. How can she roll off her tongue something false to Theo?

Yet, has Anahid found other Armenians, her father, one or both brothers? Did not Anahid say in Constantinople: if I knew where they were, I would go now?

She wills it to be so, the best solution she can think of.

She mentions the Dôme to Katya while they wipe glasses. 'Slim, leggy girl?' Katya recalls. 'With an artist? Last year. He seemed crazy about her. Lucky thing. They danced the tango. Didn't know she was your friend.'

On the fifth night as she drags herself up the staircase, home, a smell pervades her nostrils, stronger than the usual stale cooking and latrines. Somebody is slumped on the floor outside her door, knees drawn up.

'Anahid?' The knob of dread feels as if it will prise her apart.

She crouches, holds her breath against fetidness. Anahid's eyes are closed, face streaked with dirt, hair matted. She touches Anahid's shoulder. Anahid edges away as might a trapped animal.

'It's only me,' she whispers. 'What happened? Can you stand up?' She turns from the stink.

Anahid twists onto all fours, pulls herself to her feet as if the effort costs more strength than she has. 'They said I was mucky.'

They? 'You are rather.' Did Antoine throw her out?

Anahid goes inside, movements those of someone who isn't sure how her body relates to the space it's in.

Mère Catherine makes the same cross-sign as the woman in the church. *'Mon dieu!'*

'She's had an accident.'

After *mère* Catherine has gone, she fills a bowl with water. She peels off Anahid's clothes; there are bruises and scratches on limbs caked with dried mud, blood, stickiness. She who has always hated mess washes Anahid, wipes every moment of recent days as if Anahid were a baby.

She helps her to bed next to Theo, tucks the covers around them.
She is shaking.

In the morning, Anahid is coughing, deep, rattling, face burning; she does not even sit up.

'A fever,' *mère* Catherine says. 'It will come out. The body will heal itself. She's young. She'll fight.'

She looks at the sleeping figure, remembers skeletal arms when she undressed Anahid. 'I must stay with her.' She cannot expect *mère* Catherine to care for Anahid and Theo. Earlier, he kissed Anahid's cheek and whispered: Mamana's still resting.

'I will take *le petit*,' *mère* Catherine offers.

'Can you remain with them both while I cycle to the shop and say what's happened?'

Vera Davydovna's eyebrows arch. 'Neither of you?' She is fastening a hatbox; vermilion nails dart around blue satin ribbon.

'I can't leave her.'

'At least do some sewing.'

She agrees to three black bodices for the ogre's henchmen in *The Firebird*; puts them in the bicycle's pannier.

She calls at the restaurant.

In the church, she stands facing the screen. Please let Anahid be all right.

She stops at the baker's for a baguette, hurries home.

She puts on another sweater, starts work. Braid entwined with silver has been pinned on the shoulder to be stitched to the waist. She pricks her thumb, sucks it, grimaces at the sour taste. She listens to the stertorous rise and fall of Anahid's chest in sleep; waits for, cherishes, each respiration as Anahid releases it.

Anahid's breathing breaks on a cough.

She shivers with unease, pulls the chair nearer, dips a cloth in water, smoothes Anahid's forehead. She holds Anahid's hand; it lies against hers like a wounded bird.

Anahid moves; her mouth twitches; sounds, hardly speech, crawl through her lips; mumblings become speech, Armenian.

Anahid looks in her direction although not at her, or anything. '*Baba!*' Anahid shouts, 'Mama!'

Baba, *Mama, I can see you. Your faces tell me you are without trouble. So you are not angry with me. Are you the only ones? Even when I turn over, close aching eyes, you are there. Can I be with you? How? Every breath rips me. My head is burning. Somebody is sitting here. Esther? My friend. Has she found* Baba *and* Mama, *and made a home for us all together? Rearranged the pile of stones so it is a house again?*

Mère Catherine taps on the door; she is carrying a bowl covered with cloth. 'Some soup.' *Mère* Catherine puts it on the table.

'Is Mamana still tired?' Theo wants to know.

She crouches to him. 'Yes, darling.'

She kisses him; love rinses her.

When *mère* Catherine has taken him back upstairs, she eats; raises Anahid into a sitting position, spoons some into her mouth, but it dribbles down her chin.

Anahid gasps as if the effort is more than she can bear.

Don't try to feed me. I was all right in my comfortable ball. Don't do anything. Just leave me to drift. I have been disturbed; my skin aches, is on fire ... Antoinou ... coca...

Anahid's head flails on the pillow. 'Coca ... Antoinou ... coca.'

Coca?

Anahid is crying, gasping, struggling.

She holds Anahid's wrists, steadies her until Anahid subsides, whimpers, coughing.

Afternoon light fades.

Night passes, Theo with *mère* Catherine.

Coca?

Cocaine? Madame de Chelles' butler: it'll do wonders for your playing. Anahid's behaviour; the missing money, to pay for cocaine?

Another day ends.

Sometimes it is dark, or light whispers at the window but not for long.

Anahid opens her eyes. 'Esther.'

She sits close; joy blossoms that Anahid recognises her.

'Esther!' Anahid's effort to speak drags each breath. 'Not ... Antoine's ... fault.'

'Did he give you cocaine?'

'Coca ...'

If she sees Antoine again ... If? She *will*. She'll describe to him what he's done to Anahid. When will she? She does not want to leave her.

Baba, *Mama, you are still there, waiting for me. But I cannot come to you like this. There are things ... so many ... memories ... weighted on my chest. I am not your Anahid, your good girl. I am ... you would disown me if you knew ... I must tell ... I must ...*

'Esther.' Anahid's voice is faint.

She holds Anahid's hand.

'Esther ... priest ...'

Panic kicks her stomach around. She rushes up the staircase to *mère* Catherine.

'You know where to go, Esther?'

'Yes.'

Theo is seated at *mère* Catherine's table, swinging his legs, dunking bread in warm milk, humming a tune of his own making.

'We'll make a cake,' *mère* Catherine says. 'For his birthday.'

Today? She has forgotten, lost all semblance of time.

'I'm five,' Theo adds with an air of achievement.

She kisses him. 'Happy birthday, darling.'

Sunlight is beautiful and orange, cold on her skin as she cycles across the river. Wind plucks tears from her eyes. If the priest is not in church, where will she find him?

She rests the bicycle against the bottom of the steps, runs up into the dim interior. She slows, faces the screen. He is lighting a candle. Her heart leaps. She stays where she is rather than disturb him.

He turns, walks towards her.

She explains why she is there.

He smiles. 'My *nyana* was Armenian, when I was a little boy in Tiflis.'

The capital of the Caucasus, almost home; where Sasha trained at the Military Academy.

'Father Vasily,' he introduces himself. 'I must collect some things first.'

I remember – before everything – can visualise the stone cross, each point branched into two like a leaf. And the ikons. My favourite was Our Lady, tilted head framed by rows of golden half-circles and regarding me with great compassion, hands on her chest. I can see her now and confess, for Baba *and* Mama *are still there. I cannot reach them. There is nobody to hear what I say. I am talking into darkness. I am quite alone.*

Mère Catherine retreats with Theo when Father Vasily arrives.

She wonders what to do, sits by the door.

At the bed, he takes out of his bag an ikon which he holds near Anahid's closed eyes. 'Anahid.'

Anahid looks at him. Armenian stutters from her, gathers pace, and she is crying, coughing; when she stops, he puts the picture to her mouth.

He speaks in Russian, words of absolution, making the cross-sign over Anahid.

The strangeness of the ritual enfolds her. Tears roll to her neck.

'She is peaceful,' he says. 'We can do no more. Except pray.'

'I am willing her to be all right.'

'These things are not in our hands. Do you wish me to stay?'

'No. Thank you.'

'Come to me if you need me. If I am not in church, my home is next door. If I am not there, give a message to my wife.'

It is done. Everything. My life in Persia and since. Now I can see you clearly, Baba, *Mama. Hold your arms out to me. Show me the way. Esther ... I don't want to leave you ... but you have Theo. Love him, Esther. Always ...*

She sits by Anahid's face, entwines their fingers.

Anahid's eyelids flutter open, the blue of Van glazed, but a smile at the corner of her lips. Don't abandon us, Anahid. Me. Theo. Don't.

'Esther ...'

'You're going to be better. We'll make you strong again ...'

But she is talking to herself, into a void, for Anahid's eyes have closed.

Anahid's body trembles, as in a sigh, and is still.

A few days later, she and Theo move to Pleyel, with a tart from *mère* Catherine, and their belongings in the Constantinople suitcase. Even if she could afford the rent, the rue du Cardinal Lemoine is silent without Anahid, cold biting through the walls.

The nights after Anahid died, she sat, arms round Theo, until she fell asleep. The empty bed, which *mère* Catherine made with clean sheets and cover, seemed a reproach that she had not been able to save Anahid; to disturb it, a desecration.

Father Vasily arranged Anahid's burial at saint-Etienne-du-Mont. She stood in the drizzle with *mère* Catherine and Theo as the plain coffin was lowered into the mud, and Father Vasily said prayers in Russian and French. When she turned to leave, Vera Davydovna was a short distance away, black lace over head and shoulders.

Too wrapped in exhaustion and grief to visit Antoine, she hoped Vera Davydovna had told people; the news would spread.

The studio already has a table and iron stove. At the market, she buys a mattress and pillow, a couple of chairs, a three-drawer chest, and pays two men – who have heavy, drooping moustaches – a franc to carry them up. She folds Anahid's clothes and bits of material; the scorched pink slipper and embroidered silk.

Theo sets out the tin soldiers. 'Is Mamana really not coming back?'

She sits on the floor beside him. 'No, darling.' She repeats Father Vasily's words, 'God needs her.'

'So do we.'

'We have each other.'

'You won't die, will you, Mama? Or if you do, I will as well so we'll always be together.'

'I won't, darling.' She hugs and kisses him, clings to what Father Vasily said: we can only believe it is for the best, that she is in a better place.

She weeps at night; her respite, sleep which gives no rest.

In the mornings, she cycles past the *gare* saint-Lazare to La Topaze, Theo perched in front against the handlebars. Vera Davydovna frowns: a child in a fashionable dress-shop? Theo sits in the corner with *Le Chat botté*, which *mère* Catherine gave him, and whispers to Babou and Bébé.

'He's a poppet,' Vera Davydovna concedes every lunch-time as she takes from a drawer the key to lock up.

They call on *mère* Catherine with the tartdish and stay the minutes that politeness dictates; a light seems to have gone from the old lady's eyes.

When she plays the *Fantasie,* she thinks no longer of Kemal and their passion in Anatolia, but Anahid, her sole friend for nearly eight years, without whom she would not have Theo. In the opening movement, she slumps, sobbing. Theo climbs onto her lap. She seizes his little body in the brown jacket Anahid lined with yellow, and clutches him as if drowning in the realisation she will never again speak to Anahid, feel Anahid's warmth in bed.

Monsieur Tournon offers her and Theo his guest room.

'We're managing.' She can hear Liliane: can you afford to be proud?

Theo looks up at him. 'When Mama practises, I sit under the piano to listen. She got a box from the market. If I stand on it, I can just see out of the window.'

He pats Theo's head.

On the way to the rue Daru, Theo says, 'They talk funny at the restaurant, and the *patronne* at the shop.' When Vera Davydovna addresses her in Russian, she answers in French.

'They're from Russia.'

'Where's that?'

'Across the mountains. The old country.'

Theo repeats her words.

She picks what she tells him but will not lie to him. 'It was years ago. Very hot. And we ate fish freshly caught, and men worked to get oil from the ground.'

He informs the tin soldiers, 'We're going to Russia to catch fish, and we'll make a home in the mountains.'

They walk in the shady gardens of the Tuileries, where Theo spots the first snowdrop. 'Let's take some to Mamana,' he suggests the following week. With two bunches, they cross the river to saint-Etienne-du-Mont, and she marvels at his acceptance. Yet, that evening, he sobs against her chest, 'I miss Mamana.'

She clasps him, and they cry together.

When the weather is warmer, he sails his toy boat in the Tuileries. They watch barges unload bricks and sand on quays in front of the Louvre. 'We'll buy a bucket and spade,' she promises.

In June, Nadia writes: ... *I have not been well with blood pressure, and so for a complete rest and change and escape from the heat, we are going to Lake Annecy, where mountain air will be beneficial. The boys are coming with us, although Jacob is reluctant. He will be leaving school and beginning work, simply an expansion of what he has been doing in his spare time by the water.*

Another reason I shall be glad to go is that the town authorities are thinking of ways to attract more tourists, as they call them, visitors who come for the sun and to make their skin brown, which seems to be a sign of status, that you have the means to travel from your northern home. Very vulgar. The Negresco is to remain open through the summer. There are to be concerts, parades, dances, and a gala. Standards in dress have fallen appallingly; people wear less and less. Lots of money to be made, says Jacob. I am pleased he will not be here for a while. Anton is more serious and hopes to continue studying. Would you like to spend a few days with us before we leave?

She cannot afford the fare. Neither does she want to be away from La Topaze, the piano, and the restaurant, or to see places and people where she was with Anahid, or anything to disturb the fragility of a world without her.

Sponsored by Monsieur Tournon and Father Vasily, she applies to the *mairie* for French nationality papers. She registers Theo to start school in the winter. Theo Dubois. She has seen the surname on shopfronts. It seems ordinary enough.

THIRTY-SEVEN

Smyrna, western Anatolia, summer 1926

He wakes to his tunnelling scream and Fikri shaking his arm.

'Easy now,' Fikri whispers.

He opens his eyes, blinks, but the child's image is still there. He glances round at ten comrades crouched or curled in a stinking cell lit by a high window the size of a piece of bread. He shifts onto his haunches rather than sit in his own filth. His heart bumps as the nightmare recedes. Until the next time.

Banging went on through the darkness hours, more scaffolds, which mean hangings at dawn. They never know who it will be. The Progressive Republican Party, toasted into being with wine from Fikri's grapes nearly two years ago, became a vipers' nest; we have allowed ourselves to be exploited as a cloak for terrorists, Fikri snarled. The ghazi's net was wide and savage, scooping up anyone suspected of connections with the Party for failing to report the plot to kill him.

For three weeks, trials have dragged on, each prisoner presumed condemned unless he can prove himself innocent, although no witnesses are permitted. Those that aren't put to death or gaoled are sent into exile. Sometimes, men are acquitted only to be re-arrested on a minor infringement.

He has been cleared of complicity in the conspiracy; he had not been guilty.

'You shouldn't be here,' Fikri says. Fikri's lips are swollen, teeth broken, where guards manhandled him else they be informed on for lack of zeal.

'Keeping you company.'

'I shan't appeal,' Fikri tells him. 'They executed those who did.'

What is there to live for, he asks himself, in this parody of what they fought for?

'When they let you go, get right away,' Fikri insists. 'Find a boat that's leaving.'

'I'll wait for you.'

'No!' Fikri clasps his arm. 'You'll be watched. There'll be a next time, and they'll catch you. He's out of touch with the country's feeling, a victim of his suspicions.'

He remembers endless games of poker, its excitement preferable, the ghazi maintained, to bridge's many rules. The ghazi liked to win but often swept chips together and cancelled all debts; he dealt similarly with people's lives, made his own laws.

Bolts are pulled back. He turns to look. Blood pounds in his temples.

The guard intones, 'Ahmet, Halil, Kemal. Sharp now!'

Fikri pushes him to his feet. He follows Ahmet and Halil.

'Ahmet, Halil.' A finger points along the corridor, but he is thrust up narrow stone steps, those he came down weeks ago.

Someone opens a door. He walks through into the amber light of dawn.

Nobody is with him. He is not being taken to a scaffold. He checks behind him. No-one. Not even the *imbat*, that vicious wind, has come to greet him; well, he doesn't mind that.

He is free.

He starts to the waterfront, the smell of rotten plankton never sweeter. He thinks of *An-nè*, hopes his father has relented and moved to Trebizond to the rest of the family. Forgive me, *An-ne*.

His pace quickens, the nearest he will ever be to running.

THIRTY-EIGHT

Paris, early 1927

On his sixth birthday, Theo starts school. She cycles from there to the shop, misses his warmth on the bicycle; hates releasing him to the world of other people. Birds huddle on bare branches. A hearse pulled by black horses passes her, reminder of Anahid's death a year ago, not that any is necessary.

'Rémy and Jules both have a papa,' Theo tells her one Sunday afternoon as they walk along gravel paths in the *parc* de Monceau. They come here every week and count the columns of the colonnade by the lake, which today is surrounded by daffodils and birdsong. Green dusts the trees. 'I said I used to have Mamana,' he adds, 'and God needed her so she went to heaven, and now I just have Mama, but we take flowers to where Mamana rests.'

Her stomach flops in anticipation of his question.

'Rémy and Jules say everybody has a papa,' he pursues.

'Yes.' Perspiration spreads across the back of her neck and under her arms.

'Where is mine?'

Who is she to think of? Not her brother. Kemal, as she cherished him those months in Anatolia? Because to her, Theo means love?

'Did he die, my papa? Is he with Mamana? Did God need him, too?'

'No, darling. Not that I'm aware. He's a soldier. They have to fight where they are sent.'

'Will he ever stop doing that and live with us?'

'I don't know, darling. As we're not sure, we have made this life for ourselves without him.'

For nights, she lies sleepless, Theo beside her: is it better Theo should believe his father dead rather than hope he might return, only to wonder if he is alive, where he is, why I didn't mention him, and why he never came to Paris to be with us?

Back from school with Theo one June afternoon, she finds a young man standing on the pavement outside Pleyel, peering through the window. She runs the last few paces. 'Jacob?'

He turns. Black eyes widen with a smile. 'Sis!'

He is taller than two years ago. He enfolds her as if to prevent escape; smells of sweat, garlic, tobacco. Tobacco? He is fifteen.

'I could have written, sis, but didn't want you to feel you had to go to trouble or do anything different.'

She lingers in his embrace, eases him to arm's length. 'I can see you still spend a lot of time outdoors.'

'*Bonjour*,' says Theo.

Jacob crouches to him, ruffles his hair. '*Ça va?* You probably don't remember me.'

'*Si!*' Theo insists.

They kiss on both cheeks.

Jacob straightens, touches the embroidered collar of her blouse. 'Ana was in something like this.'

Her throat catches. Tears trickle down her face.

'Hey, sis!' he hugs her.

'Is it wrong to wear her clothes,' she sobs into his shoulder, 'to keep a little of her with me?'

'Of course not. I'm nothing but a clod.'

'Weeks can pass without my crying until the smallest thing pushes me over.'

'Sometimes, we're sad together,' Theo says.

'I'm sorry,' Jacob comforts against her hair, an arm round Theo. Jacob dries her skin with a fingertip. 'Mama and Philippe are going to Annecy again.'

'How is she?'

'As you remember her. Vague, yet at other times quite normal.'

'Her heart? Is it all right?'

'Providing she doesn't have too much excitement.'

They are still on the pavement. 'Come in. I don't know where we're going to put you.' She leads the way up the stairs. 'How long are you staying?'

'Till you kick me out.'

She unlocks the studio and goes in with Theo. Jacob stands in the doorway.

'Mama plays the piano,' Theo volunteers.

Jacob pats Theo's head. 'Yes, she does. I see what you mean, sis. I could always sleep underneath it.'

Only now does she notice he has no luggage. 'You're just as you are?'

He grins, and she can forgive him anything. 'I've got some money.' He fumbles in his pocket. 'I can buy a change of clothes in the morning.'

'Has something happened, Jacob? Last year, you went with Nadia and Philippe.'

He whistles through his teeth. 'It was so dull I couldn't bear it. Anyway, they're going next month.'

She waits.

'Oh, I thought I'd visit you ... and,' he taps the side of his nose, 'I needed to get away for a while. An American lady of ... a certain age ... no, probably not much older than you ... becoming a bit too ... interested.'

'Jacob!'

'Don't be shocked. It's not unusual. You drive them around, they treat you to a meal, tell you their sad story ... and ...' He shrugs.

'Does Nadia know? She doesn't have time for Americans.'

'Mama? No. Not that she'd retain it, anyway. But until she forgot, she might be unhappy, and I wouldn't do that to her.'

'What about Anton?'

'I don't think he notices Americans. He'll accompany Mama and Philippe to Annecy. He'll read to Mama, and walk with Philippe while she rests, and write letters in Russian. He doesn't seem to have any French friends. All from the old country.'

Theo is playing with his soldiers. 'I remember those,' Jacob says. He sits on the floor alongside Theo. 'The paint's worn off.'

'You said the old country,' Theo looks at him. 'Mama calls it that.'

'What have you told him?' Jacob asks her.

'Heat, sea, fish, oil.'

'And?'

She shakes her head.

'This is the river,' Theo explains. 'And these men are trying to capture the other side. Like my papa does.'

Jacob takes Theo to school in the mornings, wanders down to the Seine, talks to fishermen under the *pont* Neuf. He often comes back with a few francs; the first day, he bought a silk screen from the market in the rue des Martyrs: to give you a bit of privacy, sis. He replaces her at the restaurant so she can practise. Sometimes, Theo remains with her; after she has put him to bed, she sews for Vera Davydovna or lets out his shirts and trousers. She hates snipping Anahid's dainty stitches; her own can't compare.

When Theo's summer holiday begins, he and Jacob go to the water or the park and feed the mallards with yesterday's bread while she practises. Pleyel are opening a concert hall in the rue du faubourg saint-Honoré in October. Monsieur Tournon hopes she will play a Beethoven concerto there; she has started work on the third.

'You can be heard on the pavement,' Jacob tells her. 'Sounds like a performance. People stop, just stand, listening.'

'One day, they'll have to pay.'

He pats her shoulder. 'That's the spirit, sis.'

She is able to accept invitations to soirées until August, when most of the *gratin* decamp to the mountains, the spas, or Deauville and Trouville.

Jacob takes Theo to the cinema to see *The General* starring an American actor called Buster Keaton. It is Theo's first moving picture. He comes back jumping and waving his arms in imitation of a man riding a horse, and brandishing imaginary guns, and making shooting noises. 'My papa's a soldier,' he says.

Sometimes, Theo is invited to Rémy's after school. When Jacob has returned home – lured by the prospect of a southern winter rather than shiver towards October – Theo can walk to Pleyel on his own if Rémy's mother crosses the road with him.

Today, she knows from the shadows' slant on the wall that he is usually back by now. She has spent hours on the first movement of the third Beethoven concerto. She stands up, flexes her shoulders.

On tiptoe, she can look out of the window at the pavement. Theo is chattering to a man who has greying hair. He bends as he listens to Theo; is dressed in workman's blue jacket and trousers. She is about to run downstairs to fetch Theo when the conversation comes to a halt, and they shake hands in farewell. Theo disappears indoors; boots sound on the staircase.

'Who was that?' she asks him.

'He was there when I returned. I thought he might cry. I told him it was my mama, and she practises a lot. He talks funny but is nice. He has an outdoors face the same as Uncle Jacob.'

A boy like any on the streets here or in Marseille … whose mama plays the piano so exquisitely, with such feeling … in an attic. Is beauty which can move a man's soul and bring tears to eyes that have seen too much that is ugly, hateful, is this to remain shut in, a caged bird that longs to be free and enchant the world with its song?

Have those fingers also stitched brightly coloured shorts and yellow shirt with patterned pockets? Can he imprint on his mind the image of this happy child five minutes' walk away and hope to erase the one from Smyrna?

In his cell-like room in the basement of the hotel in the passage Jouffroy, he fixes the mirror atop two boxes so he can shave. He has already dispensed with his moustache in the western fashion at the *patron*'s request; a useful disguise, too, although the Macedonian he met in Marseille assured him Lucifer himself would never find him in Paris.

From Smyrna, that summer morning more than twelve months ago, he earned his keep to Greece once they'd thrown a bucket of water over him and found spare clothing. He was only in Piraeus a few weeks: ancient hatreds were raw, a million Greeks ejected from Turkey, where their ancestors had lived for three thousand years and, by the peace settlement at Lausanne, forced to Greece, where they were – like himself – derided as Turks and filthy refugees. He stayed the winter in Naples. The chance came for work on a freighter to Marseille. There, he passed his days stacking in the warehouse of a cotton merchant and his nights in a slum behind the port. This is how it's going to be, a ceaseless unbelonging, rootlessness.

The music he heard, standing on the pavement, ripples through him; a mountain stream in Anatolia, constant, perpetual, refreshing to the soul.

He combs and parts his hair on the left, washes his hands, puts on his white waiter's jacket and, lastly, white gloves. The first evening, the *patron* studied him from head to toe: there's still enough of the Orient in you to fascinate the ladies. But you will make no advances. Understand?

Advances? Is this the military? He nodded, had a second's recollection of the hodja who used to chastise him in Macedonia.

The *patron* hadn't finished: a hint of passion and you will be dismissed. Should a lady wish to see you again, that is up to her. Not you.

Passion? Could it be summoned from oblivion, from Anatolia, as unreachable as is that country to him? He did agree to an afternoon rendezvous with a pretty girl who slipped him a perfumed card bearing an address on the rue de Maubeuge. She turned out to be quite plain and older than shimmering sequins had suggested. As he knelt astride and undressed her at her urging spread-eagled on a Tabriz carpet, he realised blond was not her natural colour. Tears, protestations of gratitude and love, of chasteness – which he didn't believe – since her husband's death after the war, were more than he could stomach. When, the following week, she entered the hotel on the arm of a uniformed officer, bile rose in his throat at French swagger in Constantinople; he was thankful she ignored him.

His *permis de travail* declares him to be Camille Moulin. He adopts an impassive demeanour. Let the mystery of the East remain.

He does not return every afternoon to the rue de Rochechouart. Old habits die hard: he varies his routine. He goes into the reading-room in the Bibliotèque Nationale a few streets away. There, in two exercise-books, he writes stories of his childhood. From a stall by the river, while barge horns sound their mournful music, he buys a school writing-primer; practises western script, thinks it would be easier if Turkish were written that way rather than in Arabic. The fashionable shops on the boulevards bring to mind the Grande Rue de Pera when he was a cadet. He wanders through passages, dilapidated labyrinths of glass-covered arcades, and imagines himself in the Stamboul bazaars.

A fellow-waiter, a Frenchman who was decorated for service in a cavalry regiment, invites him to help in his garden in Montrouge, beyond the city boundary; the man has a thin, kind face; the bald top of his head shines under hair slicked across it.

The passion he finds in himself is for growing things; that of someone who has spent too much time in harsh, barren places.

Leaves on the trees turn infinite shades of red, yellow, brown, and fall to the ground. The days become shorter, chillier; an autumnal melancholy pervades the streets and parks. He thinks of Marseille's sail-boats and tugs, forts and sleepy quays and warm evenings; remembers the constant sewage-smell from the gutter down the middle of the pavement outside his room; recalls the fights: Algerians, Greeks, Italians.

If he had not come here, he would never have heard the music that now haunts him.

Theo is on the stairs. He is carrying a packet.

'Don't go out without my knowing, darling.'

'You were practising, Mama, and I couldn't interrupt you.'

Out of the corner of her eye, she had been aware of him. 'You went to talk to the man?'

'This is from the garden of a friend he helps sometimes.'

On the paper is written in large, uneven letters: *pour la gentille pianiste*. Theo stands beside her, watches her look inside to find two onions; soil clings to hairy roots.

'He said the maid could make soup for my papa's dinner. I told him we didn't have a maid, and my papa was a soldier and I'd yet to meet him.'

'You must thank him if he's there another time.' Or she should. She smiles. Her first gift from an appreciative audience. The chef at the restaurant can use them.

'Mama!' Theo scampers across the room.

She continues playing. Theo speaks to her. She nods. Repeats the passage. Again. Again. Until it's part of her, absorbed into her bloodstream, flowing along veins to her fingertips.

She stops. Theo isn't there. She goes to the window. He's talking to the same man.

'Mama says thank you for the onions. They had soil on.'

'What about cabbage? There are plenty in my friend's garden. I could bring one.'

'We always eat at the … here she is! We'll ask her.'

He turns from the boy to the woman who has stepped through the doorway.

He has the feeling his heart is not beating, every vein, muscle, sinew, suspended in the previous breath.

'Mama! This is Camille, who gave us the onions. He wants to know if you like cabbage.'

She looks at a clean-shaven face, lined, tired. And sad. Under bushy, greying brows, black eyes burn and, having found hers, hold them.

'Esther?' he whispers. 'Esther *Hanum*?'

She moves her lips in those long-relinquished syllables. When she speaks, her voice is hardly there. 'Kemal.'

His mouth opens in a fraction of a smile, as if he has forgotten how and is just trying.

Theo has taken her hand. 'Mama?' He glances from her to Kemal and back. 'Mama?' he repeats. He regards Kemal, 'You're my papa! Papa! You've returned to us and given Mama a surprise.' Theo lets go of her and stands by Kemal, fingers on his shabby sleeve.

No, Theo. No. This is not him. But her reply is incapable of ordering itself into speech. What does come out is, 'This is Theo.'

Kemal crouches to him, rests on his cheek a scarred, gnarled hand with soil-encrusted nails, distended wrist; this shell of a man, of the officer she married in Teheran.

In French, he says to her, 'He looks like you,' with the formal *vous*.

Not me but his father, his real one, my twin-brother. But the words barely form, banished to the furthest recesses of memory. The weight of the deceit she is allowing, and must perpetuate, presses on her as if it will crush breath from her. She closes her eyes, cannot bear Kemal's unshed tears. Can he forgive me for not trusting him enough to wait in Constantinople?

She manages a smile. 'Thank you for the onions.'

He inclines his head, a gesture that reaches across years to her from Teheran and an Ottoman captain with a waxed moustache.

They are never alone. He meets her at the end of every morning outside the shop. In the narrow street, they stroll past art galleries and studios, and into the rue de Courcelles where ponies harnessed to carts trot in front of imposing buildings. In the *parc* de Monceau, it does not seem strange to walk alongside him – not behind as she did in Teheran – oblivious to office-workers enjoying their lunch-time and a snatch of early winter warmth; or to speak French – his careful, quaint – as though they have always intended to.

'I cannot give up the piano, Kemal. So I must practise.'

'I would not ask you to stop. You have extraordinary talent. Halidé said you were good. But I had no idea …'

She smiles as she recalls playing Mozart on the untuned instrument. What will be Kemal's reaction if she tells him? Will he see it as a slur on his father? 'It was very out of tune,' she ventures. Kemal's face creases in amusement. Her heart flutters, lifts. 'I had the impression Halidé was offended when I told her. I didn't seem to make her understand they need tuning.'

Kemal laughs, transformed. 'Father wouldn't have known the first thing. He bought it because he enjoyed buying, particularly anything from Europe.'

He grows serious, a cloud passing over the sun. 'Esther, this drive to modernise, westernise Turkey, abolishing the fez and religious schools, has simply amounted to getting rid of the fallen empire's traditions, as a lover casts aside his beloved's possessions. Fear and brutality have filled the void. And you,' he adds, 'you discard everything that was Russian?' His brow furrows.

'I have made a life here. Theo must have roots, a sense of identity, belonging, and they are in Paris. In the future, this will be his past. Not what happened earlier.'

Sometimes, they sit in silence as if they have nothing to say, aware of words' inadequacy. She remembers their loving under a velvet Anatolian sky, softness around his eyes, beneath his ears, his lips' sweetness; fears such recollections, avoids touching him beyond a handshake of greeting and farewell, afraid to lose the world she has built for herself.

'Where did you stumble across him?' Vera Davydovna wants to know with a skittish expression.

She explains about the pavement outside Pleyel.

'Very romantic.' Vera Davydovna chuckles. 'Better than the husband?'

'It is him.'

'You're a deep one. So, same question.'

She summarises a street fight in Teheran.

Vera Davydona's mouth narrows to a straight line; she shakes her head, draws breath, turns away.

She wonders how Vera Davydovna met the spouse Anahid paired with Monsieur Diaghilev; if Vera Davydovna is happy, and what there is at home each evening. What is happy?

She plays the slow movement of the third Beethoven concerto for Monsieur Tournon. At the end, she is weeping. When she raises her head, he is standing by the piano.

'Esther?'

'Theo's father has returned.' The lie spoken. Kemal is meeting Theo from school and taking him to the park.

'I'm so pleased. Before Christmas, I shall go to Switzerland. For good.' Monsieur Tournon spreads his hand. 'The apartment will be free.'

She clutches at the fringes of her existence. 'We haven't decided what to do.'

'There are no photographs, Mama.' Theo snuggles next to her on the mattress.

'No.'

'Why not?'

'They're expensive, and we've never had much money.'

'Rémy's *maman* and papa have lots. In frames.' Theo enunciates the last word as if it is the highest luxury to which anyone can aspire.

Rémy's father has a schoolmaster's salary. 'We'll have one taken,' she promises.

'And frame it?'

'Yes.'

'Was Papa always a soldier?'

'Yes, darling.'

'But now he's stopped.'

'Yes.'

'Tell me about the old days, Mama.'

'What do you mean?'

'You and Papa. Before you came here.'

'It's a long time ago.' He doesn't know what to ask, she frets, just feels there's something missing. What can I say? She puts her arms round him. 'Go to sleep.'

'We can't afford it,' she insists to Kemal the following week. They are walking in the park. Theo is at Rémy's.

In a pressed suit, elbows shiny from previous wearers, Kemal was shown into Monsieur Tournon's salon at the end of her lesson. Monsieur Tournon repeated his offer of the apartment.

'Yes, we can. You will be paid for this concert. There will be more. You will take pupils. I have my stories.'

'Your?'

He describes afternoons in the Bibliotèque Nationale.

We could continue the rest of our lives, she thinks, discovering things. A journey.

'And he will forward us two months' rent,' Kemal adds, 'to celebrate what he calls my return.'

'It's charity. I pay my own way.'

'It's a gift. Esther, can you not receive as well as give?'

They stand in fading winter sunlight by the first column, the only people here. She looks at him, at the face whose every detail and texture she imprinted on her mind as she said farewell to him at his brother's house in Trebizond. A fine, dry snow has started to fall, dusting the gravel like sugar. She smoothes it from Kemal's shoulders.

He clasps her hand, raises it to his cheek.

They turn towards the boulevard, streetlamps' yellow beams harsh in the silvery landscape.

THIRTY-NINE

Paris, 1998

On the way back from Père Lachaise, I stopped to meet a friend for oysters followed by lamb curry, among the art deco columns of La Coupole where, traditionally, Russian artists used to gather.

I don't recall my parents going there. They didn't socialise much or mix in émigré circles, content with each other and me in the apartment in the rue Viète. My father made me a wooden theatre, and we created scenes for my tin soldiers, who changed into farmers, merchants, fishermen. His *Stories from the Mountains* remained in print until the war. Enduring memories are his liquorice-smelling tobacco – which he used to get from a Turkish dealer beyond the boulevard Raspail – and vegetables and salads from his allotment. Mama didn't cook: we always had a housekeeper; one of them stitched costumes for my characters.

On concert days, Papa bought Mama flowers. They have their own language, he told me: pansies, fond thoughts; lilies of the valley, return of happiness. He used to offer her sprigs of the latter on the first of May, and tulips on her birthday and for the piano competition she ran every spring. When he sat with her at home, an arthritic hand over hers, I sensed a bond, a mutual understanding such that as an adult I would marvel that two people could be so close.

A few weeks after Papa died, I listened to Mama play the opening movement of Beethoven's Moonlight sonata. She turned to me: it's like on a lake, she said. There were tears in her eyes. She never seemed to me to grow older; her figure merely became more fragile, her face more slender and peaceful.

Yet, following separation during my childhood, they must have had to adjust. It can't have been easy. An occasion has stayed in my mind. It was my birthday, the anniversary of Mamana's death, the second it would have been as we were living in the rue Viète; the previous year, Mama and I had put snowdrops on Mamana's grave, and visited *mère* Catherine to share with her the cakes we had bought.

I overheard my parents; Mama was telling Papa what she and I were going to do.

'On his birthday?' Papa's voice rose. 'He's seven, for heaven's sake. And you'd drag him to a cemetery? To a servant's grave? I thought you wanted to forget the past. We'll take him out, find some delicious food … and don't say we can't afford it.'

Mama's sobs punctuated his anger. I rushed to the salon, fists clenched to protect her from this big man who had come to live with us; who insisted I sleep in my own room and not with her, was making her cry, and referred to Mamana as a servant.

I stopped on the threshold. They were by the window, Mama's piano between us.

'And why is she Mamana?'

'It was always ... we were alone ... just the three of us ...'

I hurried to check on Babou and Bébé, and my characters; went back to see what had happened as it had gone quiet.

They were still standing, arms round each other. Mama's head was against Papa's shoulder. Aware of me, he stretched an including hand. I stood in their embrace and felt a storm had passed.

This afternoon my daughter called with her youngest child, named for my uncle in Nice who changed from Jacob to Jacques Marcaud when he became a French citizen before the war.

Around that time, Uncle married a local girl and set up his taxi and garage business, to which he was delighted to add Papa's Renault in 1940. My parents and I had left Paris that spring, ahead of the invading Germans, and travelled to my grandparents. Unsure whether their French nationality would be rescinded, my parents applied for visas for Spain and Portugal. They crossed the Pyrenees along an old smugglers' route, and on to the Portuguese coast where they took the Clipper, the seaplane – more expensive but less risky than the boat – from Lisbon to New York.

There, they stayed with a kinsman of my mother. He had emigrated as a youth and started selling socks on the street at five cents a pair, from which he built up one of the city's largest clothing companies. She had never met him, but my parents were welcomed as long-lost family. Mama gave several recitals.

I joined the maquis guerrillas in the thickets behind Nice. Both my uncles were *résistants*. Anton had converted to the Orthodox Church and become a priest; his home was safe house for Jews escaping to the Spanish border.

My parents and I were reunited in Paris after the Liberation. The Gestapo stamp was on the front door of the apartment in the rue Viète. The Germans had taken the dinner and tea services, and linen. Not the china, Mama sobbed in disbelief, trailing a finger through dust on the table. The following year, I offered her a couple of Limoges plates, better than the stolen Sèvres. Her eyes smiled. You are a darling, she said, as she touched the fluted edges.

My fascination with the past was my living. In a dark suit, clean-shaven and smelling of musky cologne, with slicked-back hair – Paris's answer to Humphrey Bogart – I worked for an antiques dealer. The walls of our second-floor atelier in the rue de Vaugirard were lined with leather-bound French and Italian classics. I added to the Limoges for my mother. I described or even showed my parents anything exotic I came across. I remember a crimson porcelain egg – Mama smoothed the gilt straps that encased it – and telling her about a Kirman rug's arabesques and gardens. Another time, there was a Persian miniature mounted between two sheets of glass: a lad with black curls and a hawk, sitting under an almond-tree; the reverse, calligraphs in red and gold. I never felt in her, or my father, a yearning to be elsewhere.

My uncles journeyed by train to Paris for Papa's funeral and, twelve months later, Mama's; carbon copies with their walking-sticks and berets; Jacques, a twinkle of appreciation for the ladies despite tears on his cheeks for his dear sis; Anton, concerned for our wellbeing, a reassuring hand on the arm of the flustered young priest at the Russian church.

Anton is the letter-writer. I hear from him every few weeks. Both widowed, he and Jacques meet each midday in a café behind the Promenade des Anglais in Nice for a glass of marc, and on to a daughter's – they have several – for lunch.

My grandson Jacques is eight years old and, secretly, my favourite. While his mother was in the kitchen this afternoon, he climbed onto my knee. I ruffled his hair, identical creosote-colour to mine at his age when Uncle Jacob used to do the same with: *ça va, jeune homme?*

To Jacques, however, I said, 'So, what have you been learning at school?'

He regarded me with night-sky eyes. They lit up as he replied, 'History. The Silk Road.' He added, '*Pépère*, tell me about olden days when you were a little boy.'

I began, 'Well, it was indeed a long time ago,' just as Mama used to say to me. 'Wait a minute.'

I went to my bedroom and returned with the photograph I've always loved – in its gilt frame, now tarnished – which I have kept on top of a chest of drawers since bringing it from the rue Viète. 'That was me,' I pointed, 'when I was almost your age.'

'With your *maman* and papa?'

'Yes.' Mama was seated. Her dress – I remember it was pale-blue – had short, capped sleeves, and the neck was cut in a low V. She wore a pendant my father had given her. In a lounge suit, he stood close behind her. I was by her knee, Papa's left hand on my shoulder. We were looking at the camera, not smiling in the way people do today, yet with optimism, contemplating the moment to be recorded forever.

Mama had written on the back of the frame: *With Kemal and Theo, December 1927.*

Jacques touched the glass. '*Pépère*,' he said to the child I had been. He glanced up at me. 'I shall grow to be like you, shan't I?'

'Of course,' I laughed. 'There's something else I'll show you.'

From my bedside drawer, I removed the scorched slipper wrapped in embroidered silk. I imagined, as I had so often, a night escape from a burning house, deaths of family, neighbours, beloved servants, things too terrible ever to be spoken of.

I placed the slipper with Mama's pouch of sand and a lock of hair, and took the embroidery to Jacques. 'My mother made this when she was a girl,' I told him. 'It's silk.'

He passed his child's fingers over the vine-leaves and yellow tulips. 'Silk,' he repeated, awe in his voice as he held the material. 'Was she a princess, your *maman*?'

'No, but she was very special.'

There was a glimpse of Mama in his smile. 'This is real history, *pépère*. Can I take it to school tomorrow?'

About the author

Born and brought up in Worcestershire, Janet Hancock trained as a teacher in Oxford and worked in Warwickshire, France and Hampshire before moving to Dorset over 30 years ago. For many years, she taught English in the south of England to military officers from the Middle East and francophone Africa.

She has had poetry, and prize-winning and shortlisted short stories published in online and print anthologies. Her novel *Beyond the Samovar*, set in Russia and England 1919-20, was published in 2019.

She enjoys choral and chamber singing, cultivating the walled courtyard garden of her Edwardian townhouse, walking with others in the countryside, and choosing books for small family-members.

The West in Her Eyes is her second novel.

www.resolutebooks.co.uk

Acknowledgements

Thank you to all who read drafts, partials, chapters, pages: Matthew Branton, Valerie Bridge, Kathy Butler, Richard Foreman, Nancy Henshaw, Åse Johannessen, Diane Morrison, Margaret Wiwczaryk; to all at Dunford Novelists and Dunford online; to David Caddy and all at the White Horse workshops.

Thank you to Suzel and Michel Daverdin, who gave up a Saturday to walk with me the same Paris streets as Esther and Anahid; to their son, Pascal, who knows the city like his pocket, as they say, and led us to the best pit stops.

Thank you to Christine Brienne for an interesting conversation about marc which, like brandy, is a digestif rather than an apéritif. We decided that if Jacob and Anton – old men – enjoyed a glass before lunch, we should let them.

Thank you to Gill Reeves, formerly of the Dermatology Unit at Poole Hospital, for a helpful chat about skin marks.

Thank you to Claire Dunn, Ruth Leigh, Sarah Nicholson, Edward de Chazal, Lindsay Rumbold, and all at Resolute Books.

Thank you to Charlotte Mouncey – www.bookstyle.co.uk – for the cover design and typesetting.

Thank you to everybody who asked how it was going and showed an interest.

And to Ken, who read an early draft and would have loved to see the book.

Glossary

à la Franga (Fr.) in the western (French) fashion
au revoir, mon brave (Fr.) goodbye, my hero
aviateur (Fr.) airpilot
baba (Turk./Arm.) father
baryn (Russ.) man of good breeding
barynya (Russ.) woman (pl. *barynii*) of good breeding
baryshnya (Russ.) young unmarried woman of good breeding
bonjour (Fr.) good day (as a greeting)
bonne nuit (Fr.) good night
bonsoir (Fr.) good evening
café crème (Fr.) coffee with cream
caneton au sang (Fr.) pressed duckling
ça va, jeune homme? (Fr.) all right, young man?
c'est un beau bébé (Fr.) he's a beautiful baby
cinquième (Fr.) fifth (arrondissement)
décédé (Fr.) deceased
divan (Pers.) a long seat
douleur (Fr.) pain
elle est juive (Fr.) she's a Jewess
enchantée (Fr.) delighted (when introduced to someone)
Ermeni (Turk.) Armenian
fine à l'eau (Fr.) brandy and water
flics (Fr.) police
framboise (Fr.) strawberry

gare (Fr.) station
gazoz (Turk.) carbonated sweetened lemonade
gimnaziya (Russ.) grammar school
grand-maman (Fr.) grandma
(grand-)mère (Fr.) (grand)mother
grippe (Fr.) influenza
hanum (Turk.) form of address towards a married or mature woman
île (Fr.) island
il y eu un massacre (Fr.) there was a massacre
imbat (Turk.) a cooling wind in the Levant
impasse (Fr.) blind alley
incroyable (Fr.) incredible
j'ai fait Verdun (Fr.) literally, I did Verdun
Je Sais Tout (Fr.) I know everything
köftes (Turk.) savoury meat rissoles
le Chat botté (Fr.) literally, the booted cat; Puss in Boots
le petit (Fr.) the little one (child)
lokum (Turk.) Turkish Delight
magasin (Fr.) shop
mairie (Fr.) town hall
maman (Fr.) mummy
ma petite Nadia (Fr.) my little Nadia (as a term of affection)
mastika (Pers.) resinous golden crystals with a sweet aromatic flavour
mon adoré (Fr.) my darling
mon (ma) chéri(e) (Fr.) my dearest
mon chou-chou (Fr.) my pet (as a term of affection)
moy(a) (Russ.) my

oeufs en gelée (Fr.) eggs in aspic
para (Turk.) a small coin
patron(ne) (Fr.) owner
pension (Fr.) boarding school, boarding house
pépère (Fr.) grandpa
permis de travail (Fr.) work permit
pilav (Turk.) spiced rice with poultry, meat or fish
pont (Fr.) bridge
pour la gentille pianist (Fr.) for the nice pianist
regarde, qu'elle est belle! (Fr.) see how beautiful she is!
sale Russe (Fr.) filthy Russian
si! (Fr.) yes (in reply to a negative statement)
thalassa (Gr.) sea
thé à l'anglaise (Fr.) tea the English way
Un Bon Petit Diable (Fr.) a clever little devil
vous (Fr.) you (formal)
yali (Turk.) summer residence

Bibliography

Memoir

Berman, Leonid, *The Three Worlds of Leonid*, Basic Books, 1978.

Bunin, Ivan, *Cursed Days: A Diary of Revolution*, Phoenix Press, 2000.

Burnaby, Frederick, *On Horseback through Asia Minor*, O.U.P., 1996.

Chary, Pauline de, transl, *The Diary of Nelly Ptashkina*, Jonathan Cape, 1923.

Dunsterville, General L.C., *The Adventures of Dunsterforce*, Edward Arnold, 1920.

Hemingway, Ernest, *A Moveable Feast*, Arrow Books, 1994.

Loti, Pierre, transl. Marjorie Laurie, *Aziyadé*, Kegan Paul International, 1989.

MacDonell, Ranald, *And Nothing Long*, Constable & Co. Ltd., 1938.

Nicolson, Harold, *Some People*, Pan Books, 1947.

Orga, Irfan, *Portrait of a Turkish Family*, Eland Books, 1988.

Orga, Irfan, *The Caravan Moves On*, Eland Books, 2002.

Price, Morgan Philips, *Dispatches from the Revolution: Russia 1916-1918*, Duke U.P., NC, 1998.

Price, Morgan Philips, *My Reminiscences of the Russian Revolution*, Allen and Unwin Ltd., 1921.

Rawlinson, Lt.-Col. A., *Adventures in the Near East 1918-22*, Andrew Melrose, 1923.

Rice, Tamara Talbot, *Tamara: Memoirs of St Petersburg, Paris, Oxford and Byzantium*, John Murray, 1996.
Sackville-West, V., *Passenger to Teheran*, Hogarth, 1926.
Sava, George, *The Healing Knife*, Faber and Faber, 1938.
Tolstoy, Alexandra, *The Last Secrets of the Silk Road*, Lyons Press, 2003.

Exile
Beaton, Roderick, *George Seferis: Waiting for the Angel*, Yale U.P., 2003.
Beevor, Antony, *The Mystery of Olga Chekhova*, Penguin, 2005.
Glenny, Michael, and Stone, Norman, *The Other Russia*, Faber and Faber, 1990.
Marsden, Philip, *The Bronski House*, Flamingo, 1996.
Raeff, Marc, *Russia Abroad: A Cultural History of the Russian Emigration 1919-39*, O.U.P., 1990.
Zinovieff, Sofka, *Red Princess: a Revolutionary Life*, Granta, 2007.

Russia
Baedeker, Karl, *Russia: A Handbook for Travellers*, London, 1914.
Bradley, John, *Allied Intervention in Russia*, Weidenfeld and Nicolson, 1968.
Bradley, John, *Civil War in Russia 1917-20*, B.T. Batsford, 1975.
Mawdsley, E., *The Russian Civil War*, Allen and Unwin, 1987.
McCauley, M., ed., *The Russian Revolution and the Soviet*

State 1917-21, Macmillan, 1975.

Shukman, H., ed., *Encyclopaedia of the Russian Revolution*, Blackwell, 1989.

Suny, R.G., *The Baku Commune*, Princeton U.P., 1972.

Persia

Byron, Robert, *The Road to Oxiana*, Picador, 1992.

Ruthven, Malise, *Freya Stark in Persia*, Garnet Publishing Ltd., 1994.

Wynn, Antony, *Persia in the Great Game*, John Murray, 2004.

Anatolia and Constantinople

Hopkirk, Peter, *On Secret Service East of Constantinople*, John Murray, 1994.

Kinross, J.B., *Atatürk: The Rebirth of a Nation*, Weidenfeld and Nicolson, 1964.

Lewis, Bernard, *The Emergence of Modern Turkey*, O.U.P., 1961.

Marsden, Philip, *The Crossing Place: a Journey among the Armenians*, Flamingo, 1994.

Milton, Giles, *Paradise Lost: Smyrna 1922*, Sceptre, 2009.

Pamuk, Orhan, *Istanbul*, Faber and Faber, 2005.

Rogan, Eugene, *The Fall of the Ottomans*, Penguin, 2016.

Shipman, Pat, *The Stolen Woman*, Bantam Press, 2004.

Suny, R.G., *They Can Live in the Desert but Nowhere Else*, Princeton U.P., 2015.

Ure, Sir John, *In Search of Nomads*, Constable, 2003.

Walker, Christopher, *Visions of Ararat*, I.B. Tauris, 2005.

France

Culbertson, Judi, and Randall, Tom, *Permanent Parisians*, Robson Books, 2000.

Krase, Andreas, *Atget's Paris*, Taschen, 2004.

Poisson, Michel, *The Monuments of Paris*, I.B. Tauris, 1999.

Rose, June, *Suzanne Valadon: The Mistress of Montmartre*, St Martin's Press, 1999.

Souhami, Diana, *Gertrude and Alice*, Phoenix Press, 2000.

Fiction

Bernières, Louis de, *Birds Without Wings*, Secker and Warburg, 2004.

Croutier, Alev Lytle, *Seven Houses*, Simon and Schuster, 2003.

Karnezis, Panos, *The Maze*, Vintage, 2005.

Macaulay, Rose, *The Towers of Trebizond*, Flamingo, 1995.

Marcom, Micheline Aharonian, *Three Apples Fell from Heaven*, HarperCollins, 2000.

Nicolson, Harold, *Sweet Waters*, Sickle Moon Books, 2000.

Pamuk, Orhan, transl. Maureen Freely, *Snow*, Faber and Faber, 2004.

Rabinyan, Dorit, transl. Yael Lotan, *Persian Brides*, Canongate, 2004.

Said, Kurban, *Ali and Nino*, Vintage, 2000.